Praise for

True Mates

"From the first page to the last, the book is fortified with humor, passion and drama."

– *Literary Nymphs Reviews*

Nikolai's Wolf

"I love the way Zena Wynn has made the story come alive for me. I could barely pull myself away..."

– Dianna, *Night Owl Reviews*

Claiming Shayla

"[W]ill make you reach for a glass of wine, and settle into your comfy chair to read."

– *Long and Short Reviews*

Recommended Read! "[T]his book was even more than I had hoped for. In fact I read it twice, back to back within days of receiving it."

– Rose, *TwoLips Reviews*

"Amazing story, loved every morsel."

– Emily, *Sensual Reads*

"You better make sure you have a fan close at hand or a sexy werewolf of your own."

– Katie Cody, *The Romance Reviews*

LooseId®

ISBN 13: 978-1-61118-980-3
TRUE MATES: CLAIMING SHAYLA

Originally released in e-book format in May 2012

Cover Art by Valerie Tibbs
Cover Layout and Design by April Martinez

Printed in the U.S.A. by
Lightning Source, Inc.
1246 Heil Quaker Blvd
La Vergne TN 37086
www.lightningsource.com

True Mates

CLAIMING SHAYLA

Zena Wynn

Dedication

To my sister, who waited three long years to find out "What happened to Shayla?" I hope the story was worth the wait.

True Mates: Claiming Shayla

Six weeks ago, Shayla Morgan, geek extraordinaire, fled the tiny mountain town of Refuge, North Carolina, as though the hounds of hell—or one horny werewolf—were on her tail. Now the time has come to return for her cousin's wedding and pay the piper in the form of one determined, red-haired wolf-shifter who believes she's his mate.

After the hell of his childhood, Rory McFelan, alpha of the Sparrowhawks, is determined never to mate or reproduce. That was before the Creator dropped one feisty, irritating human female—with a scent his wolf wouldn't let him ignore—into his path right before a blue moon. In the few short days it took the full moon to wane, Rory found himself mated, with a pup on the way and his mate gone.

Getting her back is the easy part. Keeping her is more difficult. He'll have to fight demons—his and hers—his pack, her family, and an unknown enemy determined to destroy him, any way they can.

Claiming Shayla was instinct. It's keeping her that's proving to be a challenge.

Chapter One

She stood under the shower, washing the musky scent of cum and sweat from her body. The hot water beat down on her, loosening muscles sore from days and nights of marathon sex. The glide of the cloth across her clit caused her to hiss as the overly sensitive bundle of nerves reacted by shooting a streak of fire straight through her womb. "No! You've had enough," she told it. As it was, she wouldn't be walking straight anytime soon.

It was hunger that finally drove her out of the shower. If she didn't get some food into her system soon, she'd pass out. She'd expended too many calories and eaten nothing to replace them. Her stomach cramped, a reminder of its emptiness. She rubbed her abdomen, trying to soothe the knotted muscles. "And you, give me a second, will ya? Let me get out of the bathroom, and then I'll feed you."

Already mentally cataloging the contents of the refrigerator, she opened the bathroom door. He was on her in an instant. Before a cry could escape, he had her back pressed forcefully against the wall beside the bathroom door. His menacing growl sent chills down her spine. Lifting her to eye level, he spoke out of a mouth already partially shifted to wolf, revealing a jaw full of razor-sharp teeth. "You washed off my scent."

Before her mind finished deciphering what he was saying, his tongue was in her mouth and his cock in her pussy. All thoughts of food forgotten, she wrapped her legs around his waist and hung on.

"More. Need more," he growled. He grabbed her by the thighs and bent her in half until her knees pressed against the wall along the sides of her torso, holding her immobile.

Not being a contortionist, the position should have been uncomfortable, but she was too aroused. Her nails dug into his shoulders as her head bounced off the wall with each upward thrust. She fought him, wanting to move, needing to move like she needed her next breath.

She could feel her orgasm building, tightening every muscle in her body. She couldn't catch her breath. It felt like she was going to explode. She opened her mouth to scream...

Bzzzzz! Bzzzzz! Bzzzzz! Shayla Morgan jumped as her cell phone vibrated, goosing her. Shit! She'd been dreaming. Again. This had to stop. She looked around to see if anyone noticed her strange behavior. A crowded plane was not the best place to have a wet dream. No one was looking at her, thank God. That meant she hadn't cried out in her sleep...this time.

Her breathing was labored, just as in the dream. Her nipples were tight and so sensitive even the gentle abrasion of her T-shirt irritated them. Her clit throbbed. She was right on the edge. Just one stroke, one simple touch and she would explode.

Bzzzz! She jerked again and snatched her cell phone out of her cargo pants' thigh pocket. A new text message was in her in-box. She didn't recognize the number but retrieved it anyway, needing a distraction.

Need you.

What the hell? Must be a wrong number. She shoved the phone back into her pocket. It would be another forty-five minutes before she could get off the plane. She should have brought her laptop or a book to read. All this sitting would drive her crazy, and she couldn't chance taking another nap.

Bzzzz! She jumped again. What now? She took out her phone and pressed the Display Message button.

Want you.

Same number. It wasn't familiar. She didn't even recognize the area code. She closed the phone. Before she could stick it back in her pocket, it vibrated again. Eyes narrowed, she flipped it open.

Mine.

The hairs on her nape rose. Thumbs moving rapidly on the keypad, she typed, *Who's this?*

Mate.

Shayla shook her head. It couldn't be him, the one who was still haunting her dreams three weeks later—Rory McFelan.

Mate who?

The reply was swift.

Shayla. Mate. Mine.

Oh damn. It *was* Rory. Her cousin Kiesha must have given him her number. She stared at the message. As she did, the curve of her neck throbbed, a reminder of the marks on her shoulder. Time to stop the madness. She punched the words in the keyboard.

Not yours. Sex. Fun. Over.

There. That should be plain enough.

Agreed. Claimed. Mine. Forever.

Then again, maybe not. She'd forgotten whom, or rather, what she was dealing with. The man was possibly more stubborn than she. Her conversation with Kiesha came back to her.

"So, if I were to find myself extremely attracted to a shifter and wanted to indulge, I could do so as long as I didn't let him bite me?"

"Shay, don't even think about it. If you're attracted to one of them and you don't want to find yourself mated, don't let them close to you. A strong physical attraction is a major sign of a true mate. It's not simply a matter of not getting bit. If you have sex with one, you'll be so caught up in the pleasure that you'll never notice him biting you, not until it's too late," Kiesha warned. "This is no time to indulge your curiosity."

"They're that good in the sack?" Shayla asked as her neglected libido raised its head in hunger.

"Shay, seriously, this is not something to play with. These guys are serious, and they play for keeps. They won't put up with your games."

Shayla had ignored the warning and indulged her curiosity at the first opportunity that presented itself. Three days and four nights of continuous, mind-blowing sex had been the result. Almost a month later and she was still dreaming about it. She shivered, and her clit pulsed again, begging for attention.

Bzzzz! Bzzzz! She looked down to see a new message.

Waiting. Will claim what's mine.

Well, hell. Now she'd gone and done it. Kiesha was going to kill her. In three weeks' time Shayla was heard of anyone accomplishing it, although no shifter would be crazy enough to try. Though they'd all been taught about true mates and how the process worked, none of them believed mating was possible with someone not of their species, not even the elders who'd taught them, so there was a lot he didn't know.

"How long has she been gone?"

"A little over three weeks now."

Rory could almost see Caleb's mind working, examining this information from every angle and calculating what impact it would have on the pack. His intelligence was the primary reason Caleb was his second, not to mention he was a damn strong wolf. A good man to have at his back.

Finally Caleb whistled. "She's strong."

"Damned strong…and cunning," Rory informed him, feeling the same sense of reluctant pride he'd felt since Shay's escape. That she'd managed to fight off the mating fever long enough to sneak away from him without his knowledge, even with his enhanced senses, still astounded him.

"Wait a minute. If she ran, how'd you get her to agree to come here and take this job for you?" Caleb asked.

The same wicked smile from earlier crossed his face. "She doesn't know it's me. I used the pack's lawyers to negotiate the contract."

Caleb whistled again. "This ought to be interesting."

They both fell silent.

"Again I ask, are you sure this is wise, bringing her here, with all that's going on?" As the head of security, Caleb had every right to question him. The pack was a mess. He knew it. Caleb knew it. Hell, even the pack knew it. Not only were the women fighting, but there was an undercurrent of rumblings questioning his ability to lead. There were always dissidents in any pack, but lately their numbers seemed to be growing. Even as distracted as he'd been, he'd noticed.

He debated telling Caleb the whole of it but in the end settled for simply stating, "I've no choice."

Caleb silently absorbed this. "You told Mac any of this?"

Michael MacDougal, his third in command. Not by choice but by pack hierarchy. "No."

"Hmm, if she's really your mate, he'll know as soon as he gets a whiff of her. So will the rest of the pack."

"That's what I wanted to talk to you about. I need you to keep this quiet, at least until I'm ready to make an announcement."

Caleb's lips quirked. "That will be difficult with the way everyone runs in and out of here." As alpha Rory had to be accessible to the pack at all times, which frequently meant little to no privacy.

"All I'm requesting is a few days. Give me a chance to get my mate settled. As far as everyone else is concerned, Shay is the consultant I hired to streamline the pack's computer systems, nothing more."

"And how do you plan to explain her staying with you here, in the house?"

"Easy. She's human. They'll expect me to keep her close, to make sure she doesn't discover what we are," Rory answered.

Caleb sighed. "I'll do what I can to keep everyone away. You know once the truth comes out, the council will want to vet her, make sure she's suitable to be the pack's alpha-fem."

"Unnecessary. The true mate bond supersedes council authority," Rory reminded him.

"They'll still try."

"Let them." The smile on Rory's face was lethal.

* * * *

Urrpp. Urrpp. Shayla hung on to the sides of the toilet as the contents of her stomach forcibly ejected themselves. *Urrpp. Urrpp.*

"God, please let this be the flu. Bird flu, swine flu, any kind of flu, as long as it's the flu."

It had to be the flu. She'd picked up a bug somewhere, and it was just now making itself known. A bit of medicine, a lot of rest, and she'd be fine.

You're never sick.

Okay, so normally she was disgustingly healthy, but there was a first time for everything.

You don't have any flu symptoms.

Fatigue, nausea, and vomiting—they're all flu symptoms, and these she had in abundance.

Where's the cough, body aches, and fever?

So it was just a mild case of the flu. That meant she'd get over it that much sooner.

You've been throwing up for a week. Your breasts are tender, and you missed your period.

That didn't mean anything. Lack of sleep combined with the stress she'd been under the last few weeks would be enough to make anyone miss a cycle or two. Besides, she'd never been regular.

Her conscience was quiet.

Shayla squirmed. Even she didn't believe the lie. She'd always been as regular as clockwork, no matter what was going on in her life. *Shit! Shit! Shit! I'm pregnant*. If she could have, Shayla would have slammed her head on the porcelain rim of the toilet until she knocked herself unconscious. Unfortunately doing so wouldn't change a thing.

She was so stupid. Damn her curiosity. People always warned her that one day it would get her in trouble. What the hell was she to do now? This was not supposed to happen. All she'd wanted to do was scratch an itch, satisfy her curiosity, and move on. Instead what she'd done was make a life-altering decision.

Abortion was *not* an option.

Shayla laid a hand over her stomach, fingers spread wide in an unconsciously protective gesture. Poor kid! What kind of life would it have with *her* for a mother? She was enough of a freak without throwing the kid's father into the mix. A genius and a werewolf. God help it. The poor thing wouldn't stand a chance.

Shayla flushed the toilet and pushed wearily to her feet, this afternoon's bout of sickness over. Everyone was right. She *was* weird. She couldn't even have morning sickness like a normal woman. Who ever heard of "morning sickness" that struck in the afternoon?

I need time to think, time to plan.

But time was something she didn't have. She was due back in Refuge tomorrow. She'd hurt Kiesha enough by delaying her arrival until the day before the wedding. If she'd told her about the situation with Rory, Kiesha might have understood, but then she'd be furious.

Now she had a wedding and a very determined, very possessive werewolf awaiting her arrival. She shuddered, and her stomach heaved again just thinking of Rory's reaction when he learned of his impending fatherhood. She'd never get away from him now.

This was one time she'd better have her shit together and know what she was doing.

* * * *

The next day Shayla stopped the rental in front of Kiesha's house, nervous for the first time in remembrance about seeing her family. Inside were her parents, Kiesha and her fiancé, Alex Wolfe, and who knew whom else. She wiped sweaty palms on her pants as she gazed at the closed front door.

In no rush to see them, she flipped down the visor and took in her appearance. Her thick, silky black hair had grown like weeds, and instead of its usual short, spiked style, she wore it pulled back into a ratty ponytail. Today's hair gel color was hot pink to go with her black and pink fatigues and hot pink T-shirt. Her complexion was a bit more yellow than normal, and there were dark, raccoonlike circles under her rounded, brown eyes. Usually she wore her African Asian heritage well, garnering a lot of second looks and even a few modeling offers. Today was not one of those days.

Shayla flipped the visor back into position and sighed. She would feel a lot better about facing everyone if she'd been able to devise a plan of action. The best she'd been able to come up with was to get through the weekend without anyone discovering her pregnancy. Oh, and to avoid Rory at all costs.

While she realized she needed to tell him about the baby they'd created, she couldn't do it right now. She was too raw and still uncertain how she felt about the situation. It wasn't like she'd planned on being a mother—*ever*. This was a major blip in her life-map configuration. So 'scuze her if she simply wasn't ready to factor his feelings into the equation. When she'd had time to adjust and was more in control of herself, well, *then* they could discuss it.

As she procrastinated, trying to work up the courage to exit the car, the front door opened and Kiesha stepped out. No more lingering. If she stayed in the car any longer, Kee would get suspicious. Planting a smile on her face, Shayla grabbed her overnight bag, laptop case, and purse and opened the car door.

It's showtime!

"Shayla Nei Morgan! It's about time you showed up." Kiesha's hands were planted on her hips, making her pregnant belly protrude more.

Shayla winced inwardly at the sound of her full name. "Sorry, Kee. The project took longer than I thought or I would have been here sooner. You got everything done? Was Mary Elizabeth able to help you?" While awaiting her answer, she reached into the backseat of the vehicle and pulled out her suitcase, dropping it on the ground and extending the handle so she could roll it to the door.

"Yeah, she was a big help, but it wasn't the same. She's my best friend, but you're family. We've been planning this day since we were kids."

She stopped before Kiesha, dropped her belongings, and gave her cousin a big hug. "Yeah, but when we were kids, we never imagined the groom would be a werewolf," Shayla said drily.

"True." Kiesha laughed. "And the wedding was supposed to be a double."

"Me? Married?" Shayla gave a shudder that was only partially fake, unable to imagine it.

"That's what I said, and you see what happened to me. Just wait. Your day's coming."

At one time she would have agreed. That was before discovering how difficult it was to find a man completely accepting of her, weirdness and all. Letting Kiesha's statement go without comment, she picked up her things and allowed her cousin to drag her into the house.

The house was amazingly silent considering all the people that were supposed to be here. "Where's Mom and Dad?"

"Uncle Frank got delayed. Some hush-hush project he's working on and couldn't leave. They won't make it in until tomorrow afternoon, just in time for the wedding."

Good. Not that she didn't want to see her parents, but the less people she had to pretend for the better, especially when these were the people who knew her best. "Okay, that's the 'rents accounted for. Where's Alex and everyone else?"

"Alex is in the kitchen—"

"Of course," she interrupted. "Where else would he be?" Kiesha hated cooking. Fortunately for her, Alex loved to cook. It worked well for them. "So I take it the prerehearsal brunch has been changed to something else? What's our itinerary now?"

"We're meeting at the church this evening to do a quick run-through, then coming back here for dinner."

"And my dress?"

"Already in your room, hanging in the closet." Kiesha laid a hand on Shay's arm. "You're sure you want to stay here? Since Shannon moved in with Nikolai, the house is empty."

Puzzled, Shay asked, “Aren’t Alex’s parents coming for the wedding?”

Kiesha snapped her finger. “That’s right. I forgot, but I’m sure they wouldn’t mind putting you up. You could stay in the basement. Lord knows, with all the stuff Shannon added, it’s like a mini-apartment down there.”

“*No!* I mean, that’s okay. I’d rather be here with you.” Shay scrambled to catch the bags that slipped from her lax fingers before her cousin noticed her knee-jerk reaction at the mention of the basement where she and Rory had—

She immediately shut down the rest of that thought.

Having already taken steps to lead her to the first-floor guest room where she’d be staying, Kiesha stopped, turned back, and looked at her strangely. “Shay, are you all right?”

“I’m fine. Why do you ask?”

“*Why do I ask*?” Kiesha looked behind Shayla, then all around her. Turning her piercing, brown-eyed gaze back to Shay and pinning her with a look, she asked, “All right, you imposter. Where’s my cousin and what have you done with her?”

Shayla giggled nervously and fidgeted under the intense scrutiny. “Kee, I’m fine. Really. Just tired. Remember I flew across the country after working around the clock trying to finish in order to make it here in time. A good night’s sleep and I’ll be back to my usual self.” The lie Shay had told Kiesha about why she’d not been able to come early to help with the wedding preparations as planned had turned into a self-fulfilling prophecy. Due to the severe morning sickness she’d been experiencing, she’d gotten seriously behind on her project.

Kiesha leaned in until she was only inches away, causing Shay to draw back and hug her laptop case to her chest. “That explains the dark circles under your eyes. What about the yellow tinge to your skin?”

“Hellooo, I’m half-Japanese. Remember?” She shook her head and went to walk around Kiesha, mentally willing her to let it go.

“Shay…” Kiesha growled as she stepped into her pathway, hands on her hips.

Shayla sighed heavily. Of course Kee wouldn’t. “I picked up some kind of virus while away. I’m over the worst of it, but my stomach’s still a bit unsettled.” She wanted to whoop for joy as the lie rolled off her tongue. Though unplanned, it was perfect. It would explain any sickness she experienced this weekend that couldn’t be hidden.

Kiesha’s eyes narrowed. Whether in concern or because she suspected the falsehood, Shayla couldn’t tell. Just when she was ready to push past her cousin and continue toward the bedroom, Kiesha spoke. “As long as you’re feeling better now.”

“Much. Now let’s go so I can put this stuff down and see my outfit. It had better be as nice as you described. You know how I feel about wearing dresses. Wedding or not, if it’s hellish, I’ll show up in my fatigues. I’m sure I have some that will fit your color scheme.”

“It’s gorgeous, and quit whining,” Kiesha commanded as they entered the room. “The guys won’t be able to keep their eyes off you.”

“As long as it’s only their eyes. They touch without permission and somebody’s going to draw back a nub,” Shay warned, eyes narrowed.

Kiesha rolled her eyes. "I'll be sure to warn the pack. Although…that no-touching rule is going to make dancing difficult."

If Rory's there, dancing with other males won't be an option. "I'll give it careful consideration," Shayla lied.

She set her bags on the bed while Kiesha went to the closet and opened it. The dress she removed was a dream. Halter-topped with a plunging back, it was a deep, ruby-red satin that shimmered and flowed in Kiesha's hand. "*Kiesha.*"

"I know, right? Didn't I tell you not to worry? All the dresses are styled the same and made with the same material, but in different colors. Mary Elizabeth's is emerald, and Shannon's is midnight blue. My dress is gold."

Shayla fingered the fabric. "They're going to be so beautiful in the candlelight."

"That's what I thought. I had everyone's shoes dyed to match. The heels are high but thick, so you won't have any problems walking in them."

"I'm wearing my boots, remember? You promised."

"Yeah, but I really didn't think you'd go through with it!" Kiesha exclaimed.

Shayla held out her hand. "Hi, I'm Shayla Morgan. Have we met?"

Kiesha slapped her hand down and rolled her eyes. "Okay, so I should have known better." She sighed and tucked a loose curl behind her ear. "At least the dresses are long and loose enough that the boots won't show."

Releasing the gown so that Kiesha could put it away, Shayla said, "I'd better go speak to Alex before he thinks I'm still mad at him." A month ago Alex had tried to set her up with some of his shifter buddies on the sly.

Kiesha had caught on to what he was doing and rushed Shayla out of the house before they arrived.

As they left the room, Shayla thought about it. It was Alex's fault she was in her current predicament. If Alex hadn't called for some of the alpha males of his pack to come over, they wouldn't have chased her and Shannon. Rory wouldn't have fought for her, and she might not have stopped disliking Rory long enough to realize she was attracted to him and act on it. Yeah, blaming Alex was sounding better and better.

"I wouldn't blame you if you were."

Shayla stumbled before righting herself. Was Kiesha reading her mind?

"What Alex did was just wrong. I told him he'd better not pull another stunt like that this time or there'd be hell to pay," Kiesha continued sternly, not noticing her sudden lack of coordination.

"He does something stupid like that again and next time I won't be so forgiving." The point was moot now, but Kiesha didn't know that.

"Hey, I learned my lesson," Alex told Shayla as she entered the kitchen. "Let's leave the FBI out of this."

When she'd first met Alex, Shayla had threatened to hack into the Federal Bureau of Investigation's system and add him to their most wanted list if he ever did anything to hurt her cousin. It was a valid threat, one she was more than capable of accomplishing. "Lucky for you I've decided to forgive and forget. Besides, if anyone is pissed, it should be Shannon."

"For the last time, I didn't know she was coming with you. I thought she would stay home under lock and key like any other sane, unmated she-wolf would when there was a blue moon and she was in heat."

"Hey! Don't drag me into this," Shannon told Alex.

Shayla jerked awkwardly in Shannon's direction. "Shannon! I didn't know you were here." She reached out and punched her cousin in the arm. "Kiesha, why didn't you tell me Shannon was here?" Damn, Shannon was Rory's baby sister, and the two were extremely close.

Does she know about Rory and me? Taking a deep breath, Shay counseled herself not to panic, knowing shifters could smell fear.

As she and Kiesha approached the center island where Alex was cooking, the phone rang. "I'll get it in there. The darn thing's been ringing off the hook all day." Kiesha disappeared into the office.

"How have you been, Shay?" Alex looked up from the pot he was stirring as she sat down.

Shayla could feel Shannon's gaze on her, and it made her twitchy. "Good." She forced herself to take a seat at the island and casually lean an elbow on the countertop.

Does she know? She tried to view Shannon's expression out of the corner of her eye.

"Hmm, you look rough. Have you been getting enough sleep?"

The question snapped her attention back to Alex. Damn, she'd forgotten he was a doctor. She was very careful with her answer. "I picked up one of those stomach bugs while I was gone, and my stomach's still a little sensitive but other than that, I'm fine. Just extremely tired. I worked crazy hours trying to finish on time."

Alex's eyes crinkled in concern. "Are you sure you're over it? The last thing Kiesha needs is to be sick, especially while she's pregnant." He placed the lid on the pot, leaned closer to her, and took a deep breath.

"Kiesha's safe. If I were contagious, I would have stayed away," Shayla assured him. "What? Why are you looking at me like that?"

Alex studied her like she was a puzzle he couldn't quite figure out. "There's something different about your scent. I can't put my finger on it."

"It's my lotion. I'm using a new brand." From what she'd been told, Shayla had concluded that the mating mark must leave behind some type of scent identifier that other shape-shifters recognized. To be safe, she'd hunted until she found a brand of perfumed lotion that didn't make her gag and slathered it on.

"No, that's not it. There's something else. Shannon?"

As Shannon approached from her seat at the breakfast nook near the window, Shayla conquered the urge to slide out of the chair and move away. *Breathe. Don't do anything to make them suspicious.*

Shannon walked right up behind Shayla and pressed her nose against the skin of her neck, right below the unlotioned hairline. Shayla froze. It felt like even her heart stopped beating.

It seemed a lifetime but was probably only seconds before Shannon lifted her head and moved to face Shayla. With her eyes gazing directly into Shayla's, she told Alex, "She's not sick."

She could see the knowledge shimmering in Shannon's eyes. Shayla opened her mouth, the word *don't* on the tip of her tongue as she reached out beseechingly to stop her.

"She's pregnant," Shannon stated.

"Who's pregnant?" Kiesha asked from behind.

Chapter Two

Kiesha's question cut through the tense silence like a knife.

Alex watched Shay's face close up tighter than a rock wall and just as hard. It was clear by her very lack of expression that her pregnancy was not open for discussion. Glancing at Shannon and then Kiesha, he didn't believe they got her silent message, or maybe they were just ignoring it.

"Shannon?" Kiesha asked curiously.

Shannon shook her head, still engaged in her staring contest with Shay. "Nope, not me."

"But it can't be...*Shay*?"

When Shay didn't respond, Kiesha moved to stand next to Shannon. "Shay, are you pregnant?"

Shayla finally ended the contest with Shannon by briefly closing her eyes. "I don't want to talk about it."

"But..." Kiesha began.

A very firm, "No."

"Shay, if you're pregnant..."

A surge of supernatural power suddenly swelled in the room, making his skin crawl. It was coming from Shayla. "I *said*...I *don't* want to discuss it." Her voice came out in a guttural growl, and her eyes flashed to gold and then back to brown. He doubted Shayla was aware of what she was doing.

Shannon obviously felt it too, for she took a cautious step back and pulled Kiesha with her. Alex's wolf came to attention. New shifters, especially those as unaware of their power as Shay seemed to be, were aggressive, unpredictable, and potentially dangerous.

Kiesha's mouth opened. Alex cut her off. "Kiesha, leave it alone. She doesn't want to talk. Stop forcing the issue."

If his mate continued to push, Shayla's wolf might see it as a challenge and attack, either to establish or determine its dominance over Kiesha. The vibes he felt coming off Shay indicated that already her wolf was a force to be reckoned with, and Kiesha was still mostly human.

Kiesha turned on him. "I'm not *forcing* anything. She's my cousin. We don't keep secrets from each other."

"And I'm sure she'll talk when she's ready. Right now I don't think she is." Alex nodded toward Shay, silently urging Kiesha to note her expression.

The phone rang in the background. Kiesha hesitated, obviously torn. Her gaze bounced from him to Shay to the office, and back to Shay again. Finally she gave in to its urgent prompting and took off for the office den.

"I know about you and Rory," Shannon said quietly.

"That's my cue to leave. I'll go see if Kiesha needs help." Alex turned down the stove and left the room. Shannon was also an alpha and her mate a vampire. Between the two of them, she was more than capable of handling Shay if her wolf got out of hand.

* * * *

"What did he tell you?" Shayla didn't want to discuss this but sensed that unlike Kiesha, Shannon wasn't going to let it go until she'd said her piece.

Shannon shook her head and took a cautious step forward. "Rory didn't say anything. I figured it out on my own."

Shayla felt a little twinge in the region of her heart. Surely that was relief she was feeling and not...*disappointment?*

"You're his mate," Shannon continued.

"No, I'm not. We don't even like each other," Shay disputed.

"Rory claimed you," Shannon insisted.

Shayla's eyes lost focus as she thought back to that time. "That was just the effect of the blue moon madness. You're the one who told me how it affected shifters. He'd never have touched me otherwise."

Shannon disagreed. "It was more than that. You're his one, his true mate. I know it, but more importantly, Rory knows it."

"Even if I believed in all this true mate, true love crap you guys keep spouting, it doesn't apply to me. The whole thing is just a fluke of nature, chemistry. Rory doesn't want me, not really. I'm too..." She shook her head. "He just wouldn't," she finished sadly.

Shannon's eyes softened, and she gave Shayla a look of understanding. "Shay, I know exactly how you feel. I..." She glanced around furtively. "Let's go to your room. There's a few things you need to know, and I don't want to chance us being interrupted." *Or overheard* was left unsaid.

Shayla turned and led the way to the guest bedroom, situated off the living room. Once they were both inside, she shut the door. Then, as an afterthought, locked it. "You were saying?"

Shannon leaned against the dresser, watching her carefully. "I know what it's like to be different."

Shayla snorted. "Of course you do. You're a shape-shifter."

Shannon shook her head violently. "No. That's not what I mean. Even among my own kind, I'm an anomaly."

Interested, Shayla crossed to the bed and sat, drawing up her leg to prop her chin on her knee. "In what way?"

"In wolf packs, strength and cunning are everything. Strength determines your ranking in the pack and cunning your ability to maintain it. So being strong is a good thing, unless you're a female."

"They want the females to be weak?" Shayla asked, startled. This contradicted everything she knew of wolves.

"No, that's not what I mean. They admire strength in females too—within reason. A strong female means strong cubs. What they don't like are females that are abnormally strong, like me. I'm as strong as Rory, which meant not only was I the alpha-fem—the strongest female—but I was also stronger than every other male in our pack."

Shay bit her bottom lip before stating, "I don't see what the problem is. You just said strong is good."

The side of Shannon's mouth quirked up in a wry grin. "How do you feel about weak men? You know, men you can run all over."

Shayla winced. “I see what you mean. If a man is weaker than me, I can’t respect him. I’ll walk all over him, do whatever I want to do and dare him to take exception to it.”

“Exactly,” Shannon said, grinning hugely. “With shifters, it’s even more important that the male be stronger than the female, or at least equal to her in power.”

“Why is that?”

Shannon shrugged. “If the wolf can’t respect its mate, it has a nasty habit of killing them.”

“Well, hell! That’s mighty efficient of it,” Shayla said drily.

“What it is, is a huge pain in the ass,” Shannon corrected. “Until Nikolai, I didn’t think I’d ever find a man that could handle my wolf, and I didn’t want some male’s death on my conscience.”

Shayla sighed and rubbed her weary eyes. Man was she tired. “As happy as I am for you and Nik, what does this have to do with me and your brother?”

“I know you, Shay. The hair, clothes, and abrasive manner? That’s just camouflage to hide what I’m guessing is an extremely high IQ. Don’t you see? The very thing that makes you stick out like a sore thumb among humans is highly prized among wolves. Your intelligence and strength are what Rory needs. He’s alpha. That means not only is he strong, but he’s smart as well. He has to be to lead the pack. You’re perfect for him, his equal. He couldn’t have found a better match if he’d gone looking for one,” Shannon said earnestly.

Shayla was shaking her head by the time Shannon finished her little speech. “Perfect? I don’t think so. Maybe that vampire of yours has addled your brains.

Don't you remember all the fighting we did? Rory and I couldn't even be in the same room with each other without going for each other's throats."

Shannon laughed softly. "That's because you're too much alike, which only proves my point."

When she continued shaking her head, Shannon came and sat beside her. "Look, I'm going to tell you some things that Rory and I rarely discuss with others. At one time my mother *might* have been strong, but loving my father made her weak. My father, Magnus, only mated her because she was the first female to conceive from his seed, but she wasn't his mate and she knew it. They both did, and we all suffered for it. My mother, because she loved the bastard dearly, even knowing he despised her. Rory, because my father was determined to beat any hint of supposed weakness out of him. I was basically ignored, because I was a female and therefore beneath his notice."

"Your father was abusive?" Shayla tried to keep the distaste from her voice. Her parents were both so loving she couldn't quite wrap her mind around the horror Rory and his family must have lived with on a daily basis.

"Verbally and emotionally, but not physically or sexually, thank God—with me at least. It didn't help that he was also the pack's alpha, so there was no interference from the others. Dad called it 'toughening us up.' Ma was too busy trying to please him to stand up to him and was no protection for us at all. Rory protected us as best he could, mostly by taking the brunt of his ire whenever possible."

Shannon sighed deeply and seemed to shake off the bad vibes these old memories were resurrecting. "The reason I'm telling you this is because growing up the way we did left scars. Rory's so afraid he'll turn out like our father that he's refused to mate. But I think that's only part of it. I suspect the real reason is that he's never met a woman tough enough to stand up to him the way you do. He respects you. Yes, you aggravate and annoy the hell out of him, but that's because he's not used to anyone like you. No one's ever stood toe-to-toe with him before, man or woman. He needs that in his life. You challenge him, and that's a good thing."

She grabbed Shay's hand. "All I ask is that you give Rory a chance. With Nikolai being a vampire and me being a wolf-shifter, I didn't think things could ever work between us. There were too many problems, too many reasons why we as a couple didn't make sense, but it works. The Creator doesn't make mistakes, so it will work for you too. And remember, this is more than about the two of you. There's a baby involved now. One that deserves to know its father, and Rory is an excellent father. I know because he raised me."

"Shannon, I have no intention of denying Rory his child. I know he or she will need both of us. As far as a relationship between us goes, even if I wanted to give Rory a chance, I can't. I begin a new six-month assignment on Monday."

Shannon dropped her hand like it was hot, and scowled fiercely. "Can't you tell them you changed your mind? That circumstances have arisen that make it impossible for you to accept the job?"

"I wish I could, but the contract's ironclad and there are no loopholes. It was so detailed I hired a lawyer to look at it before signing. The only reason I agreed to take it was because the money was too good to pass on. At least I'll still be in the area."

Shannon perked up, her manner suddenly intent. "What's the name of the company that hired you?"

"Sparrowhawk, Inc."

A strange expression crossed Shannon's face, and her mouth dropped open. She seemed to convulse right before bursting into peals of laughter. "Spar…row… hawk…Inc.?" Shannon struggled to get out, still laughing so hard she was in danger of falling off the bed.

"Why? What have you heard about them?" Shayla was puzzled at her bizarre reaction, beginning to get annoyed.

"What…have…I…heard?" she gasped, laughing too hard to finish. "Oh God, this is too funny," she added when she'd calmed, still wiping tears from her eyes.

Eyes narrowed in displeasure, Shay asked, "Mind sharing the joke?"

"Shayla." She giggled. "You're working for Rory."

* * * *

Hours later Shay entered the small church where the wedding was being held, still pissed that Rory had managed to outsmart and outmaneuver her. Able to think circles around most individuals, her ego was smarting at being bested. She refused to acknowledge the tiny spark of respect flickering to life deep inside.

Fortunately Kiesha had lain off. Shayla didn't know what Alex had said to make Kiesha give her space, but it worked. Instead of nagging her, her cousin was giving her wounded looks, as if she needed one more person to worry about. Now she simply hoped Kee had enough sense to keep her mouth shut around Shayla's parents. As traditional as her mother was, if she knew her daughter was pregnant, she'd turn this wedding into a double.

It didn't help that she and Shannon were the last to arrive. Shayla strode up the aisle of the church, trying to ignore her churning stomach. *Please, not again.* The last thing she needed was for her morning sickness to reappear. She'd thrown up once already at the house, causing them to be late.

Scanning the participants standing at the altar, her gaze came to a screeching halt when it landed on Rory. Their eyes connected. Lust slammed into her so hard that she grabbed ahold of the pew to keep from toppling over.

Images of their last night together bombarded her mind in full Technicolor, with all the associated textures and smells. The present faded as she was thrust back into the past…

* * * *

She lay on top of Rory, their legs tangled together and her head on his chest while she recovered from their last round of sex.

"I need to go upstairs," she told him, lazily twirling her finger in his dense red chest hair.

"It's still not safe. Besides, I like you right where you are." His large, calloused hand stroked her bare skin from shoulder to hip.

"I like it here too, but"—she stuck out her tongue and licked his left nipple—"I don't want to miss my flight. That means I need to pack tonight."

He stiffened beneath her. "You're not going anywhere." It came out in a growl.

"Down, boy." She patted his shoulder. "Don't go all caveman on me. This was fun, but I have a job to do. Vacation time's over."

Rory gripped her by the shoulders and dragged her up his body until their faces were level. "You belong to me. Forget the job."

"My job is how I earn my living."

Rory's grip tightened and a hint of fang showed at her words.

Shayla narrowed her eyes. "Watch the grip, wolf boy. Don't make me hurt you. I belong to myself. No man owns me."

"Mine," he growled, his eyes beginning to glow.

"I don't think so, Neanderthal. Them days are long gone." She placed her knee right over his groin and applied a hint of pressure. "Let go or lose something very important to you," she threatened.

Rory glared back, taking her measure. His eyes seemed to dare her to do it. More than willing to call his bluff, she applied steadily increasing pressure.

His anger a tangible thing, he released her. Shayla scrambled quickly to her feet and headed for the door, feeling his gaze drill a hole in her back. As she reached out a hand to grab the doorknob, she called back over her shoulder, "I figured you'd see things my way."

Rory was on her in a heartbeat, driving her to the floor on her knees. He yanked her hands behind her back, forced her shoulders to the carpet, and kneed her legs apart.

His roughness caused her pussy to cream. "Let go." Her voice came out a breathy moan. Oh yeah, that was convincing, she thought.

"Mine!" He drove into her tender muscles with one sharp thrust, sliding in to the hilt, and proceeded to set a punishing rhythm.

"No," Shayla complained even as her pussy tightened around him, gripping him harder with each stroke.

"Mine! Say it!"

"I won't!" She tugged on her arms, trying to free them. Then she leaped forward, attempting to escape. She wanted him and wanted this desperately, but needed to make him fight for it—fight for her.

Rory growled as her movement dislodged his cock, a sound so terrible it caused the hairs on her arms to raise. He caught her by the waist and pulled her back. "Submit!"

"Make me," she foolishly challenged, twisting her body this way and that, trying to gain the leverage she needed to scramble forward on her elbows.

With a roar, Rory's arm hooked her low around her torso, and her knees left the floor. He impaled her on his shaft and held her to him, his claws digging into her hips. His other arm caught her across the shoulders as he lunged forward and pinned her to the carpet, his teeth locked in the tendon between her neck and right shoulder. His body enlarged, expanding in and around her as he partially shifted.

Shayla screamed her pleasure. Yes! This was what she wanted. This was what she'd fought for. Rory, completely out of control.

"Shayla mine. Say it!"

"Yes yes yes," she babbled. "Yours. Shayla yours."

He grunted his approval, clutched her head by the hair, and tugged it up and to the side, baring her left shoulder. Then he bit her. Marked! She'd been double marked. Damn, there'd be no escaping him now.

Bright lights burst behind her eyelids as her body exploded. Her throat locked up tight as her body seized, then shook violently…

A tiny alarm sounded at the back of her mind but was quickly smothered. It was difficult to think with her body continuously convulsing. Another voice, one she'd never heard before, spoke. "*Bite. Claim. Mine.*"

She played with his neck, licking and nibbling, occasionally scraping the tendon with her teeth. *Claim Rory?* Was that something she wanted to do?

Rory's hands gripped the cheeks of her ass, pulling them apart while he held her to him, spiked by his pistoning cock. He shifted angles and hit something inside that caused her back to bow and her nails to dig into his skin, drawing blood. "Shit!" She screamed the profanity into the night as another orgasm ricocheted through her body.

His claws dug into the sensitive inner area lining her rectum, hard enough to sting but not pierce through the skin. The hint of violence thrilled her, and her greedy pussy tightened on his cock.

"Bite me!" His voice joined with the one in her head. *"Bite him, mark him, make him ours."*

Shayla pulled back and shook her head, confused. There was something she was supposed to remember. Some reason why she shouldn't. She couldn't think, and she desperately needed to.

"Bite me!"

"Bite. Mark. Claim."

Their voices blended together, and something broke loose inside of Shayla. It rose to the surface, and her vision changed, colors bleeding to gray. A growl started low in her chest, swelling until it rolled out of her throat.

"*Bite me*!"

Instinct took over and Shayla lunged. She clamped her teeth down on the tendon that connected his neck and shoulder, biting him so hard she broke skin and his blood filled her mouth.

Rory howled triumphantly. "Mine," he roared as he shifted into his half-man/half-wolf form.

The feel of his fur growing against her tongue caused Shay to jerk her mouth free.

He lifted her off him and over onto her stomach. Pulling Shay to her knees, he locked his teeth on her shoulder and drilled her from behind. Their mating was raw, intense, primal, and when it was over, all Shayla could do was lie there, drained.

He'd reversed their positions so she could sprawl on top of him instead of the hard ground.

"Never again. I won't let you go. You're mine."

Shayla shivered at the certainty she heard in his voice. Something had just happened. Something important, but she lacked the cognitive ability to decipher it. She was too tired. Shifting her head to a more comfortable position, she yawned and felt her body sink deeper into his. "Where are we?" She yawned again and felt her eyes closing.

He raised his head and looked around, the movement jostling her, and she grumbled until he settled back down. "Playground."

"Umph." Consciousness faded as all her sleepless nights caught up with her in rush.

* * * *

Shayla woke to the tantalizing scent of bacon passing back and forth beneath her nostrils. Before she was completely alert, hunger took over and she'd snatched the slice of bacon out of the air and stuffed it into her mouth. As she chewed, she debated whether she wanted to satisfy her appetite or her need for more slumber. Hunger won, and she held a hand out for more.

"If you want it, you have to open your eyes."

Rory! Sleep was looking better and better. Mentally she reviewed what she remembered of last night while pondering the wisdom of facing him without all her faculties intact. Her conversation with Shannon and the scene at the playground all flashed through her mind in a matter of seconds. After that she drew a blank.

Where am I?

"Shayla, I know you're awake. You've slept all night and half of the day. If you plan on making it to the wedding on time, you need to get up. I'm perfectly content to let you sleep the day away, but your family might take issue with it."

At that her eyes popped open. She jackknifed into a sitting position, holding the covers to her chest, and immediately wished she hadn't as the room spun round in circles. Putting a hand to her head to hold it in place, she closed her eyes until the dizziness faded. Damn, she knew better than that. Sudden changes in position, especially going from lying to sitting, always upset her equilibrium, courtesy of her pregnancy.

"Are you all right?" She felt his hand settle on her shoulder, steadying her. She must be swaying.

"I'm fine." *Not*...but she didn't want to get into it with Rory right now.

"If you say so. Here! You'll feel better once you eat." He plopped a plate down onto her lap.

The smell of meat caused her to open her eyes once again. The plate was loaded with sausage, bacon, seared strips of steak still dripping blood, and scrambled eggs.

Her stomach gave a loud rumble, and she swore something shifted inside.

"I'm not really a meat eater," Shayla told him, watching in horrified fascination as her hand—independently of her mind—reached out and snatched a piece of steak and brought it to her mouth.

Once the meat touched her lips, it was gone, and so was the rest of the food. She scarfed it down in a flurry of movement. The fork fell unnoticed onto the bed as Shayla ate with her hands. She was licking the grease off her fingers when she remembered Rory. One glance showed he was amused by her appalling display.

"Want more?" He wiggled his eyebrows and held aloft another plate full of the same.

Not even close to being satisfied, with a muttered, "Thanks," she forced herself to calmly remove the plate from his hand and continue eating. She was halfway finished before she noticed the unused fork. No sense worrying about it now, she thought with an inward shrug.

When she was done, weariness rushed over her and a huge yawn cracked her jaw. She dropped back onto the pillows and allowed her eyes to drift close.

"It's obvious to me from the way you demolished this food that you haven't been feeding our babe properly."

And as simple as that, sleep was the furthest thing from her mind. Shayla tapped her heels together three times and made a wish. Cautiously she peeked one eye open, and then the other. Damn, Glinda was wrong. She was still here. *Where's a pair of red magic slippers when you need them?*

"You know I'm pregnant?" She popped herself on the forehead. "Of course you know. It's that damn nose of yours. You probably knew before I did."

Rory set the plates on the side table and leaned over her, a hand on either side of her body. "Aye, I know. How long have you been aware, and when exactly were you planning on telling me?"

His scent overwhelmed her, and another hunger rose to the surface in a rush. Not ready to have this discussion, she let lust consume her. Mentally she flipped through her arsenal of feminine wiles, pulled out her sexiest come-hither smile, and allowed it to form on her face. Then she reached out and grazed his torso with her nails, beginning with his ripped abdominals, past bulging pectorals, to settle on his rock-hard deltoids.

"Stop trying to distract me. We need to talk." He grabbed her hands and pushed them down to her sides, holding her in place.

Determinedly Shay wriggled around and kicked with her feet until the covers slid down around her waist. Arching her back to draw his attention to her bare, puckered breasts, she licked her lips and exhaled his name on a sigh. "Rory."

"No, Shay."

"Fuck me."

He growled, and she felt her cream coat her thighs. God, she loved it when he went primal on her. His nostrils twitched, and his eyes began to change, the gold edging out the hazel. To add to the temptation, she spread her legs wide and shifted around under the sheet until even she could smell her arousal.

"We will discuss this," he stated as he snatched the sheet off the bed and looked down at her naked body.

Shay's gaze followed his, and she noticed her pubic hair was already glistening with moisture. Only this man had the power to make her this wet without even trying.

Rory stood and yanked down the zipper of his faded blue jeans. The bulbous head of his engorged cock popped out to bob against his abdomen. He snarled as he shoved the pants down his legs. "Don't think you'll control me with sex. We will discuss the babe and our future together."

"Whatever, just get that cock in me where it belongs."

He planted a knee on the bed. "As long as you realize—"

The phone rang.

"Don't answer," Shayla commanded, already reaching out to pull him over her.

He glanced at the caller ID. "It's Alex, probably wondering where we are."

Loyalty to Kee warred with lust while the phone continued to ring. She noticed the time on the bedside clock. Darn, they really didn't have time to fool around. The wedding was scheduled to start at six. It was almost three now. Finally she pushed Rory away with a sigh. "Better answer. If you don't, they'll keep calling."

Chapter Three

Sitting on the edge of the mattress, Rory snatched up the receiver and snarled, "McFelan."

"Hate to interrupt the happy reunion, but your mate's parents have arrived and are asking questions. My mate's ready to kill someone. You think you two could put a halt to the festivities and get here?" Alex asked.

Rory gazed at Shay, who was still laid out like a veritable banquet before him, and mentally calculated how much time he had to feast and still arrive on time. "Fifteen minutes and we'll be on our way."

"Make it five and I'll keep Kiesha from castrating you as she's threatening to do."

Rory's eyebrows shot to his hairline. "Ten minutes and remind your mate we're family now."

Alex choked on a laugh and started coughing. "Yeah, that will go over real well. How 'bout I wait till after the wedding to let her know that little tidbit?"

"Fine, whatever. Clock's ticking," he reminded Alex. As he went to hang up the phone, he heard Alex call, "Rory?"

"Yeah?"

"No claw marks. The dresses Kiesha picked out are pretty revealing." Alex disconnected.

Rory scowled at Shayla as he tossed the phone back in the cradle. "What does your bridesmaid's dress look like?"

She stared at him like he didn't have all his faculties intact. "What! What did Alex have to say?"

"Your parents are asking about you, and your cousin's homicidal. Now answer my question. Just how revealing is the dress you'll be wearing?"

She tried to jump up from the bed. "My parents are here? We've got to leave, now! Where are my clothes?"

He snatched her down onto the mattress and pressed her flat on her back. "We'll get to that in a bit. First I want to know about this dress."

She glared up at him as he loomed over her. "Do we really have time for this? Where are we? I assume we're not in Refuge or Kiesha would have come pounding on the door. How long of a drive is it? Shouldn't we be leaving? The wedding will be starting soon."

He held her stare before flicking his gaze to the clock. Damn it, she was right. They needed to leave. He'd told Alex ten minutes, and he'd already wasted three. Coming to a sudden decision, he stood, reached down, and scooped Shayla up in his arms and strode toward the bathroom. "You're right. We'll discuss it on the way there."

He carried her straight into the shower and turned the water on, laughing when she shrieked and tried to climb his body to get away from the cold spray. As the water warmed, he maneuvered Shay until her legs were around his waist with her ankles locked at the small of his back and his cock deeply embedded inside her warm, wet sheath.

She gasped and then asked on a moan, "I thought we were leaving."

"I can multitask. Can't you? Grab the shampoo bottle and wash your hair," he ordered.

"You want to see multitasking?" she challenged.

Shay leaned back into the spray, and it was his turn to groan as her small, rounded breasts with their taut, brown areolae and nipples were put on prominent display. Her cunt rippled around him, gripping and releasing in a manner that stole all the fluid from his mouth. He stood with his feet apart, legs braced, and gripped her by the waist, supporting her back as hot-pink-colored water ran down her body and out the drain. Of their own accord, his hips made mini jabbing motions. He loved the feel of this woman, the way her tight, velvety sheath gripped him like a glove, milking him. Loved the feisty way she opposed him at every turn. He'd never be bored with Shay. Angry, frustrated, bemused, but never bored.

She lifted her arms to wash her hair, and his gaze became fixated on the pure pleasure in her expression. She was such a hedonist when it came to sex. Mating with Shay was like nothing he'd ever experienced before. In the past he'd had to temper his strength, leash the beast, even with female shifters. Shay took—no, demanded—all of him, no holding back.

Bending his knees, he leaned forward and latched on to one of the nipples brazenly on display, drawing strongly.

Shay balled up her fist and popped him upside the head—hard. "Watch it, buster. That hurts."

He released her breast, making a small popping sound. "Are they tender?" He glanced from her chest to her face.

"Like you wouldn't believe."

He grunted, inwardly pleased at this small sign of the changes her body was going through. He lightened his touch and smiled when she moaned and her sheath tightened. Shayla undulated her lower body in a circle, and he lost it. He swung her around so that she was braced against the wall. "Hold on," was all the warning he gave.

Shay was right with him every second, going over the edge into a screaming orgasm just moments before he spurted inside her. He leaned against her, breathing heavily. Annoyingly she pushed and shoved on his shoulders.

"What!" he snarled.

"Parents, wedding, Kiesha? Helloooo, we have to go."

"Shit!" He lowered Shay until her feet touched the floor. If he thought he could get away with it, he'd take her back to bed. He wasn't nearly satisfied.

She washed quick and climbed out of the shower, smelling of the soap she'd washed with. His wolf urged him to snatch her up and scent mark her again. He resisted. They really didn't have time, but tomorrow was a new day and they had the rest of their lives. He allowed the thought to comfort him.

"Where are my clothes?" Shay faced him in the center of the bedroom with the towel wrapped around her.

"What's left of them is in the trash," he stated shortly.

"I can't go to Refuge like this." She swept a hand down her body, emphasizing her current state of undress. "Did you at least grab my suitcase?"

His only thought after she'd crashed was of finally getting Shay where she belonged, at home in his bed. "Didn't have the opportunity."

"What am I supposed to wear?" she demanded, hands on her hips.

"I'm sure there's something here that will fit you." He walked into the closet and came out with a black tux to find Shay glaring at him, an evil glint in her eye.

"If you think I'm wearing something an old lover left behind, forget it," she said on a growl.

"Feeling possessive?" he teased. When she snarled at him, he laughed. "Shay, I'm alpha. This is the pack house. We keep clothing here in a variety of sizes since shifters have a nasty habit of losing theirs."

"I knew that," she muttered.

"Down the hallway to the left you'll find the storage room. Pick something. And don't take too long. I'll be ready to roll in ten."

Shay flipped him the bird as she walked out of the room.

* * * *

Shay woke as the vehicle slowed and came to a stop. Once again she'd been aware of little of the drive from Rory's town to Refuge, having knocked out almost before they got rolling. "Why are we at the church?"

"Shannon called while we were en route and stated that she'd bring your things here and save time. She said to tell you Kiesha excused your absence by telling your parents you'd started your new work assignment."

She stretched and yawned before gazing out the windshield through sleepy eyes. "I'll have to thank them. God, I feel like I could sleep for a week and barely make a dent in all the rest I've lost this past month."

He lifted her chin by a finger, tilted her head in his direction, and studied her face intently. "After this is over, I'll make sure you get rid of those dark circles under your eyes. I'll take good care of you and our cub."

Shayla was proud of herself for not flinching at the mention of her pregnancy. Then she had a thought. "Don't you dare mention any of this to my parents," she growled.

Rory met her stare for stare until she found herself looking away. He captured her chin between his thumb and index finger and turned her head back toward him. "When you're ready, we'll announce it together. This is your cousin's day. I have no intention of doing anything to take away from it."

Shay breathed a sigh of relief. The last thing she wanted right now was to have a knock-down, drag-out brawl with Rory over this. "Kiesha's already pissed with me for not telling her. I just can't handle any more grief," she found herself explaining.

He released her. "Let's go. They're waiting."

Rory opened the door and got out while she sat there looking at the church. Inside were the people who knew her best, the ones who loved her most. Their opinions were very important to her, but right now she could do without their alarmed inquisitiveness if her condition became known. Her father would go into protective mood, demanding Rory take care of his "responsibility." Her mother, who had a streak of traditionalism a mile wide, would be in raptures over Shay finally "settling down with a nice man and starting a family."

She snorted. As if by any stretch of the imagination Rory could be considered *nice.*

Then there was Kiesha, her cousin who loved and annoyed her the way an older sibling could. They'd shared everything through the years, but for the first time she understood and appreciated Kiesha's reticence to share when she'd first hooked up with Alex. It wasn't so much reluctance to dish but an "I don't know what the hell is happening myself so how can I rationally discuss it with you" type of thing. Too bad she'd nagged until Kiesha had no choice but to talk.

Payback was a bitch, and payment was due.

Her door swung open, and Rory stood in the opening. "You going in or you gonna sit here till the wedding's over?"

Snapped out of her thoughts, Shay noted the way he hovered protectively over her, the possessive glint in his eye. "Don't do that in front of my parents."

"What?" He looked confused. It was not a good look on him.

"That"—she waved a hand, indicating his facial expression and body posture—"whole possessive vibe you've got going."

His eyes widened in surprise, then narrowed. "I'm a wolf, babe. It's in my DNA."

"Yeah, well, tone it down or something, will ya? Mom's already going to be on the whole 'when are you going to get busy producing grandkids, Shayla' kick. I don't need you giving her ammunition," she snarled as she slid out of the truck.

He backed up to give her room. As she pushed past him, he murmured in her ear, "Only around your parents and only because you're covered in my scent."

"Damn it, why didn't you tell me I stink?" she asked just to piss him off.

He growled. Shay smirked even as her pussy creamed. Damn she loved yanking Cujo's chain. He was so easy. She picked up the pace, finally feeling a bit more like herself. She didn't even grumble when his arm shot past her to pull the door open for her.

Shannon met them at the door. "It's about time you two showed up."

"Hello to you too. Where's the bloodsucker? Asleep in his coffin?" Rory asked his sister.

"Don't mind him. He has penis envy. Everyone knows vamps are at the top of the paranormal food chain, which means they do *everything* better," Shay stated. Glancing past Shannon, she called out, "Hey, Dad," effectively cutting off the snarling comment she knew Rory was forming.

"You'll pay for that later," Shannon murmured as Shay brushed by, headed for her father.

"Aye, she will," Rory confirmed.

Shay certainly hoped so. Otherwise what was the point?

As her father enfolded her in his embrace, she could feel Rory's gaze. Ignoring wolf man for the moment, she concentrated on her dad, whom she hadn't seen in a while. He pulled back and stared down at her face. "Baby girl, you work too hard."

She shrugged away his concern. "I got sick on my last assignment. Stomach virus. Still getting over it," she explained.

"Kiesha told us. You'd better get in there before the Drill Sergeant comes looking for you." He gave her a gentle shove in the direction she assumed held the rooms Kiesha and the other girls were changing in.

"I'm going, and I'm telling Mom you're calling her names again," she teased, then jumped out of the way of the playful swat he aimed toward her butt.

Shay crossed the foyer, headed for the door in the corner that her father had indicated. Shannon left Rory's side and joined her. The minute the door closed behind them, Shannon laid a restraining hand on her arm. "You marked him."

"I…it just happened. I couldn't control myself," Shay explained.

"Does this mean you're staying?" Shannon's solemn gaze showed her concern for Rory's well-being.

"Yeah," Shayla slowly responded. "I guess it does. There's more than me to think about, you know? Got to do what's best for the little one."

"And what about you? Despite what I said earlier, Rory would hate it if the only reason you're with him is because you're pregnant."

"He…your brother…" She stopped, not sure how to put it in words. "He intrigues me, makes me crazy. I like yanking his chain, making him lose control." She sighed, frustrated. "He affects me. I'm not sure how this will all play out. I don't know. Maybe there is something to this true mates stuff."

Shannon's smile lit up the hallway where they stood. "It's a start. Long as you don't run, everything should work out fine."

Shayla snorted. "This is me you're talking to. I'm more likely to head into trouble than to run from it." Hell, most times she was the one who'd started it.

Shannon laughed and threw her arm around Shay. "Welcome to the family, Sis."

"Yeah, well, just don't say anything like that in front of my parents. I'm not ready for them to know yet," Shayla warned.

"Having met your mother, I understand completely. Are you sure she isn't a shifter? She's alpha enough. Doesn't say a lot, but the look on her face…" Shannon shuddered. "That woman could teach a wolf a few things."

"My father didn't call her the Drill Sergeant for nothing. She has eyes like a hawk and this way of issuing orders that has you obeying before you even realize what you're doing," she said with a roll of her eyes.

"Like I said—alpha."

"I'd better get in there before she comes looking for me." Shay motioned for Shannon to lead the way. "How's Kee?"

"Steady. Still worried about you but trying to hide it. This whole wedding thing is just a formality," Shannon stated as she came to a halt in front of an unmarked door.

"For you shifters, maybe, but not for Kiesha. She's been dreaming of this day her whole life," Shay commented as Shannon opened the door.

As soon as she saw her mother, Shay squealed, "Mommy," like the geek she was and ran to give her a hug.

"Shay-Nei." Her mother hugged her tight, then pinched her cheeks. "Look at these dark circles. You work too hard. When are you going to quit this gypsy lifestyle, settle down with a man, and give me some grandkids? You're almost thirty."

"Moooom," she groaned. "It's been almost a year since we've seen each other, and you're already starting in on me?"

"I'm not getting any younger. Neither are you. Kiesha's found a nice young man of her own. Why can't you?"

"Her next assignment is nearby in Tennessee. She'll be there for six months. Maybe she'll meet a nice man, Auntie," Kiesha said.

Glancing over her shoulder, Shay gave Kiesha evil voodoo eyes. When her mom went into raptures, ruminating on the possibilities, she turned where her mother couldn't see her, pointed at Kiesha, then put her hands to her throat, miming choking motions. Kiesha's gaze dropped meaningfully to Shay's stomach, and she arched an eyebrow. The message was clear. With a sigh of defeat, Shay looked around for her dress.

"My brother lives there. In fact, that's who Shay will be working for. He's single, and they seemed to hit it off fairly well when she was here a few weeks ago," Shannon added with a sly grin.

"Really?" The glance her mother gave Shay was speculative. "And he's single, you say?"

"Owns his own construction business and has partnerships in quite a few of the other local businesses," Shannon stated.

"Best of all, he's not scared of Shay," Kiesha said with a smirk.

Grinning, Shay's mother said, "I want to meet this man. Is he coming to the wedding?"

"He's in it," Kiesha said. "He's paired with Shayla."

I'm going to kill them, the both of them, as soon as this thing is over, Shayla thought to herself.

"And what's this young man's name? And why is he still single if he's so eligible?" her mom asked suspiciously.

'Cause he's crazy mean and no one would have him? Shay quickly muffled a laugh at her thoughts. If she commented in any way, it would just encourage her mother, so she got her dress and acted oblivious to the conversation around her.

"He wanted to make sure I was taken care of first. We shared a house until recently. Actually Rory practically raised me. He'll make a good father," Shannon said.

Shayla rolled her eyes.

"He's become a good friend of Alex's in the short time I've been here," Kiesha stated. "I can vouch for his character. I think he's a good match for Shay. She needs a firm hand, and he can definitely handle her."

Come on, guys, laying it on a bit thick, aren't you? Shay snorted.

"Did you say something, Shay-Nei?" her mother asked.

"Hmm? Oh, just that I don't remember this dress being this loose," she responded, thinking quickly. Kiesha looked over as her mother and Shannon came close.

"Turn around," her mother commanded.

As she spun, her mother ordered, "Hold your hands out."

Shay did as she was told. "Is it really noticeable?"

There was a brief knock, and the door opened to admit Kiesha's best friend, Mary Elizabeth. "Hey, Tameka's here," Mary Elizabeth announced as she stepped to the side. Behind Mary Elizabeth stood a slender black woman with a hesitant look on her face.

"Oh great. Shay, Auntie, this is Tameka. She's going to be doing my hair. Tameka, this is my cousin Shayla and her mother, Kiyona. Did you bring the stuff?" Kiesha asked.

"Right here." Tameka held up a square, plastic container that looked sort of like a toolbox.

Things got a bit hectic. Kiesha and Tameka were discussing hairstyles. Her mother sent Mary Elizabeth to get the seamstress to take in her dress while berating Shayla about her poor eating habits. Alex's mother, Mona, came into the already crowded room to see how things were progressing. But the shit really hit the fan when her mother absolutely refused to let her wear her combat boots under her dress.

By the time her dad knocked on the door and said they were ready, Shayla had a massive headache.

* * * *

The wedding ceremony passed in a stomach-churning blur. Despite his promise, Rory kept making eyes at her whenever their gazes connected. She tried not to look at him, but he was in her line of vision and did everything he could to make sure she saw him. In addition she could feel her mother's stare like an itch between her shoulder blades.

Her shoes pinched—she'd lost the battle over her boots—making her feet hurt. Just her rotten luck that she and her mother wore almost the same size and she'd had an extra pair of pumps in the car. There wasn't enough time to drive to Kiesha's and pick up the shoes matching her dress, so Shay wobbled down the aisle on three-inch stilettos, praying she wouldn't fall and embarrass herself. Simply making it to the altar was a challenge. Flowers in one hand, dress in the other to prevent tripping over the hem, she kept her head lowered, watching the placement of her feet in the carpet in the candlelit church while valiantly ignoring her mother's whispered hisses of, "Lift your head up, Shayla. Stop looking down."

Despite her misery, she couldn't help but smile when Alex bent Kiesha back over his arm for the kiss after they were pronounced man and wife.

The end was in sight. Alex escorted his new bride out of the church, the photographer snapping pictures the whole way. Then went Mary Elizabeth and her mate, a bear-shifter named Hugh. Shannon and some guy she didn't know were next. Shay wondered where the vampire was. Still home in his casket? The sun was setting outside, so he should be rising soon.

Rory held out his arm, and she laid her hand on the sleeve, leaning a bit heavier than she wanted as she gathered her dress in the same hand that was holding her bouquet. He leaned close to her ear. "You okay?"

"Damn shoes are killing my feet," she complained. She caught her mother giving them an appraising look out the corner of her eye and abruptly pulled away. Shay would have tipped over if Rory hadn't caught her. "She's watching," she muttered out the side of her mouth.

"Who?"

"My mother. She's matchmaking."

He grinned. "With me?"

"It's not funny," she hissed. "Your sister and my cousin put her up to it. They were singing your praises. It was enough to make me sick."

"Look at it this way. She won't be upset when she finds out about me and the babe," Rory stated.

She didn't remember the aisle being this damn long. If she didn't get out of these shoes soon, she was going to hurt someone. Finally they reached the exit and joined the rest of the wedding party in the reception line. Shay immediately stepped out of her heels.

She was bent over, rubbing the toes of her left foot, when her mother's commanding voice rang out as she passed. "Shay, straighten up and put those shoes back on your feet."

A growl slipped out as Shay glared at her mother's retreating back.

"I heard that," her mother called over her shoulder.

She muttered some very succinct curse words under her breath as she stuffed her abused feet back into the torture devices masquerading as shoes.

"You don't have to put them on if they hurt," Rory stated.

"Yeah, I do. I wouldn't put it past her to come and check." As much as Shay loved her mother, a little bit of her presence went a long way. Now she remembered why they hadn't seen each other in a year.

As soon as the last person cleared the line, Kiyona went into drill sergeant mode. "You there, clear the area. It's time for pictures."

Rory whistled under his breath. "Your mother's something else."

"Right now I wish she were *somewhere* else."

Kiyona got a few startled glances, but everyone obediently moved off the steps. Then came the poses. The bride and groom. The groom with his parents. The couple with his parents. The couple with Shay's mother and father. The bride with her bridesmaids. The groom with the groomsmen. It went on and on, in every combination possible.

"All right, everybody back in the church," Kiyona ordered.

They trooped back inside, the beleaguered photographer having lost control long ago, if he ever had it. Everything was repeated. Shayla knew she'd be seeing cameras flash in her nightmares.

"Shayla, the man said smile! That is not a smile."

Shay told Shannon through clenched teeth, "I'll kill her. You eat her. No body, no evidence."

"But lots of witnesses," Shannon reminded her.

"They won't tell. Hell, they might even help."

Just when she was tempted to make good on her threat, her father came to the rescue. "Okay, that's enough. I'm sure the kids are tired and hungry and so am I. They've been at it an hour. The guests are waiting."

Thanks, Dad, she mouthed.

He winked in return.

Everyone, including the photographer, heaved a sigh of relief as he led her mother off. Shayla promptly came out of her heels, and she noticed Mary Elizabeth and Kiesha doing the same.

"Don't your feet hurt?" she asked Shannon.

Shannon held up the hem of her dress, revealing the dainty, slipperlike flats she wore.

"Bitch," Shayla groused.

"And proud of it," Shannon responded.

"You know, agreeing with me just takes all the fun out of insulting you," she complained. Right then her stomach growled loudly.

Rory was suddenly by her side. He put a hand under her elbow. "Come on, let's go get you fed."

"Wait, let me grab my shoes," she protested as he tugged, pulling her along behind him.

Rory went back and scooped them up. "You riding?" he asked his sister.

The reception was being held at a nearby community center. "I drove," Shannon answered.

"We'll see you there." He rushed Shay out of the church.

At the top of the stairs, Shay pulled on his arm. "Stop. Give me my shoes. I'm not walking on that with bare feet." *That* was the pebbled driveway leading to the front of the church.

He didn't even pause. Rory swung her into his arms and kept walking.

"Put me down. My parents..."

"Will just have to deal."

Shay subsided. It's not like she wanted to walk anyway, not with the way her toes were throbbing.

"I can't believe you wore those things," he continued angrily.

"My mother made me."

He glanced down at her in surprise. "Do you always do what she tells you?"

"No, but I didn't figure Kiesha's wedding was the time to get into it with her."

He grunted in reply. His ground-eating stride rapidly ate up the distance to the truck. Rory opened the passenger door and set her on the seat. Before she could slide around, he reached down and massaged the toes and arch of her left foot. Shay fell back onto her elbows as a moan of pure pleasure left her lips. "God, that feels good."

"Aren't you supposed to have on stockings or something with those shoes?"

"I didn't have any. I was supposed to be wearing my boots. The heels wouldn't fit with the socks I had on," she stated wryly.

He switched feet, and Shay let her head relax back, staring up at the ceiling. Now that her appendages didn't hurt so much, she realized she was getting nauseated. Her mouth filled with saliva, and she swallowed repeatedly.

"What's wrong?"

It continually amazed her how attuned Rory was to her every nuance. "Stomach."

His gaze sharpened. "It pains you?"

She shook her head. "Sick."

"The babe needs to eat. Bend your knees." She curled so that both feet rested on the seat, and felt Rory arranging the skirt of her dress around her. "Don't move," he ordered before closing the door.

She didn't intend to. With the bile churning, it felt like the slightest movement on her part would upset the delicate balance and she'd hurl. He came around and slid into the driver's seat, lifting her head so that it rested in his lap. After starting the engine and backing out of the parking space, he laid his hand on her stomach and gently massaged the tense muscles.

"Damn town doesn't have a fast-food joint," he complained.

Shay placed her hand on his, entwining their fingers. "It shouldn't take long to get to the reception, and then I can eat. Kiesha's not going to prolong things. Alex will ensure it since she's pregnant too."

She closed her eyes and did her best to relax in the few minutes she had before they arrived. Shay must have been more tired than she realized, because the next thing she knew, Rory was lightly shaking her shoulder. "Shay, wake up. They're lining up to go inside."

She cautiously rolled to a sitting position and ran her fingers through her hair, smoothing the curls into place behind her ear. She'd wanted to add ruby-colored streaks to match her dress. Yet another thing her mother had vetoed.

The door opened, and Rory reached in to lift her out. When she was stable on her feet—once more in the damnable heels—he placed his hands on the sides of her neck and used his thumbs to raise her chin. "We don't have to do this if you don't feel up to it. I can take you straight to the table and fix you a plate. Alex will understand."

Alex would, but her parents wouldn't. Such action would cause more trouble for her than it was worth. "I'm fine. The nap and the foot rub helped." She glanced over his shoulder. "They're waiting."

Chapter Four

Rory led her across the parking lot—asphalt this time, fortunately—and they took their position. Both sets of parents were escorted inside, then Shannon and her partner, followed by Shayla and Rory, with Mary Elizabeth and Hugh bringing up the rear.

Mary Elizabeth and Hugh, as maid of honor and best man respectively, sat at the high table with Alex's and her parents. Shannon, the guy with her—what *was* his name?—Rory, and Shayla sat at a reserved table to the side. They remained standing and clapped as Alex and Kiesha walked in. Her cousin was beaming. Marriage looked good on her.

As soon as everyone was seated, Rory stepped away from the table. Shay caught him by the arm. "Where are you going?"

"To get you some food."

"The bride's table is supposed to eat first."

He shook her loose. "Screw that. Your health and the well-being of our child are more important than protocol."

Realizing he was prepared to make a scene, Shay let him go. Maybe he could slip over to the buffet table and back with none the wiser. She turned to Shannon and asked, "Where's Nik? Shouldn't he be out his coffin by now?"

"He's on the way."

"I'm surprised he wasn't with you at the ceremony. The whole sunlight thing got him, huh?"

Shannon laughed. "Sunlight doesn't hurt him, just makes him sluggish. He stayed away because he knows he makes a lot of the shifters uncomfortable."

"How are they adjusting to you mating a vamp?" Shay was curious. There had been some problems in the beginning because so many people were against it.

"The people that matter are for it. Everyone else…" She shrugged.

"I hear you."

Shayla played with the silverware, wishing Rory would hurry. She was starving, and the smell of all that meat was making her salivate, in a good way this time. The MC—an older black lady Shay had never met—was droning on in the background, announcing the order of events. Just as she released the wedding party to go fix their plates, Rory returned to the table with hers.

It was piled high. There were meatballs, chicken wings, riblets, some type of pastry that looked like it contained meat, seafood salad, and more. Shayla picked up her fork and calmly jabbed it into a meatball before bringing it to her mouth. She forced herself to eat slowly, knowing her mother was watching.

For a species that felt marriage was unnecessary, these shifters certainly knew how to plan a reception. The food was delicious, the decorations exquisite. Through closed double glass doors she could see a pool. Floating in it were flowered wreaths with tea-light candles lit in the center. Spaced evenly around the perimeter were torches, the kind that repelled flying insects.

The inside was decorated just as nicely. There was a stage on which a live band played. To the left a long table contained a mountain of wedding gifts. The table to the right held a huge three-tiered wedding cake adorned with pink rosettes. The center was open, forming a floor for dancing.

There must be over a hundred guests present, seated in groupings of eight at round tables. Each table had a floral centerpiece made of some flower Shay didn't know the name of but could see was very pretty and delicate. The jewel tones of their bridesmaid's dresses were repeated throughout the room. Coupled with the soft lighting and artificial candlelight, it gave the room a romantic feel.

Nikolai arrived while the guests were being served. The guy with Shannon quickly decamped, leaving the vampire his seat. Watching the two of them together, she could clearly see how in love they were. She wondered if she and Rory would ever look like that; then she snorted. Not bloody likely. Shannon and Nikolai were too sappy for words. She looked around the room. All the mated couples were, including Kiesha and Alex, and Mary Elizabeth and Hugh. It was enough to make a girl gag.

Shay leaned back in her chair and let the conversation wash over her. Now that her stomach was full, the nausea was gone and sleepiness had returned. Rory reached down, lifted her legs into his lap, and rubbed her calves. The tablecloth hid what he was doing, but at this point she really didn't care if her parents saw.

She propped her arm on the table, rested her cheek on her fist, and semidozed through both the maid of honor and best man's toasts, the cutting of the cake, and the tossing of the bridal bouquet and garter belt. Shay roused when Rory lowered her legs and stood. "Time to do our duty."

Shay reluctantly slid her shoes back on her feet and allowed Rory to lead her to the dance floor, where Kiesha and Alex along with both sets of parents were already dancing. They danced quietly through the rest of the set. Then came the rounds of switching partners, until each of the wedding party had danced with everyone else. By this time some of the older guests had left, Alex's parents among them.

Shay's parents approached. "Baby girl, your mother and I are getting ready to leave. We're hitting the road tonight. Our flight leaves in the morning, early. I wish we could stay longer, but I've got an important meeting I have to attend and your mother needs to prepare for the next semester."

"Okay, Daddy. Call me when you get in so I don't worry."

Shay's mother pulled her to the side. "Shannon's brother…*very* nice. He's interested too. It shows. You better snap him up."

"Moooom."

"You do what I tell you," she scolded.

"I don't think so." Shayla had to protest. If she agreed, her mother would be suspicious.

"Rory!"

"Mom, don't," Shay protested as her mother motioned for him to come over.

"Ma'am?" The glance he slid Shayla was questioning.

"You take good care of my girl while she's working for you. Introduce her to some nice men. A girl like my Shay-Nei has a lot to offer, yes?"

"Yes, ma'am. I'll see to it," he responded in his most solicitous voice. Shayla narrowed her eyes at him.

"Come on, Kiyona, let's go. We have a long drive ahead of us," her father said.

"Take care. Don't forget to call," Shay admonished as hugs were exchanged.

"We won't. Bye," her dad said. Her mom nodded her head in Rory's direction, smiling meaningfully, before her dad grabbed her by the arm and pulled her away.

"Bye," she echoed as they left.

As the underage and the elderly left and only the in-between remained, the atmosphere changed. Ties and jackets came off, and abandoned heels littered the floor, partially hidden beneath the trailing edges of tablecloths. A bar was set up in the corner, and the doors to the pool area were thrown open, letting in the cool night air. The bright lights were turned on, and some industrious males began taking down the unnecessary tables, increasing the dancing area.

Shayla looked around avidly, sleep forgotten. These people really knew how to party. The band switched from the easygoing, laid-back tunes they were playing to hard rock. The singles among them joined up into couples or, in some cases, threesomes. From the amount of sexual tension in the air, quite a few of them would be getting lucky.

With both sets of parents gone, there was room at the main table for the rest of the wedding party, so they gathered their things and joined Kiesha and Alex at the head table. She was calling it a table, but it was really three in a U formation, with Alex and Kiesha at the top. Shayla sank into the seat next to her cousin, and Rory, never far away, settled on her right.

"I am never getting married," she told Kiesha. "That woman is insane. I don't know how you stood it."

Kiesha looked to where Shay and Rory's hands were linked on the table. Now that her parents were gone, the man was indulging in his need to stake a claim, especially with all the horny wolves on the prowl. Not that they were a concern. One glance followed by a sniff and they stayed away. Maybe there really was something to this marking business. "What about Rory?"

"We'll live in sin. It'll give her something to pray about. Hell, she's getting a grandchild out of the deal. That ought to be enough." Shay rolled her shoulders, trying to loosen the tension.

"You know your dad won't go for that. He'll come after Rory with a shotgun," Kiesha stated with a laugh.

Rory stirred. "I don't think I like the sound of that."

Shay rolled her eyes at him. "You're a werewolf. Suck it up. It's not like a bullet will kill you unless he uses silver."

She could feel all of them gazing at her in stunned dismay.

"Shay, we really have to do something about your preconceptions," Alex said.

"Yeah. For one, Nikolai does not sleep in a coffin and sunlight won't kill him," Shannon stated.

"She thought that?" Nikolai asked.

"Yes, she asked if that's why you weren't at the wedding," Shannon responded.

“And while we heal superfast, enough bullets in the right body part will kill us just as much as anyone else,” Rory added.

“Really? Man, I didn’t know that, but…you guys do turn hairy during a full moon, right? And Nik, being the undead evil and all, doesn’t being on holy ground bother you?” Shay asked, a bewildered expression on her face.

There were groans from the shifters at the table and what sounded like a snarl from Nikolai.

“No, Shay. Where are you getting this stuff from?” Alex asked.

“I researched vamps and shifters online, where else?”

They all started talking at once, only to quiet when Mary Elizabeth burst out laughing and Kiesha joined her, almost falling out of her chair.

“You shouldn’t laugh at her, Mary Elizabeth. She doesn’t know,” Hugh scolded.

“She’s not laughing at Shayla,” Kiesha denied. “She’s—we’re—laughing at you. You guys are so gullible. Shay, stop messing with them.”

Shay gazed blandly at each person in the group. “I don’t know what she’s talking about.”

Alex’s suspicion showed on his face. Hugh looked confused. Shannon’s expression showed she realized she’d been had. Nikolai was hard to read, but Rory? His eyes were narrowed.

“Shay’s a genius. She probably knows more about your species than you do yourselves,” Mary Elizabeth said while wiping tears from her eyes.

“My area of expertise is computers,” she loftily informed them.

"Yes but Auntie Yona's is genetics, and she taught you all she knows. Don't tell me you haven't done DNA testing on Alex. You can probably tell us what this child I'm carrying will look like and which characteristics of ours it will have," Kiesha finished with a chuckle.

As the grumbling rose from the paranormals sitting there, she decided retreat might be in order. "Traitor," she grumbled at her cousin as she rose from her seat.

Rory tightened his grip on her fingers. "Where are you going?"

"Bathroom." Her look dared him to make something out of it.

He released her as Kiesha said, "I'll join you. My bladder's about to burst."

"Count me in," Mary Elizabeth added. "You coming?" she asked Shannon.

"Might as well."

As they walked off, she heard Alex telling Rory, "I don't envy you, my friend. She's going to turn your pack upside down."

"They could use a good shaking up," was his response.

As they crowded into the restroom, Shay realized she really did have to go. While she stood washing her hands at the sink, Shannon said, "I can't believe I fell for that. After all the questions you asked me about shifters and vamps when you were here the last time, I should have known you knew better."

"It's that expression she gets on her face," Kiesha said. "You know, the 'I really don't know, please educate me' look? She does it so well."

"Shay plays stupid better than anyone I know," Mary Elizabeth informed them.

Shay shrugged. "What can I say? It's a gift."

"Well make sure you use that 'gift' of yours when you meet Rory's pack. Let 'em underestimate you," Shannon said.

"I thought you told me they respected intelligence and strength," Shay asked, confused for real this time.

"They do, but they also admire cunning. If you go in there acting clueless, you'll discover faster who's on your side. They'll relax their guard if they think you aren't a threat," Shannon concluded.

"You make it sound like she's going into battle," Kiesha said, looking worried.

"She is. The Sparrowhawks aren't like the Ravens. If she comes on too strong, Shay's going to be challenged for her alpha-fem position, true mate or not. But if she plays dumb, they'll understand Rory protecting the 'puny human.' Shay will have a chance to learn who her enemies are, and she'll have some, believe it."

"That's terrible," Mary Elizabeth said.

"What's worse is that as alpha, Rory's slept with over half the females of the pack at one time or another. Many of them are still hoping he'll choose them to be his mate. They aren't going to be happy to see Shay, and they're sure to try to discredit her and make her life miserable if they possibly can."

"Well, hell, Shannon. You couldn't have mentioned all this earlier when you were convincing me to give Rory a chance?" Shay asked.

Shannon gave her a lopsided grin. "I didn't want to scare you off."

"Anything else I need to know?"

"Yeah. Don't go in the basement," Shannon said, her expression as serious as Shayla had ever seen.

"What's down there, the boogeyman?"

Kiesha and Mary Elizabeth laughed. Shannon did not.

"Something like that," Shannon agreed.

"We'd better go before the guys come looking for us," Kiesha interrupted.

Shayla trailed behind the others, curiosity working overtime. First chance she got, she'd have to take a little look in the basement. That's what Shannon wanted her to do, right? She had to know telling Shay not to do something was like waving a red flag at a bull. The results were almost guaranteed.

As she neared the opening to the pool, she noticed a tall, lean figure standing in the shadows that was vaguely familiar. Shay thought she knew him, and that in and of itself was enough to capture her attention since she didn't know many folks in Refuge. In actuality the only people she knew were in the wedding party, which meant this guy wasn't from here. Why was he lurking, and how was it that no one—werewolves and vamps included—noticed his presence?

No time like the present to find out.

She detoured away from the others and headed straight for him. If he noticed her approach, it didn't send him running. As she drew near, recognition struck like lightning. "*Conor!* Dude, you're here! Why are you hiding in the shadows? Come on out." She launched herself at him, grinning and hugging him tight.

This Indian was a favorite of hers. Kiesha had thought him old and senile in a harmless sort of way.

Shay thought Conor was a hoot and he told the best stories.

He hugged her back, his grip strong. “Shayla Nei, I see you’ve found your mate. Pregnancy becomes you. You glow.”

Shay didn’t even question how he knew. Back in Pirate’s Cove he’d always done things like that, just popped out with some bit of knowledge. Used to freak Kiesha out, but of the two of them, her cousin had always been the doubter. If Kee didn’t believe in it, it couldn’t exist, and there was a lot of stuff she didn’t believe in. Or there used to be before she’d ended up mated to a werewolf.

“Nice job, by the way, what you did for Kee,” she complimented him as she gazed up at him from within his loose embrace. Conor was responsible for Kiesha meeting Alex.

He grinned, and she caught a glimpse of his slightly crooked front tooth. “She was the catalyst. Look at all that’s happened since she’s arrived.”

“While I’m happy for Kiesha and Mary Elizabeth, I think you went a little too far with the matchmaking when you threw me into the mix,” she groused, not truly angry.

He threw back his head and laughed, causing his silver-streaked black hair to float around his shoulders and the fine wrinkles around his eyes in his deeply tanned face to scrunch. He really was a stunningly attractive male, even if he was at least as old as her father. “You are just what that red wolf needs. The Creator makes no mistakes.”

“He might need me, but what am I getting out of the exchange?”

Conor gazed down at her, his black eyes deep and mysterious. "Someone who loves you totally and completely, just the way you are. Never forget that, Shayla Nei, no matter how rough things get. It will all be worth it in the end."

Hearing the warning, she asked, "What's coming?"

His eyes seemed to lose focus. "You must fight to hold on to what is yours. Treachery surrounds you. Only by uniting together will you be victorious." His gaze drilled into hers with laserlike precision. "Show no mercy. Your daughters' safety depends on the decisions you make now."

Before she could press for more details, she was snatched back against a hard, muscular chest and strong arms wrapped securely around her from behind. Rory. She'd know that chest rumble anywhere. With a wave of her hand, she introduced them. "Rory, meet Conor, the man responsible for Kiesha and Alex and, consequently, you and I meeting."

The growling stopped, and a stunned silence followed. "*The* Conor?"

She leaned to the side and glanced up at him. "Alex told you about him?"

He looked down at her, eyes still rounded in shock. "Uh...Conor's a legend among our kind. Until Alex told me differently, I didn't think he was real."

"A legend? Come on," she scoffed. Turning to Conor, she said, "Don't get me wrong. You're one of my favorite peeps in the world, but a legend?" She shook her head and chuckled.

The grin he gave her in return said Conor shared her amusement.

"Shay, who are you talking...Conor!"

She reached out and slapped her cousin's arm. "Kee, why didn't you tell me he was coming?"

"I didn't know. I didn't even know he knew I was engaged. We didn't see him in Pirate's Cove when Alex and I returned to pack up my condo." Kiesha appeared totally bemused.

"*This* is Conor?" Alex asked. Startlement gave way to the same awe Shayla saw on Rory's face.

"Oh, not you too." Shay rolled her eyes. "What is it with you people? He's a man, not God. What's with all the astonishment?"

Conor's features seemed to shimmer and blur. In a matter of seconds his slightly hunched shoulders straightened, his graying hair turned black and curled, and his attractively wrinkled face unlined, becoming youthful. The end result was a man so devastatingly handsome it made Shay's mouth drop open. "Okaaay, I didn't know he could do *that*!"

"Damn," Kiesha muttered, equally surprised.

On second thought Shay wasn't sure why she was stunned. If the man had teleported Kiesha five states away in the middle of the night to meet her mate, as Kiesha suspected, neither of them really should be astonished at Conor magically altering his appearance.

Mary Elizabeth, who'd just walked up with Hugh close behind, said under her breath, "Hubba, hubba," and fanned her face.

Shay was distracted from her own shock by Nikolai. He strode up to Conor, went down on one knee, placed his fist on his chest, and bowed his head respectfully. "Sire."

"Nikolai!" Conor said with a big grin and held out a hand to him. Nikolai stood, and the two clasped forearms.

"Sire as in *king*?" Shay asked.

"Why don't we all sit down while Nikolai—or Conor—explains," Alex suggested. The ones Shay identified as pack immediately complied.

Rory led Shay to the table, giving Conor a wide berth. Shay looked over her shoulder and winked at Conor. When she noticed Nikolai watching, she crossed her eyes and stuck out her tongue at him. Nikolai was so dignified and formal in his old-world way, Shay couldn't help but try to loosen him up. Shannon burst into laughter when she saw.

"What are you doing?" Rory asked.

"Nothing," Shay responded innocently. "You know since he and Nik are family, that means Conor's related to you as well, don't you?"

"Shay…not another word."

"I'm just saying…"

"Shay!"

She hummed the theme to *The Addams Family* under her breath, smiling wickedly when Rory's chest rumbled with a low growl. He pulled out a chair, sat, and tumbled her into his lap, snarling when she tried to scoot into the empty seat next to him. Figuring she'd done enough for the moment, she subsided. Besides, he smelled really good. Shay turned her nose into his neck and inhaled, then licked the skin for good measure. Rory was instantly hard beneath her hip.

"Shayla, behave, *please*." Rory sighed. "I'd like to hear this."

She muttered under her breath but settled down. Now that her belly was full and bladder empty, another need was making itself known. She felt her sex clench. This Conor thing better not take too long.

When only Conor remained standing, he asked Alex, "What is it you would like to know?"

"How is it that you're able to identify potential true mates?" Alex asked.

"And why do you smell like a wolf-shifter when you're a vamp?" Rory added.

"He was talking to Alex, not you," Shay couldn't resist pointing out.

The man shushed her. Shay would have commented, but Kiesha was glaring at her. Okay, so this whole thing might be a little important. She could tangle with Rory later. Shay wrapped an arm around his neck and leaned against him, squirming as she tried to get comfortable. Sitting on Rory was like sitting on concrete. There was no give, no softness in his body. He shifted until she was held securely in his arms with her back against his chest, and she sighed. She wasn't completely satisfied with her position, but this was as good as it got.

RORY EXAMINED CONOR as he stood before them. The man was an enigma, and he didn't like puzzles. Even his wolf senses couldn't detect exactly what Conor was. It didn't help that his scent kept changing.

"My mother was a wolf-shifter, my father a vampire."

Conor's words caused an explosive reaction. Furious outbursts and heated denials filled the room. Even Shay quit her squirming, sat up, and took notice. A vamp and a shifter breeding? Impossible. His da had been well versed in the old ways and he'd never mentioned it being possible, but if it were...

His gaze shifted to rest on Shannon.

One voice rose above the rest. “Vampire and shifter matings are forbidden.”

“Aye and there’s a reason that is so,” Conor said quietly. “I, and others like myself, are the reason it was forbidden. Imagine a being with the combined strength of a vampire and shifter and none of the weaknesses.”

A weighty silence filled the room. That would be one damn powerful being, Rory thought.

Conor looked Rory in the eye. “You’ve the right of it. A damn powerful being indeed,” he said. “Such matings were rare. Offspring even rarer, but it happened. Like shifters, vampires mostly kept to their own kind. Then the plague hit, annihilating humans and decimating our old, females, and young. No species was exempt from the carnage.”

A gloom settled over the room. Even the lighting seemed to dim.

“Only the strong survived. Those that were left focused on surviving, rebuilding their clans, families…packs.” Conor’s gaze scanned the room. “Instead of pulling together, it was every man…every species for himself. What resources remained were fought over, many times to the death. The weak got weaker and the strong…more vicious.”

His focus turned inward. “Out of the darkness stepped a leader, a being like myself, both shifter and vampire. He managed to unite what was left of the packs, convincing them that the path to survival lay in banding together. Laws were written and obeyed or death was swift. ‘Protect the young and elderly, our women treasured above all.’”

Rory stirred at the familiar tenets. He wasn't the only one.

"The wolf-shifters began to grow and thrive. Others noticed. Some of the other groups allied themselves and strengthened as well. Others remained apart, isolating themselves. Some died out…or were never heard from again."

It was as quiet as the grave in the room. Barely a breath could be heard.

"Among the vampires a leader arose, only she wasn't as…benevolent. For her it was all about power. Like Mangus, Fiala was half-vamp/half wolf-shifter. Unlike Mangus, she ruled by might. Those who opposed her were captured and killed. She wasn't satisfied simply having vampires under her thumb. She wanted to rule the world."

"Sounds like she had a screw loose," Shayla murmured.

"There was a war," Conor continued.

He heard Alex declare softly, "The vamp-shifter wars."

Conor nodded abruptly, acknowledging Alex's comment. "Many fled…hid. My parents among them. Fiala was finally overthrown, but by that time vamps and shifters alike had grown to fear and hate half-breeds such as myself. We were hunted. Matings between the two species were forbidden. My father died protecting us. By then I was old enough to hide what I was, mask my scent. My mother found a pack that took us in, and I was raised as a wolf."

"That answers one question," Rory stated. "What about the other?"

"I'm somewhat of a genealogist. As a near immortal, I've had plenty of time to indulge my habit," Conor said.

Shayla snorted. "The man's a freakin' psychic, is what he is."

"That too." Conor smiled and his eyes...their color changed and began to swirl and glow. Rory clutched his mate to him, a hand pressed protectively against her stomach where his cub rested. He tensed, ready to move at a moment's notice.

"Cool trick with the eyes. What else can you do?" Shay asked, sounding impressed, to Rory's disgust.

Conor threw back his head and laughed, a deep belly chuckle that released the tension in the room.

When he stopped, his eyes were back to normal. Or what Rory assumed was normal. With this guy, it was hard to say.

Shay's teasing and Conor's response must have been a signal for the rest of the room. Questions began to fly, people calling out over one another to be heard. Shay leaned forward and rested her elbows on the table, propping her chin on her hands as her head turned this way and that, trying to keep up with who was speaking. Rory's gaze was immediately drawn to the long line of her spine, bared by the haltered gown she wore. Its V-shaped back stopped right above the swell of her ass, making him wonder what she wore underneath.

The thought of her naked beneath the silky material made him harder, tighter, and he suddenly realized it had been much too long since he'd buried himself within her satiny sheath. Losing all interest in the conversation swirling around them, he glided his hands up the sides of Shay's body, feeling for underwear. Finding none, a small growl rumbled out of his chest and he prodded her with his raging, temporarily confined hard-on.

The perfume of Shay's arousal filled the air in response, and a hard grin crossed his face. Firmly gripping her hips, he rubbed her against his bulging crotch and ran the point of his tongue up the middle of her back to just below her neck. Rory could feel her heat, smell her dampness.

Shay's breath caught on a small moan, and she rocked on him in microcircles. He trailed his lips from her nape to her left shoulder, where one of his marks was prominently displayed. He tongued it, knowing it would spike her arousal. Rory slid his hand inside her dress and around to her stomach, and glided the flat of his palm up until his fingers rested just below her breasts.

"Rory." She groaned his name. Straightening, she relaxed against his chest and tilted her head to the side, granting him unhindered access.

He murmured his approval and, as a reward, lifted his thumb to lightly stroke her beaded nipple.

Shay reached over her head and grabbed him by the hair, yanking his lips to hers. Their mouths fused together, the passion bounding back and forth between them, building higher and higher each round. Rory reached for Shay's dress, intent on dragging it up her hips and burying himself in her from behind, when a sharp pain in his leg snapped him out of his lust-induced craze.

Rory swung around with a snarl.

Alex had his hands raised, a rueful expression on his face. "Sorry, but you're putting on a show."

"You *kicked* me!" Rory all but roared.

Alex shrugged. "Just following orders." He pointed.

Rory's gaze followed Alex's finger to see his baby sister frowning at him. "Get a room already." A quick glance showed him they had the attention of everyone.

"I believe that's exactly what I'll do." In one smooth move, he rose to his feet with his mate in his arms. "It's time I took my family home."

"My things!" Shay exclaimed.

"Already in the truck," he announced as he strode out of the room.

"Shay, call me," were the last words he heard as the door closed behind them.

Rory's stride rapidly ate up the distance to the truck.

Chapter Five

Rory stood at the stove, reminiscing about the night before as he cooked breakfast meat. What he thought would be a night of hard, pounding sex had fizzled into nothing, his mate having fallen asleep on the ride home. The man part of him demanded he wake her and finish what they'd started. The wolf overrode it, more concerned with the well-being of his mate and cub than his own physical needs.

Suddenly his nose twitched and his beast stirred. Above the savory aroma of sausage and bacon cooking, he smelled something even more tantalizing. His mate. His aroused mate. Breakfast would have to wait.

He turned off the stove and removed the frying pan from the burner. Turning in the direction where Shay's scent was the strongest, his breath caught and his cock rose strong and proud.

She stood in the doorway in one of his dress shirts, unbuttoned down the middle. One hand played with the folds of her sex while the other toyed with a peaked, dusky brown nipple. His gaze reluctantly rose from that mouthwatering sight, and his eyes met the focused, golden-eyed stare she fixed on him. She didn't say a word. None was necessary.

Rory prowled to her, stopping mere centimeters away so that his now throbbing erection brushed the back of her hand. He reached up and pushed the shirt off her shoulders. It fell to her elbows and hung there around her hips. She was completely bare underneath.

Leaning forward, he licked the mate mark on her right shoulder, then bit down hard, teeth sinking in, breaking the flesh. Blood flooded his mouth. One of Shay's hands wrapped around his cock and squeezed. A growl rumbled from deep in her chest. An answering one sounded from his wolf. He felt the prick of tiny claws on his flesh, and the hint of violence in her touch excited him.

Rory released his hold on her shoulder and swirled his tongue over the wound, both to help it heal and because the taste of her blood turned him on. Prying her hand from his penis, he captured both of her wrists and held them over her head, pinning them alongside the wall. At the same time he covered her mouth with his. The kiss was raw, brutal.

Shay rose to her toes, arched her mound, and rubbed it against his cock. As her needy whimper filled the air, she tugged on her arms and, when he wouldn't release them, snarled into his mouth. He nipped her lower lip, a warning, a reprimand. In turn she bared her teeth and lunged for his face, mouth wide open.

Rory jerked away, eyes narrowed. A rumble began in his chest before emerging as a full-throated growl. She was testing his beast, challenging his dominance over her. It was there in the way she matched him glare for glare. He growled again, and she growled back, teeth still bared, still fighting to reach him. Her eyes had gone pure wolf. She was strong but no match for him, and he could see that the knowledge infuriated her beast.

At that moment the kitchen door swung open and Caleb and MacDougal walked in. Caleb, smart wolf that he was, stopped in the doorway, sniffing the air before his apologetic gaze locked on them near the entrance to the dining room. MacDougal continued on into the house, headed toward the stove. "Smells like we're in time for breakfast. Nice tits," he commented, giving Shay's body a thorough perusal.

"Maybe we should come back later," Caleb said, retreating for the door, which still stood open, eyes glued to Shay's half-naked body.

Shay's stare traveled from Caleb to MacDougal, and her scent increased. A flood of moisture coated his cock where it rested between her legs along her slit. She dared to look at another male with desire in his presence? When he could smell the other males' lust as they gazed at his mate?

His beast broke free. "Mine," he roared.

He flipped her around, ripped the shirt off her back, and took her down to the floor onto her knees. Forcing her legs apart, he impaled her with one deep thrust. She bucked and fought beneath him, but he swiftly overpowered her. Teeth locked on to her shoulder, he rutted on her like a beast gone wild. There was no thought or reasoning left within him.

Intent on proving his claim without a doubt, he pounded into her until she relaxed, arched her back, and raised her ass while whimpering, accepting his dominance. Raising eyes gone totally wolf, he stared at his men, daring them to challenge his claim. Caleb raised his hands and withdrew slowly until he was out the door. MacDougal smirked, crossed his arms over his chest, planted his feet, and watched, eyes still full of lust for Shay.

MY MATE.

He roared again, flashing his fangs in challenge as Shay shuddered beneath him, her pussy clamping around him like a vise as she came with a muffled scream. Growling low in his throat, eyes locked with his third, Rory pulled out and stroked his cock with his fist, spewing cum all over Shay's back and ass, scent marking her so there'd be no doubt to whom she belonged.

MacDougal snorted and finally strode from the house. Watching him, Rory knew one day he'd have to do something about him. He wouldn't continue to allow challenges to his leadership. His father would have already killed MacDougal by now. His thoughts were interrupted by Shay scrambling away from him. As soon as she gained her feet, she scampered off, running up the stairs. She never looked back.

Rory flinched at the sound of an upstairs door slamming.

What had he done? He looked at his hands with the claws still extended and thought back on all the times he'd seen his father do this very same thing to his mother. A man he'd sworn he'd never be like. With a cry of self-directed fury, Rory slammed his fists on the floor.

Slowly, cold resolve filled his being. It was his responsibility—no, his duty—to protect his mate, even from himself. Knowing what he had to do, he went to the kitchen wall phone and jabbed in a number. As he'd hoped, Kiesha answered the phone.

"Come get your bitch of a cousin. I no longer want her," he snarled into the receiver and slammed the phone down before she could respond.

His beast let out a mournful howl that Rory refused to give voice to. He forced himself to walk out the door, shifted to wolf, and took off running into the woods surrounding the house, trying to exhaust himself enough to forget that he'd just sent away the best thing that ever happened to him.

* * * *

Shayla rested her flaming cheeks on the cold tile of the shower while hot water poured over her. She, who didn't embarrass easily, was mortified. She'd had sex—in front of witnesses!—and she'd never been so turned on in her life.

She groaned and brought her hands up to cover her face.

For all her bold speaking and thinking, she knew she really wasn't the sexual libertine she pretended to herself and everyone else to be. Despite how brazenly she acted, this was over the top, even for her. Her sexually free attitude was simply a facade to keep men away. Most guys were intimidated by a more sexually experienced woman, afraid they couldn't measure up and not willing to take the risk. The ones who were attracted to the challenge Shay managed to scare off in other ways.

With the exception of Rory, the guys she'd previously allowed into her bed were major geeks and nerds like herself. Maybe they were a bit immature, but they didn't think her weird or strange because they were weird themselves. They'd have never considered turning sex into a spectator sport. Well, they might have considered it but definitely wouldn't have the balls to do it.

Shay didn't know which embarrassed her most: the way she'd literally preened under the lustful gaze of those two guys seeing her naked, or her reaction to Rory spurting his seed all over her body. She shuddered, but not in revulsion. He'd scent marked her to show his possession of her—something she'd read about in her study of werewolves—and she'd reveled in it. Almost turned and begged him to do it again.

Shay shook her head. And to think at the wedding reception they'd said that stuff she'd found on the Internet was pure fiction.

Kiesha had explained that as a result of her mating with Alex, she was slowly becoming a shifter. Hell, Conor had explained the process to Shay long before Kiesha knew who Alex was, back when she'd thought Conor was an amusing older gentleman who told the most fascinating stories. While Shay knew to expect the change in her DNA, no one had warned her that her very personality might change. That's the only explanation she could find for her odd behavior.

She'd been acting like a bitch in heat ever since Rory first laid his hands on her.

Even now she didn't want to wash his scent off, choosing instead to rinse the semen off. She reluctantly left the shower, knowing she couldn't hide in here forever. She would have to face the man at some point. Once again it was time to put her game face on. It wouldn't do to let Rory know the effect he had on her. The braggart would never let her live it down.

Shay wrapped a towel around her body and exited the bathroom, expecting to find Rory waiting for her. Instead the bedroom was empty and her cell phone was ringing. She lifted it off the bedside table and glanced at the display. Shannon. "Hey! Are you calling to see if your brother and I managed to kill each other yet?"

"*What the hell is going on there?*" Kee blasted, almost piercing her eardrum. "Pack your bags. We're on our way."

"*Kee?* Aren't you supposed to be on your honeymoon? And why are you calling from Shannon's phone?" Shay asked, confused.

"We're not going anywhere until we find out what's happening," she heard Alex say.

Alex was on the phone too?

"I'll be there as soon as *someone* tells me how the hell to get there. If you won't go with me, Alex Wolfe, I'll take some of the guys," Kiesha snarled.

"Kiesha, before you go running off, let's find out what the situation is," Shannon stated calmly.

"Kiesha, I can't allow you to do that. You'll start a pack war if you do," Alex reasoned.

Situation? Pack war? Huh?

"Fuck that! This is my cousin we're talking about. If you and Shannon won't tell me how to get to her, I'll find someone who will. Someone has to know where that fucker lives," Kee said.

"Hey, watch it! That 'fucker' is my brother," Shannon protested.

"Kee, be reasonable," Alex cautioned.

"That's easy for you to say. She's not your kin," Kiesha shouted.

"No, but Rory's mine and I know he wouldn't hurt Shayla," Shannon argued. "Especially not when she's carrying his cub."

"Guys, what—" Shay said.

"Oh, but he has no problems doing it when she's not?" Kee sarcastically questioned.

“Ladies, we still don’t know—” Alex began.

“I can’t believe you said that,” Shannon said on a growl.

“I should have followed my first instinct and castrated the bastard when I found out Shay was pregnant,” Kiesha snarled.

Okay, this was rapidly getting out of hand. Shay put her fingers between her lips and let out a shrill whistle into the phone. Her action gained immediate silence. Before anyone could say something else, she asked in a calm voice, “Would someone care to tell me what this is all about?”

When both Kiesha and Shannon began to make a heated response, she cut them off. “Alex, you tell me since you seem to be the only reasonable one at the moment.”

“Rory called Kiesha and told her to come and get you,” was his reply.

“No, he didn’t. First he called her a bitch, and *then* he told me to come get her. That he didn’t want her,’” Kiesha snarled.

“He said *what*?” Shay asked, her voice faint with shock.

“You heard me. He doesn’t want you there. I told these two…two…”

She heard Alex growl a warning.

“I told *them* what he said. However, neither one of them will tell me how to get to you, and they refuse to come and get you themselves,” Kiesha finished angrily.

Someone took a deep breath; then Shannon said, “Shayla, why would Rory tell Kiesha such a lie? I know he wants you. The man mourned the whole time you were gone. I've never seen him as content as when he's with you. What's going on?"

"I don't know, but I intend to find out," Shay said as bewilderment gave way to anger.

"Who cares why he said it? The fact is he did, and I don't want her there," Kiesha said.

"Kiesha, I keep telling you, we can't interfere with the bonding process," Alex reminded.

"When it comes to the Raven pack, I'll stay out of it, but when it's my cousin, there's no way in hell I'm sitting back and letting her get hurt," Kiesha stated firmly.

"Kee, I got this," Shayla inserted in a no-nonsense tone of voice.

"But—"

"No, Kee. I don't know what's going on, but I'll handle it," Shay said.

"But Shay—"

Alex cut her off. "Kiesha, she said she'd handle it."

"Fine!" Kiesha slammed down her receiver, and Shayla flinched and jerked the phone away from her abused eardrum. Hell, she'd really have to do some fence mending with her cousin later.

"Let us know if you need anything, Shayla. Despite what I said, if your safety depended on it, I'd start as many wars as necessary," Alex said before he too disconnected.

"None of this makes sense. My brother loves you," Shannon stated when it was just the two of them.

Shay sank onto the side of the bed. "He does?"

She knew he was possessive of her, or rather the baby, but love?

"Yes, told me so himself. I've never seen him like he was while you were gone. He was grieving. Rory…and his beast," Shannon said with great certainty. "Did anything happen?"

"He…we…I…" She broke off, her face hot like it was on fire. Taking a deep breath, she forced herself to continue. "He might have lost control, a bit."

"Oh. Shay, are you sure you're all right? Because the only reason I can think of that would cause a male shifter to send his mate away is fear—for her safety."

"Shannon, you know Rory wouldn't hurt me."

"I know he wouldn't, but does he?" Shannon paused to let that sink in before continuing, "Call me if you need me."

Shannon's question gave Shayla something to consider while dressing before going downstairs to find her mate, who had some serious explaining to do. She wasn't sure at what point she'd switched from merely tolerating this relationship for the sake of their baby to actively wanting it, but she wasn't letting go, especially not if he loved her. She'd seen—first with Alex, then with Hugh—how shifter males were with the women they loved. She'd never thought to experience it for herself, with any man, but if what Conor and now Shannon said was true…

She thought about how tender and caring he'd been with her since her return. He was still as possessive and sex-crazed as ever, but there was a new element in his touch. She'd thought it was because she was pregnant, but maybe it wasn't. Shannon knew him best. If she said Rory loved her, it must be true.

So what's this all about?

The man knew exactly what he'd been doing. He'd called Kee and got her all riled up, knowing with her protective nature, she was the one most likely to take exception to his words and come to the rescue. Then he'd run like the coward he was. She couldn't find him anywhere in the house, and she'd looked everywhere—with the exception of the double-bolted door she assumed led to the basement and its mysterious contents.

Shay wasn't going chasing all over the countryside after him. One, it was a good way to get lost, and two, the man had to come home sometime. Right now she had more important matters to attend to, like her empty, growling stomach.

* * * *

Rory silently padded toward the house. He was weary, his coat filthy, covered with dried blood from the brambles and thickets he'd run through. His paws were sore and tender. He'd deliberately run through the roughest terrain he could find, making trails where there were none. He hadn't eaten all day, barely drank any water, and even now the thought of food held little appeal.

At least his mate and unborn cub were safe.

It was his only solace. The hope he'd clung to as day slowly faded to night. For that small comfort, he could live with the pain. Deal with his beast that howled with grief and snarled in fury every time he thought of the mate he'd sent away or got a whiff of her scent, still on his body.

He shifted at the back door and paused, gathering himself to enter his once more empty house. As he opened the door, Shay's scent hit his nose like a hammer.

Altogether she'd been here less than twenty-four hours, and yet her sweet fragrance saturated the building. Shay and... He sniffed the air. *Popcorn?*

Then he heard it. The television was on. Quietly closing the door, he crept into the den, unable to believe what his senses were telling him. Stunned, he stopped in the arched entry and stared. Shay sat, leaned back in his favorite black leather rocker-recliner, a bowl of popcorn in her lap, eyes glued to the screen. She was completely and totally oblivious to his presence.

Why was she still here?

He'd planned it perfectly. Kiesha should have swooped in and snatched her up. Once she finished telling Shay what he'd said—and probably a few things he hadn't—Shay should have left in a fit of fury, especially after his earlier treatment of her. He didn't understand.

What went wrong?

"We need satellite. The reception here sucks." Shay's voice broke into his musings.

"What are you doing here?" he snarled, trying to ignore the way his beast almost quivered with joy at her presence.

"I live here." She tossed another handful of popcorn into her mouth and noisily munched on it.

"I don't want you here." He choked out the lie.

"Tough." She didn't even give him the courtesy of looking at him as she made her pronouncement.

Frustrated and angry, he stalked into the room until he towered over her, blocking her view of the television. She leaned to the right, and he moved with her. Then she leaned to the left, and he did the same.

Finally she huffed and glared at him. "Do you mind?" she barked.

"Yes, I do. For the love of God, woman, have you no sense of self-preservation? Leave now before I hurt you worse than I already have," he snapped.

Shay looked him dead in the eye and...*laughed*. In his face, and no light chuckle either. This was a "slap your leg, bend over at the waist, laugh till you cry while gasping for breath" type of laughter.

He stood there feeling foolish and more than a bit perturbed. Putting on his fiercest, cruelest expression—the one that sent grown male shifters running for safety—he planted his hands on his hips and glared her into submission.

Or that was the plan.

Shay took one look at his face, and the laughter that was tapering off exploded into life again. He growled, breathing heavily through his nostrils, and resisted the almost overwhelming urge to shake her silly. He was Rory McFelan. Alpha of the Sparrowhawks. Son of the most feared wolf-shifter in the tristate area, and she dared to laugh at him?

Shay snorted while drying her cheeks with her palms, smearing butter on one as she panted, trying to catch her breath. She laid one hand on her chest and held the other out beseechingly. "Sorry," she gasped. "Give me...a moment...to compose...myself."

She closed her eyes and inhaled deeply a few times before finally seeming to calm. When her gaze once more fell on him, she snickered briefly before firmly clamping her lips together. He could still see the merriment in her eyes, though.

"You mind telling me what the hell is so amusing?" he snarled, left eye twitching, so furious that he was dangerously close to shifting.

"The idea of you...hurting me." She chortled again, as though she found the very thought of it absolutely hilarious.

Her amusement and the certainty behind it confused him and had the effect of defusing his anger. Head tilted to the side and eyes narrowed, he waited until she quieted. "I hurt you. You whimpered." Of this he had no doubt. He'd thought of little else all day.

"I screamed too." She paused and seemed to consider. "Maybe it was more a howl than a scream." She thought a bit more, then shook her head. "Either way, it had nothing to do with pain," she assured him.

Floored, he could do nothing but stare—again. "What are you saying?"

Her face turned red. Was Shay...*blushing?* He didn't think she knew how.

Turning her head, she gazed over his shoulder and mumbled something.

"What did you say? I didn't catch that."

She huffed and drilled her gaze into his. "I said *I liked it*, okay? And if you dare laugh, you'd better learn to sleep with one eye open for the foreseeable future."

It took a minute for the meaning of her words to sink in. Then another minute or two for his perception of his world to readjust. She wasn't hurt? She'd actually liked the brutal way he'd claimed her in front of his men? Enjoyed it even?

Slowly a cocky grin spread across his face.

Shay slapped the arm of the recliner. “I *knew* I shouldn’t have told you!”

“What? I didn’t laugh,” he protested, still grinning with delight.

She glared at him. “No, you’re smirking. It’s annoying as hell.”

As she set the nearly empty bowl on the nearby side table and lowered the foot of the chair, the realization struck that his mate, the woman he loved, wasn’t leaving. She wanted to stay—with him. He’d given her a prime opportunity to escape, and she hadn’t taken it. Never mind the contract. Shay had to know he wouldn’t have held her to it if he was the one forcing her to leave. She hadn’t even mentioned it, and as in demand as her services were, he knew she didn’t need the money from him. No, she was here because she wanted to be.

The wonder of it all astonished him, and a surge of lust hit him so hard he almost fell to his knees under the force of it.

Shay rose regally from the chair and sauntered up to him. When she was inches away, she smiled, an evil and malicious grin. That was the only warning he got before her booted foot slammed down on top of his bare toes.

“*O-o-o-w! What the hell was that for*?” he roared as he hopped on one leg, cradling his abused and crushed foot in his hands, the other hand instinctively leaping to protect the family jewels in case the crazy woman decided to knee his dangling balls.

“For involving my cousin in our business, asshole.” She kicked the shin of his standing leg with what felt like steel in the toe of her boots and shoved, upsetting his already tenuous balance. "And that's for calling me a bitch."

As he crashed to the wood floor, she stepped around him, pausing as she reached the archway to call out, "Take a bath; you stink."

She walked out of the room humming a happy tune, leaving him on the floor cursing. And to think, mere seconds ago he'd been happy to see the little she-devil. He must have lost his mind.

Much later, after showering—damn, he had been a bit odorous—and eating the food Shay had so considerately—considering the way she'd attacked him earlier—cooked and left in the microwave for him, he climbed naked into the bed beside his mate as she read some information technology magazine.

"You stayed," he marveled again, now that his toes and shin were no longer throbbing with pain.

"Yeah…well…" She floundered. "I'm not that easy to be rid of." She set the publication aside and turned off the lamp.

They lay silently in the dark, two almost-strangers connected by the child growing in her womb and the fragile bond getting stronger between them.

Shay's voice broke the silence. "Who were those two guys?"

Instantly jealousy arose. "Why?"

"Considering you fucked me silly in front of them, I think it only fair that I know their names."

He grunted, knowing she had a valid point. Grudgingly he responded, "The one with the dreads is Caleb, my second. The big, burly guy is MacDougal, my third." At the thought of Mac, Rory remembered his borderline defiance. The man hadn't outright challenged him. He was too savvy for that, but his small displays of disrespect could be just as much, if not more, detrimental to his position as alpha.

“Do they make a habit of walking in without knocking?” Shay asked.

Still pondering his options, Rory absently answered, “This is the pack’s house, and we’re their alphas. All are always welcome here.”

“Hmm…”

Rory rolled to the center of the bed and tugged Shay until her back was flush with his chest. The events of the day catching up with him, he yawned and blinked tiredly. He snuggled closer and buried his nose in her neck, inhaling deeply. Her scent filled his nostrils. Soothed by her presence, he drifted off to sleep.

* * * *

Shayla woke, lying on her stomach, facedown in the pillows. There was a heavy weight on her. Rory was using her as a pillow. She could hear and feel his breath on her back. Her bare back.

Where was the nightshirt she’d come to bed in?

Then a more disturbing realization occurred. There was something wet on her skin. Almost like…

“Ew ew ew ew ew! Get it off me!” she shrieked.

Rory shot up, braced protectively on his forearms above her. “What! Huh! Where?” Glancing over her shoulder, she could see his head twisting to and fro as he tried to determine the source of the threat.

“Get. It. Off,” she snarled. Shay shifted to reach her hand behind her to point at the offensive material—no way was she touching it—and it began to travel. Shuddering in disgust, she added, "Now!"

He looked at where she was pointing. "That? That's what you're carrying on about? It's just a bit of drool."

Offended, she asked, "Do you know how many germs are in the human mouth?"

The mattress shifted as Rory settled on his side next to her, head propped on his hand as he studied her. "You don't mind my germs when I'm kissing you, or when my mouth is between your thighs. Hell, I've had my cock in your mouth and you didn't complain. What's the big deal?"

"It's spit. On my skin. It's disgusting," she gritted out between her teeth. It was crazy, she knew, but she had a thing about other people's saliva being anywhere on her body. "Wipe it off, please," she gritted out.

Instead he took a finger and drew circles in it.

"Stop that!" She wanted to slap his arm, but if she moved, it would travel.

"Babies drool, Shay, especially when they're teething. On your neck, face, the hand that they gnaw on. What are you going to do when it's our cub? Freak out like you're doing now?" he asked curiously.

Shay tried to hide the shudder of revulsion that went through her body. That was a major reason she didn't do babies and puppies. They both slobbered. It was enough to make her gag. "I'm not freaking out. I just don't want your disgusting body fluid on me," she countered.

He sighed. "You're not making sense. Cum is also body fluid, and I spewed it all over your back." He leaned forward and sniffed. "I can still smell it on you. That tells me you didn't wash it off. What's the difference?"

The difference was she didn't have a phobia about sperm. No, she didn't have *any* phobia. She didn't fear anything. It was totally normal to dislike spit, especially when it was on her person. "Never mind. I'll get it off myself."

She eased to the edge of the bed, trying to keep her back as straight as possible. Shay managed to get one foot onto the floor before she felt the insidious slide of fluid in the crease of her spine. She immediately froze. Her stomach lurched and she whimpered. Swallowing hard, she bit back her pride and pleaded, "Rory, please, *please* clean it off me. I'll repay you however you say, only you have to get it off."

"This is really bothering you, isn't it?" he mused. "Don't move."

Moving wasn't really a concern. Even though the position she held was awkward, Shay's muscles were locked into place. She heard water running in the bathroom. The thick carpet muffled his footsteps, but she felt Rory's presence a second before a warm, wet cloth landed on her back. She relaxed as he soaped her down.

"There. That should be better. Wait a moment and I'll rinse it off."

She lay there as he returned to the bathroom, rinsed out the rag, and wiped the soap off her back. As he walked off, she slowly rolled to her stomach and rose to a seated position, bracing herself for the teasing to come. She'd revealed a weakness to Rory. Any second now the gloating would begin.

From the sounds, Rory was taking care of his morning needs. She glanced around for her nightshirt and found it ripped into pieces on the floor. She had a vague memory of Rory removing the offending material from her body, deep in the night while mumbling something about scent and skin. Before she could rise to go get another shirt, Rory returned.

"Hungry?" He stood naked in the doorway, his cock stretched out before him. As always, the sight of him aroused her hunger. One that had nothing to do with food.

She paused with one foot on the floor, searching his expression. Was this a setup? Did he think to lull her into a false sense of security and mock her when her guard was down? It's what she'd do.

"Shay, I can smell your arousal. If you want food, speak now. In another minute I won't care about your empty stomach." He slowly stroked his erection from balls to head, his gaze narrowed on her breasts.

Staring at his stroking fingers, she watched, wishing it were her mouth. But first things first. "That's it? You're just going to let it go? No tormenting me about earlier?"

His hand halted midmotion. "Shay, look at me."

"I am." Rory's fist had stopped right below the crown. The head of his penis was purplish-red and glistened with precum leaking from the eye. She wanted a taste. Shay found herself moving forward, unaware of anything until her knees hit the floor.

"My face, hellcat. Look at my face." She could hear the amusement in his voice.

Only Rory could make something like being called *hellcat* sound like an endearment, Shay mused. She crawled forward, eye on her prize. Deep inside, something flexed its muscles, then stretched. Shayla halted, a bit disconcerted, but then the scent of Rory's arousal hit her nostrils. She continued, her movements fluid, more animalistic. Someone was growling, and dimly she recognized the sound as coming from her.

Rory tangled his fingers in her hair, and tugged until her eyes met his. “Why did you expect me to tease you?”

What was he blathering about? She tried to lower her mouth and capture what she wanted.

Rory shook her head. “Shay! Answer me; then you can have my cock.”

Shay saw the determination in his eyes, heard the resolve in his voice, and that thing inside of her retreated enough for her to think. She focused on the conversation. “Because that’s what you do.”

“That was before, when I was still trying to fight fate. I thought I could escape my destiny.” His solemn gaze traveled all over her face. “I was a fool to try and deny the best thing that’s ever happened to me. You’re mine. I won’t make fun of your weaknesses. That’s not what mates do.”

Shay literally felt her heart melt. Who knew the big lug had a romantic streak in him? On the heels of that emotional rush, her arousal came roaring back. Her mouth watered. She brought up her right hand and captured his cock, giving it a gentle squeeze and a slight tug. “Mine.”

Rory’s eyes began to glow. “Yours,” he confirmed as he pulled her head toward his straining erection.

Shay stuck out the tip of her tongue and drew it over the slit, tasting his essence. The slightly salty, musky flavor burst in her mouth, causing her to want more. She twirled her tongue around the head before delicately lapping at him like a cat.

She could see the tension in his body, feel the aggression he was trying to contain. Instinct and something else pushed her. He was holding back. He thought she was too weak to handle him.

Unacceptable.

She wanted, no, needed all of him. He had to know she was strong enough to take all of him. All he had to give and more besides. She wouldn't settle for anything less. There would be no more repeats of yesterday.

"Shay!" A growl, a command.

Shay twirled her tongue around the head before letting his penis rest in her mouth. She didn't close her lips. Didn't move in any way. As the moist heat of her breath flowed over him, she gazed at his expression from beneath her lashes. Rory of the blue moon would have already rammed it down her throat. This Rory stood here bristling, containing the fury of his lust, waiting on her to do to him what she willed.

"Suck my cock!" he demanded, his body vibrating with the need to use force.

Instead Shay pulled her mouth away and crawled closer until she was resting on her knees before him. Then she placed suckling kisses all over his shaft and balls. Fisting his cock at the base, she traced bulging veins upward to the sensitive ridge circling the head. With the tip of her tongue, she flicked it, keeping the pressure light.

By now Rory's face alternated between red and white, and his nostrils flared. She could feel the tiny prick of claws in her scalp. He snarled, and she caught a glimpse of fang.

"Push him. Make him dominate and prove his strength. Show him we're worthy mates."

Shay didn't know where the thought came from, but she was in total agreement. Shifting minutely closer, she drew the tip into her mouth and lightly suckled while licking the underside of his cock. Her fist on his cock, positioned near her mouth, kept the shaft, which was expanding and getting harder by the moment, out.

Rory gave a low, vicious growl, and Shay rolled her eyes up. He glared at her. His normally hazel eyes were gold and glowing, just a hint of pupil remaining. In response she gave his cock a hard squeeze and sat back, hands on her thighs, smirking. Knowing it would infuriate him. Knowing the alpha in him would demand her submission.

He butted his penis against her closed lips, silently demanding she let him in. Still smirking, she rubbed her closed mouth over the tip. Then, unable to resist, she swiped a taste of precum with her tongue before quickly withdrawing. With her gaze she deliberately challenged him to loose his wolf and be the mate she needed him to be.

Rory's left hand held his cock while the right one shot out and grabbed her by the jaw. The intense pressure of his grip forced her mouth open. Holding her still, he thrust his cock into her mouth and then moved his left hand to keep her in position, gripping the back of her head firmly.

Refusing to surrender too easily to what they both desired, Shay used her tongue and teeth to block his passage while shoving back, resisting the pressure of the hand on her head. He was still holding back. Still taking it easy with her. She could feel it in the way he was being so careful with the claws she could see, fully extended but not pressing into her skin. The cautiously forceful way he pressed his hips forward, thighs locked against the urge to viciously thrust and take what he wanted.

Snarling, Rory commanded, “Take it! Take all of it.”

Shay arched one eyebrow, her message clear. *Make me.*

He closed his eyes, face raised to the ceiling as he fought with himself. Tiny hairs sprouted along his arms and chest, thickening to form a pelt. She inhaled, and he smelled wild, with a hint of feral underneath. The muscles in his forearms expanded until they resembled cords. Shay recognized the signs. His beast was fighting to break free.

Chapter Six

The thing she knew to be the wolf, what Kiesha had warned her about, stirred inside. Instead of fighting it or freaking, Shayla encouraged its presence. *"Make him give us what we want. I know you know how."*

It came forth in a rush, and Shay sensed its anger, its hurt. Its mate—their mate—had tried to send them away. Their mate considered them weak, unworthy of standing at his side. They had to prove him wrong. If they failed, others would know. Their pup would be unprotected, fair game. They had to prove they were alpha enough to handle and hold him, or another would be chosen.

Strength shot through her body. Shay's mouth tingled, and her jaw felt funny. Her fingers, which were digging into Rory's thighs, grew claws. Using the power of the wolf, Shay jerked away and twisted free, landing on her hands and knees. Her vision faded to gray, and when she raised her head, the world looked different. Crouching low, ears pointed, she growled—showing plenty of fang. Deep inside herself, Shay gave control over to her wolf, her analytical mind documenting and cataloging every sensation and reaction for future study.

Despite her now black-and-white vision, Shay knew the eyes that focused on her were pure gold, not a hint of pupil remaining.

"Don't do this, Shay."

The she-wolf snarled again, the sound deep and vicious, and gave a minilunge, snapping her teeth before returning to her crouched position. *Oh yeah, we are so doing this.*

Rory dropped down on all fours. His wolf came in a rush of power that swept over the she-wolf, making her fur stick out on end. While he was still off balance, she darted forward and tried to clamp down on Rory's overly large muzzle with her much smaller mouth, drawing first blood.

The wolf easily twisted free, and in the process his massive hindquarters slammed into the she-wolf's right flank, sending her skidding into the chest of drawers as she scrambled for purchase on the wood floor. Something crashed, and there was the sound of breaking glass as the wood shuddered from the impact.

"Shay, don't make me hurt you."

"You can try." She was unsure if her thought would carry to him the way his did to her.

The she-wolf found her balance, spun around on her paws, and quickly went on the offensive again. She charged the wolf, mouth open, fangs bared. The wolf met her, and they both went up on their hind legs. The she-wolf leaned in, trying to lock fangs around any portion of the wolf she could reach. The wolf, using his superior size and strength, body slammed her and stepped back, his posture aggressive.

The she-wolf came to her feet and attacked again and again and again. Each time, Rory's wolf flicked her off, tossing her with the ease a mastiff would use routing a pesky little terrier. The she-wolf slid into the dresser, the nightstand, the closet, the bathroom...all over the room, but still she rose onto four paws and came charging back full of snarling fury.

The scent of blood was in the air. Rory's, not the she-wolf. He was so obviously careful of her that it made the she-wolf even angrier and out for more blood than the little she'd managed to nip here and there. By God, he would treat her as an equal.

"Shayla, control your wolf!"

Shay snorted. *"I'm not the one that dissed her."* Apparently the maxim about hell having no fury like a woman scorned applied to all females, no matter the species. Shay could say one thing about her beast: what she lacked in skill, she made up for in sheer determination. The outcome of this battle may have been predetermined, but Rory would have to fight for his victory.

Tired of going for the throat, the she-wolf switched tactics. Taking advantage of her shorter stature and smaller size, she aimed for the legs. Attacking from behind, she finally managed to get a good grip on one of Rory's hind legs and bit down hard, shaking her head and worrying it like a dog with a chew toy.

Rory let out a howl of pain. Finally she had his attention. His muzzle whipped around, fangs bared. The she-wolf let loose and danced out of the way. Rory lunged, and they met in a snarling tangle of biting teeth, grappling like two furry sumo wrestlers.

With a menacing growl that spoke of his waning patience, Rory caught the she-wolf by the throat and took her to the ground on her back, standing over her braced on all fours, fur bristling. The she-wolf twisted from side to side, bringing her hind paws up to scratch at his tender underbelly and hopefully break free. He was having none of it.

"Enough!" The thought blasted through Shay's mind, and she winced.

His jaws tightened; his fangs pierced the skin. No fool, the she-wolf ceased her struggles and relaxed her neck, baring it in surrender as she whimpered. For a long moment Rory didn't move, and his bite didn't lessen. Then the she-wolf whined.

Finally the wolf loosened his grip and licked the bites on her neck and then her jaw and mouth. With his muzzle, he nudged her until she stood. She licked his face, showing her submission. As the wolf walked around her, he rubbed his body along hers, sharing his scent and showing his affection.

He came to a halt at her rear and sniffed her sex. The she-wolf stood still, waiting eagerly for him to mount her. The weight of his larger body settled against her, his penis penetrated her sheath, and he began to hump. The whole thing took less than a minute before the hot wash of his seed splashed against her innards.

Deep in the she-wolf, Shay found the whole thing fascinating in a freaky kind of way. *I have to tell Kee about this.*

Finished, the wolf backed away. There was another brief flare of power. The wolf shimmered and disappeared; an angry and aroused Rory took his place.

"Shift back to human," he commanded. With his face blotchy and eyes still glowing, Rory might be in human form, but his beast was clearly in charge.

Uh-oh. Confess that I don't know how to change back or let him think I'm defying him? Hmm…

Shay glanced again at his furious countenance and decided on the latter. She plopped down on her haunches, tilted her head to the side, and let her tongue hang out.

Rory's eyes narrowed in stunned disbelief. A growl rose up out of his throat. "Mate, shift *now*!"

There was such force to his command that Shay felt a dizzying rush; then found herself naked on the floor, on her side, huddled in the fetal position, shivering. *Damn, I should have picked option one. That hurt!* Now that she was human, her whole body was one big ache.

RORY PLANTED HIS hands on his hips, looked down at his quivering mate, and sighed. "Woman, I swear, I don't know if you're a blessing or a curse," he muttered as he reached down and scooped her into his arms.

He laid her gently on the bed and came down behind her, curling his body protectively around her own.

"What the hell did you do?" she asked through teeth that chattered.

"Forced a change," he murmured, more interested in getting her warm than conversing.

"How?"

"I'm alpha. It's one of the perks." He chafed her skin, rubbing her arms and legs to get the blood circulating. Forced changes were painful and not something he liked to do.

"And the thought projection thingy?"

He had to think about that one for a minute before he understood. "It's how we communicate in shifted form."

"So when I shift, everyone can hear my thoughts?" She sounded a bit horrified by the idea. He couldn't help but smile.

"No, only when you project them."

"Sooo…you couldn't hear what I was thinking earlier?"

He fell silent. While he hadn't heard actual thoughts, through their still developing mate bond he could feel what she was feeling and had a pretty good idea of the thoughts rolling through her head. But he wasn't about to tell her that. With Shay he needed every advantage he could get. No doubt, the woman kept him on his toes. She was constantly testing him, keeping him off balance. He never knew what to expect next.

If his ma had challenged Da the way Shay had him, instead of bending over backward trying to please the man, maybe she would have gained his respect—and love. Rory froze at the disloyal thought.

Shay rolled over. "Before you get angry again, most of that wasn't me. It was her," she defensively denied.

Rory blinked. "Huh? What?"

"Uh, never mind. What were you thinking about? That's a strange expression on your face." She studied him intently.

"My parents."

"Oh." She looked like she wanted to say something, but thought better of it. *Shay, holding back?*

"What?" he asked again, this time suspiciously.

"Nothing."

"Don't give me that. That's woman code for 'beg me long enough and I'll finally spit out what I was dying to say all along,'" he grumbled, glaring at her.

"Fine," she bit out. "Shannon told me about your parents, and what I don't understand is how they ever hooked up to begin with. They sound totally mismatched. I mean, here's Shannon telling me how you guys value and respect strength, and there's your mother barely able to stand up to your father. What was the attraction? And how'd she end up pregnant? Can't you guys tell when someone's in heat? Don't condoms work for shifters like they do humans? And who the hell told them to get married? Statistics show that marriages that begin because of an unplanned pregnancy rarely work and end up making all parties miserable, even the children." Shay's eyes rounded, and her mouth snapped shut. She laid a hesitant hand on his arm. "I'm sorry. That's none of my business. I didn't mean to criticize."

He stared at her, not saying anything while his mind raced. Shay brought up things he'd never considered. Silently he rolled off the bed, went into the bathroom, and began filling the tub with water. He'd always known his father took his mother as mate because it was the only way to claim him. In the shifter world, the only way for a father to claim his pup was to mark the mother as his mate. Bastard sons weren't recognized by the pack and couldn't inherit, no matter how exalted his parentage. And above all Rory's father had wanted an heir to succeed him.

But for the first time Rory wondered just how his mother had ended up pregnant. He knew Shannon had and quite a few of the pack still believed him to be infertile, but the truth was he stayed well clear of any female bearing the slightest whiff of being in heat. With his sensitive nose, he could always tell. It simply wasn't possible to trap a shifter male through unplanned pregnancy, which, coupled with their immunity to most diseases, was why they didn't use birth control. *All* pregnancies were planned and highly anticipated by both parties.

"Rory?"

Shay's feelings blasted through the mate bond, the strongest he'd ever felt them outside of when they'd both been in wolf form. She thought she'd offended him or hurt his feelings and wasn't sure how to approach him.

"Come get in the tub, Shay," he said as he reached down to turn off the faucet.

"Rory," she said his name again, standing hesitantly in the doorway. "I..."

His beast became agitated. His mate was unsettled, uneasy, and he was the cause. It was unacceptable.

Rory crossed over to Shay and kissed her lingeringly. When he finished, his penis prodded her tender belly. "It's okay. I'm okay. I'm simply thinking, and you're bruised and sore. Come get into the tub."

He caught her by the hand and led her over to it. Casting her a sweeping glance that noted every mar and red spot, he added Epsom salts to the water before lifting her by the waist and into the tub.

She hissed, and her nails dug into his forearms. "It's hot," she complained, looking ready to climb back out.

"It will feel good once you adjust," he informed her as he stepped into the oversize claw-foot bathtub behind her, arm outstretched to prevent her from escaping.

He settled against the back of the tub, one hand gripping her ankle. When she made no move to sit, he gave a jab to the bends in her knees and caught her as she fell, shrieking and cussing a blue streak. He maneuvered her into the V of his thighs and held her securely by the waist until she quit fighting.

He was ready to hold her head under water before she finally ceased acting like a cat thrown in the bath. She gave a great big huff and, relaxing against his chest, sarcastically asked, "Happy now?"

He merely grunted. She'd splashed out a great deal of the water. With his foot he nudged the hot water spigot, much to his mate's dismay. She drew her legs up to her chest and turned sideways on his lap to escape the encroaching heat, squealing.

He sighed deeply. "You are such a girlie girl."

Shay growled and sank her teeth into his chest.

Grinning because he knew it would infuriate her, he said, "I know you want my cock, but you can't have it until some of these wounds heal."

As she was sputtering, he abruptly slid down, leg extended to turn off the faucet. Shay gasped and clutched him around the neck. Rory's grin grew as he chuckled aloud.

"Evil bastard," Shay muttered into his throat.

"Your evil bastard," he agreed, running soothing hands over her body.

"Hmph."

After a few minutes she finally stretched out and relaxed with her body lying on his, her head on his shoulder. Rory closed his eyes, enjoying the soothing heat and his mate's nearness. Warm, moist air filled the room like a sauna.

He thought Shay was asleep before her voice broke the quiet. "What were you thinking about earlier?"

Once again his mind plunged back into the past. "My parents," he murmured. "Their story doesn't make sense. I never really thought about it before. Simply believed what I was told."

"By whom?"

As Rory reflected, he realized no one had ever told him how his parents ended up together. What he knew was speculation and conjecture gleaned from comments made over the years. "Random comments," he admitted. "I thought I knew, but now I'm not so sure."

Shay tilted her head, and he could feel the weight of her stare. Looking down, he met her concerned gaze. "Does it really matter? You're not your father, and I'm nothing like your mother. Besides, they're both gone now. Their answers died with them."

No, it shouldn't matter, Rory thought to himself, but somehow it did. His thoughts fragmented when Shay rose and straddled him, reaching for the soap. Her slit nestled right along his cock, and he had to remind himself that now was not the time. Shay was hurting and weak from her first shift, which she'd handled like a pro. He'd have to warn her about the dangers of giving her wolf too much control.

"Let me." He took the bar from her and lathered his hands. Though he wasn't able to do as his libido demanded, he could still satisfy his need to touch.

"I can..." she sputtered, reaching for the soap.

"Shay." That's all he said, and she instantly subsided. Good. She was learning.

He washed her from head to toe, and every luscious inch in between, making no attempt to keep his actions practical and impersonal. He desired her and wanted her to know, so he stroked and fingered and lingered until she cried out her release. Satiated, her body went limp, and she fell into his waiting arms.

Rory hauled her out of the water, dried her quickly, and tucked her into bed. She'd expended a lot of energy. A nap to recharge and food to refuel were in order. While she slept, he'd handle the food part of the equation.

* * * *

Someone poked her—repeatedly.

"Get up! You're in the alpha's bed. He doesn't let anyone sleep here but himself," the female hissed.

Tired, still more asleep than awake, Shay rolled away from the irritant.

The poking commenced again. "Move it! You have to leave."

Shay opened bleary eyes to find a young, petite, obviously fake blonde with dark brown eyes and naturally olive-toned skin leaning over her. She hated blondes, even dyed blondes, she mused. Especially ones that looked like this one, all cute and perky, even when she had a fierce frown on her face. With her hair in a high, bobbing ponytail, she looked like an escapee from summer cheerleading camp.

Never at her best when first awakened, Shay snarled, "What is your problem?" Then, as her vision cleared and she got a better look, she added, "And where the hell are your clothes?" Damn, she did not need proof that Skipper's blonde hair was dyed.

Skipper frowned. Before she could answer, Rory spoke from the doorway. "Ashley, what are you doing here?"

Ashley? It figures. A cutesy name for a cutesy girl.

Ashley immediately dropped to her knees and, after crawling over to where Rory stood, rubbed her nude, nubile young body on his leg. "I came to clean, alpha," she stated softly, her hands rising to clutch Rory's upper thigh.

Shay's eyes narrowed at the location of said hands and found herself watching in angry disbelief as Rory patted the woman on the head as one would a puppy. "You should have been instructed not to come. Go home. Caleb will inform you when it's time to return," he said in a gentle tone of voice.

"Yes, alpha," she responded meekly. Ashley rose to her feet, managing to rub the entire length of her body against Rory's in the process. As she turned to leave the room, she made certain her pebbled breast brushed his equally bare chest. The only reason Shay was still lying in bed and not tossing the bitch out on her ass was because although she could smell the chick's lust from where she sat, she knew Rory barely noticed. His focus was on Shay.

When she stepped past him, her trailing hand lightly brushed the front of his zippered jeans. *Oh. Hell. No.* Did that bitch just cop a feel? And had he allowed it? Shay heard growling and realized it was coming from her.

"Since you're awake, are you ready to eat? Breakfast is almost done. Everything's finished but the eggs," he asked.

"She *touched* you."

"What?" From his expression it was evident he didn't know what she was talking about.

"That bitch. She rubbed all over you like a cat," she expounded since he seemed to be clueless.

"Ashley? She's just a child." He shrugged dismissively. "It didn't mean anything. I'm her alpha. She's a shifter. It's what we do. Get dressed and come downstairs. You need to eat." He turned and left the room.

That easily, he dismissed her concern. Shay stared at the spot where he'd stood, face blank, mind racing. How Rory could have missed the smell of Ashley's desire, she didn't know, unless as Shannon had stated, he was so used to women throwing themselves at him it no longer registered. According to Shannon, he'd slept with half the women of the pack already. Ms. Young Thing obviously wanted to be included on that list.

At least he'd never brought them to this bed. That's what some women would be thinking. Shayla wasn't inclined to be as generous. The man was a dog, and the problem with having a dog was that you never knew when you'd step in leftover shit.

Despite her ever-increasing hunger, Shayla sat on the side of the bed pondering her situation. She was mated to and pregnant by a man she was sure she would eventually come to love, but…

She sighed. Mated didn't mean married. According to Kiesha and Mary Elizabeth, the true mate bond was more binding than marriage vows and more permanent than a marriage certificate. She'd thought it must be true when, just two nights ago, Rory'd declared, "*I won't let you go. You're mine.*" But twenty-four hours later he'd shown his statement for the lie it was by trying to get rid of her.

Where was the security or permanence in that?

She thought about her parents' relationship. Her mother was a geek of the highest order. Not only that, she was manipulative and controlling. But her dad loved her. Thought the sun rose and set on her mother. That didn't mean he took her shit. He put his foot down when necessary, and her mother allowed it because she knew, to the depths of her soul, that there was nothing Shay's father wouldn't do for her. They were in it for the long haul.

Shay wanted the same thing for herself even though she doubted she'd ever find it. Men like her father were rare. Then along came Rory and this true mates crap and for a while, Shay had allowed herself to believe.

"*He loves you, Shay,*" Shannon had told her. So had Conor. But was it love?

Maybe Rory did love her. But was he committed to her the way Alex was to Kiesha and Hugh to Mary Elizabeth? That's what she needed to find out.

* * * *

Ashley eased down the stairs and stood quietly at the bottom, out of sight but listening. As soon as she heard Rory heading her way, she crept out the back door, shifted seamlessly to wolf, and took off running. Cutting through the backyard, she entered the woods and kept running full-out until she reached her destination.

Taking a moment to catch her breath, she made sure she wasn't seen before approaching the door. The knob pushed down under the weight of her paw, and the door opened easily.

"Well?" he asked, one brow lifted expectantly.

She changed back to her human form and pushed the door closed with her foot before walking over to where he stood, a cup of coffee cradled in his hands. "The rumors are true. The human female was in his bed."

He studied her, his gaze dropping to her taut nipples before flicking back to her face. "Did Rory see you?"

Ashley slowly glided her wet tongue around her lips, smiling inwardly as his eyes followed. "He caught me in his room."

His gaze sharpened. "Did he suspect?"

"No, alpha. I told him I was there to clean. He believed me." She shifted her balance from one leg to the other, and the scent of her arousal rose. His nostrils flared.

"You did good. Ready for your reward?"

"Oh yes," she moaned.

"Get on the table. Let me see how ready you are."

Ashley stepped backward until the edge of the table hit the back of her thighs. She hopped on top and scooted so that she was no longer balanced on its rim, then lowered her body to its surface. Slowly, teasingly, she drew her knees up, exposing her needy snatch.

"My, you are ready." He rubbed his cock from balls to head as his gaze centered on her slit. "Hungry for me, my sweet?"

"Yes, alpha." She reached a hand between her legs and parted her nether lips enticingly.

"Is that where you want me?" His hand continued its stroking. "Does your greedy little pussy want my big, thick cock?"

He was big, and thick. His penis slanted up at the tip, capable of doing magnificent things when plunged inside her body. "Please," she responded, ready to beg.

"You want me to ram this thick piece of meat into your sopping pussy, don't you? Look how wet you are for me. I'm the only one that knows how to fuck this cunt properly, give it to you nasty, the way you like, aren't I?"

"Yes, alpha. Just you. Give it to me, please."

He approached where she lay and ran his finger down her center from clit to anus. She arched into it with a hiss. "You are needy, aren't you? Here, let me give you what you want."

Lining the bulbous head with her opening, he rammed it inside, not stopping until he was fully embedded. She let out a keening cry at the delicious pleasure-pain of it. "You like that, don't you? Take more."

He withdrew and slammed home again, and again, until he was pounding inside her. It still wasn't enough. He lifted her legs and instantly went an inch deeper.

"Harder. Fuck me harder, please," she demanded.

He gave her what she asked for, plunging rapidly inside her with the full force of his body. Ashley screamed and clawed the table as she came. He kept battering at her, wringing out another orgasm.

As she came down from her high, she felt his body tense as his cock expanded. "Pull out," she quickly reminded.

Another two pumps of his hips and then he pulled away, shooting his seed on the floor. She rose onto her elbows. "Did you get any cum inside of me?" They couldn't afford for his scent to be recognized on her.

He stood there shuddering as he jerked on his erection, loosing the last of his release. Gazing at her through slitted eyes, he admitted, "I'm not sure. But just to be on the safe side..." He went to his knees and buried his face in her cunt.

* * * *

Shay clumped down the stairs sporting a red T-shirt and red and black cammies, mind still troubled. If their relationship was to work, Rory would have to learn not to disregard her insights and to respect her opinions. Simply because she was a novice at being a shifter didn't make her an imbecile. She was highly intelligent and had good instincts. She knew what she saw and what she smelled. Ashley's actions weren't simply that of one shifter seeking ordinary affection from another.

Shay had watched enough nature documentaries to know that wolves in the wild often rubbed against other pack members for affection, belonging, and as a means of identification. Pack had a smell. What she'd seen was none of that.

She thought back to Conor's statement about treachery surrounding them and that they'd have to stick together in order to be victorious. Hard to do when your mate thought you were a naive twit.

Earlier this morning her furry counterpart had taken a stand and earned Rory's respect. The woman could do no less. While her wolf relied on sheer dogged determination, Shayla would use the one thing that had never failed her—her brain.

She needed a plan, but before she could come up with a course of action, she needed information. In a sense, Rory was right. There was a lot she didn't know about being a shifter or being a Sparrowhawk, but she would learn. She would watch, take notes, and not take anything at face value. She didn't know who the enemy or enemies were, but when the time came, she'd be ready.

In the meantime she was here to do a job. It was time to get busy on it.

"There you are," Rory said as she entered the kitchen. "I was getting ready to come and get you."

She took a seat at the table and waited until he'd placed a plate in front of her to say, "Where's the equipment you set up? I'm ready to begin work."

"You need to rest," he stated as he set a glass of juice and another of milk in front of her before sitting across from her.

“I’ve rested,” she said around a mouth full of bacon. “That’s all I did yesterday and this morning. Now it’s time to do what you contracted me for."

“Your work doesn’t officially begin until Monday. If you’re feeling energetic, why don’t you take today to settle in? Unpack and I’ll throw your suitcases in the attic, then give you a tour of the house.”

She thought about it for a moment, not telling him she’d seen every room in the house yesterday when she searched for him. “And where do you suggest I put my clothes?”

He stared at her, nonplussed. “In our room, where else?”

“So it’s *our* room?”

His eyes narrowed. “You try sleeping somewhere else…” He shook his head. “What’s wrong with you? What happened to the woman who calmly announced that she lived here and wasn’t leaving?”

“Last night you were being stupid, and I was mad.”

He crossed his arms and settled back in his chair, rocking on its two hind legs. “And today?”

Shay shrugged one shoulder. “Today I’m wondering if you were right.”

His chair landed on all fours with a bang. “So you *do* think I’d hurt you.”

She glared at him for being dense. “No, asshole, I don’t.”

Now he just appeared confused. “Then what’s the problem?”

Shay took a deep breath and set her fork to the side. “No problem. I simply think we should take one day at a time, one step at a time. At least until we see where this is going."

Rory studied her while she played with her toast. "Finish eating. Shifting consumes a lot of energy. With the babe, you don't have any to spare."

So no protestations of dying devotion, Shay thought cynically as she resumed eating. Figures. *Get a grip. Shannon already told you the man has issues. Between his issues and your hang-ups it's a wonder you two have made it this far.* With a sigh, Shayla conceded that this was true. If they didn't get their act together, this was going to be one messed-up child, she mused.

When she finished, Rory took her plate and utensil and loaded them into the dishwasher. "Drink your milk," he commanded.

Shay screwed up her face and did as he commanded without complaint, something that would have shocked everyone who knew her.

"I need to call the pack's midwife and have her check you out. You haven't seen a doctor yet, have you? Prompt medical attention is essential for a healthy pregnancy."

Shayla's temporary obedient streak came to a halt. "No."

"What do you mean no?" he asked, his eyebrows scrunched.

"Just what I said. N. O. You need it in another language? *Nein. Nyet.*" She crossed her arms over her chest and settled more firmly into her seat.

His mouth opened to say something, closed, and then he shut his eyes and appeared to be counting under his breath. "Why, Shay?"

"I'm not opposed to medical treatment, but when it comes to my health and the welfare of this child, it will be handled by someone with a string of letters behind their name, preferably OB-GYN." Her set gaze dared him to state differently.

"Shay, our midwife has lots of experience. She's been delivering pack babies for over twenty years. She knows what she's doing. You think I would trust you or our child to simply anyone?"

She shook her head. "Not happening. I don't care what you say. You want me to see someone, take me to Alex. I know he's certified. Checked him out myself."

"Fine," he growled. "I'll take you to go see Alex. Get ready. We roll in five." He stalked out of the kitchen.

Chapter Seven

A brooding werewolf. Now there's an interesting sight. Shay watched Rory's reflection in the window.

"Shouldn't we have called first and made an appointment?" she asked.

"No. Your cousin's his mate. He'll see you. Besides, I'd rather Kiesha not know we're coming. She's a bit…bloodthirsty," he finished with a grimace.

"That's what happens when you act without thinking, dumb-ass."

"Evil bastard, asshole, and now dumb-ass. Any other names you'd like to call me, *mate*?" Rory asked in a silky, if menacing, tone of voice.

Shay pretended to think on the matter. "Hmm, that's it for now. At least it is until the next stupid thing you do," she finished.

"That's it," he muttered. "Tell me how you really feel about me."

With a sigh, Shay scooted closer and laid her hand on his thigh. "Not you," she admitted, "but your actions." She rested her head on his shoulder.

He covered her hand with his own, and nothing more was said until they arrived. It was nice, Shay reflected. She'd heard of companionable silences, but this was the first one she and Rory had experienced. Only now that the clinic sat in front of them, he was tensing up. The shoulder she leaned on and the thigh her hand lay on felt like rocks. Deep inside where she was bonded to him, she could literally feel his aggression rising.

The small parking lot was rather full for a Friday afternoon, but somehow she didn't believe that was Rory's issue. Personally she hated waiting in doctor's offices. They really should have called first and made an appointment, but it was too late to argue now. They'd driven almost an hour to get here, and he was determined that she see someone today. So it was sit here and wait or see his pack's midwife.

Shay mentally debated the pros and cons of staying. Neither she nor Rory made a move to get out of the truck. She knew why she hesitated but had no clue what his problem was. Finally she asked, "What's wrong?"

"He's going to see you. Touch you," he growled.

"Alex's a doctor. That's what they do, especially for this type of exam." Shay didn't particularly like the idea of Kiesha's husband seeing her—the whole thing was creeping her out—but she couldn't tell Rory that, not when she'd insisted Alex be the one to do the exam. Damn, now she was tense and the tiniest bit nauseated.

Rory snarled. Actually snarled.

Shay turned to look at him. Meeting his gaze, she realized Rory was no longer home behind those eyes. Rory's wolf's golden-eyed gaze stared back at her. *Lord, spare me from possessive werewolves.* "We can go home. I'm sure the baby's fine," she offered.

A growl rumbled from his chest. She could see the wolf's possessiveness over his mate fighting with his concern for his cub. He couldn't go inside with his wolf this close to the surface. He'd scare the staff, be kicked out, and then all hell would break loose. She needed to calm him somehow. Shay rose to her knees on the bench seat and rubbed her cheek alongside his, the way she'd seen wolves do, hoping to calm him.

It did and didn't work.

Shay found herself plastered to Rory from chest to pelvis as he pulled her to him in an inescapable grip. Feeling his claws on her butt, she quickly shrieked, "Don't rip my pants."

The world tilted, and she found herself on the seat below him. As Rory attacked the button and zipper of her pants, Shay rose on her elbows, trying to see if there were any witnesses to what was surely about to take place. Having her body put on display once was enough, thank you very much. If the wrong person came along, they'd get arrested for indecent exposure. If that happened, Kee would tease her mercilessly, forever.

"Down." One hand pressing firmly against her chest ensured she obeyed while his other stripped her pants and panties from her legs. At least he left her upper body clothed. Thank God for small favors.

A slash of his claws and his jeans fell open, revealing his already heavy and bobbing cock. Shay hoped he had another pair in the truck. Rory parted her thighs and then he was between them. "Mine," he pronounced as he entered her with one determined thrust.

Good thing she stayed in a perpetual state of arousal with this man or she would never have been able to take him. If Rory's wolf was running the show, all it was interested in was staking its claim. Come to think of it, that's all the man was usually interested in as well. Then Shay lost the ability to reason.

* * * *

Hours later Shay entered the house, still in a state of shock.

A whistling Rory closed the door behind her. "Guess I'd better get started on the nursery. With the way time's flying, our cub will be here before we know it. I was thinking of opening the wall between our room and the one on the right. I can close off the hallway door and leave the only access through our bedroom. Just for the first year or so; then we'll move him across the hall. I think two's a good age, or sooner if you get pregnant again. I think we should have more than one cub, don't you?"

He didn't stick around for an answer. Instead he wandered up the staircase muttering about safety gates and baby proofing.

Shay drifted into the living room and sat staring out the picture window. She didn't see the vibrant greens and browns of the surrounding hills and forest. All she could hear was Carol's voice saying, *"Well, you're definitely pregnant."*

Shay couldn't believe she'd forgotten Alex and Kiesha were gone on their honeymoon. Since they'd driven all that way, she'd agreed to let Carol, a nurse practitioner and certified nurse midwife, do the honors.

Thinking she was pregnant and having it confirmed were two different things. Nothing like hearing a heartbeat to drive home the fact that she was really going to be a mother. She didn't even have nine months to get used to the idea. According to Carol, her pregnancy was progressing more like a shifter than human.

Normal gestation for a human female was forty weeks. For shifter females it was more like thirty. That meant in four to five months, she'd be delivering. Figured she couldn't even do pregnancy like a normal human. But then, when had the word *normal* ever applied to her?

Her body jostled as the weight of Rory lowering to the seat beside her dented the cushions. "Somehow I'm sensing you're not sharing my excitement."

Shayla shrugged. "It just hit me. I mean, I knew I was pregnant. All the signs were there, but...*I'm pregnant!* This is really happening. What do I know about being a mother?"

Rory put his arm around her and tugged her to him. "I'm sure you'll do fine. Every first-time parent feels that way. You think I'm not nervous about being a father?"

"Please." She rolled her eyes. "If there's any part of this equation I'm not worried about, it's you. Shannon said you practically raised her. Our kid will be lucky to have you as a father. I'm the one most likely to make it need therapy."

He tucked his face against her nape and squeezed her so hard the breath left her body in a rush. "Can't breathe," she gasped.

Immediately his hold loosened. After a while he raised shining eyes and said in a hoarse voice, "Thank you. You don't know how much that means to me."

"It's the truth," she stated, waving aside his gratitude.

He shook his head but didn't argue. They sat in yet another companionable silence, each busy with their own thoughts. Rory broke it when he said, "I might have some experience with little girls, but I know nothing about raising boys. Being one doesn't count."

"Good thing it's a girl."

"Highly improbable. Shifters aren't known for their female offspring. Most likely it's a boy."

"That's what you say. Excuse me if I choose to believe Conor instead," she told him.

He turned her face so that he could look her in the eyes. "*Conor* said we're having a daughter?"

"Actually he said daughters, which I assume meant plural, not possessive, but I'm not sure if he means now or accumulatively speaking," Shay said with a shrug.

"He's a seer," Rory murmured, speaking to himself. Then his gaze sharpened. "Did he say anything else?"

"You must fight to hold on to what is yours. Treachery surrounds you. Only by uniting together will you be victorious. Show no mercy. Your daughters' safety depends on the decisions you make now." Conor's words flowed through her mind.

She debated. Alphas were protective of their packs. Kee and Conor had both taught her pack meant family, and as their leader, Rory was like their kingly father. *But I'm Rory's mate and as such, his first priority. If not me, then definitely our child.* But still, she didn't really know Rory. Yes they had amazing sex and yes she was pregnant with his baby, but…

"Shay…" His tone said he was willing to push until she told him the whole.

Shay weighed her response. Conor *had* said she and Rory needed to work together. Then she remembered how easily he'd dismissed her concerns about Ashley, and it tilted the scales against Rory. "Nothing you need to be concerned about," she finally muttered.

"I don't believe you."

She arched one brow. "Sounds like a personal problem to me."

Rory glared at her, his face slowly building to a fine red color. Shay met his stare calmly. She'd tell him when she was good and ready, and not a minute before.

He took a deep breath. "Shay, mates don't withhold information from each other."

"Really? It's my understanding that mates take each other's concerns seriously." She shrugged. "Guess we were both wrong." Shay rose and looked down at him. "Since it looks like I'm staying, I'm going to go unpack…in *our* room."

He grabbed her hand as she walked past, pulling her to a halt. "I don't know what the problem is, but I promise, one day you'll trust me."

Shay tugged until he released her. "Maybe. But will you trust me in return?" At the moment she didn't think so. Their staring contested lasted a long while. Finally Shay turned away and walked off with her head held high.

Despite Conor's warning, she had a brain. She was more than capable of handling things herself. It wasn't in her nature to ask for help. She'd figure out who the threat was and bring Rory in only when absolutely necessary.

WHAT THE HELL'S her problem?

Rory watched his mate stalk away from him, bemused at how such a tender moment between the two of them could have turned into such a disaster. *Pregnancy hormones must be kicking in. Let it go.*

A minute later he charged up the stairs.

When he topped the rise, he found Shay contemplating one of the extra bedrooms. "If you prefer that room, I'll be happy to move all our things in there. Might be a little cramped…"

She flicked an annoyed look over her shoulder. "I'm checking out the storage. I doubt you have enough space in your room for both of our clothing."

"Our room," he emphasized, making sure Shay was clear on that point. "And think again. I prepared." He turned the knob and pushed opened the bedroom door with his hip.

"All the furniture is new. The dresser and nightstand on the right side of the bed are yours. I also cleared out half the closet. If you need more space, let me know and I'll move more of my stuff to another room."

As she shoved past him into the room, Rory took in the antique-looking cherry wood set he'd purchased. It had a low-profile, king-size sleigh bed, eight-drawer dresser, and five-drawer chest, which should be more than enough for them, but if not, there was still the empty two-drawer cedar chest designed for comforters. Being a shifter, with his naturally high body temperature, he never used heavy covers.

He noted Shay preparing to lift her suitcase onto the bed and gently nudged her out of the way. "I'll get this and the other one. I don't want you straining yourself."

She snorted but stepped out of the way.

As Shay unpacked, Rory tried to define what he was feeling. It was like all the random dots that made up his life were finally connected into one big, glorious picture. His mate was here, in their room, taking her first major step to settle in to their life together.

"We need to call the pack together to celebrate our mating and the coming of our young," he said as he sat on the bed near where she worked.

Shay looked up from the contents of her suitcase, a frown on her face. "Will they?"

Confused, he asked, "Will they what?"

"Celebrate. The few members I've met so far didn't seem all that joyous."

He scowled, feeling his ire rise at MacDougal and even Caleb's reaction to his desirable mate. "I'll deal with Mac later on the proper respect due an alpha pair."

Her hair fell forward when she bent over the luggage, and she shoved it back with a muttered curse before lifting a stack of folded cotton shirts and carrying them to the dresser. "And will Ashley be sitting in on this lecture?"

Baffled, he reminded Shay, "Ashley's a child."

Shay snorted. "That's what you say."

"Shay, Ashley's getting close to the age where she's old enough to be mated. She wants strong pups and a mate strong enough to protect her. It's a survival instinct. I'm the most powerful wolf in the pack. It's natural that she would make a play for me. All females do. Eventually she'll realize I'm not interested and move on to someone who is."

Shay's eyes narrowed. "While your little glimpse into the animal kingdom was fascinating, I don't like her. I don't trust her, and I always trust my instincts." She punctuated her words by slamming the drawer shut.

Rory glanced at the furniture and then back at his mate, not liking the way the heavy mirror was angled, especially after the way Shay's wolf had banged into it earlier. He went to make sure it was still secure. He didn't want it to come crashing down, but he wasn't so distracted that he couldn't feel the jump in his mate's emotions through their bond.

He thought about their earlier discussion along with her recent comments, and it clicked. Turning to lean his body against the wall next to the mirror, he watched his mate closely. "I can include her in the talk, but she's not the real problem. Is she, Shay?"

"You think?"

Hmm, snarky answer. Even without the mate bond he'd know she was irritated. What concerned him was the underlying hurt he sensed that agitated both wolf and man. Asking outright what the issue was wouldn't help. She'd only clam up like she had about Conor. He thought for a moment…

"Talking to the females might not be a bad idea. You're not only my mate but their alpha-fem. It would be a good time for you to lay out your expectations."

"Yeah, like it doesn't matter how many times you've fucked him in the past, the alpha's mated now so keep your grubby paws off," she muttered en route to the bed to gather more items.

He smiled. "I can't believe you're jealous of Ashley."

She stopped to glare at him. "I'll admit I didn't like the way she rubbed all over you like a bitch in heat—"

"I told you it meant nothing. It's something shifter females do."

"But according to Shannon, you've fucked your way through half the pack."

His smile died. "I never touched Ashley." Is that what she thought, that he messed with children? The girl was barely out of school.

"I never said you did, but it's obvious she wants her turn with the pack's stud." Her expression turned to one of disgust. "Of course, that's what happens when you mate with dogs. Always have to watch for leftover shit."

For the first time Rory considered things from Shay's viewpoint. He'd gone ballistic, and all his men had done was look at Shay. How would he feel if they'd rubbed their aroused bodies against her as Ashley had done to him? "I'm a bloody fool."

"Nice of you to finally notice."

He caught her around the waist and tugged her against his body, wrapping his arms around her hips to hold her close. "I'm sorry."

"For what?" Suspicion was evident on her face and the way she held her body so stiff.

"For blowing off your concerns about Ashley. If one of my men dared to touch you the way she did me, I wouldn't have been able to control myself."

Shay shoved away from him, and he released his hold. She paced a bit before turning to confront him. "Don't get it twisted. I'm not jealous of your perky little Skipper doll."

Rory clamped his mouth shut.

"What you do with your harem is your business…"

This time he snorted. Yeah, like he believed that. His little she-demon would castrate him if his cock so much as stood at attention for another woman.

"…but I will not tolerate being disrespected, especially in my own home, in front of my face, and definitely not by that little twit!"

"You're right."

"Does she have any idea what I could do to her? I can screw up her credit so bad she'll be an old lady before she untangled it all. I can have every law enforcement agency in this country and Europe looking for her, and she wouldn't even know why. I can erase her Social Security number out of the system or report her as dead. Let her fix that!"

"No, you're not jealous at all," he murmured, withholding a smile. Damn, his mate was vicious. His perfect match in every way.

Finally she stopped ranting and hung her head. "Okay, I'll cop to a streak of possessiveness, but not jealousy. I refuse to be jealous of that woman."

Rory slouched and hooked his thumbs in the belt loops of his jeans. "And the difference between the two would be…?"

Shay raised her head and met his inquisitive gaze with a direct stare. "Jealousy is the result of one's insecurity. My being jealous would mean I see Ashley as a worthy rival and feared her ability to steal you from me."

He straightened and crossed over to stand in front of his mate. "Then I must be the most insecure man on the planet. The thought of someone desiring you, touching you"—he gripped both cheeks—"or smelling your luscious scent"—he leaned in close and inhaled—"drives me absolutely crazy."

Then he kissed her because the thought of anyone else having Shay was intolerable.

"You're not insecure," she told him when he allowed her to breathe. "You're a werewolf. Possessiveness is coded in your DNA."

As he claimed her mouth again, he knew she was wrong. He was terrified of doing or saying something to drive Shay away, and ending up living the rest of his life mourning what might have been.

* * * *

Rory left to cook dinner and organize his *gathering*. Shay finished unpacking. As she lined her lotions, perfumes, nail polishes, and other personal items on the dresser beside Rory's, she contemplated the circumstances in her life that had brought her to this. Thoughts of being a mother made her realize she hadn't heard from her parents since they'd left the reception.

She pulled her cell phone out of her pants pocket and dialed home.

"Dad," she said with pleasure, happy to hear his voice and relieved he'd been the one to answer. "Just calling to make sure you made it home with no problem."

"Sorry we didn't call. Things got a little hectic, and I knew you were settling in on a new project. I didn't want to be a pest."

She scowled at the phone. "Dad, a two-minute call from you to say we made it home alive and in one piece is no bother."

He laughed at her scolding. "As you can see, we're fine."

Shay pushed the empty suitcase to the floor and sat on the bed. "How's your project going? You get it done?'

"Almost. Everything's proceeding on schedule. I made up the time I lost by being away. What about you?"

She plucked nervously at the bedspread. "I don't officially begin work until Monday. I'll spend the weekend settling in."

"Impressions of the people you're working for?"

Professionally or personally? Shay winced, then bit back a chuckle at her discomfort, glad her father couldn't see her face. "Not enough data to compute," she lied. "But I admire their taste in equipment." Shay always gave her clients three options when it came to purchasing the required hardware: cheap but functional, moderately expensive but will get the job done with a few added perks, and top-of-the-line. Rory had purchased top-of-the-line everything. The geek in her was impressed. The woman wondered just how much money the man had.

"Well, whatever the case, I'm sure you'll whip them into shape soon enough."

"Daddy! I'm not a tyrant," she protested.

He laughed again, then said, "Speaking of tyrants, your mother wants to talk to you."

"No, Daddy, wait! Tell her I'm... Hi, Mom." Shay stifled a long-suffering sigh.

"Shay-Nei, how's Rory? That's one nice catch. You better hook him while you can. A man like that won't stay single for long. His sister says you're staying with him in his house. You're a good cook. Cook for him. A big man like that eats plenty of food. Show him what I taught you and catch yourself a nice man."

"Mom, he's not a fish." *Wait till I see Shannon again. I have a few words for her.*

"No, he's a man, and just like fish, you need the right bait to reel him in."

Shay rolled her eyes. "Or I could bash him over the head with an oar and drag him off to my cave."

"Shay-Nei, not funny. You're already past prime childbearing years. Wait too long and you'll be too old. Your father and I want lots of grandkids. There's no time to be playing around."

Sick to death of her mother hounding her, Shay let her anger do the talking. "Tell you what, why don't I crawl naked into his bed each night while I'm here, and if we're lucky, in nine months you'll have that grandchild you're so desperate for. Then I can send the brat to you and Daddy to raise *and finally get some peace*!"

She held the phone away from her ear while her mother yelled at her. She supposed the chewing out she got was deserved, but damn, enough was enough. A woman could only take so much, and Shay had reached her limit.

Before her mother completely wound down, Shay shouted into the phone, "Gotta go. Love you both. Tell Daddy I said take care."

"Shay-Nei! Shay-Nei! Don't you hang up the—"

With an evil grin, Shay pressed the button, watched while the phone powered off, then tossed it onto the mattress. She wanted to throw it, but it wasn't her BlackBerry's fault her mother was a nag. Instead Shay rolled over, grabbed a pillow, buried her head into it, and screamed. It felt so good she did it again.

The mattress dipped, jostling her. "Was that wise?"

Shay raised her head and glared when she saw the amusement on his face. "The woman makes me crazy."

"That may be true, but she'll remember this when you reveal that you're pregnant."

Shay tried not to look as guilty as she was suddenly feeling, but apparently she was unsuccessful.

His smile fled as Rory's eyes narrowed. "When are you telling your parents about the baby, Shay?"

She shrugged. "Sometime before she begins school, I promise."

Rory closes his eyes and rubbed his forehead. "Shay, don't you think they'll notice you're pregnant at our wedding?"

Sitting up and tossing the pillow to the side, she aimed for nonchalance as she answered, "Since we're not getting married, I don't see that being an issue."

He gripped her arm as she made to rise, halting her midmotion. "What do you mean, we're not getting married?"

It was Shay's turn to narrow her eyes. "You need a hearing aid?"

He scowled. "I can hear just fine, but your words make no sense."

Shay shook him off and stood, taking a few steps to put distance between them. "We're mated. That's good enough."

"No, it's not." His words came out slow and measured as he rose to his feet.

She placed her hands on her hips and tilted her head to the side. "Well that's too bad, because I'm not marrying a man who doesn't love me!"

Rory stared at her for a full minute, mouth gaped open like a trout, face turning redder and redder. Shay mentally counted. *Five, four, three, two…*

"*Are you daft, woman?* Not love you?" He threw his arms open wide. "You think I'd be doing all this if I didn't?" he yelled.

She leaned forward and shouted in his face. "*How the hell would I know?* You aren't the sanest of men. One minute you're never letting me go, the next you're calling Kiesha to come and get me and I'm supposed to think *you love me*?" She wanted to throw something at him.

"I already apologized for that!"

"When?" she demanded, furious now.

He dropped his hands to his sides as his mouth worked.

"Exactly." She spun on her heel and walked to the dresser. *No, too many weapons.* She switched directions and headed to the window.

Behind her, Rory heaved a heavy sigh. Seconds later his image showed behind her in the glass she was looking at instead of through, his heat warming her back.

"Shayla, I'm sorry. I was wrong."

Darn tootin' you were.

"I love you so much it scares me."

Uh-huh, pull the other one.

"When we met, I knew you were the one, my mate, and I fought it with everything in me. If it hadn't been for events at the blue moon, I don't think I would ever have claimed you."

Shay frowned. *Way to convince me, stud.*

"But I did, and as a result I'm happier than I'll ever be able to show. I'm also scared shitless that I'll fuck up or worse, be the monster my father was and lose you as a result."

That caught her attention, and she turned to face him. "Rory, you are not your father. How many times do I have to say it?"

He held her gaze. "Shay, you didn't know him. You didn't live with him. When I look in the mirror, I see his eyes looking back at me."

"Well, look again or get your eyes checked, 'cause you talking like this is doing nothing but pissing me off. You think Shannon would love you if you were anything like him?"

"What about you, Shay? I'm wearing my heart on my sleeve here."

She closed her eyes. *Quit being such a wimp and answer the man's question.* When she opened them, he was still staring at her, waiting. "Maybe…I think…I don't know, okay? I thought maybe I did, but then you went and got stupid on me and pissed me off. Then I didn't know anymore. Bottom line, I'm not going to love you unless I'm sure my feelings are returned." With her eyes, she dared him to complain.

Rory's smile began in his eyes before spreading to his mouth. He stepped closer and put one arm around her waist. The other cupped her nape under her hair. His erection brushed her stomach. Why he was suddenly turned on she had no idea.

"You love me." He sounded very sure.

"I said maybe," Shay grumbled.

"That's why you stayed and why you're still here. It has nothing to do with the babe."

She scowled. "Of course it doesn't, asshole. You think I need you to raise my child?"

He smirked, and Shay, realizing what she'd said, stated hastily, "That means absolutely nothing."

"Aye, it does." He kissed the protest off her lips.

Rory stripped her shirt over her head and dived back into the kiss once her face was clear.

He backed away, pulling Shay with him until their progress was halted by the bed. “Don’t ever wear a bra. I love looking at your breasts. They make me hard.”

“Everything makes you hard.”

“You make me hard.” He sniffed. “And I make you cream. I can smell your arousal.” His smile was full of self-satisfaction.

“Beast.”

“Yeah, and you love it when I go wild.”

Since it was true, Shay didn’t see the point in arguing.

“Strip.” Rory sat on the mattress and leaned back on his elbows to watch.

Shay raised her eyebrows but obligingly removed her shoes, pants, and underwear.

“Now me.” He raised his arms. Shay straddled his lap and lifted his shirt over his head before tossing aside.

Rory bent his head, captured a nipple, and suckled lightly, releasing it with a pop. Shay grabbed his face and directed him to the other one. He toyed with it, then the folds of her sex, easily penetrating her with one, then two fingers.

Shay was lost in pleasure, riding his hand, when a stinging slap to her butt had her rearing back, fist clenched and raised, ready to strike.

“I’m not naked,” he reminded. One eyebrow arched as his gaze drifted from her face to her fist, then returned to her face.

Eyes narrowed, Shay lowered her feet to the floor and reached for the waistband of Rory’s jeans. She popped open the button, then eased down the zipper. The shiny, engorged head of his cock popped out, tempting Shay to taste.

She dipped down and swiped her tongue over the slit. When his hips jerked, she did it again, then engulfed the tip in her mouth.

Rory said something Gaelic that sounded like a curse as he lifted her off him. "Love, as good as that feels, I've something different in mind."

He gently moved her out of the way and rose to remove the rest of his clothing. Then he lay on the bed and patted the mattress. "Ride me."

Shay stood there, taking him in. He reclined like a pasha waiting to be serviced by his harem. Viewing all his manly glory—ripped abs and thighs, powerful arms and furred chest that couldn't hide the underlying muscle, a thick, swollen cock standing at attention—Shay felt like a highly favored sex slave honored to be chosen by her master.

Rory groaned, the sound part frustration, part need. "Shay, I've been dreaming of this for weeks. I'm begging you, put me out of my misery."

No, he wasn't begging yet, but he would.

Slow and seductive, Shay sank to her knees between his legs. Beginning with his calves, she trailed moist kisses and nibbles to his inner thigh, stopping short of his balls. Ignoring his increasingly impatient demands, she worshipped his legs—stroking, caressing, and rubbing her needy breasts over every inch.

When she was satisfied they'd received enough attention, she moved to his stomach and covered the surface with the same. Rory gripped her by the upper arms to maneuver her into the position he wanted, and Shay bared her teeth.

"My way!"

With a hiss that sounded more feline than lupine, he subsided, dropping his hands to dig into the mattress instead.

Shay directed her attention to his chest and the reddish-brown nipples puckered there. Straddling his thighs to give her more leverage, she licked, tugged, and basically tormented the hell out of Rory.

There was a sharp ripping sound. A quick glance revealed Rory's claws had sprouted. She smirked. "Hope you have money for a new mattress."

"Witch," he griped in a tight, husky voice.

"Yep, and loving every minute of it."

Claws were good, but Shay wouldn't be satisfied until he completely lost it. There was something about being wanted so much by a man that he couldn't control himself that just did it for her.

Bracing her hands on either side of his torso, Shay nibbled her way to his throat. She pulled a pinch of skin between her lips and suckled until a bright red mark appeared. Kissed the hollow in his neck where his pulse pounded a rapid tattoo. Licked his Adam's apple and then worked her way over to the protruding tendon connecting his shoulder and neck. As she played with it, moistening it with her hot breath and licking the sweat off his skin, Rory grabbed her thighs with his hand and thrust up with his hips. His cock slid through her slick folds, briefly catching on her opening before jumping free.

He growled.

Shay raised her head to look at him and saw eyes gone wolf and a mouth full of clenched fangs. "Want something?" she teased with a smile and canted her hips, cushioning his penis like a sausage between a hot dog bun.

"Fuck. Me!"

"In time," she promised.

His grip tightened, and his claws stung as they pricked her skin.

Shay rocked her cradle back and forth, causing his shaft to stroke her clit at just the right angle. "We've never done it slow," she mused, meeting his gaze.

Rory hesitated. She could see impatience and sheer need warring with the desire to give her what she wanted. Desire to please her won, barely, but the tide could switch at any moment. He grunted his assent and made an effort to relax. As a reward, Shay canted her hips and took him inside. Due to their angle, only the tip and a bit of the shaft sank in. Shay rode the head, patiently realigning their bodies whenever he slipped out. And she resumed tormenting his now straining neck with her bites.

"Take all of me!"

"Not yet," she murmured.

Shay never knew the mouth of her vagina was so sensitive. She was enjoying him right where he was.

"Deeper."

"Not…yet."

"Too much," he snarled.

"Quit…whining."

Shay worked her way up to his ear and murmured soft words, erotic words, words of love and devotion. Words she'd never have had the courage to say if passion weren't clouding her mind and lust giving her heart the boost it needed to override reticence born from an inherent need to protect herself. As she spoke, she remained in constant motion, riding the same two inches until her breath came in gasps, her eyes crossed, and beads of sweat rolled down her forehead.

She was so wet. Shay glanced between their bodies. Rory's cock glistened with the juices flowing from her to pool in his pubic hair. Her scent, the smell of sex, filled the room.

Beneath her, Rory rumbled like a volcano. His dick lengthened and swelled until two inches became four. The swollen veins abraded her sensitive tissue like nubbins on a dildo, and Shay's eyes rolled back into her head.

It was torture keeping to the same steady, slow pace. Everything in her wanted to move faster, go deeper, thrust down harder, but she clenched her teeth, dug her nails in his chest, and resisted. By God, for once they were going to take their time. She only hoped Rory knew CPR because her heart was doing its best to pound out of her rib cage.

"Come, Shay."

"Not…yet." Her voice broke, and she almost sobbed from the intensity of what she was feeling.

"Come!" He reached between them, delicately folded back the hood partially covering her clit, and strummed the bud with his claw. Once, twice, three times.

Shay's muscles seized. She froze for one heartbeat, then another. Then she exploded. The force threw her shoulders and head back and ripped a scream from her throat. She lost sense of her surroundings. All she knew was the pulsing of her vagina and the pounding of her heart.

When Shay returned to awareness, she had seven feet of werewolf, drawn tight as a bowstring beneath her, and her head was pillowed on his pelted sternum. Shay licked her lips in anticipation and held on for the ride to come.

Chapter Eight

Rory gritted his teeth and forced back his wolf. It snarled and fought, but Rory's will was stronger and at this moment, what he wanted more than anything was to make love with his mate like she'd requested. Rory, the man, not Rory, the wolf. He beat it down, pushed it back, and shut it down, but the effort cost him.

"What happened?"

"What?" he bit out, still dealing with the pain his wolf had inflicted.

Shay touched his chest with a finger. "Your fur's receded." She stroked his arm down to his hand and raised it to eye level. "Claws retracted." She lifted her head and gazed at him, her face flushed and eyes lazy with satiation, brows furrowed in puzzlement. "No fangs. What gives?"

"No wolf this time. Just me."

Shay continued to stare. In displeasure?

"Is that a problem?" he asked uncertainly. Shay accepted, even encouraged his beast, but would she welcome the man?

Her expression changed to something Rory wasn't sure he liked. Something that left him feeling like a specimen under a microscope. "Why are you speaking of yourself like you're two different entities? Furry or not, it's all you, isn't it?"

Rory let out the breath he hadn't realized he was holding. "In a manner of speaking, aye." Shay accepted him, all of him. The realization had his waning arousal surging through him with a vengeance.

"What's that supposed to mean? The wolf's in you, but it's still a part of you, right?" She frowned. "Or is it completely separate? This whole shifter thing is so confusing. Is my inner wolf me, or a totally separate entity? And when I shift, does she merge with me or—"

Rory deftly flipped them over so that he was on top and rose to his knees. "Later. Right now I've something else in mind."

A slow, cheeky grin crossed her face. "Is that right? And would that something have anything to do with this?" Shay reached out and grabbed his cock in her small hand, giving it a slow pump.

Rory hissed and felt his wolf jerk on its leash. "Aye. None of that," he ordered, catching her by the wrist before she could weaken his control. "Lie back. It's my turn now."

"Like this?" Shay reclined on the mattress, arms over her head, thighs spread wide, opening her sex fully to his gaze.

He looked her over from head to hips. His, every last, luscious inch of her. The gift he'd never dared ask for, never dared dream he could have. A mate. And not just any mate—a true mate. A gift from the Creator, crafted especially for him. A woman who loved him in spite of his flaws, and if that weren't enough, a babe—the fruit of their love.

Once again doubts arose.

"I'm a hard man, Shayla," he said grimly as though confessing a great sin.

"I'll say." Shay gazed at his erection, an amorous glint in her eye. "And getting harder by the moment."

"I'll mess up," he continued. "I'm not a man of soft touches, flowery speeches, and all that romantic crap women want and need. Any tenderness was beat out of me long ago."

Shay looked him dead in the eyes. "Bull."

He shook his head, determined not to let her make light of what he was saying. "It's the truth. I won't want to, but I'll hurt you if you expect more."

She looked at him, gauging his mood, then scrambled to her knees. Instead of confronting him as he expected, she placed her arms around his neck and put her face inches from his. "I am not your mother, and you're damned sure not your father. So get that into your head, first. I know you, Rory McFelan. You're a pain in my ass half the time. You don't take shit off anyone, including me. But then, neither do I, so we're well matched there. If you act like an asshole, I'll tell you. If I want or need something I'm not getting, you can bet your sweet, luscious ass I'll demand it. I won't whine, mope, or sulk in some corner like a child. And if I do go quiet on you, baby, watch out."

It made him smile. He must be demented to find pleasure in his woman threatening him.

"Rory," she continued in her serious, un-Shay-like manner. "I see you. Yes, I give you hell, but I do it because I know you. I've watched how you are with Shannon. Paid attention to the way you've been with me since I've been back. Hell, even before I left. You're tender with those you care about. Protective, loving, in your crazy-assed 'I'm the alpha' way. It's enough. More than enough. Any more and I'd need drugs, or a really big bat, to deal with you."

Deeply moved, he reached for Shay, only to find himself shoved down onto the mattress. Shay slapped both hands on his chest and got into his face again. "Now enough with the mushy. Commence with the fucking!"

He couldn't help but laugh at the shit-eating grin she gave him. "Your wish is my command."

Shay pursed her lips. "Can I get that in writing?"

"Hell no!" he stated as he deftly rolled them so that she lay under him.

Rory made love—he savored the word—to his mate. He couldn't keep his wolf totally out of it. Strong emotions brought out the beast, and what he felt for Shay was extreme. Still, her sighs, moans, gasps—and at the end, screams—made his restraint worth the effort. The claw marks on his back along with the teeth marks on his shoulders satisfied his beast.

Later they lay entangled on the bed. Shay blanketed his body, her head pillowed on his chest. Rory leisurely stroked her spine, wallowing in the aroma of their lovemaking.

"Tell me about the pack."

"Hmm…?" he murmured, still floating in the peaceful aftermath.

"The Sparrowhawks. Tell me about them."

Rory sighed. The pack was the last thing on his mind right now. Just the thought of them was enough to give him a headache, but she'd a right to know what she was getting into.

"The Sparrowhawks are jacked up beyond all measure. For the most part their mentality is straight out of the Dark Ages. More wolves than men. The strong rule. The weak are held in contempt. Women are for fucking and breeding."

Shay propped up on an elbow and looked at him. "Sounds like redneck bigotry shit. The kind that's passed from father to son. How'd you escape?"

Annoyed, he stiffened and glared at her. "I've eyes and ears, haven't I? A mind to reason? Some glimmer of intelligence?"

When she only grinned, he calmed enough to acknowledge, "Take away the beer guzzling and rebel flag and you've the right of it."

Still grinning, she wagged her eyebrows. "Without those elements you're just a bunch of hillbillies with fangs."

He laughed, as she'd obviously intended, then sobered. "My father, he liked the fear, the intimidation. Being the biggest, the baddest. Justice—his justice—was swift and merciless and, in the past, maybe necessary. But times change and he didn't. We're no longer as insulated as we once were. Exposure is more of a concern. Our safety depends on our ability to blend with society. To be more human than wolf.

"Also, our species as a whole is dying. We don't need to speed the process fighting among ourselves," he finished wryly.

"So you're trying to modernize the pack."

"And having a bloody hard time of it," he stated with disgust. "I can't really blame them. Most of them have never been outside of these mountains. One good thing Da did was insist I go roaming. He told the council it was so I could find a mate since none of the women in the pack interested me enough. The real reason was that even then my wolf was rebelling against being under his rule. He was afraid I'd challenge him and win, and he wasn't ready to give up his position as alpha."

"Where'd you go?" Her eyes lit up, and Rory remembered all the traveling she did.

"My grandfather talked so much about Ireland, I had to see it for myself. I spent my last year of college studying abroad in Ireland. Then after graduation I spent another six months backpacking, absorbing the language and culture while working my way across the country before being summoned home." Rory paused as his mind went back to that time. "For the first time in my life I was free—from the pack, Da, and the expectations of me being the next alpha. I still worried about what was happening at home in my absence, but I could *breathe.* I ran across other packs. Saw how they operated. Realized how outdated we were."

He sighed. "Once I became alpha, I tried to put into practice all I'd learned. I'm still trying, without much success."

Shay nodded and patted his chest in sympathy. "I'll bet. People don't like change. In fact, they fight against it. 'If it ain't broke, why fix it?'"

"Because it is broke. More, it's wrong. Treating omegas like slaves, or worse, as though they're less than human? Survival of the strongest, the fittest, and the most cunning, and screw the rest? Treating women like chattel and whores instead of valuing them as the precious beings they are?" He couldn't disguise the disgust he felt with his pack and the old ways most, if not all, were clinging to with all their strength. It was a far cry from the shifter values and tenets Conor had mentioned during the reception. His pack really were the throwbacks many accused them of being.

"And yet you're more than human. You're shifters," Shay reasoned. "You can't totally disregard the wolf and its animalistic nature."

"Being shifters doesn't mean we have to live or function like animals."

"Rory, underneath these civilized veneers humans wear, all men are animals. Shifters simply have an added dimension."

He eased Shay to the side and sat up, running a hand through his hair. "What are you saying, Shay? Since we're nothing but animals, we might as well act like ones?"

"No!" She placed her hand on his shoulder blade. "That's not what I'm saying at all. I don't like you being so…disheartened, I guess, that they're not evolving as fast as you'd like. You're doing a good thing. The Sparrowhawks have been operating the old way for how long?"

He glanced over his shoulder. "Generations. Long before my great-grandfather left Ireland for these fair shores, bringing his pack with him."

"So we're talking your father, and his father and his father before him. Several lifetimes. You thought to break that, change that in how short a period?"

Rory turned, leaned down and pressed a slow, lingering kiss on her mouth. "Thank you."

She ran her tongue around her lips before pressing gently on his chest. Once he reclined again, Shay snuggled close, facing him. "So you're alpha, and I'm your mate. That makes me…?"

"Mine."

She punched him in the stomach. “No. In the eyes of the pack?”

“Still mine,” he said with a grin.

Shay rolled her eyes. “What’s my title?”

“Alpha-fem,” he answered, still smirking.

“Right. Shannon said something about that. But what role do I play in the pack? I assume everyone has one.”

He spoke slowly, feeling his way. “You’ll rule the females, unquestionably. There may be some friction at first. Some testing to see what you’re made of. Some resentment. Because you’re an outsider, human—take your pick.”

She frowned. “Only the females? With the Ravens, Kiesha leads by Alex’s side.”

“The Ravens are more progressive than the Sparrowhawks, and even at that, I’m sure Alex eased her into it. There would have been a period of adjustment, for both Kiesha and the Ravens. One step, one change at a time. Isn’t that what you meant before?”

Shrugging, she asked, “What about the males? What reaction do you expect from them?”

He held her gaze, waiting to see her reaction. “They’ll sniff at you. Testing of a different sort.”

“To see if they can get to you through me?”

“That’s part of it. Shay, you’re a very beautiful woman. One any male would desire. On top of that, I chose you. That makes you the prize—a highly desirable one. You’re strong, intelligent, sexy, everything a male shifter looks for in a mate. If they can steal you away from me…” He left Shay to connect the dots.

Her nose wrinkled as though smelling something unsavory, and a fire burned in her eyes. “Great! Nothing I’d like more than a bunch of horny werewolves trying to get between my legs. Unless, of course, it’s a bunch of jealous bitches—with claws, I might add—who’d kill to trade places with me.”

“No one, male or female, will lay a hand on you.” The mere thought of it had his wolf in his throat.

She patted his chest. “Down, Cujo. You can’t protect me. Not from this. Doing so would make me look weak.”

“You’re my mate. You carry my child under your heart. I bloody well can and will keep you safe.” Rory felt his eyes go wolf, and the tips of his fingers prickled, claws waiting to spring out.

She narrowed her eyes in such a way that he knew, just knew meant he wasn’t going to like what came next. “Respect is earned, not forced. Eventually, I’ll have to stand on my own.”

Though it went against every protective instinct in his body, Rory knew Shay was right. But still… “You’re human. Not only that, you’re mine to protect.”

Snorting, she responded, “That’s fine as long as your idea of protection doesn’t cause me to lose face.” Suddenly she sighed and inched closer. “Rory, I know enough about shifters to know that anyone wanting to get to you could do so through me. Granted, you’d make them wish they’d never been born before you kill the bastard and anyone associated with him. But afterward, once the anger abated, grief—the crippling kind—would hit and most likely you’d be done for. In this relationship, I’m the weakest link.

“I also know enough about animals, canine in particular, to know you can psych them out. It’s all in the attitude. If you treat me like I'm powerless, then in their eyes that's what I'll be. I'm not saying throw me to the wolves—no pun intended—but I need you to stand back and let's see what happens. I guess what I'm really saying is give me a chance to show I'm strong enough to stand by your side."

Rory thought about it. He could understand her not wanting to appear weak. Could he suppress his protective nature enough to give Shay what she needed? "I can't promise anything. You're my mate. Protecting you is as natural to me as breathing. It's instinctive to all shifter males. Not doing so would send the message that I don't value you, that you aren't truly my mate. Shifter males protect their own."

He could almost see the wheels turning in her head as she considered his words. He went on. "Think of how Alex is with Kiesha, Hugh with Mary Elizabeth, even the vampire with my sister. Do you honestly think I could do or be anything less with you?"

Shay sighed as she rolled her eyes. Finally she said, "You're right. You do what you do, and I'll handle the rest."

He cupped her jaw. "As stated, there'll be some friction at first. A period of testing and adjustment because I've been without a mate for so long, and because I've made known my intentions never to take one. You and the babe will be a shock, but they'll get over it and if they don't, they'll deal with me."

She considered his words. "What about the enemy within?"

Her words threw him. "What enemy?"

"Your enemies," she clarified, her gaze intent.

Her expression indicated there was some bit of knowledge she wasn't sharing with him. He wanted to ask, to push. Instead he decided to bide his time. Build trust between them and the rest would come.

"Everyone has enemies, and every pack has dissenters. If I'm not powerful enough to hold the pack and protect what's mine, then I don't deserve either one of you."

Eyes narrowed, Shay pointed a finger at him and commanded, "Watch your ass."

"Yours and mine, always." Rory patted the body part in question. Though she smiled, she still seemed worried.

Part of him was offended. "Shay, I've been alpha more than eight years. You think someone handed me the position? I had to kill for it, my own father, and while I was still tired from the battle, had to take on five others who thought they were the better wolf for the job. In the years since, I've proven by combat and by wits that I'm more than tough enough, powerful enough to hold it."

Rory rolled away from her, intending to get out of bed and put space between them. How dare his own mate doubt his abilities? How dare she think him too weak, too feebleminded to protect her and their babe?

"Rory…" Shay laid a hand on his arm. He shook it off and made to rise. Suddenly her arms were around his neck as she gripped him in a headlock.

"Oh no you don't!"

"What the bloody hell is wrong with you?" He pulled on her forearm. In response she tightened her grip to near strangling and wrapped her legs around his waist.

"You're not going anywhere until we finish discussing this like rational adults. Well, I'll be rational. You try not to be so hardheaded."

"I'm done with this subject," he grunted, still trying to pry her loose.

"I'm not." She bit his ear—hard. "Think, damn it. Shove your ego to the side. Do you think I'd be here with you in the midst of a bunch of freaking werewolves who want my blood if I thought you couldn't keep me safe? Hell, Rory, you fought off two horny wolves for me, or don't you remember? You think I'd have been screaming your name at the top of my lungs if I hadn't believed you'd do otherwise? And that's when I thought we hated each other's guts."

The reminder of that night, the first night of the blue moon, calmed him. "Then what's this about?"

"Conor."

He stiffened and dropped his hands to his sides as the lightbulb in his head clicked on. Looking straight ahead, his tone neutral, he asked, "Are you ready to tell me now what the seer said?"

Shay was quiet. Through the link, he could feel the war going on inside of her as she debated whether or not to trust him with the truth. *Tell me, baby*."

She released her hold, and the mattress shifted as she retreated, putting space between them. Rory turned and caught her by the wrist. "Trust, Shay. That's what relationships are built on."

She tilted her head to the side, her gaze bouncing between his hold on her wrist and his eyes. He knew the minute she dropped her guard. Felt it deep within as their mate bond strengthened.

"Don't get crazy," she warned.

"I won't," he promised.

"I'm serious."

"I know."

She narrowed her eyes in stern warning. "You blow up at me, and I'm going to be pissed."

"Shay..."

"Oh, all right," she said with a sigh. "I'm paraphrasing, but Conor said for me to be careful. That I'd be surrounded by treachery and that my safety and the safety of our daughters depended on you and I working together to defeat the enemy."

Rory stared, unable to believe he'd heard right. Then what she said sank in.

UNDERNEATH HER BREATH, Shayla counted down. "Ten, nine, eight, seven, six, five, four, three—"

Rory surged to his feet, and the words that came out of his mouth had even her flinching. He paced across the room and back. It was more of a prowl, that of a caged predator. Suddenly he spun and pinned her with a glare. "Why didn't you tell me earlier?"

"You've already tried to send me away once for my protection."

He visibly winced before shutting his eyes. Rory pinched the bridge of his nose and took a couple of deep breaths. "Shay, that was completely different."

"Uh-huh." She made certain he saw the skepticism in her facial expression.

He stared a moment, shook his head, then resumed pacing. A thought must have struck, for he paused midstep before turning to face her. "That's why you refused the pack's midwife."

"Yes."

"And why you were suspicious of Ashley," he continued.

"No."

"What do you mean, *no*?"

"I already told you my reasons for disliking the..." Biting back the word she wanted to used, she finished with, "skank."

He waved the Ashley issue away. "You said Conor told you not to trust anyone in the pack?"

Shay shook her head. "I told you I was paraphrasing. His actual words were, 'You must fight to hold on to what is yours. Treachery surrounds you. Only by uniting together will you be victorious. Show no mercy. Your daughters' safety depends on the decisions you make now.'" She left out the part about Rory loving her totally and completely, just the way she was. It wasn't pertinent to their current conversation, and Conor had proven to be right about Rory loving her.

Rory let loose with another string of words. And she thought she knew how to curse. Compared to him, she was a naive amateur. She waited for him to settle down. When he quieted, she told him, "You can't talk like that once the baby gets here. She'll have a potty mouth."

Nonplussed, he stared at her.

"Besides you promised not to blow up." She pointed at him. "You, Mount Saint Helens, just erupted all over the place."

"You can't tell me my family's in danger and not expect me to react!"

Shay arched an eyebrow and waited for him to calm. He looked like he wanted to hurt someone. Then he eyed the wall. "You punch a hole in that wall and you'll have to fix it…tonight."

The look he shot her should have singed the hair on her head. He paced in short, angry strides, back and forth. Shay placed some pillows behind her back and propped against the headboard, ready to wait him out.

After about five minutes of muttering and movement, he stopped with his back to her and clutched two handfuls of hair. Good thing he was a werewolf. If he kept pulling like that, he'd go bald. Finally he came and sat on the bed beside her.

"I don't know if I completely buy into all this mumbo jumbo stuff—"

"You mean like werewolves and vampires being real?" Shay murmured wryly.

"But…he's right about one thing. We're a unit. Two halves of a whole. For this…us…to work, we have to learn to trust each other. And we can't keep secrets," he stated with a pointed stare.

She met his gaze with a bland expression, knowing she damn well would continue to determine when and what to share with him. An open book she wasn't, and neither was he.

Before the silence could drag out too long, she asked, "So what's the plan?"

When he didn't say anything, she added, "You do have a plan, don't you? We only have five months to figure this shit out or some folks are going to start dying. I will not have my children threatened."

Rory seemed to come to some inner decision. The lethal smile that crept into the open boded ill to whomever it was aimed toward. Anyone else viewing it would have been chilled. "I'll handle it," he said. His tone was equally deadly.

Shay felt the pulse of temper tattoo a beat in her left temple. "You mean *we'll* handle it, right? Mr. We're a Unit, Two Halves of a Whole?"

He scowled. "No, I don't. This half of our *unit* knows where the threat lies, so I'll take care of it. No need to involve you and the babe."

"Excuse me, but the word 'treachery' implies that you don't know who the enemy or enemies are. You only think you do," she snapped.

He leaned forward and planted his hands on either side of her hips. "I know my pack. I not only rule them, I live and grew up with them. I know who's the most likely to want to do you harm." His hazel eyes bled to gold, and a hint of fang showed in his mouth.

"And if you're wrong?"

"I'm not!"

"But if you are? This is my life you're talking about."

"Wrong! It's our lives because you are my life," he roared as he shot to his feet.

Talk about taking the wind out of someone's sails. His words weren't flowery, but they were heartfelt and knocked the building anger right out of her. She no longer felt like arguing. Besides, Conor had said the decisions *she* made would be the determining factor.

"You're right." Her tone was so calm, so reasonable it had him observing her suspiciously. Probably waiting for the catch. "Your child and I are hungry. Feed us."

Without waiting for him to react, Shay rose and went to one of the dressers, pulling out a pair of shorts and a tank. She still smelled like sex and Rory, but the scents appealed so she dressed without washing. She turned to find him still standing there.

"Food," she prompted and, as her gaze fell on the discarded luggage, added, "and do something with those."

Muttering something about pregnancy, mood swings, and incomprehensible women, Rory snagged his pants from the floor, donned them, and then snatched up her suitcases.

"The small one fits inside the larger for storage," she told him.

From the doorway he glanced over his shoulder at her and snarled, "I'm not a bleeding idiot!" before leaving the room.

Patting her still-flat stomach, Shay told her child, "Your daddy's pissed with me. Let's give him a little time to calm."

She remade the bed and rearranged the items on the dressers. Then went into the bathroom and straightened the medicine cabinets. While she worked, she went back to her earlier line of thought.

The decision she'd made. Hmm…

What she'd told Rory was correct. She did trust him to protect her from any and all threats of which he was aware. The problem was Rory had a huge blind spot when it came to his pack.

In this area she had an advantage. Sort of. Since she didn't know the people, she could be more objective. Of course, her unfamiliarity with the pack was also a huge drawback. How did she distinguish between normal and suspicious? Maybe this was why Conor said it would take both of them. Rory's knowledge coupled with her objectivity.

The smell of marinara sauce drifted into the bedroom. Dinner was almost done.

Sighing, she gave the thoughts circling in her head a break and went down to join her mate. "Can I help with anything?" she asked as she entered the kitchen.

"No, I have it." His tone was brisk but not angry. The space from each other had helped, as she'd hoped it would.

Rory gestured her to the table. He served up the spaghetti, then joined her. "Let me know if the tomato sauce gives you a problem. Some pregnant women find it too acidic."

Shay poked at a piece of ground beef with her fork. "You have so much meat in this, I doubt it will be an issue."

He grunted in reply. A comfortable silence settled as they ate.

After the worst of her hunger was sated—she hadn't lied about being hungry—Shay waved her fork at Rory. "Tell me more about the Sparrowhawks. Who are the major players and what do you think of them?"

The fork paused halfway to his mouth as he looked at her. "Why?"

She chopped up a few more noodles as she answered. "Because I'll be meeting them—" She broke off as she remembered Rory said he was calling the pack together but didn't say when. "When exactly are we having this little shindig?"

"Tomorrow night."

"*Tomorrow*?" Her eating utensil clattered onto the table. "Why so soon?"

"This is a small town, a small pack. Word travels quickly. I wanted to have you to myself for a few days before having to share you with the others. That won't be possible now that members of the pack know about you. Better to take control and make an official announcement."

Shay rubbed wearily at her forehead. "All the more reason for you to give me an idea what to expect."

Rory nudged her fork closer and motioned for her to continue eating. He waited until she'd eaten another mouthful to respond. "Wouldn't you like to form your own opinions of them?"

Shay held up a finger until she'd swallowed. "I will, but forewarned is forearmed."

"Makes sense. Something I'd do myself." He rose, went to the refrigerator, and pulled out a gallon of milk.

"If that's for me, I'm not drinking milk with tomato sauce."

Rory ducked inside and came out with a bottle of apple juice instead.

"Don't you have any punch, lemonade, soda? Anything with sugar?" she demanded.

"This is better for you." He poured her a glass of the juice, grabbed a bottled water for himself, and returned to the table. "Where do you want to start?"

She motioned with the fork. "Who takes over if you're"—she searched for and discarded several words before settling on—"incapacitated?"

He arched a brow. "It's not that simple. There'd be fights to see who'd take control of the pack if I'm no longer able to lead."

Shay thought for a moment. “Your second—what’s his name?—he wouldn’t automatically step into the gap?”

“Caleb Jones,” he supplied.

“The dude with the dreads?”

He nodded. “In the short term, as second he could act on my behalf.”

“And who’s his backup?”

Rory frowned. “MacDougal, my third.”

He didn’t seem to like this MacDougal guy too much. The tone he used when he said Caleb’s and MacDougal’s names was totally different. “Ranks are based on strength, right?”

“Yes.”

“So who’s after this Mac guy?’”

“If we’re speaking pecking order based solely on strength, next would be Wesley. He’s one of the council. A strong beta, but brash and impulsive. His wolf is powerful but unseasoned in combat.”

“Is he one of the shifters you fought when you assumed leadership?”

Something flashed on his face. “No.”

Hmm, something there. Something Rory didn’t want to talk about. “You said there were five contenders,” she probed. “If Wesley wasn’t one of them, then who?”

Rory looked over her shoulder. “MacDougal.” The response was clipped.

When he fell silent, Shay pushed a little harder, aware she was treading on dangerous ground. “Caleb too?”

He shook his head. “No. He’s never wanted to be alpha.”

It was obvious he didn't want to talk about it. Should she let it go? Shay wanted to. She could literally feel his agitation, his internal distress. But what if one of these guys hadn't let go of the desire to be alpha? What if they were going about it in a subtler, more treacherous way? She couldn't take that chance.

"And the others?"

"Dead," he stated flatly.

Shay felt her eyes bulge, and her mouth dropped open. "You killed…?"

Rory lifted his head, and she trailed off. His eyes were pure gold. But what got her was the pain in them. "Aye. I killed five men that night. Four of whom their only crime was wanting to improve their status within the pack. My first official act as alpha was to ban dominance fights to the death."

"Shannon said your father forced you to kill him," she stated slowly.

"He set the terms of the battle, yes. To the death. No surrender."

Shay placed her hand on top of his fisted one where it rested on the table. "I'm sure, if there'd been any other way, you would have taken it."

Rory gazed at his hands, flexed them a few times before holding them up. "There's blood on these."

"Did they give you a choice?" she asked quietly. "Any of them?"

He swallowed hard, then placed his hands under the table, out of view. "No." When he looked at her again, his eyes were bleak. "My mother called me a murderer. Screamed it at me."

Shay felt such rage it was a good thing the woman was already dead. Shay would have killed her otherwise. "She was wrong," she bit out. She wanted to curse, but more importantly, Shay wanted to soothe her hurting mate.

"I could have walked away."

"Could you, really? And leave the pack you grew up expecting to lead to someone else? And Shannon—don't alphas typically mate the strongest female? Could you have left your sister unprotected?" Shay knew the answer. Rory knew, but he hadn't accepted it yet.

"No." It came out strangled.

"Then you had no choice. Are you going to eat that?"

Rory frowned at his half-full plate. "I'm no longer hungry."

Shay rose and gathered both their plates. "Where's the foil?"

He grabbed her wrist and held it so that her plate lowered to the table. "You need to eat to keep up your strength."

"I've had enough. I ate more than you." She tugged free and placed the leftovers on the countertop, then hunted in the pantry until she found what she was looking for. After putting the food away, she took a dish towel, moistened it, and wiped down the stove and table.

"You don't have to clean after me." Rory rose to help.

"And you don't have to slave for me. I'll do my share." She took one last glance at the room to make sure everything was in place. As she tossed the dish towel into the sink, she told him, "Let's go take a shower and snuggle. It's been a long day."

Chapter Nine

Shay's dreams were filled with dark and disturbing, yet strangely erotic images. She woke with a gasp on her lips and a fire between her legs. In the way of dreams, all faded but one startlingly vivid picture of Shay on her hands and knees while a half-shifted, furry Rory claimed her from behind as the faceless members of their pack watched angrily. Shay found herself rubbing enticingly against Rory's morning erection, strategically positioned between the crease of her buttocks.

"Does my hellcat want her kitty stroked?" Rory asked in a low, rumbling murmur. The heat of his breath on her earlobe sent a shiver racing through her.

"Your mate wants your cock in her pussy," she half pleaded, half demanded, arching her hips to get that hard, thick part of him where it would do the most good.

Rory trailed his hand down her stomach to lazily stroke her clit. "And does my mate want it hard and fast, or long and deep?"

"Decisions, decisions, decisions," she gasped out. "Why can't I have both?" Shay rocked forward and backward, unable to determine which she wanted more, the finger shooting sparks through her or the head of Rory's penis teasing her opening.

"Greedy this morning, aren't you?" he asked with a husky chuckle.

"Very." She reached an arm behind her and caught a handful of his hair, adding a small tug for emphasis as she ordered, "Now give me what I *need*!"

"Your wish is my command."

"Can I get *that* in writing?"

"After I'm dead and gone," he promised as he lifted her leg and curved closer, sinking his shaft deep. They both moaned at the contact.

"Deep enough?"

"Let me see." Shay swallowed. "I don't taste you at the back of my throat, so no."

"Darling, if you want a taste of my cock, I'm in the wrong end." He nibbled on her neck and pinched a nipple, but otherwise didn't move.

Shay canted her hips and pushed back. "Don't toy with me, wolf boy. Give it to me."

"Like this?" Rory braced a hand on the mattress, lifted his hips, and thrust deep.

Matching his movements, Shay nearly hummed in pleasure. Instead she taunted, "If this is the best you can do, I guess it will have to suffice."

"Feeling sassy, huh? Brace yourself." He shifted them until Shay was on her belly, shoulders pressed to the mattress, ass in the air. Shay felt his fingers part her sex where they'd been joined, widening her opening for his possession.

She pressed her forearms down and dug her fingers in, readying herself for the pounding to come, only to almost leap out of her skin when she felt the broad swipe of Rory's tongue. "Ahhh! Rory, what are you doing?"

"Eating breakfast. Now be quiet!"

He took his time, capturing every drop of cream her body produced. Incoherent, Shay wondered if this qualified as the long or the deep, as the tongue he used couldn't possibly be human and reach the depths of her core as it did.

Just when she was ready to come out of her mind, he stopped. Shay emitted a small scream of protest. He growled in response, his breath hot on her pussy. One last swipe of the tongue curling around her clit set her off. Shay bucked in his hands, her squeal muffled by the bed.

Rory rose over her, and Shay felt the bulbous head of his erection nudge her nether lips. As he tightened his grip on her hips, the pinprick of his claws nipped her skin. His muscles tensed, and the phone rang.

"Answer and die!"

He slid in an inch. Shay tried pushing back to take more, but Rory held her still. The phone rang again.

"You wanted long," he reminded in a gravelly voice.

Another ring.

"I wanted hard and deep too. We did the long. Give me the rest."

The answering machine clicked on, loudly in the room. "*Rory, I know you said not to bother you, but we have a situation at the McCormick site. You better get down here quick. The city inspector's here, and it's not looking good.*"

Rory's body tensed. Then he lunged for the phone, cursing. A rapid-fire conversation followed, and minutes later he was dressed and striding out the bedroom door, casting one longing look at her still-naked form

Shay sighed. So much for morning nooky. Next time she'd pick option A instead of being greedy and wanting it all. She roused her still-quivering flesh and trudged into the bathroom to shower. Then she cooked and ate a full breakfast, heavy on the protein. Rory still hadn't returned by the time she cleaned the kitchen, so she took advantage of the opportunity to give Shannon a call.

Shannon's cell phone rang a number of times before her groggy voice answered. "Shay?"

"Keeping vampire hours now?"

"Vampires aren't the only nocturnal being. Wolves are too." She yawned. "How are things with my brother?"

"Fine. He gets a little stubborn sometimes. Nothing a good two-by-four upside the head won't cure."

Shannon chuckled. "I'll remember that the next time we get into it." She could hear Shannon moving around, the whisper of bedcovers. "Seriously, Shay, is everything okay between you?"

"He said he loves me," Shay heard herself admit. And this, she realized, was the real reason she'd called.

"You don't believe him?"

"Yes, no…maybe. I think he believes it."

"But you don't."

Shay sighed. "Honestly, I don't know what to think. Part of me thinks, if he really loved me, he wouldn't have tried to get rid of me. But another part of me knows that was simply Rory being stupid and in a strange way, it is actually proof that he does."

"Did he ever say what that was about?"

Face flaming, Shay explained how Rory had claimed her in front of his men.

"Oh man. No wonder he went off the deep end," Shannon murmured.

"I'm the one that was embarrassed," Shay muttered.

"No, Shay. I'm not making light of what you may have felt. It's just that, well, my mother was a very beautiful woman. Even as she grew older, men would make plays for her. My father's answer was to publicly claim her, every time. When I was younger, it would horrify me. As I got older, I realized she provoked him. Rory swore never to be like our father, in any way. Now do you understand?"

"Yes." The idiot. "No offense, Shannon, but the more I hear about your father, the less I like him."

"Try having to live with him. You know, Shay, I used to blame my father for a lot of things. It's only since I've been with Nikolai that I realize how much of a role my mother played in my father's behavior. Their relationship was really sick and sometimes twisted. It left scars on us. Be patient with Rory."

There was a small pause as Shay let that sink in. Then, unable to hold it in anymore, she hesitantly asked, "Shannon, can I ask you a question?"

"Sure."

"You told me about you and Nikolai, how you came together. What convinced you his love was real?"

"Boy, you don't ask easy questions." She was quiet for a bit. "I think the first thing to catch my attention was that Nikolai wanted me, in spite of my wolf, not because of it. And he stopped having sex with me," she added with a laugh.

"What!"

"After my heat had passed, he stopped. Oh, we kissed and touched, but he refused to mate with me.

Nikolai *romanced* me instead. Said he didn't want sex clouding my mind. That he wanted me to come to him out of love, not lust."

"Rory's introducing me to the pack tonight," Shay blurted.

Shannon, well used to Shay's manner of conversational ball play, bounced right along with the change of topic without a quibble. "He called a howl? You want me to come?"

Shay thought for a moment. "While I'd welcome the support, I think you being here would send the wrong message. I need to handle this on my own. I just wish I was more confident in my relationship with Rory."

"If you change your mind, let me know, and Shay, the rest will come. Give it time."

Time was the one thing Shay didn't have.

"Since you don't want me there, tell me how I can help," Shannon said.

"I need information. I asked Rory what to expect, but he's a man. They don't see things like women. Give me a handle on what to expect and who to watch out for."

They spoke for another half hour to forty-five minutes before Shayla was content that she had the knowledge she needed to handle the coming night. Once she hung up, she realized Rory had been gone now for three hours. Rather than sit in the house and twiddle her thumbs, Shay decided to go outside and explore the grounds.

She tucked her cell phone in her shorts pocket and made sure both the front and rear doors were unlocked before venturing out. Stepping off the front porch, Shay walked into the yard before turning to study the structure. The house appeared to be a ramshackle hodgepodge of additions that had been added to the main one-room log cabin and modernized. Between the basement, the main and upper levels, the building could comfortably house twenty. The kitchen and main rooms were huge. Shay knew that upstairs were seven comfortable bedrooms and four bathrooms.

Shay glanced over the yard. The front lawn was manicured, containing trees and rocks and a bubbling brook running on one side of the property. A few feet in any direction and the land sloped up, fading into trees. She walked down the drive to the one-lane road and glanced in either direction. Though she could see no houses, she noted a few driveways branching off, indicating the presence of neighbors.

Turning, Shay took one of the paths leading around to the rear of the house. At first glance the backyard appeared to be more rugged, less cultured and slightly overgrown, but someone had installed a freestanding wooden swing in the midst of it. Shay sat and set it in motion.

In the calm quiet, Shay reflected. What direction did she need to take next? Her family wasn't particularly religious, but Auntie Miri had been, or at least she'd become that way after her husband died. She'd dragged Kiesha and Shay with her to a little Baptist church. Shay hadn't really minded going but had felt obligated to complain because Kiesha had.

One sermon in particular had stuck with her through all these years, the one on reaping and sowing. The minister had taught it in such a way that even as a child she'd understood the concept. Everyone reaps what they sow so be careful how you treat people, because what you do to others comes back to you threefold.

Based on what the minister had taught, Shay had a decision to make. She could continue to sow mistrust, disbelief, and fear into her relationship with Rory and receive a crop full of the same. Or she could believe in him, in his love for her, and the mate bond forming between them. An intelligent woman, something she prided herself as being, would do the latter.

Shay rocked in the dappled sunlight, face lifted into the breeze, and allowed the rest of her doubts and concerns to drift away.

* * * *

It was late afternoon before Rory arrived home, dirty, sweaty, muttering angrily about code inspectors who don't know their assholes from their armpits. Dinner simmered on the stove. Shay spared him a glance from the computer game she played at the kitchen table.

"Shower first, then dinner."

Rory stopped and looked around. "You didn't have to cook."

She shrugged. "You worked. I cooked. It's not like I had anything else to do."

He scrubbed his face with his hands. "I'm sorry I had to run off—"

"Don't," she interrupted quietly. "It's your job. I understand. There will be times when I'm called off to handle a project. Will I need to apologize for doing my job?"

"No." He frowned. "We need to discuss the amount of traveling you do."

Shay smiled. "After you shower. We're on a schedule. What time is the pack arriving?"

He cursed. "I forgot. They're not coming here. We're gathering at our meeting place in the woods."

Shay had a flash of her dream and prayed it wasn't a premonition, though she'd never been prone to them. "Um, about tonight. There won't be any public claiming, will there?" she couldn't help but ask.

Rory's forehead scrunched. "Claiming?"

"Fucking—you and me—in front of the pack."

He sputtered, "No! Where would you get a ridiculous idea like that?"

"You haven't been very forthcoming about tonight's festivities. What am I supposed to think?"

"Not that." He bent over, undid the laces of his work boots, toed them off, and set them by the door before rising and placing his hands on his hips. "We'll go, I'll introduce you to the pack, the council will acknowledge our mating, and the pack will submit to the alpha pair."

"You make it sound simple. A mere formality."

He began unbuttoning his shirt. Shay's gaze was drawn to the flesh being slowly revealed. "It will be."

She squeezed her thighs together. "Hurry up and get clean. I'm hungry."

Rory glanced at the clock over the stove. "Be down in a few."

Shay rose, gave the food a last stir, and turned off the burners on the stove. As the sounds of the shower reached downstairs, she set the table with place mats, ice-filled glasses, napkins, and silverware. By the time Rory's footsteps sounded on the stairs, she was scooping food onto dinner plates.

"Smells good. I could eat a deer. Didn't get a chance to eat today," he said as he sat.

Shay set a plate heaping with food in front of him, then went to the fridge to get the sweet tea, pouring them both a glass before placing the pitcher on the table. She picked up her plate and settled beside him.

Rory glanced from his to hers. “I thought you were hungry.”

“I am,” she stated. “I never said for what.” The look she shot him was scorching.

His fork hung forgotten halfway to his mouth as his eyes narrowed, arousal tightening his features. Shay nudged his arm. “Eat. You’ll need your strength.”

They ate in silence. When Rory’s fork scraped the now empty porcelain, Shay rose and held out her hand. “More food?”

“No.” His gaze was intent as he handed her the plate.

As she set it on the countertop, she asked, “Tea?”

“No.”

Hands braced on the counter behind her, she commented, “You still look hungry.”

“I am.” He slowly rose to stand.

“There’s ice cream,” she offered.

He stepped toward her, shaking his head.

“Cookies?”

“Later.” He trapped her against the sink.

“The table—”

“Can wait.”

“Oh thank God.” Shay dived into his arms. “I’ve been going crazy all day.” She tugged on his jeans, frantic. “Inside me now. No foreplay.”

A few swipes of his claws and Shay's clothes were shreds. He lifted her by the waist, and Shay wrapped her legs high around his. Hands gripping her butt, Rory swung around and began to lower her.

"Not the table," she squeaked.

He smoothly switched directions and braced her against the wall. "Free my cock."

Shay reached a hand down and pushed at his briefs. "Why are you wearing underwear? You never wear underwear."

His cock sprung free and slapped her mound. Rory readjusted his hold, warning, "Hold on."

The first thrust made her see stars. The second had her crying out his name. Then Shay held on as Rory took her the way she'd wanted to be taken since waking that morning—hard, strong, and deep thrusts that filled her to the brim and hit every hot spot. His pubic bone applied steady friction to her clit. Shay clawed his shoulders and, when the pleasure reached crisis point, buried her teeth in his neck. Rory howled as he came, grinding his hips sharply into her. Legs limp, they slid bonelessly to the floor, panting.

Rory rested his forehead against hers. "If this is the way you greet me, I need to get called on emergencies more often."

"Yeah…well…" Shay, her brain fried, was too sated to think of a good comeback.

Eventually she caught her breath, planted her feet on the floor, and shoved up. The angle left her naked, glistening sex in Rory's face. Not one to miss an opportunity, he immediately latched ahold with his mouth, licking and sucking.

Shay let her head slump to the wall, angled her hips to give him greater access, and closed her eyes on a sigh of pleasure. No man had ever loved her the way this one did. The sex alone was reason to stick around.

Rory lifted her right leg onto his shoulder. Already weak-kneed with pleasure, Shay shot out both arms and called a warning. "I'm going to fall!"

Rory reclined on the floor, pulling Shay with him so that she straddled his face. For a brief moment Shay had a vision of his men walking in on them again, then all else was forgotten. She arched her spine, lifted her face to the ceiling, and let the orgasm rush over her.

After crawling from beneath her, Rory bent and picked her up, cradling her in his arms.

"Where are we going?"

"To bed to finish round two in comfort."

"Whoopee!"

* * * *

Much later in the truck, Rory kept sending scowling glances at his mate. "I can't believe you wore that."

"It's just a skirt—"

"That barely covers your ass," he muttered.

"And a tank top—"

"So thin I can see the outline of your nipples," he snarled.

"—and I'm wearing your shirt to cover it all," she reminded. "You keep clawing the clothes off my body and soon I'll be forced to walk around naked."

In truth the ensemble she wore wasn't that revealing. What was making Rory's cock hard was the excuse for panties Shay almost wore beneath the denim and the knowledge that with one tug, she'd be bare for his possession.

He'd told Shayla there'd be no public claiming of her tonight, but by God's truth, he'd didn't know how he was going to keep his hands off her, especially once the celebrating began. An alpha taking a mate was a joyous occasion in any pack. According to his father, the Sparrowhawks had celebrated for a week when his parents mated, resulting in several matings and a few pregnancies. In addition, Shay being pregnant meant the future of the pack was well secured.

He believed much of the unrest among the older members would now disappear. They knew the importance of the pack having an alpha pair. Tonight there would be revelry, some of it sexual in nature. Shifters as a species didn't have any qualms about public nudity, and the Sparrowhawks weren't particularly private about sex. His father had seen to that.

Thinking about it, Rory wished he could have held this at the house where they could party in style with barbecue, beer, and dancing. But the pack couldn't celebrate until their mating had been formally recognized by the council. In addition, as grounded in tradition as his people were, they wouldn't be happy unless he made the announcement of his mating at the official meeting place where his father and grandfather and every other member's mating had been made since settling in this territory in the 1800s. Maybe when they were done, he'd invite the entire pack to the house.

He drove up the narrow, winding road several miles before turning onto a deliberately overgrown track barely visible from the street. Even if any curious person noticed it, the rough terrain suitable only for pickups or four-wheel drives would quickly discourage them from going on.

Rory felt uneasy, his wolf agitated. Reaching out through the bond, he sensed Shay's tension rising the closer they came to their destination. He reached over, snagged her hand off her lap, and brought it to his mouth for a kiss. "Calm down."

"I am calm."

He let the lie go. She'd see soon enough there was no reason to worry. "I can't wait to show you off to my pack. My beautiful, sexy mate, Shayla Morgan, soon to be Shayla McFelan."

Rory released her to turn into a small clearing where several all-terrain vehicles were already parked. Once he cut off the engine, he undid both their seat belts. "Come here."

Taking her hand again, Rory tugged Shay to him and lifted her onto his lap, then simply held her close. She settled in his arms with a sigh. "Maybe I am a *little* nervous."

"It's just a formality, Shay. A necessary evil, if you will, to be dispensed with so we can get on with our lives together."

"I know," she said, but her tone stated otherwise.

Instead of decreasing, her anxiety escalated. To settle his wolf, whose agitation was also amplifying, he tugged on his link to the pack, only to discover the edginess he was feeling wasn't emanating from Shay at all. Both of them were feeding off the pack, which was filled with uncertainty, dismay, and in some, downright anger and distrust.

Shay stroked the side of his face, capturing his attention. "You're snarling," she told him.

"I'm reading the pack. They're not happy." It didn't even occur to him to keep it from Shay. They were a unit now, and mates didn't keep secrets from each other.

"Did you expect them to be?"

"Yes, damn it!" He slammed his hand on the dashboard. "They're supposed to be happy and excited for me, not all this bullshit I'm sensing."

"Maybe some are, but you can't blame them for being uncertain, or even suspicious. I'm an unknown. Human. They don't know what to expect."

"That's no excuse. They—"

Shay silenced him by slanting her mouth over his. She slid a hand into the hair at his nape and deepened the kiss. His dick, always semiready where his mate was concerned, went stiff as a board. In seconds their tongues and teeth came into play as the kiss turned ravenous.

When they broke for air, he reminded reluctantly, "They're waiting."

"Let them." Shay climbed to her knees before shifting to straddle his lap. With the movement, her skirt rose until the crotch of her thong was visible. "You've felt what they're feeling; now let them feel us through the bond. Feel how right we are for each other. Let them see it doesn't matter what anyone thinks or how they feel about our mating. It's here to stay."

Then she worked that oh-so-short piece of denim material over her hips to her waist and ripped the crotch out of her panties. The scent of her arousal filled the cab.

"You're sure? One of my men or the council may come looking for us if we don't appear soon. They know we're here. They can sense me just as I can sense them." Even as he spoke, he stroked the soft curls between her legs.

Shay untied the knot on his shirt she wore and shrugged it off as she glanced out of all the windows. Seeing no one about, she whipped her tank top over her head, tossed it to the side, then slid her arms inside the sleeves of his shirt. Anyone observing them would see his white dress shirt and not the bounty he saw—perky, brown-tipped breasts, skirt bunched high, and the moisture-slicked curls between her legs beckoning him.

"Last chance," he warned, feeling his beast rise.

In response Shay bared her shoulder and tilted her head to the side. "Mark me."

Wolf off its leash, Rory lunged forward and sank his fangs into the tendon between her shoulder and neck, feeling in that moment more vamp than shifter. Shay let out a soft, gasping moan that went straight to his cock, and reached up to clutch his hair in a tight grip while rocking her sex on the hard bulge in his pants. "God, that feels good," she panted.

"This will feel even better." He eased a hand between them and undid his pants. His engorged cock sprang free, right into Shay's greedy little hands. In an instant she had him positioned for penetration. As she lowered, Rory surged up, clamping hard hands on her hips to keep from bucking her off his lap. Their ride was short, rough, but extremely satisfying. When it was over, they wore matching bite marks and the scent of sex clung to them.

He blasted the link with his pack wide open. *This, this is what my mate gives me. This is what you in your selfishness seek to deny me!*

Rory made sure they felt the love, peace, joy, and sheer contentment he found in Shay, and his displeasure that anyone would seek to disallow his right to be loved and love in return. Then he shut the link down, shut them out.

"What was that?" Shay asked, rubbing her chest lightly.

"You felt it?" he asked, surprised she was sensitive enough to pick up on his psychic connection with the pack.

"Some. I could tell you were communicating with someone and whoever it is, you're not happy with them. Of course, this scowl would have told me that." She kissed the side of his mouth and did a little shimmy on his lap, smiling when he hardened inside her again.

Still frowning, this time at his mate, he asked, "Are you always going to use sex to coax me out of my bad moods?"

She arched a brow. "It works, doesn't it?"

Smiling reluctantly at her logic, he brushed a lock of hair out of her face and said with a sigh, "Put your shirt back on and straighten your clothes. Let's get this over with and go home."

PISSED ON HER mate's behalf, Shay did as instructed. Shannon was right. The Sparrowhawks weren't simply going to welcome her with open arms, no matter how much Rory might wish differently. Hence this little lovemaking session she'd engineered. She needed to rub it in their faces that she and Rory were mated and nothing they said or did would change it.

"*Show them graphically you two belong to each other,*" Shannon had said. "*Wear his mark proudly. Arrive at the howl covered in his scent. Be obvious. Let them all see your mating's a done deal.*"

With Shannon's instructions ringing in her ears, Shay used her torn underwear to wipe the excess cum from between her legs, then tucked the scrap of material in her front skirt pocket. She tossed Rory's shirt to the side and slid on her tank, knowing it left her shoulders bare and marks visible. Over the course of the last few days, Rory had marked her so many times that the scars were visible to the naked eye, despite the healing saliva in his glands. Wearing his possession like a shield of armor, Shay indicated she was ready.

"You going like that? What happened to the shirt?"

Shay wrinkled her nose. "That thing swallowed me."

"And you'd rather be half-naked instead?" he asked, scowling at the length of her skirt. "When you're not wearing panties?"

"I'm covered," she argued, glancing down to be certain.

"Barely."

"I thought you shifters considered clothing optional," she teased.

"As long as it's not my mate, I do."

Laughing, Shay reached in and grabbed his shirt, tying it around her waist. The material fell to her knees, covering all but a small portion of her thighs in the front. "Better?"

His gaze fell to her breasts, and her nipples responded by tightening. With a sigh, he muttered, "It will have to be. I just hope no one dies tonight. Pack's small enough as it is." Rory placed his hand on her lower back and escorted her forward.

As they shoved through the heavy foliage with Rory leading the way, Shay caught a branch before it could slap her in the face. "You guys ever think of trimming the underbrush or cutting back the overgrowth?"

He glanced over his shoulder. "We get a lot of tourists in the area. The last thing we want is some noisy human, thinking they've found a new hunting or hiking trail, discovering our existence."

"Other than the noisy human comment, which I'll let slide, that makes perfect sense, but still, do you have to keep it this bad?" She slapped at a bug that landed on her arm.

"It gets better up ahead."

He was right. A few yards ahead they stepped out into a large clearing with a knoll in the center. The area was filled with people standing around in groups talking. The minute she and Rory came into view, Shay found herself the center of attention. Their animosity hit her like a body blow.

"*Show no fear. Don't let them sense any discomfort or uneasiness you might be feeling. Shove it down, way down inside and lock it away.*"

As Shannon 's words drifted to mind, Shay straightened her shoulders and slid on the attitude that came as naturally to her as breathing. She didn't walk. She strutted into the midst of them like she owned the place and the people and didn't care who didn't like it. These people didn't know her, and she wasn't here for them. They could take their hostility, their suspicion, and stuff it where the sun didn't shine.

A path opened before them. The loud talk dropped to barely a murmur. King of all he surveyed, Rory led her through his people. She'd seen the concerned brother, the nagging pest, the lover and caretaker, and his wolf and half-shifted forms, but Shay had never seen him in true alpha mode.

Once they reached the centermost, highest point of the rise, Rory turned to face them, holding Shay with her back to his chest. He looped one arm across her chest, and the hand of his other rested on the slight swell of her belly; his hold was both protective and possessive.

Shay relaxed, allowing Rory to support her weight as she glanced over the motley group. Upon closer examination, Shay discovered they weren't as intimidating as they'd originally appeared. Well, as long as she didn't think about the fact that the majority of those present could rip her throat out before she could blink.

The members present comprised all ages and races, though there were very few young children. The ones she did see were male. Some of the women offered hesitant smiles. The younger, unmated—Shay assumed from the way they were acting—males were checking her out: face, tits, and thighs. Males were the same everywhere, no matter the species.

Standing to Rory's right were the men he'd previously identified as his second and third, Caleb and MacDougal. To his left were three older gentlemen, which by process of deduction and Shannon's detailed descriptions, Shay concluded must be the council. They reeked of arrogance and barely concealed hostility. Shay smiled, a big teeth-baring grin, laughing inwardly when the middle one stiffened in outrage.

Rory did some type of metaphysical mumbo jumbo that had her heart pounding faster and the hairs on her arms and nape standing at attention. One by one, silence fell as gazes lowered in recognition of his power.

"Tonight I introduce to you your alpha-fem. My mate, Shayla Morgan!"

Chapter Ten

The small spattering of tepid applause ended abruptly when one of the men to the left stepped forward and boldly—albeit stupidly, in Shay's opinion—proclaimed, "She's not your mate until the council officially recognizes her as such."

Shay remembered her conversation with Shannon. "*Beware the council, Shay. If they refuse to recognize your mating, then some of the more die-hard traditional members of the pack won't either. Your pup will be labeled a bastard and considered not fit to lead the pack when the time comes. More importantly, the men will consider you usable and the women will consider Rory fair game. Now Wesley, the youngest and most arrogant of the council, will be against the mating simply because he didn't sanction it first. He's been full of himself ever since he was given the position.*"

"Protocol demands that the council vet her, make sure she's suitable to be your mate *before* you claim her," the oldest-looking member of the council stated harshly.

"*Graham is the pack's historian. You'll know him instantly as he's the oldest. He'll be against the mating because he's a bigot. Hates humans, vampires, women…almost everyone.*"

So the old Native American-looking dude was Graham, Shay thought, as a few low murmurs rose from the group.

"I'm alpha," Rory reminded in a quiet, deadly tone.

Graham sniffed. "Be that as it may, how do we know this woman, this human"—he spat out the word *human* the way a racist would say *nigger*—"is capable of being the alpha-fem the pack needs?"

Shay felt the pinprick of claws biting into her skin. Behind her, Rory burned like a furnace. She felt a light sheen of sweat break out where their bodies touched. His chest vibrated with a barely contained growl. Pushing aside her own outrage, Shay prepared to enjoy the show.

"You dare to question my judgment?" Rory asked in that same quiet voice.

"That's what it sounds like to me," Shay responded.

When Graham's eyes narrowed on her in intense dislike, she smirked. No sense wasting time getting the old dude to approve of her, and really, Graham was just the kind of tight-ass Shay liked to mess with. Their reactions were so comical.

He flushed red and snarled, "As elders, we have a responsibility—"

"Don't preach responsibility to me. Remember who established your positions and gave you those responsibilities...and who can take them away," Rory said sharply.

"Uhm, guess you heard that," Shay murmured, pursing her lips.

Graham shot a venomous glance at Shay.

"Rory, Graham, let's all calm down. Rory, why don't you tell us why, after all this time, you selected this charming young...woman to be your mate," the remaining councilman said.

"Bertram is usually the voice of reason, but don't let his calm nature fool you. He won't like you and Rory mating any more than the others. He'll simply use a different, more subtle approach to voicing his displeasure."

"And while you're at it, tell us how you expect her to bear you the pups you need to succeed you as alpha," Wesley added.

"She can't. Human females are incompatible with shifters. Everyone knows this," Graham said.

Stupid asses, couldn't they smell she was already pregnant? And these clueless idiots were the people Rory counted on to help him lead the pack?

"Graham's right. Humans are for fucking, not mating," MacDougal stated.

"*Et tu, Brutus*?" Shay asked drily, unsurprised by the lack of support coming from Rory's third. And she didn't appreciate the lascivious look he gave her. Again Shannon was right on the money.

"MacDougal will be against the mating because with Rory mated, the chances of him ever becoming alpha grow slimmer and further away. He'll go ballistic when he discovers you're pregnant."

"Maybe it's time for some new blood. After all, his sister proved her unnaturalness, and Kian... Well, need I say more?" Graham stated sourly.

Oh shit, he did not go there. Rory's going to blow a gasket, Shay thought and braced for impact.

It was the pack that erupted. People arguing for and against the mating. Shay only caught bits and pieces. They seemed divided on the issue of whether or not as alpha, Rory should be allowed to pick his own mate without interference, as his father and grandfather had. Others seemed disturbed that he'd chosen a human to mate with and not one of their own. Yet another group seemed to feel that this latest decision of Rory's was proof that he needed to step aside and let someone more capable lead the pack.

The only person who seemed unaffected by the chaos was Caleb. He stood alert, intent, and bodyguard ready. Watching him, Shay doubted he missed a thing. He was aware of who was for and against Rory, and if anyone made the mistake of moving toward them, he was going to be there first.

They grew louder and louder. Some of the men broke into fights. Instantly Caleb was a shield in front of them. Shay stared around in amazement. Dang, Rory had said his pack was fucked-up, but this was beyond all comprehension. Good Lord, no wonder Shannon had decamped as soon as the opportunity became available.

"*Enough!*" Rory's voice roared out.

Some of the women and men quieted, but a good bit continued their "discussion" as though he hadn't spoken.

"I said, ENOUGH!" A wave of power shot out of him so strong Shay had to grab hold of him to keep her knees from buckling. Everyone else fell like dominoes, one after another, from the weakest to the strongest, until they were prostrate on the ground.

What the hell was he doing, and did she have that power too? It was a handy little trick.

"Shayla is my one, my true mate, given to me by the Creator. She already carries my cub in her womb." He pointed to the council. "You *will* recognize my mating, or

I'll rip out your puny little spines and shove them down your whiny little throats."

Well, that settled that, Shay thought.

"Impossible. True mates are a myth," Graham unwisely responded as he pushed up to his knees.

"Are you calling me a liar?" Rory gently nudged Shay to the side and started toward Graham. One look at his face and Caleb and everyone else cleared out of his way.

"You owe me, old man," Shay muttered as she dashed around in front of her furious mate.

"Shay, move!"

Shay held her hands out in a placating manner. "Now, Rory, I realize he's a major pain in the ass, but you can't kill him."

"Aye, I can," he said grimly as he stepped around her.

She darted back in front of him. Why didn't the old fool run? Didn't he realize how close to death he was?

"Don't defend me, *human*. If I die, I die with honor having spoken the truth."

"It's not the truth, you fool. What kind of historian are you? Over in Refuge, the Ravens' alpha found his true mate—a human—and his best friend, a bear-shifter, found his, another human female. Hell, even the Ravens' beta found hers, a human male. Are you really that stupid that you don't know any of this?" Shay huffed out, her efforts to physically restrain Rory having little impact.

There was a gasp from someone and some excited chatter among the group. Shay, being a little preoccupied, didn't look to see what stirred them up this time. Her feet slid on the ground as Rory moved forward determinedly.

"Rory, stop, and I'll do you right here and right now!" she cried out a bit desperately.

He halted. Molten gold eyes fixed on hers. "What?"

"Me, you, right here, right now. A BJ, my ass in the air, whatever you want. Just don't do anything we'll both regret later."

The man cocked his head, but it was his wolf staring at her.

"Anything," she tempted and brought her hands up to her breasts, lifting them as an offering. Damn people didn't even want her as their leader and here she was, trying to protect one of them.

His gaze dropped to her puckered nipples, then past her to Graham.

"Uh-uh. Eyes on me, big boy," Shay ordered and dropped a hand to cup his balls.

The pack seemed to be holding its collective breath, waiting to see what he would do.

Rory's attention snapped back to her. She slid her hand up his shaft and gave it a firm squeeze.

"On your knees."

Careful not to flash anyone, Shay did as directed. The sacrifices she made…

"Suck my cock."

Shay undid the snap on his jeans and then hesitated with the zipper between her fingers. "The old man lives?"

He snarled. Being no fool, Shay narrowed her eyes and told him, "Not until I have your agreement."

He visibly struggled—lust or angry retribution? Shay licked her lips, and the lust won, barely. Taking his abrupt nod as assent, Shay freed his cock and immediately deep throated him.

She heard someone say, “Damn.”

Another male groaned.

“Shit, she can be my mate.”

Like before, Shay felt her wolf preen at being the center of so much masculine attention. When her wolf tried lifting Shay’s butt in the air to present herself enticingly for mounting, Shay slapped her down. *“Down, girl. We have a man, the strongest one here. I’m not giving the rest of them a glimpse of the goods.”*

In retaliation the bitch blasted open the bond between her and Rory’s beast. His emotions swamped her, and Shay went from mildly aroused to burning hot as his anger-tinted desire washed over and through her. She moaned around his cock as her pussy caught fire. The scent of her need rose in the air like an aphrodisiac, and her traitorous wolf shimmied in delight. In a small portion of her mind, Shay was appalled. This wasn’t supposed to happen.

Lust boomeranged back and forth between them, amplifying with each round until it spilled out over the pack. Someone—Caleb?—howled. Then a chorus of howls broke out. It sounded as if the whole pack joined in.

Rory snatched Shay off him and flipped her over onto her knees in a dizzying rush, yanking her ass in the air even as her forearms hit the ground. She cried out as he plunged into her, pounding furiously. His clawed hands gripped her, pricking her skin through the denim while his heavy balls slapped continuously at her mound, spanking her clit. The erotic sounds of wet flesh smacking together filled the air. Guttural grunts sounded from Rory.

Shay heard herself pleading and egging him on. "More! More! Yes! Yes!"

She forgot about how exposed she was and who might be looking at her. All she knew was that this was her man, her mate, and he was claiming her in the most primal of manners in front of his pack. Announcing his possession and daring anyone to challenge it, challenge him.

An orgasm burst through her, the sudden violence of it taking her by surprise. Shay screamed even as her wolf howled in delight, her position as alpha bitch secured.

The lower half of her body was lifted higher in the air as Rory's size and mass increased in a full half-shift. Shay shuddered and braced, her pussy slickening even more to accommodate him. Call her crazy but she loved it when he went werewolf on her. He planted a hairy hand on the ground in front of her face as he bent over her. Anticipating his next move, Shay tilted her head to the side, baring her shoulder.

Pain struck as his canines sank deep. "Shit!"

Her wolf went crazy. Shay's vision faded to shades of gray and black. Her nails became claws, and her gums tingled. The rich, dark scent of moist soil, decomposing foliage, and surrounding flora filled her nostrils. For a moment Shay feared her beast would overpower her and shift to the forefront, but instead it rode right beneath her skin, sharing the experience.

Rory threw back his head and roared as he thrust one last time, deep inside, holding stiff as if frozen. Inside Shay, his cock gave little jerking pulses as he emptied.

Withdrawing, he kicked out of his jeans, shifted to wolf, and howled before running deep into the forest. The rest of the males shifted and ran with him.

Senses wide open, Shay felt Rory's joy in the night, in running with his brothers. She also felt and for the first time understood his bond, his connection with the Sparrowhawks. She'd been wrong earlier. Instead of a king with his subjects, Rory was a father with his children. He cared for them. Wanted the best for them and felt responsible for them the way a parent feels responsible for his offspring. It was beautiful and hit Shay on an emotional level she'd never experienced.

Her wolf retreated enough for Shay to realize she was still on her knees with her ass in the air. Hastily she straightened and tugged down her skirt. While she untied Rory's shirt from her waist and slipped it on, the women, in various stages of disarray, crowded around. A quick glance revealed someone had taken the children away. Hopefully before things turned X-rated.

"You took an alpha in full rut," a young, pretty blonde said, looking and sounding awed.

"Yeah…well…" Off balance and trying desperately not to show it, that's all she could say.

"Big whooping deal. She can fuck. That doesn't make her alpha-fem," another said.

"Yana, you're just jealous he didn't pick you," another stated boldly.

As Yana glared at the girl, Shay rose, not willing to be at a disadvantage.

So this is Yana, Shay mused. She looked like a Playboy bunny: big breasts, small waist, flared hips, pouty mouth, and sultry, tousled brown hair that gleamed even in the hazy twilight.

"Watch out for Yana. She's had a thing for Rory for as long as I can remember and will make trouble if she can. Yana's strong. Strong enough to be an alpha's mate, and she knows it. Worse, she makes sure everyone else knows as well. I'm sure she stepped up to be alpha-fem as soon as the pack realized I was gone."

"I take it Yana's one of the many women Rory's screwed?"

"Worse. They were an item before Rory became alpha. Magnus made no secret that he thought she'd make an acceptable mate for his son."

"So she's strong, power hungry, and had your father's approval," Shay concluded.

"That sums it up," Shannon responded.

"She ever try you?"

The laugh Shannon emitted had Shay's brows rising. "Once."

Grinning evilly, she asked, "Whipped her ass, didn't you?"

"I didn't have any more problems," Shannon acknowledged, and no matter how much Shay pleaded for the details, that's all she would say.

Shay tuned in to hear Yana declare, "*I'm* the strongest female."

"Were."

All eyes turned to Shay. Yana pushed her way forward until she stood directly in front of Shay. She was a good five to six inches taller, about five-nine or five-ten. "What did you say?" she asked in a dangerously low voice.

In the same quiet but firm tone she'd used before, Shay repeated, "Were. You *were* the strongest female, after Shannon."

Yana bristled visibly. "You think you can take me?" Her eyes began to subtly glow, and her body seemed to shimmer. Shay could feel Yana's wolf readying itself.

Looking inwardly at her own beast, Shay was secretly amused and, if she was honest, relieved to feel her wolf yawn and glance disdainfully away from Yana's perceived threat. Since brawn obviously wouldn't be needed, she could use her preferred method of dealing with issues—brain.

Shay watched the reactions of the other women as they subtly rearranged themselves, making room. She took note of those who angled closer to Yana in silent support. A few moved closer to Shay, standing slightly behind and to the left. The majority retreated a short distance away, clearly waiting for the outcome before choosing a side.

"It doesn't really matter what I can or can't do, now does it? It won't change your situation or give you what you want. If, by some miracle, you manage to defeat me, Rory still won't be your mate and he'll kick your ass for touching me," Shay announced calmly.

Her direct stare coupled with her ultraconfident manner caused Yana's wolf to visibly falter. The shimmering stopped, and her eyes seemed to short-circuit as the glow flickered a few times before fading away. Shay, by not responding as Yana so obviously expected, put the woman in a precarious position. Test her and risk humiliation being defeated by a human female? Or prove she was stronger than Shay and have the alpha unleash his fury because she'd touched his mate? Shay watched the battle play out on Yana's face. The whole time, Shay held her gaze, face impassive, body relaxed, as if she couldn't care less what Yana decided to do.

Yana glanced uneasily at her friends. As one, they lowered their gazes to the ground. A couple even took a few steps to put a bit of telling distance between them.

Hmm, no help there. Shay almost smiled.

The silence became awkward.

Another woman, an older one who'd sided with Shay, stepped forward. "Pay Yana no mind. If Rory had wanted her—wanted any of them—he would have chosen a mate. They're just jealous he went outside the pack to pick a woman, and rightly so. We need new blood," she declared. "My name is Laurie Bell, and I wanted to applaud you for what you did. Graham's a fool but he's my brother. I thank you for saving him."

Laurie Bell, with her softly lined face, reminded Shay of that saying about southern ladies—a velvet glove encasing an iron fist. Upon closer inspection, she could see the slightest resemblance between the two. Native American like her brother, Laurie Bell's hair hung in a thick, dark wave down her back, liberally streaked with gray. Her slim body was encased in a pair of straight-legged jeans and a western shirt.

"Laurie Bell is the pack's midwife. She delivered over half the pack and doctors the rest whenever there's a need. Her words have power. Get her on your side and she'll run interference with the council. Show her respect, but don't brownnose. She respects people who keep it real."

Shay waved her thanks away. "I did it for Rory. If he'd let his anger get the better of him, he'd suffer for it later."

"Exactly so. You know your mate well. I'm happy to see Rory made such a wise decision in his choice of mate. It bodes well for the pack. Now, let's settle over here while we wait for the men and you can tell me how you two met and why he hasn't brought you to see me to make sure your pregnancy is progressing properly."

At Laurie Bell's words, several gasps sounded and Shay could literally feel the stares directed toward her belly. Had they not heard Rory's announcement? Why the big surprise? Disregarding the now chattering women, Laurie Bell pushed through them and went to the knoll and sat, patting the ground beside her. With an inward shrug, Shay ignored the cum still leaking down her thighs and followed.

"It's not Rory's fault. My cousin's mate is an ob-gyn. I insisted on going to see him," Shay answered. Then launched into the tale of how she and Rory first met.

Laurie Bell laughed merrily as Shay described kicking Rory for invading her personal space, sat spellbound as she described the events of the blue moon, and her mouth literally dropped open when Shay admitted to escaping while Rory was asleep. Laurie Bell's reactions were so entertaining Shay couldn't help but tell her about Kiesha's wedding and some of her and Rory's more amusing interactions since they'd been back together.

When she finished, Laurie Bell sat wiping tears from her eyes. "Oh my dear, you are indeed a breath of fresh air and exactly what that troubled young man needed. I have no doubt the Creator brought you two together."

* * * *

Pregnant! That bitch was ruining everything!

Ashley eased away into the woods. Once far enough, she shifted and ran through the woods and upstream a distance before branching off onto a little-known deer track. There she slowed to a walk, listening to make sure no one else was around before coming into a small, heavily thicketed clearing before a shallow cave.

As she sat waiting, another wolf, this one a large male, brown in coloring, approached from the west. He strode confidently into the clearing and entered the cave. After another glance around, she shifted and followed. Wesley had already shifted to human and stood waiting, hands on his hips and wearing a scowl.

"You fucked MacDougal," he stated coldly.

"Yes, alpha," she said with eyes lowered. "He came to me. To refuse would have brought unnecessary suspicion on myself, but the whole time he was in me, I thought of you."

"Fair enough," he acknowledged. He crowded her smaller, slighter body against the cave's wall and stuck a hand between her legs, roughly inserting two fingers. "But this is mine. Remember that when others are pawing you."

"Yes, alpha," she gasped. Ashley spread her legs and arched her hips, riding his thick digits.

He watched his hand. "Look how nice and slick you are. Your pussy's always greedy for my cock, isn't it?"

"Yes," she hissed.

He tormented her a minute more before lifting her by the waist. She eagerly wrapped her legs around his torso. The first thrust nailed her to the wall. Pinning her in place with his body, he slammed into her. His heart beat a rapid tattoo as his hot breath scalded her ear. She squeezed her inner muscles, knowing it drove him crazy.

"Your pussy is the best I've ever had," he murmured. "Hot, tight, and wet. So responsive. I could fuck you all day and night."

She whimpered and dug her nails into his shoulders. Then she gave little gasping moans, slowly increasing in volume. Following her cues, he increased the pace and force of his thrusts.

"Yes! Yes!" she cried out passionately. "So good."

Ashley clenched around him, tightening her pussy like a vise, knowing he was reaching his limit and wanting to hurry him along. She moaned again for good measure.

He reached a hand between them and stroked her clit. "Come now!"

On a gasp that was real, Ashley fell apart, coming hard.

He bucked once, twice, then groaned low and long. His muscles slowly lost their tension, but before he collapsed, he lifted and carried Ashley to the sleeping bag they kept in the cave for this purpose. She was too sated to worry that he'd come inside of her.

Lying together, Ashley cuddled close and whispered, "She really is pregnant with Rory's child. He wasn't just saying that to appease the council."

He stiffened, his eyes opened wide, and she could see the shock in them. "She must really be his mate." There was more silence before he said, "Kill the woman and Rory will be easy. Of course, I'll have to play with her first. Did you see the way she swallowed him whole? And that ass…" He actually shuddered. "Yes, I definitely want a taste of her first."

Ashley watched Wesley through narrowed eyes. *Arrogant fool! How dare he insult me like this!* Nothing of her fury showed on her face or in her manner. She was very good at hiding her feelings and lying without a betraying scent. "Alpha"—she almost choked on the title—"touch his mate and he'll kill you," she reminded in a soft voice.

"He'll try," the braggart proclaimed.

Ashley's quick, agile mind went to work on this newest wrinkle. "If you really want the woman, I can help."

"How?" After a moment he asked more suspiciously, "Why?"

She rose gracefully to her knees and bent over, mouth level with his cock. "Whatever you need," she breathed, watching him stir, "I provide. Whatever you want"—she trailed the vein to the ridge of his penis with her tongue—"it's my pleasure to give to you."

While she went down on him, Ashley mentally reviewed her options. Wesley was proving to be a bit unreliable. Typical male. It was time for a backup plan. By the time she straddled his body and took him inside, she had her new strategy in place. As she rode him, Ashley explained how Wesley could snatch the human.

* * * *

Rory trotted into the clearing to find his mate sitting, surrounded on all sides by the women. He tested their bond for any hints of distress emanating from Shay and found she was mostly amused. While she was occupied, he went to where his pants lay, shifted, and dressed.

The other men came and did the same, and soon were leading their mates away.

Figuring he might as well face the music, he strolled over to Shay and Laurie Bell, who were having an animated conversation about graphic art, of all things.

"Laurie Bell." He nodded respectfully in greeting. Holding out a hand to Shay, he said, "It's time to go." She allowed him to help her up.

He reached to do the same for Laurie Bell, but she was already standing. "Rory, you have a lovely mate. I look forward to seeing more of the both of you." She kissed both of their cheeks and then headed in the direction of most of the others.

Only Rory, Shay, and a few stragglers remained, standing in the weak moonlight of a half-moon.

"So"—Shay began—"color me confused. Have we been officially recognized or not?"

Rolling his eyes, he tugged Shay behind him, waving absently at the chorus of good-byes that rang out. The whole way he wondered how he was going to apologize for doing exactly what he'd promised he wouldn't—claim Shay in front of the entire pack.

"Have we?" she persisted.

"The council doesn't matter. The pack does. They'll have to fall in line."

He pushed through the woods, moving slowly, aware Shay's night vision wasn't as good as his.

"But Shannon said—"

He stopped abruptly and turned to her. "When did you speak to Shannon?"

"Today, while you were gone."

Tensed, he asked, "Is she okay? Does she need anything?"

Shay gave him "the look." The one that said he was a few cards short of a full deck. "I called her. She said if the council doesn't recognize us, the pack won't either and our child will be considered a bastard."

He glanced around but, knowing his pack didn't have to be visible to be able to hear, leaned close to her ear and murmured, "Let's discuss this later when it's just the two of us."

Shay nodded and remained quiet the rest of the way to the truck. She hummed with the radio as they rode home and, as soon as they walked in the house, began stripping. She announced, "I need a shower. I reek."

"I'm sorry," he forced out. He detested apologizing but hated more that he'd broken his promise.

She paused with one foot on the stairs, shirt dangling from her fingers, and glanced over her shoulder. "For what?"

"Tonight."

"You're not responsible for the way the pack acted. You told me they were jacked up. I sort of expected their response." She continued up the stairs.

"Not that," he said, a hint of the annoyance he felt slipping out. Did he have to spell it out? Part of him said let it go. It didn't seem to be bothering her, so why push the issue? But Rory wanted trust between them. That being the case, just "letting it go" wouldn't work.

She stopped several steps above him and turned to face him fully. "Then what?" she asked impatiently.

"The sex," he ground out. "I said I wouldn't, then did anyway."

The skin between her brows furrowed. "But I pushed you into it."

The reminder brought him up short. Confused, he stated, "You did, didn't you. Why?"

"Can we discuss this in the shower? I've been sitting on the ground in the dirt, leaves, and God knows what else. I'm really grungy."

Knowing if he got anywhere near her wet, naked body, talking was the last thing he'd be interested in, Rory told her, "Go ahead. I have something I need to do down here first."

Shay ran her fingers through her hair, muttering when a clump of dried, brown leaves fell to the floor. "Fine. What the hell is a city girl like me doing in the woods at night? There'd better not be any bugs in my hair."

Chapter Eleven

Rory stood watching the sensuous sway of Shay's hips until she disappeared from sight. Then, realizing he was hungry, he went into the kitchen to prepare a late-night snack. Shifting always burned a lot of calories, which was why shifters tended to be lean and muscular, and he needed to refuel.

Ten minutes later, he had a plate full of meaty sandwiches on the table along with a bag of cookies and a cup of milk. Shay joined him wearing another of his shirts. Though he loved seeing her in his stuff, to needle her he said, "You've seemed to acquire a fondness for wearing my clothes."

"That's because you have a fondness for ripping mine off," she shot back.

He grunted rather than acknowledge the truth of her words.

"You didn't want a shower?" she asked while pouring herself a glass of milk.

He shook his head. "Too hungry. I'll clean up after I eat." Rory motioned her to a chair. "Hungry?"

"I'll take some cookies." She grabbed a handful of the chocolate-cream-filled sandwich cookies, twisted one open, and licked the cream filling, just like on the commercials. He couldn't help but smile.

"So did they recognize us or not?"

His smile faded. "Shay, as alpha, I have final say in all things. When I established the council, I gave them some of my minor duties to give them something to do and to free my time for more important matters. They've never had a say in my choice of mate.

"Recognizing you as my mate is to their benefit, not ours. The council needs me. They rule on my authority. I can and will disband them in a heartbeat if they cross me."

"So basically they're just figureheads?" she asked, grabbing another cookie.

He rose to pour Shay another glass of milk. "No. Shifters believe elders should be respected. These men are all that remain of the Sparrowhawks' male elders. By giving them a title and duties, I hope to show them respect and at the same time teach the younger ones how the elders are to be treated."

"What about the women?" She dipped a cookie in *his* milk and popped it in her mouth.

Amused at her actions, he answered, "From what I could see, you did a good job of winning them over."

"That's not what I'm talking about. Do none of the women have power? Oh, and thanks for leaving me alone with women who could tear out my throat in the blink of an eye," she groused, frowning at him.

He smirked. "None of them are that fast, and as long as all the men were with me, you were safe."

Shay stared, her mouth gaping the tiniest bit, before she snapped it shut and shook her head.

"What?"

She examined him. "You don't get it, do you?"

He arched an eyebrow. "Get what?"

"Women. Don't you realize in ninety percent of all species, females are the most deadly, the most treacherous?"

Rory frowned, mentally reviewing the women of the pack. "The strongest one of them is a beta, at the most. You're an alpha like me, or will be once you learn how to tap into your wolf. Besides, you're my mate. They wouldn't dare touch you."

Shay snorted, ending in an amused chuckle. "God, you are so clueless it's funny."

Offended because she was calling him stupid, he tried to puzzle out what she meant, but honestly in this he *was* clueless. Male shifters were much stronger than females. It was the men of the pack he needed to watch out for.

Shay twirled her tongue around the cookie, catching the cream on its tip before pulling it into her mouth with a look of carnal ecstasy on her face. The sight reminded him of the way she'd looked sucking his cock earlier. Immediately he lost his train of thought as the majority of his reasoning power pooled below his waist.

"Don't worry. I handled myself. How'd your run go with your friends?"

The question snapped him back, and he shrugged, baffled and slightly uncomfortable. "It was a run. We shifted, ran until we got tired, then came back to the women."

Shay made a small humming sound, eyed him for a moment like she was trying to see into him, then selected another cookie.

Rory decided he didn't even want to know what that was about. His stomach growled, reminding him he'd prepared food but had yet to eat. He took a sandwich and snagged a handful of cookies before his mate could consume them all and began eating.

He'd devoured two sandwiches, drank his first glass of milk and poured another, and was munching on cookies before Shay spoke again.

"I've been introduced to the pack. Now what?"

"Now we get back to normal."

Shay tilted her head to the side. "Do we have a normal?"

"We will. I'll show you the different business systems the pack uses so you can get started on a program that will integrate them all into one, or at least let them speak to each other, and I need to get back to work. Half days, at least. I can do paperwork here at the house so I can be available to answer any questions you might have. I've seen how involved you get when you're working on a project, so don't worry about the house. Ashley's paid to keep it clean. When you're ready, I'll let Caleb know it's okay for her to return."

Through the bond, he felt her instant and vehement recoil. "It's just the two of us. I don't need anyone cleaning behind me."

Rory tried not to frown. This mate business was tricky. He thought she'd be glad not to do housework. But if that's how she felt... "It's your house. Your choice, but..."

"But what?" she asked, eyes narrowed suspiciously.

With a sigh, he admitted, "Ashley's father was one of the men I killed during the challenge. In the beginning I paid her to clean as a way of earning extra money for her family. Now she uses the money to help with college expenses."

Shay bit her lower lip and stared hard at the table. Finally, after the silence had drawn out, she said, "Fine. She can clean, but I don't want anyone in our room, for any reason. In fact, I prefer she not come up the stairs at all."

"I'll let her know upstairs is off-limits."

"And she needs set working hours. No coming and going as she pleases. That goes for the rest of the pack as well."

"Shay—" He was already shaking his head.

"No, on this I'm adamant. My house, remember? The howl aside, if I want to screw you on the kitchen table, I don't want to worry about someone walking in on us—again," she said pointedly.

He conceded her argument was valid. As alpha, Rory felt he should be accessible to the pack when he was home, but as a mated man, he did have a right to privacy. "What if we have a few hours a day where the pack can simply drop by without notice, but the rest of the time they have to call first?"

"Why can't they call first all the time?"

He sighed and wearily rubbed his forehead. "Eventually we'll work our way to that, but for now let's ease them into it. By mating, I've already introduced a lot of changes to the pack."

"I'm sure the women would understand. The men should too," she argued. "You don't go dropping in on them willy-nilly, do you?"

"If I need to."

She stared at him until he admitted, "Okay, very rarely. Usually I call first."

Shay jabbed a finger at him. "See, that's what I'm talking about."

"You're right. I'll talk things over with Caleb and MacDougal—"

"We'll talk things over," she pointedly interjected.

"We'll," he corrected. "Between the four of us we should be able to come up with a plan."

Shay laid her hand on top of his. "Rory, I'm not trying to be a pain or come between you and the pack. I get how you feel about them. Felt it tonight through the bond. You're a good alpha. However I can't get Conor's warning out of my mind. I'd rather err on the side of caution than relax my guard and discover the hard way I trusted the wrong person."

The reminder was like a punch in the guts. Rory brought her fingers to his lips and kissed them. "You're right. We'll do whatever you think is best. No one is going to harm our child."

* * * *

Ashley fluffed her tousled hair and tweaked her nipples good and hard before knocking on the door. While waiting, she bit at her full lips to give them the pouty look men seemed to find sexy. It was late, a little after midnight, and though there were no lights on inside, she could hear the low murmur of the television—wrestling.

When MacDougal opened the door, she gave him her most enticing smile and asked in a low, throaty voice, "May I come in?"

In answer, he widened the opening.

She stepped in and glanced around curiously, having never been inside. Unlike Wesley and the other leaders, MacDougal never paid her to keep house for him, preferring his privacy.

"Did I wake you?" As a lineman for the electric company, she knew he worked early hours. She'd made it her business to learn everything she could about him.

"No. Just catching some tube before calling it a night."

Ashley turned to face him, playing with the drawstring holding the front of her low-cut blouse together over her breasts. "I can't stop thinking about tonight," she confessed.

Truth. Though she'd made several subtle plays for him in the past, tonight was the first time he'd shown any interest in her.

He crossed his arms and leaned against the door. "Yeah?" he asked, sounding only mildly interested.

Cautiously she licked her lips and added, "You made me feel things I've never felt before and…" She allowed her voice to trail off, and glanced away as though nervous.

"And…" he prompted, watching her closely.

Careful, she warned herself. MacDougal was strong, cunning, and wouldn't be easily led by his cock like Wesley. As though she were shy, she bounced her gaze all around the room before meeting his through lowered lashes. "Can we do it again?" she asked hesitantly.

"I like to be in control," he warned.

She licked her lips again, the act real this time as she remembered the way he'd held her down, her wrists bound by one large hand as he'd fucked her hard. "I know." She gave a small, delicate shudder as cream slicked between her lower lips.

His gaze homed in on the crotch of her Daisy Dukes, and she knew he could smell her arousal. “Are you willing to submit to me?”

“Yes,” she answered, allowing a small bit of her need to sound in her voice.

“Take off your clothes.”

She whipped off her shirt, dropped it to the floor, and pushed down her denim shorts. She wore no underwear.

“Kneel.”

She was panting as she sank gracefully to her knees. Wesley was a mature, experienced lover, but he was old. Michael was young and virile. She wanted him with a desperation she was only beginning to realize.

“Suck my cock.”

When he didn’t move, she crawled forward on her hands and knees, climbed her hands up his legs, and freed his penis from his jeans. He was already erect, a small bead of precum on its tip. Not as indifferent to her as he was pretending to be. More confident at this sign that she was getting to him, she took her time, licking and savoring him. It surprised Ashley to find she was more interested in his pleasure than showing off her considerable skills in this area.

“That’s it,” he praised when she deep throated him. “Take it all.” He grabbed her hair and wrapped his hands in its length, trapping her head and holding her still for his gratification. Then he began thrusting in long, slow strokes.

Ashley closed her eyes, breathed though her nostrils, and let him fuck her mouth. He got a little rough toward the end, but his roughness excited her. She wanted to touch her clit and stroke her pussy but thought he would object. When he came, she swallowed, then sucked his softening penis for more cum.

"Greedy bitch, aren't you? Get up."

As she rose, she managed to rub her breasts along the length of his body. Then she stood, eyes lowered, awaiting his command.

"Go to my room, lie on the bed, and wait for me."

Her cream coating her thighs, she did as he instructed, following his scent trail to where it was the strongest. The mattress, unsurprisingly, was king-size, sitting on a four-poster frame. Ashley climbed on, crawled to the middle, and lay on her back. Above the bed on the ceiling was mirrored tile.

When he entered the room, she had the fingers of her left hand buried in her cunt while her right hand tweaked her nipple, watching herself get off in the mirror. He let her play for a bit, then commanded, "Hands outstretched."

She indulged herself with one last, lingering stroke before obeying. He bound her hands and feet, then stood studying his handiwork. Ashley gave a little tug on the scarves, testing the restraints.

"They'll hold until I release you. Still want to do this?"

"Oh yes." She was so turned on her pussy was on fire. He had to fuck her soon.

He stroked a finger down her slit, and she arched into it with a gasp. "If I had more time, I'd drag this out. See how much you can take." Her sex clenched as she moaned. "But I work tomorrow so…"

He mounted the mattress between her legs, pumping his thickly veined cock. "Since you took the edge off, prepare for a long, hard ride." He propped a pillow under her ass to angle her body like he wanted.

After rubbing the tip through her cream-slicked slit a few times, he asked, "Ready?"

"Yes!"

Her first orgasm hit almost instantly. As promised, he took her on a good, long ride, full throttle. Ashley came twice more before Michael finally stiffened above her. His sweaty body collapsed on top of her, driving the air from her lungs. Her breath came in shallow pants until he recovered enough to move and release her bonds.

He returned to lie at her side, idly caressing the hair on her mound. She spread her legs wider and tilted her cradle, humming in appreciation of his touch.

"That was good. Good enough to repeat. What do you say? You wanna be my bitch?"

"Yes, alpha," she answered softly.

There was a pause as he stiffened. Then he thrust two fingers into her sheath and gave her clit a twirl with his thumb. "That's a good bitch," he murmured.

Gotcha! Ashley smiled inwardly in satisfaction. The seed was sown. Now all she needed to do was water it and watch it grow.

* * * *

"I had an epiphany tonight," Shay declared.

Rory chuckled as he climbed naked into bed beside her, smelling of soap and water. "And what was this revelation?"

"At the howl tonight I felt my wolf. She got off on being the center of attention, on knowing the males wanted her. And later, while we were having sex, she..."

Shay searched for a word. "Gloated, I guess you could say. 'Look at me. See who I am? I'm the alpha's bitch, top female.' At the time it shocked me. Later I got to thinking about it and wondering about your mother."

He slid down until his head was propped on his hand, and stroked her thigh in random patterns. "In what way?"

"Tonight while we were talking, Shannon said now that she is older, she realized your mother instigated a lot of the public interactions between your father and her."

"Shannon's mistaken."

"I don't know, Rory," she said, shaking her head slowly. "I realize I wasn't here and didn't witness it, but I know what I felt inside of me tonight. If her beast was in any way the same, if it felt it had something to prove..."

"And yours did?" he asked.

"You saw how they reacted to the idea of me as your mate. How against it they were." Shay paused to let a thought simmering in the background come to the forefront, then continued thinking aloud. "The 'look at me' wasn't directed at the men. It was for the other females of the pack—her competition."

"I never wanted any of them," Rory interjected.

"That doesn't matter. To my beast the other females were rivals. And you said yourself your dad only mated your mother because she was pregnant. If that's true..." Shay stared off into space, trying to imagine it.

"What do you mean if?"

His question, the tone of it, brought her attention back to Rory. "Well"—she frowned—"you really don't know, do you? I mean, did your father ever say, 'Son, the only reason I mated your mother is because of you'?"

"Don't be ridiculous."

"Did your mother?" This time his response was slower. "No."

"Then you don't really know for sure, do you? But you got that impression from someone, somewhere along the way. If that's what the pack also thought, it means she constantly had to prove she was worthy—of being the alpha's mate, being alpha-fem, basically everything." And wouldn't that be a bitch, she thought, having to constantly prove the unprovable.

Rory's brow wrinkled in thought.

Unreasonably irritated and scowling at the thought of it all, she turned on Rory. "Where'd you get an idea like that anyway?"

"My uncle, Wesley."

At the simple response, Shay froze, her mind blank of all but one thought. "You have an uncle? I thought there was only you and Shannon."

Rory pushed to a seated position, his turn to stare in disbelief. "I have family—a sister, a brother, uncle, cousins—"

"Hold up!" Shay held out a hand like a police officer commanding traffic to stop. "*Brother*?"

He shifted, and an expression crossed his face that she couldn't decipher. "They mentioned him tonight," he said finally.

She searched her memory and came up empty. "When?"

"When Graham questioned the wisdom of keeping me as alpha—as if they had a choice," he scoffed. "He mentioned Kian and Shannon, remember?"

"No," she admitted, "but then I was so busy waiting for your explosion over what he said about Shannon, I didn't pay attention to anything else."

He arched an eyebrow in response. Shay waited and, when Rory didn't say anything, asked, "So where is Kian, and why haven't you—or Shannon, for that matter—mentioned him before now? Does he know about me and the baby? How old is he? When can I meet him?"

Again with the strange expression. Why doesn't he want to talk about this? Can't he see I'm curious? He met my family. At that last thought, Shay glared at him, sending her determination to get answers through their bond.

When he winced, she knew he got the message. With a sigh, he glanced away. "Actually, he's here."

Her eyes narrowed. "Here…where?"

Still he didn't meet her gaze. "In the house. He lives here."

"I've been all over this house and never…" Her eyes met his, and she trailed off. In a sudden flurry of movement, she shot to her knees. "The basement? Your brother lives in the *basement*?"

Rory watched her warily. "It's not what you think."

"You don't know what I think!" *Oh my God! Kian's been here in the house this whole time, and Rory didn't tell me. What else don't I know?* She took a calming breath and ran her hands through her hair. In a lower, less sharp tone of voice, she said, "All right. I'll bite. Why does your brother live in the basement? The one I was warned by Shannon to stay out of?"

"Shannon said that?"

When she only glared at him, he said, "Shay, you're judging a situation you know nothing about."

"I don't remember making any judgments, just asking questions. So enlighten me already," she commanded.

He shoved his hair out of his face. "Kian's...different."

Should she ask the obvious? No. She stared, her impatience pulsing between them.

"Kian doesn't like being around people, not even the pack, so I don't force him."

"I'm not people. I'm family, or at least I thought I was," she muttered.

"Shay, don't make this about you. It's not."

Insecurity raised its ugly head. Rory never wanted a mate, pups. Like his father, was he making the best of a bad situation by doing the honorable thing? "You're ashamed of me."

He reared back. "What? No! Where the hell did you get an idea like that?"

"What else am I supposed to think?" she shot back. "He lives right here in the house, and you haven't introduced us."

"Did you hear nothing I told you? Don't make this about you, Shay, 'cause it's not. Ashamed of you? Hell, I claimed you in front of my men, my whole pack!" He got off the bed and paced, frustration in every stride.

He was so irate, so outraged that Shay immediately felt foolish. "You're right. I'm sorry," she added before he could build up a full head of steam.

At her words he halted with his back to her.

My God, she wondered, was this how Rory's mother had felt? This constant sense of insecurity that rose at the oddest moments? How many times had his parents had this very same fight? How many times had Rory's father had to reassure his mate that she was the one he wanted? Worse, how long before he tired of it—her constant need for assurance, her lack of trust—before he tired of her?

The thought had her feet moving. Laying her hand on his shoulder, Shay made herself vulnerable in a way she never would have believed she could a month ago. "I'm trying to believe you love me, that this true mates stuff is the real deal. It's not easy. Just like you thought you'd never mate, I never believed I'd find a man who could accept me—all of me. No one has before, so if I forget sometimes, just be patient with me. It will eventually sink in."

Rory turned and pulled her into his arms. "Believe it. Believe me."

She sighed and snuggled close. "When you think about it, we've spent what? Two weeks together? You have to admit this has all happened really fast. Eight weeks ago I didn't even know you existed, and now we're mated, with a child on the way."

He rested his chin on her head. "You're right. I guess it's easier for me because I always knew there was a possibility—however slim—that I'd meet my one. Remember, I told you how I fought my reaction to you and would have continued fighting if the blue moon hadn't happened." When she stirred, he held her still. "Not because of you, but because of me. You deserve better."

Rory's chest expanded as he took a deep breath and let it out in her hair. "Then you left, and that changed everything."

"Not everything. You tried to send me away," she reminded him, some part of her still unable to let it go.

He leaned away and cupped her chin, lifting her face so she'd meet his gaze. "You have your fears. I have mine. We'll face them together."

Shay was smiling as Rory led her to the bed and pulled her onto his lap. "I need you to understand about Kian. I'm very protective of him. As I said, he's different."

The man had a way of messing up her head. She scrambled off his lap and went for the door.

"Where are you going?" Pure exasperation.

"I want to meet him."

"Shay, for the love of God, it's one in the morning," he called out.

She heard him, but she was already out the door, jogging down the stairs. He came charging after her. "Shay, leave him alone."

Shay spun to face him. "We're family now. Kian's this baby's uncle. He lives in this house—my house, you said earlier. You think I'm going to have someone living here I haven't met?"

Their wills clashed.

Rory took a deep breath, then tried reason. "I'm not trying to stop you from meeting Kian. I'm saying do it at a more reasonable hour. Would you appreciate being wakened to meet Kian if the situation was reversed?"

Decisions, decisions, decisions…

Sanity trumped curiosity. "Fine," she said grumpily as she turned and started back up the staircase. "But I'm wide-awake now. You're going to have to put me to sleep."

He smiled wickedly as she came even with him. "I'll think of something."

* * * *

Rory awakened with Shay sprawled across his body, sleeping with the abandon of an exhausted child. He shifted her to the side, giving a mild grunt of pleasure when she briefly clung to him before allowing him to be removed from her grasp. On some level not apparent when awake and alert, his wary mate accepted him. Usually their positions were reversed, and he woke clinging to her as though afraid she'd slip away from him during the night—again.

He studied her face, not liking the dark circles visible under her eyes. His mate wasn't resting enough. Nor was she eating enough, he decided after examining the rest of her. She'd lost weight. Pregnancy was hard on a woman, and Shay had the added pressure of carrying a shifter child. Her metabolism must be off the charts. Shay's former eating patterns weren't enough to provide proper nutrition for both her and the babe. The woman had been a vegetarian!

Alex's second said Shay was doing as well as could be expected under the circumstances. He'd still like to have Laurie Bell look at Shay, for his peace of mind. Not that he doubted Carol's capability, but he preferred one of his own—a trusted member of his pack, he added mentally as he remembered Conor's warning to Shay.

He rolled out of bed and paused at its side as Shay sent a hand seeking his warmth, waiting until with a sigh, she pulled his pillow close and buried her face in it. Definitely bonding, he thought. If he wanted his mate to eat properly, he better go downstairs and get breakfast started.

After a short trip to the bathroom, Rory silently grabbed a pair of jeans and a T-shirt from a drawer and eased out of the room. Moments later he was downstairs headed for the kitchen when a knock came at the front door.

He sniffed. Laurie Bell stood on the doorstep. Rory switched directions and went to allow her entrance. "Is there a problem?"

"Morning, alpha. Sorry to disturb you so early, but I thought your mate could use this." In her hand she held a clear baggie of loose herbs. "For her pregnancy. She mentioned being tired. This should take care of the problem."

"Thank you. I'll give it to her. You coming in?"

"No, I'm on my way to work." Laurie Bell ran *All Naturale*, a shop catering to, as she called it, folks wanting to get back to nature. "Tell her to seep it in a tea for three to five minutes and sweeten with honey. She's to drink it two to three times a day, or whenever she needs a pick-me-up."

"I'll let her know. Did she mention having you examine her?" he asked curiously. The two seemed to have hit it off last night. Maybe Shay wouldn't be so reluctant if he broached the subject again.

Laurie Bell's mouth crooked ruefully in a smile. "She mentioned her fondness for professionals with alphabets after their name. Don't worry," she added when he frowned. "A lot of folks prefer someone with a degree and formal training over someone to whom the knowledge is passed down from generation to generation. My feelings aren't hurt." She turned to leave, then paused. "Did you realize the door was locked? I was going to leave it in the kitchen with a quick note but couldn't get in."

Rory felt a flush of embarrassment rise from his neck to his face. “Aye,” he said simply, hesitating to elaborate until he’d discussed it with his men.

Laurie Bell laughed and gave him a wicked smile. “Good for you both. I remember what it’s like being newly mated. The last thing you want is someone walking in on you at an inappropriate moment.”

Air went down the wrong pipe, and Rory immediately began to choke.

Both Laurie Bell’s brows rose in contemplation. “I see. Well…” Obviously fighting back a smile, she said, “I really need to go or I’ll be late. Tell Shay I said hello.”

With a quick wave, she was gone.

Rory glanced at the herbs in his hand, wondering how he’d convince Shay to drink them. Shay didn’t strike him as the back-to-nature type, although she had been a vegetarian, so maybe she’d be open to drinking the herb tonic.

He went into the kitchen and prepared a breakfast of bacon, sausage, eggs, and toast. Shay appeared in the doorway while he was scooping up the eggs. “Do I smell bacon?”

“Hungry?” he asked, glancing over his shoulder.

From the looks of her, Shay hadn’t done more than run fingers through her hair. Her eyes were still heavy with sleep, and there was a pillow crease on her left cheek. She was in another one of his dress shirts, barely buttoned and slipping off her right shoulder. She looked sexy as hell.

“Starved,” she acknowledged, crossing over to the table.

When she sat, he handed her a teacup. Shay blinked at it owlishly. “What’s this?”

"Herbal tea," he stated matter-of-factly as he went back to the stove. Rory watched out of the corner of his eye as Shay sniffed the contents.

"What's in it?" she asked suspiciously.

"Something to give you energy." He took down two plates and filled them with food.

"Uh-huh, but what's in it?" Shay dipped her finger inside the cup and brought a drop of liquid to her tongue.

He wanted to laugh at the expression on her face. It couldn't taste that bad. "Drink it, Shay."

"I'd rather have coffee." She pushed the cup away.

"And I'd rather my mate not have dark circles under her eyes and be so tired she can barely see," he countered. "Now be a good mate and drink all your tea; then you can eat." He held the plate up as an enticement.

Shay snagged the cup by its holder and dragged it to her. As she contemplated the tea, she said, "If I don't drink this, you wouldn't really make me go without eating. It's like, against the mate code of honor or something."

Because what she said was nothing less than the truth, Rory tried bargaining with her. "I took you to see Alex when we have a perfectly good midwife here in the pack. Now I'm asking you to return the favor and drink the brew Laurie Bell recommended for you."

Shay frowned. "Laurie Bell gave you this?"

"Yes. She dropped it by this morning on her way to work."

Her gaze met his, bounced to the food, the cup, and back to his again. Then she sighed. "Fine. I'll drink the stupid tea."

Waiting until she'd drained the cup, Rory set a full plate in front of her and joined her at the table. As half the food disappeared, Shay's eyes gradually became more alert. Either the food or the tea, or a combination of the two, had done the trick.

Suddenly her head snapped up. "Kian," she said and began to rise from her seat.

He gestured with his fork. "Sit. Eat."

"But—"

"Unless you plan to meet him like that," he added, flicking his gaze up and down her body, drawing attention to her attire.

Shay glanced down at herself, flushed a brilliant shade of red, then sat.

Rory wisely held in his smirk.

After another few mouthfuls of food, Shay said, "You never did say what's so special about your brother."

"He's mute," Rory said flatly, watching Shay closely for her response.

There was an expectant silence; then Shay said, "That's it?"

"Isn't that enough?"

She scrunched up her face. "I thought you were going to say your brother had some severe physical or mental problem that made him unable to function. But mute…?" She shrugged. "So he can't talk. What's the big deal?"

Rory gaped. He simply couldn't help himself. "It doesn't bother you?"

"No. Does it bother *you*?" Shay asked pointedly.

"No, but then he's my brother. Others in the pack aren't as welcoming."

Shay snorted. "Big surprise there."

Rory studied her. "It really doesn't bother you?"

"No, Rory, it *really* doesn't. It wouldn't bother me no matter what disability he had. I don't discriminate. In fact, whenever I'm home long enough, I volunteer my time at the local children's hospital, working with special needs kids."

Rory sat back, admittedly astonished by this bit of insight into the woman he loved. "Maybe it's because you're human," he mused.

"What does my being human have to do with anything?" Shay asked, making Rory realize he'd spoken that last thought aloud.

Rory tried to put into words something he'd never had to explain. "As a species, shifters are strong, faster, *better* than everyone else."

The ferocious frown on Shay's face showed she took exception to his words. He hurried on before she could interrupt. "What I mean is because of our healing abilities, we don't suffer the normal defects and diseases humans are used to dealing with. So when one of us is born…" he hesitated, then continued, "*different*, we don't know how to react."

"By different you mean flawed."

He winced. "Yeah."

"That's asinine," she said, angry sparks in her eyes.

He shrugged. "Are humans really so different, Shay? How many humans avert their gaze when they see a less than perfect specimen of the species? Some even go out of their way to avoid the disabled as though the disability were somehow contagious."

"You're right," she admitted, then sighed. "Well, at least Kian and I have something in common."

He arched a brow. "And what might that be?"

"Neither one of us is crazy about your pack," she said before heading upstairs to dress.

Chapter Twelve

An hour later Rory and Shay stood at the entrance to the basement level. The door had four deadbolt locks and appeared to be made of steel. Shay knocked on it to be sure. Definitely metal.

Amazed, she asked, “Are you trying to lock him in or keep others out?”

“Keeping others out. Kian’s free to come and go as he pleases.”

“How? I’ve been here a week and never seen this door opened,” she muttered at his back.

“There’s an exit at the rear of the house. Stay close,” Rory called over his shoulder as he turned the key in the last lock, pulled open the door, and started down the dark stairwell.

Shay was right on his heels, curiosity driving her.

At the bottom of the steps was another door with even more locks, reminding Shayla of Shannon’s basement room. “What is it with you people and basements locked up tighter than Fort Knox?”

He tossed a glance over his shoulder. “After what happened during the blue moon, you need to ask?”

Okay, so it was a stupid question.

"Each pack maintains a minimum of one secure room for shifters out of control. It's to protect them and to protect the pack. The Sparrowhawk pack has two," Rory explained.

"And this is one of them," Shayla concluded.

"No, this is Kian's room. When we get inside, stay by the door until I tell you it's okay to come forward," Rory said as he opened the door and walked inside.

As Shay entered behind him, something in the shadows moved. The biggest black wolf she'd ever seen in her life emerged out of the shadows and into a beam of sunlight. Her breath caught, and she edged closer to Rory, forgetting his earlier instructions. He reached back a hand and nudged her gently until she stood partially behind him.

"Kian, I want you to meet my mate, Shayla. Shay, this is my brother, Kian."

Kian came forward, and Shayla stared into eyes so pale a blue they were almost translucent. There was feral intelligence in his gaze. On all fours, his head nearly reached her shoulder, and even his shiny, thick pelt couldn't disguise that his body was a lithe mass of muscle. Her fingers clinched on Rory's waist, nails digging into his side.

"Hold out your hand," Rory instructed.

Shay glanced at him sharply. *Hold out her hand?* What, like she was meeting the family pet? Troubled, she reluctantly did as instructed.

Kian's nostrils flared as he took in her scent, and he came even closer, his massive head lowering until his snout was even with her belly. Then he swung his gaze to Rory's.

"That's right," Rory stated as though he were answering a question. "Shay's pregnant with my cub."

The wolf, Kian, looked at her again; then his gaze met Rory's and something seemed to pass between them. In the sunlight Shay could see Kian's belly and fur vibrate, but no sound emerged. It took all Shay had not to run when he came nearer and rubbed his body against hers, marking her with his scent. Dang, he was huge. Bigger even than Rory in wolf form.

Did this mean she was accepted? If so, why hadn't he shifted and greeted her properly?

Kian nudged her hand with his snout. After a brief glance at Rory to check his reaction, she reached out a hesitant hand and rubbed him behind his ears like she would any dog. He tolerated her touch for a few, brief moments, then disappeared around the corner into the shadows. Very anticlimactic. Not what she'd expected at all.

Now that Kian was gone, she took a longer, more thorough look at her surroundings. What she saw—or rather didn't see—pissed her off. She'd believed, since Kian resided here, that the setup would be like a small apartment efficiency. It wasn't. There was no couch, no television or stereo, no dressers or bed. Just a measly, bare mattress thrown on the floor in the corner. And unless they were hidden around that corner, there were no kitchen appliances. She couldn't even hear the hum of a refrigerator.

"Your brother lives like an animal," she snarled at Rory before spinning on her heel and charging up the stairs.

"Shay..."

"I can't believe you make him live like that. I thought—no, hoped—you were better than this." In the living room she spun to face him, hands on her hips. "If, God forbid, our child comes out *flawed*"—she spat the word—"is this how you'll treat her?"

"Shay, you can't believe I'd want my own brother living like that."

She formed a V with her fingers and pointed them at her eyes. "Tell it to the eyes. I know what I saw." Shay was beyond angry, beyond horrified. She was sick. She turned her back, unable to stand the sight of him.

Between one breath and the next, he was on her. Shay let out a squeal of fear as Rory snatched her off her feet and into his arms. As he stormed up the stairs, Shay pushed at his chest and wheezed out, "Put me down."

"When I'm ready." He stalked down the hallway and stopped before a closed door. A quick twist of the knob, then he pushed the door open so hard it rebounded off the wall. Rory set her down, none too gently, and went to the closet, flinging open the double doors. Inside were rows of men's clothing—shirts, pants, suits, belts, and hats. He crossed to the dresser and began opening drawers, leaving them open. More clothes.

Confused, Shay glanced around the room. Done in shades of blue, it was a man's room. No doubt about it. The walls and dressers were stark, lacking any personal decorations such as pictures, awards, and the like. The furniture and its surfaces were pristine, but that didn't negate the empty, unused feel of the place.

"Kian's room. The one he refuses—has *always* refused—to use."

Rory stood, hands on hips, breathing hard. "The locks you objected to? They're not to lock Kian in. They're to lock us out."

Shay tore her gaze away from him to take another look at the room. "I'm sorry," she said finally, hoping he'd see the regret in her eyes. "I know what it's like to be different, to be shunned because of those differences. I projected. I should have known—"

"Aye, you should have," he snapped. Then he closed his eyes and took a deep breath. When he opened them, he was much calmer. "I'm wrong as well. It bothers me, because at one time he *was* treated as no better than an animal—by my father. And the pack followed his lead.

"I did my best to change his status. To change the status of all of those who were thought of as lesser, as lacking, within the pack. Kian refused. He prefers his wolf, and I can't—won't—force him to change, to be what he doesn't want to be."

"What happened to Kian?" she asked. "Why is he mute? Some type of childhood trauma?" When he simply stared at her, Shay said, "I know you said he was born this way, but did anyone ever say *why?* Being born mute is a rarity, even among humans. If he was deaf, I could understand it better. But he's not." Though she voiced the last as a statement, her eyes questioned him.

"No, he's not deaf," Rory confirmed.

"So what happened? What did the doctors say?"

Rory sighed and went and sat on the bed, motioning for Shay to join him. "Shifters come in four basic classifications, with varying levels within. Rogues, at the bottom, have no control over their beast. They are ruled by instinct, barely one step above our animal counterpart. Omegas have more control, but their beast still tends to dominate their human nature. Betas have complete control over their beast and know how to work with it. Alphas can not only control their beasts but are able to tap into and use the power of their beast when necessary, without giving control over to it. And then there's me. As pack alpha not only can I draw on the power of my beast—the two of us working together in harmony—but when necessary, I can pull power from the pack as well."

"Sort of an alpha's alpha," Shay commented.

"Aye, though we don't really have a name for it. Remember what I was saying about shifter females earlier?"

"About that 'survival instinct'?" she asked, making air quotes. "It's not limited to shifters. Human females tend to be drawn to alpha males as well."

"In shifters it works both ways. The higher ranked the male, the stronger the female he'll want, just like in the wild. Strong pairings produce strong offspring. It's when you start mixing ranks that things get a little iffy."

"Like your parents," Shay stated, wondering what he was getting at.

"Yes. When an alpha and an omega mate, there's no predicting the classification their offspring will fall into. That's why to ensure succession, pack alphas will only mate with the strongest female of the pack—normally."

He ran a hand through his vibrant red hair, a sure sign of his agitation. "Da lucked out with me. I turned out to be an alpha like him, although he really had no way of knowing for sure until I went through my first change at puberty."

"Your personality didn't give him a clue?"

"It gave an indication of the type of man I'd be, but there's no way to tell about the wolf until it emerges."

"So your wolf's an alpha, and Shannon's wolf is an alpha. What about Kian?"

"Kian's wolf is as strong as, possibly even stronger than mine, since he spends so much time in wolf form. But something went wrong with his human side."

Shay pondered this for a moment, letting the silence settle. "So let me see if I understand correctly. Kian's mute because your dad's an alpha but your mom's an omega, and her wolf being weak somehow caused Kian to come out with a human disability."

"Yes."

"Bullshit."

He blinked, his mouth sagging open the tiniest bit.

"Complete and utter bullshit. Genetics don't work that way."

"Maybe in humans but in wolves—"

"First of all," she cut in, "you're not wolves. You're shifters. That means you're human with a little something extra, and I beg to differ with you, but genetics work exactly the same way whether we're talking humans or animals. I don't know what caused Kian to be mute, but it damn sure skippy isn't because your momma was an omega."

Rory shook his head and opened his mouth, but Shay cut him off. "Don't you dare tell me I don't know what the hell I'm talking about. I *know*. I've run the tests. My mother's an expert, remember? You think I wouldn't have checked this shit out as soon as Kiesha told me what she was mated to, whose child she was carrying?

"If this is the kind of bullshit your parents were spouting, I'm guessing no one ever bothered to take Kian to a doctor, have him checked out. See if his problem could be *fixed*." She gazed off, staring blindly at the mirror on the dresser. "Of course you didn't. You probably don't even go to doctors. If you can't shift and heal it or Laurie Bell can't treat it, you're stuck with it."

She turned her attention back to Rory to find him sitting there, dumbfounded. "When Alex returns from his honeymoon, you take Kian to see him. Get his throat checked out. I understand not wanting to expose your secret, but there are treatments, surgeries, things that can be done to give Kian his speech."

"What if they don't work?"

Shay shrugged. "At least you'll have tried."

When he still appeared troubled, she added, "I'd have to research the affliction, but from my understanding, muteness comes in two different forms. Either there was trauma to Kian's vocal cords during birth that caused them to become damaged, or the portion of his brain that develops speech didn't receive enough oxygen while in the womb. Did something happen when he was born? Did your mom suffer some type of mishap?"

"I don't know," Rory said with a shrug. "I don't believe so."

"You weren't there when he was born?"

A strange glint entered his eyes. "Kian's older than I. Ten minutes older."

"Ten—" She stared. "Twins? You're twins?"

"Aye."

Shay brought a trembling hand to her forehead and leaned against it. The shocks were coming too fast, too hard for her mind to process. "I need a nap. My brain's fuzzy."

"We'll both take one."

As he rose and extended a hand, she gazed up at him suspiciously. “Why are you taking a nap? You don’t look sleepy to me.”

He smiled, slow and sexy. Shay felt moisture pool between her legs. “Never said I was. We’ll sleep…after.” He tugged her to her feet and into his arms, his erection a hard pole against her belly.

“Yes, after,” she agreed.

* * * *

That night after work, Caleb and MacDougal came to the house in response to Rory’s call.

Shay sat on Rory’s lap behind a mammoth desk in an utterly masculine office domain Rory stated used to belong to his father. The chair was roomy and wide, completely made of leather, and positively screamed *I’m in charge*. The dark cherry wood of the desk gleamed in the lamplight.

Opposite it sat Caleb and MacDougal, in two not nearly as imposing office chairs facing the desk. Caleb’s pose was relaxed, with both hands resting on the arms of the chair. His dark, long, well-maintained dreads were pulled back from his face in a low ponytail. MacDougal had one foot resting on the opposing knee and settled into his chair with what Shay considered an insolent smirk. She didn’t like the way he kept checking her body out, ogling as though he were visualizing her naked.

Shay observed him through narrowed eyes, making no attempt to mask her dislike.

MacDougal wagged his eyebrows at her. “Like what you see?”

“No.”

He grinned at her abrupt answer, obviously not taking her seriously.

Rory didn't keep them waiting. "For security reasons my mate has requested that access to the house be denied."

"Being led by your bitch?" MacDougal asked with a sneer.

Rory's body stilled and seemed to swell. Shay felt the heat of him increase against the skin of her back and thighs where she connected with him. "You will refer to my mate with respect, or I'll rip your tongue out of your mouth and force-feed it to you," Rory said, his wolf in his voice.

MacDougal lost his stupid grin. Though he didn't respond verbally, Shay could see a hint of contained anger in the lines around his eyes.

"Of course." Caleb spoke into the silence. "The security of the alpha pair, especially when they are breeding, is of utmost importance. How can we assist?"

The claws digging into Shay's thigh retracted as Rory relaxed. "Spread the word that from now on, anyone wishing to meet with me"—Shay cleared her throat, a pointed reminder of her presence—"with us will need to call first. The doors will be kept locked, even when I'm in residence, so they'll need to knock and be granted entrance—"

"And the locks will be changed," Shay added, looking up at Rory as she added her decree.

He frowned down at her. "I don't think that's necessary."

She arched an eyebrow. "Who all has a key to the house?"

Rory paused, then glanced at Caleb in question. Caleb didn't seem to know either. He shrugged. "When Rory became alpha, he instituted the open-door policy. No one has needed keys because the door is always unlocked."

"How old are these locks?" she asked.

Rory's brow furrowed as he thought. "They've been here since I was a child, at minimum. I don't remember them ever being changed. They were sturdy enough when I did the last remodel to leave as is."

"Then you really have no idea who could be walking around with spares. You're going back to work soon. I don't want just anyone walking in, catching me unawares," she told Rory.

"Scared of the wolves, little human?" MacDougal asked.

Shay shifted until her gaze met his, then stared until MacDougal lowered his gaze, silently acknowledging her dominance. She stared for another moment, letting him feel the weight of it, before turning back to her mate. Rory didn't comment on the byplay between her and MacDougal, but she could feel his pride in her, and his anger at MacDougal.

"She's right," Caleb said.

Shay tossed him a smile of thanks.

Rory sighed. "I'll change the locks. As second and third, you two will have a spare for emergencies—"

"No!" Shayla declared forcefully.

All eyes turned on her. "Caleb, yes. He's your second, and I know he'd sacrifice his life for yours. MacDougal, no. I don't like him, and if a knife ever sprouted from your back, I wouldn't be surprised to find him holding the handle."

MacDougal made sounds of protest. "I would never do anything so underhanded, so vile."

Shay glared at him, her dislike tangible. "You're rude, disrespectful, egotistical, and most of all, a sore loser. So you fought for and lost the position of alpha. Get over it or get out. The pack doesn't need your poison."

MacDougal's eyes widened, and his mouth dropped open. There was a choked sound from Caleb. When she glanced at him, his face was blank but his eyes danced merrily. Rory stroked an approving hand down her spine.

"Who else besides the three of us, and Shannon, needs a key?" Shay asked, turning once more to Rory.

"If you object to MacDougal, then that also leaves out the council," Rory mused.

"Those old farts? Over my dead body," Shay said.

Another choked sound from Caleb. This time when she glanced over, a smile showed. He said, "You don't have a problem speaking your mind, do you?"

"No, I don't."

"Good. When dealing with this pack, boldness is an asset," Caleb said.

"Laurie Bell," Rory said, still throwing out names.

Shay thought for a minute. "No."

"She's the pack's healer," Rory reminded her.

"I know, but unless she's psychic, she'll be coming in response to being called, including emergencies. And if she's summoned, she'll be expected. There's no need for her to have a key. Same goes for Ashley," Shay added.

At the sound of her name, MacDougal stirred. Shay noted it but was distracted by Rory saying, "Caleb, that reminds me. Inform Ashley she can resume cleaning, but she'll be on a schedule determined by my mate and her duties will be restricted to the lower levels."

Again the look Caleb gave Shay contained a healthy dose of respect and, if she wasn't mistaken, approval. "When do you want her to start?"

Shay opened her mouth, considered, then stopped when she realized she had no idea what day of the week it was. "What's today?" she asked. "I'm losing time."

"Sunday," Rory answered.

"Is Ashley paid by the hour or a set rate?"

"A flat rate. We can change that if needed," Rory assured her.

"No, I understand why you have her cleaning. I don't want her to lose money she may be dependent on. Neither one of us are messy people. Beginning next Monday, tell her she can come twice a week, on Tuesdays and Fridays, between one and four." To Rory she said, "I believe we deserve another few days of privacy before life returns to normal."

Rory smiled intimately at her, his pleasure in her desire to spend more time with him visible.

Another thought struck. "Does she cook for you as well?"

Rory shook his head. "Not for me. For some of the others, yes. I prefer to do my own."

"Me too. Okay," she told Caleb. "Tuesdays and Fridays and if we need to readjust because of her class schedule, let me know."

"Consider it done," Caleb said.

"These changes may cause problems within the pack. They've gotten used to being able to come to you whenever needed," MacDougal said without any of the nastiness he'd displayed earlier.

"They'll adjust. These aren't the first changes I've made, and it's doubtful they'll be the last," Rory told him.

"Have you confirmed that there's a threat, or are you simply being cautious?" Caleb asked.

Shay casually wrapped her arm around Rory's shoulders and dug her nails into the back of his neck. She did not want him sharing Conor's warning with these men. Yes, they were his second and third. Caleb, she believed, had Rory's best interest at heart. Or it could all be an elaborate act. Since she didn't know, she preferred to retain the element of surprise.

"My mate's pregnant. That's reason enough," Rory answered and nudged Shay, indicating he was ready to stand. When she moved, he stood, indicating the meeting was over.

Both men grunted in understanding and rose to leave. A solemn MacDougal exited the room first.

"How's the pregnancy coming?" Caleb asked Shay as they walked to the door.

"Good."

Caleb smiled. "You have any sisters or female cousins?"

"No sisters. One cousin, Kiesha—"

"Who's mated to the Raven pack's alpha," Rory interjected.

Caleb's smile turned rueful. "Oh well. Shake the family tree, will you? And if any more like you fall out, let me know."

Rory laughed. "Don't hold your breath. My Shay's one of a kind."

* * * *

They spent the next weekend out in the surrounding area. First Rory took Shay on a tour of his town. Well, he referred to it as a town, but it was more like an outlying area containing a few businesses, a post office, gas stations, and the like. The town butted up against the North Carolina/Tennessee border, near the top of a mountain, bordered by a state park on one side and a Native American reservation in the valley on the other.

"All this land and these businesses belong to the pack," he told her.

"This is a lot of territory. How did the pack manage to own all of this?" Shay asked, taking in the raw, and for the most part, undeveloped land that went on for miles.

"Most of the pack land was either purchased or bartered for by my great-grandfather with the Cherokee Nation when he first immigrated. The tribe took one look at him and his men and knew exactly what they were. In exchange for land and wives, the pack provided protection. It's one of the reasons this tribe wasn't forced west with the others and managed to hold on to their land."

Shay studied him carefully. She'd noticed the heavy influence of Native American blood when Rory had introduced her to the pack. It made sense. "Do you still have close ties to the tribe?"

He shook his head. "Not so much anymore. The growing need to keep what we are a secret damaged that relationship. Although some of the pack still have relatives on the reservation."

Next he took her by all the pack-owned businesses so that she could get a feel for their physical operation.

She'd already been introduced to their computer systems. The Sparrowhawks owned three campgrounds. The largest campsite catered to those who wanted to pitch their tents and rough it in a secure location but still have access to restrooms. The second, smaller location was an RV campsite completed with hookups, showers, and restrooms. The third contained a twenty-room, lodge-style hotel and a series of small wood cabins ranging from one-room efficiencies to two-bedroom cabins that slept six comfortably. There were picnic tables and grills spread throughout, and both the RV campsite and lodge had outdoor pools to attract summer campers.

"We're considering building some time-share condos. Those do well in this area. But the question is where. We don't want to crowd the land, and while tourism brings in money to support the pack, we don't want too many people around," he told her as they were leaving the lodge's restaurant after having a delicious lunch.

In addition to the restaurant in the lodge, the pack also owned a pancake house that was open for breakfast and lunch, and three general stores that sold everything from camping supplies to tourist souvenirs situated near each campsite.

"This is a nice little setup you have and, from the looks of it, prosperous as well," Shay commented.

"It wasn't always this way. We had the land, but it was going to waste. We opened the first campground a year after I became alpha. Two years later we opened the third. It took four years to get the lodge up and running but each is doing well, and we've managed to pay back most of the money we borrowed for start-up," Rory said.

"I recognized a lot of pack members working as employees," Shay said as Rory headed the truck toward his construction business.

"As part owners, pack gets preference when it comes to hiring, but we don't discriminate. We have a few of the outlying townspeople working for us as well. Not many folks want to work for minimum wage, and some of our businesses are seasonal. Those who need steady, higher paying employment drive over into Fort Knox or hit the tourist traps in Pigeon Forge or Gatlinburg."

"Speaking of tourist traps, I'll probably have to visit one to shop. I'm going to need some larger clothing soon," Shay said, looking down at her ever-expanding bump.

Rory reached out and laid a possessive hand over her stomach. "We'll drive into Fort Knox tomorrow and do some shopping at the mall. How are you feeling?"

She'd started out the morning with a bit of nausea. "Better. Lunch helped."

"When's your follow-up with Carol?"

"In two more weeks."

"You sure you won't let Laurie Bell take a look at you?"

Shay sighed. "I'm drinking the tea, and while I won't deny that it helps, I'm still more comfortable going to an actual doctor's office to be seen. Speaking of which, per our contract, you owe me some form of transportation."

"I don't want you riding over to Refuge without me." He brought the truck to a stop in front of a building with a sign proclaiming: McFelan Construction.

"Be reasonable. You can't keep me tethered to the house. I have friends and family in Refuge. You think I'm going to be this close to Kiesha and not visit her?"

Rory turned to her with one hand still resting on the steering wheel. "No, I don't. All I'm asking is that you don't go without me."

"Fine, but I still need a ride."

"You can have this one. I'll drive one of the company trucks."

Shay glanced around the truck and scrunched her nose. "This will do for now until I can make arrangements to have mine brought from Florida."

"Unless it's an SUV or a four-wheel drive, don't bother. Anything else is not worth having on these mountainous roads, especially in the winter when there's snow on the ground." Rory climbed out of the truck and came around to hold the door open for Shay.

"Then I guess I'm going car shopping, which I hate," she muttered.

Rory kept his truck well maintained and fairly clean, but it was obviously a work truck. The full-size pickup was difficult for someone of her height and stature to climb in and out of. She could only imagine the difficulty she'd have later in her pregnancy.

"I've introduced you to the pack and to Kian. When are you going to tell your parents about us?" Rory asked out of the blue, holding the door to his office building open for her to enter.

Shay actually felt her eye twitch. "Later." Much, much later if she had her way about it.

"Shay, I want us married before the babe arrives. I think your parents would like to be there."

She glared at him. "After the way my mother behaved at Kiesha's wedding, you can say that to me with a straight face?"

"Shay…" he chided. She hunched her shoulders.

"All right, all right. I'll do it. And when she descends on us like a plague of locusts, don't say I didn't warn you." She glanced around the interior. "The construction slump doesn't seem to be affecting you," Shay said to change the subject. The thought of confessing all to her parents caused her stomach to churn.

"No, business is good. Hold on, let me check on a few things while I'm here. My office is through there." He pointed to an open doorway, then walked over to a man at a desk and began asking questions.

There was a receptionist at the front desk giving Shayla a curious look. Shay guessed she didn't see Rory come in with too many women who were so obviously not a client.

She entered his office and spent time looking at all the plaques on the wall and pictures of projects his firm had completed. When he came in, she motioned to the walls and said, "So you do both commercial and residential construction?"

"Mostly residential, but I have taken on a few commercial projects, as well as remodels and renovations. We basically do it all and at a reasonable price. Caleb, my business partner and project foreman, has been handling things for me while I've been home working with you," he said as he settled into his chair and then booted up the computer.

"So he's your second in more than just the pack?"

"Yes." Rory scanned through his e-mails, firing off responses to a few and filing others in folders.

Shay sat on his desk and waited until he'd finished, watching him work. He loved his job, and it showed in the focus that he gave to each task. Word spread that the head boss was on-site, and there was a steady stream of visitors to the office asking about this and that. Shay sat, absorbing it all, enjoying seeing the business side of her mate.

An hour later they left and made a trip to a nearby hardware store for locks.

"You know changing the locks won't stop any shifter really determined to get in," he said.

"Of course, just like all the locked doors and windows in the world won't keep out a really determined burglar. But it will slow them down and hopefully give warning that they're coming in," she said.

He grunted, seeming satisfied with her answer.

Chapter Thirteen

Back at the house, Shay played assistant while Rory changed out all the locks, top and bottom.

"These doors are all steel with reinforced frames," he told her. "The windows are double paned and meet hurricane standards. Like I said, it won't keep anyone determined to get inside out, but it will take time and a hell of a lot of effort."

He glanced up at her. "The alpha's house is always built capable of withstanding a siege because in times of crisis, the pack runs here. Our pantries are always stocked full of food, and there's a locked storage room in the basement full of emergency supplies."

Shay nodded her understanding and glanced around. "That's why this house is so big?"

"In my grandfather's day, when most of the additions to the original cabin were made, the alpha pair, beta pair, and the elders lived in this house. Even when I was a boy, the beta pair lived here until as healer, it was determined that Laurie Bell and her mate needed their own residence. The pack built them a house not too far from here."

Shay's gaze swung back to Rory in surprise. "Laurie Bell was married to your father's beta? His second in command?"

"Yes, although my father wasn't big on sharing his authority, he did have a second," he confirmed.

There was something there, something on the edge of her mind, but Shay couldn't bring it into focus. Something Rory had said... "Did your father choose his own beta?"

"No, his position was established by pack ranking, although they were good friends, having grown up together. Actually Quintin—that's his name—and Laurie Bell were all around the same age as my father. At one time, I'm told, Da was expected to mate with Laurie Bell."

Shock rocked Shay back on her heels. "Laurie Bell's wolf is that strong?" she asked, remembering what he'd said about alphas and their mates.

Rory paused with the screwdriver in his hand. "I never really thought about it. Healers fall outside of the hierarchy, but her father was my grandfather's beta and her mother, our healer, so yes, I guess she would be."

"Didn't you say your father's beta was one of the men who'd challenged you for the position of alpha?"

A shadow crossed his face. "Yes."

"And," Shay searched the threads of her memory, trying to pull it all together, "that Ashley was the daughter of your father's beta?"

"Yes." He went back to his screwing, using a little more force than necessary.

"So that means Ashley is Laurie Bell's daughter?"

"Uh-huh. What of it?" he asked absently, his focus once more on his task.

"I'm just wondering why she didn't say anything or make an introduction." Shay thought hard. Had she even seen Ashley at the howl? She had to have been there.

Attendance was mandatory, but she'd met so many new faces. Shay honestly couldn't remember if she'd seen her.

Rory paused in thought. "Laurie Bell doesn't like to mention it, but she's displeased with Ashley. She wants her daughter to follow in her footsteps, but Ashley doesn't have the aptitude for healing like her mother and grandmother before her."

"I guess that makes sense." Shay knew all about disappointed mothers, with her mother constantly nagging her to marry and give her grandchildren. Another thought occurred. "What would have happened if Quintin hadn't challenged you? Would he have remained your second?"

Rory shrugged. "It's possible but highly doubtful. With the rise of a new alpha, everyone's position within the hierarchy has to be reestablished. Quintin might have been able to hold on to it. More likely he would have lost his position and, by virtue of age and experience, become one of the pack elders."

What would it do to a woman, Shay wondered, to expect to be alpha-fem and have her position taken by a lowly omega? Laurie Bell seemed to have adjusted well to her change in status. Of course, Shay supposed the position of healer was powerful in its own right.

Thinking about mothers and daughters and following in one's footsteps, Shay asked, "Laurie Bell ever make any noises about you and Ashley?"

"Me and Ashley what?" Rory asked blankly.

Shay rolled her eyes. "You and Ashley mating?"

Stunned amazement and a hint of distaste came through their bond. "Shay, Ashley's a child. I'll never see her as anything but."

Okay, that was certainly clear enough. Best leave that subject alone. Still trying to figure out all the intrapack dynamics, she asked instead, "If Laurie Bell and your father were supposed to mate, how'd he end up with your mother?"

"I honestly have no clue." He stood, the last lock in place. He gave the door and lock a few tests with the key. "It's near time for dinner. What do you have a taste for?"

Without hesitation, Shay stated, "Pizza with the works."

"You want to order in or eat out?"

"Let's go out. I'm not used to spending this much time inside of one place." In truth she was beginning to go a bit stir-crazy. Rory made a nice distraction, but even he couldn't keep the walls from closing in.

"I know a great pizza parlor. They serve New York-style authentic pizza pie. And after we eat, we can take in a few of the nearby attractions," he offered with a smile.

"You're on," she told him. "Let me use the restroom and I'll be ready to go."

They ate really fantastic pizza, rode bumper cars—though Rory inserted himself between her and other drivers to keep her from getting hit too hard—and played in the arcade until closing.

On the ride home, Shay snuggled close to Rory's side, listening to the romantic music playing low on the radio as the fresh air blew through the open windows. Even at this hour the traffic was stop-and-go. "You're not a bad date."

He chuckled. "Does that mean I get laid when we get home?"

"Hmm, possibly. Or I could do you now," she said, laying a hand on the bulge in his pants.

He covered her hand with his. "As enticing as that sounds, I think I'll wait until we're home. That way I can take my time, and there'll be no pesky distractions like honking horns or citations for indecent exposure."

Shay laughingly agreed and moved her hand from his crotch to lie on his hard, muscular thigh. As they rode, they spoke of everything and nothing in general, and Shay felt like she was part of a normal, everyday couple. It was nice.

When they entered the house and Rory locked the door behind them, instead of heading upstairs as Shay expected, he diverted them to the living room and went and programmed the stereo. "Let's dance," he said, holding out a hand.

Shay moved into his arms, and they drifted around the room as one slow song after another played. It was the perfect ending to a perfect evening. Rory languidly stroked her spine as they danced. She wrapped her arms around his neck and tucked her face on his shoulder, sighing contentedly when he rested his cheek on her head.

This togetherness, this sense of oneness was what she'd always thought of when she used to try and imagine herself married. Sex was great, but a woman needed more than a man who could burn between the sheets. She needed a man who knew when and how to cherish her. And when, she thought, to drive her crazy to keep her from getting complacent.

For her, Rory was that man, even if he did have a habit of occasionally turning furry.

They drifted around the dimly lit room, and as the moon rode high in the sky, they made their way up the stairs. A trail of clothes marked their passing. When they reached the bed, they were skin to skin.

Their loving was long and languid. Rory surprised Shay by staying in his skin. Only the golden glow of his eyes revealed he was as affected as she. And when they found their release, it was he who called out her name. Afterward, he held her close to his heart, his arm draped possessively, protectively around her. Shay fell asleep, feeling safe, secure, and most of all, loved.

* * * *

The next morning after breakfast and another cup of that disgusting tea, they rode into Fort Knox to hunt for SUVs. When Shay found a few she liked and Rory agreed with the price, he called in one of his men knowledgeable about vehicles to make sure the engines were sound and there were no major problems with the SUVs before finalizing the purchase.

Shay mentioned that her clothes were getting snug at the waist. That sparked a trip to the mall, where Rory loaded her down with enough items to last through two pregnancies. Glancing at some of the tentlike shirts, Shay sincerely hoped she wouldn't get that big.

Over lunch at a local steakhouse, Rory said, "We need to go next weekend and pack up your condo and bring your things here. While we're there, we can tell your parents about us."

Part of the lemonade Shay was sipping went down the wrong pipe. Once she finished coughing, Shay pinned Rory with a glare. "There's no need. My stuff is already in storage. Between setting up Kiesha's stores, going to California for six weeks, and then the contract with you, I knew I'd be away for a long period of time. I made arrangements for a moving company to pack up all my things and store them, and hired a management company to sublet my condo. So there's no rush to gather my belongings." *Or tell my parents about us.*

"And your parents?" he questioned.

"I'll tell them, eventually," she muttered.

Rory's narrow-eyed gaze had her hunching her shoulders again. "You do realize in another few months you'll be delivering our babe." He leaned forward, lowering his voice. "As it is, unless you're planning on telling them the truth about shifters, they're going to believe you've been pregnant for a lot longer than you have, and be upset that you hid it from them. And they're going to wonder why. Then their focus is going to turn on me. They'll wonder what's wrong with me that you hid our relationship for so long. And do you know how that's going to make me feel, Shay? Do you, Shay?"

She shook her head no.

"Like your dirty little secret," he said angrily.

Shay shrank back into her seat and pushed her plate away. Seemed guilt played havoc with the appetite. "All right, all right. I'll tell them. Jeez. But don't blame me when you open the door and find my parents standing on the doorstep, suitcases in hand."

Rory studied her face for a moment, then nodded. "Now that we have that settled, finish eating your food."

She glanced at the half a steak and majority of the loaded baked potato on her plate. "I lost my appetite."

"Fine. If you're not hungry, drink your tea. We'll get a to-go box for the food." He motioned to the still-steaming cup.

Shay looked at the nasty concoction and frowned. "I don't know why you brought that stuff with us today," she complained.

"Laurie Bell said for you to drink it a couple of times a day."

When she heaved a sigh and obediently picked up the cup, he motioned for the waitress, who came before Shay finished swallowing the first sip. "We need a to-go box and the check."

"Yes, sir. Be back in a moment."

While they waited, he asked, "You have any other stops you want to make while we're in the city?"

"I want to find a local health food store."

"There's one close to the house—Laurie Bell's."

Shay scrunched her nose. "No offense, but this tea is nasty. I'd like to see if someone can recommend one that does the same thing but tastes better."

He chuckled. "None taken. She's always giving me brews to drink or pills to take for this or that. Mostly I chuck them."

Outraged, she said, "But you're making me drink it? This tastes like cow piss!"

He smirked. "And you'd be knowing this how?"

She snarled. "You know what I mean. I can't believe you're forcing me to drink this stuff."

Rory pinned her with a look. "It's helping you, isn't it?"

Glumly Shay had to admit it was. She wasn't feeling as tired and run-down as she had been. "Could be the prenatal vitamins kicking in," she suggested.

"Maybe," he agreed, but a small smile tilted the corners of his mouth.

The waitress returned to the table. As she boxed up Shay's lunch, Rory dealt with the check.

Shay continued sipping and allowed her mind to wander. *Is Rory my dirty little secret? Am I ashamed of him, ashamed of my unplanned pregnancy? No, of course not. I love him, which is amazing now that I think about it. And now that I'm over the worst of the shock, I'm actually happy about this little one.* She placed a protective hand over her mildly rounded belly.

Was it wrong to want to keep what she'd found with him to herself, just a little while longer? To savor the feeling of being in love and loved? To take time to adjust to the wonder of her new circumstances before reality, in the form of her parents, intruded?

When the waitress returned with Rory's card, Shay rose, food in hand, and they exited the restaurant. Rory held the passenger door of the truck open for her, hand on her elbow to give her a boost. She paused in the opening, turned instead to face him, and placed her palm on his cheek. "You're not my 'dirty little secret.' If anything, you're my secret treasure. Is it any wonder I want more time to savor our mating before bringing my family into it?"

His pupils flared, and stunned pleasure filled his gaze. He took her mouth in a devouring kiss. Shay leaned weakly against the seat, panting when it was over.

He rested his forehead on hers. "Are you sure that's the only reason?"

She rolled her eyes. "Rory, you've met my mother. What do you think her reaction is going to be when she finds out I'm pregnant and living with my baby's father? Do you really think she's going to be like, 'Oh, Shay, that's wonderful. Let me know when the baby's born so we can come visit'?" she asked. "Hell no! She's going to catch the first flight here, and we might, *might* get rid of her by time the kid's five. That's *after* she puts both of us through the Inquisition."

He winced and drew back a bit. She could see by his expression he was remembering her mother's behavior at Kiesha's wedding.

"Now you begin to see. You think she was bad with Kee? Wait until it's our turn. Do you know how long she's been nagging me to tie the knot and give her grandkids?"

He placed his hand over her mouth. "All right. You've made your point. I'll leave it to your discretion when to break the news to your folks."

Rory gripped her by the hips, lifted her into the truck, then gently closed the door. Shay set her food on the seat between them while he came around and got in. Seconds later they were exiting the parking lot.

"Where are we headed?"

"Back to the mall. There's a health food place inside," he told her.

* * * *

"Our midwife gave me this tea to drink to help with my pregnancy, but the stuff tastes awful. It's helping, so I don't want to hurt her feelings by trashing it, but is there anything you can recommend that actually tastes good, or if not good, at least not so bitter?" Shay asked the helpful store attendant while Rory roamed the aisles.

"Did you want a tea?" he asked.

"Not necessarily. If you have something in pill form, that would be great," Shay told him. Pills had to be better than tea. She could knock it back with her prenatals, and best part, no nasty taste.

"Do you happen to know what's in the brew she gave you?" he asked as he led the way to a section of shelves labeled Pregnancy.

"No, but we have some with us if that would help," she said and called to Rory. "Give the man the tea. He wants to see what's in it."

Rory pulled a sealed baggie out of his pocket.

The attendant said, "I don't need all of it. A portion will do."

"No, please, keep it," Shay said quickly. "I'd rather have the capsules. Just tell me what and how much to take."

He took the bag from Rory, went behind the counter, and much to Shay's displeasure, took about half the potion and transferred it to a container before sealing the baggie and returning it to Rory. Then he motioned for Shay to follow and went and pulled a few bottles off the shelf.

Rory's eyebrows rose. "Shay, that's a lot of pills. Are you sure you wouldn't rather drink the tea?"

The store attendant paused and gave her a questioning look, waiting for her response.

"Pills are more convenient. If it gets to be too much, then I'll switch to the tea again."

The store attendant nodded, then told her the purpose for each herb and how many to take before pointing to a few more bottles. "These you'll want to begin taking when you're in your last few weeks. They'll help ease the delivery."

"Ease as in less painful?" she asked.

"Yes," he answered.

Shay committed the bottles to memory. Anything that would help her through the labor process was on her must-have list.

Taking the herbs to the register, the attendant pulled out a pad and wrote down the name of each and the prescribed dosage he'd give her, then made a copy of what he'd written. He handed Shay the extra. "I'm an herbalist. I'll analyze the brew she gave you and make sure I didn't miss anything. We like to work with medical professionals, whenever possible, and it's so rare to find one into natural remedies. If you won't mind giving me your name and number…?"

Shay gave him her name, e-mail addy, and cell phone number, and Rory rattled off the number to the house. They paid for their purchases, and Shay thanked the attendant profusely, holding the bag to her chest like it was precious.

As they left the mall, Rory teased, "They had some interesting items in there. There's something called 'horny goat weed.' It's supposed to increase the male sex drive."

Shay narrowed her eyes at him. "You're already a horny werewolf. The last thing you need is help in the keeping-it-up department. I wonder if they have something to keep it down?" she mused.

"We'll never know," he said, sounding smug, before he laughed.

* * * *

Sunday morning Shay awakened to a feeling of vicious nausea she hadn't experienced since her first morning in Rory's home. Lying absolutely still, she breathed softly through her nostrils, praying for it to pass.

Between one breath and the next, Rory woke beside her. "What's wrong?"

"Queasy," she muttered in a low voice.

"You need food," he stated decisively and rose from the bed.

Shay flattened her hands on the mattress out on either side of her body, trying to stabilize herself. Even that small bit of jostling had her swallowing hard, the steady stream of saliva filling her mouth adding to her misery instead of lessening it. "No food," she ground out. Just the thought of it had the acid rising to the back of her throat.

"Tea, then," Rory said, stopping to look at her. "I don't like your pallor."

"Tea," Shay agreed, knowing she needed something. "And not that mess Laurie Bell gave you. Bring me black tea sweetened with lots of honey, and dry toast or saltine crackers."

Rory brushed her hair out of her face. "Your forehead's clammy. I'm calling the midwife."

"No," Shay bit out. "It's just morning sickness. Give me what I asked for. I'll drink the tea and eat the bread and lay here until my stomach settles."

He frowned. "Fine, but if your remedy doesn't work, I'm calling her."

"It will," she assured him. When he left, Shay closed her eyes. She hated morning sickness almost as much as she hated throwing up. It was always a battle to see which was better, the constant queasiness or upchucking the contents of her stomach. If she could make herself throw up, she knew she'd feel better in minutes, but who wanted to go through the trauma?

Shay lay still and concentrated on her shallow breathing. She'd yet to take the first birthing class, but she already had the labor breathing nailed.

Rory returned in minutes with the requested items. Gritting her teeth, Shay shoved into a seated position and then froze as her stomach rolled in protest.

"Shay, you're totally white. I'm calling Laurie Bell."

She shook her head violently, eyes closed as she fought to control her stomach. "I'll be fine." She held out a hand.

"Tea or toast?"

"Toast," she whispered.

He placed a paper towel in her hand. Shay squinted at it to make sure it was dry before bringing the bread to her mouth and nibbling on it. She'd eaten her way through half the slice before holding out her free hand for the tea. Once she had it in hand, she alternated sipping the contents with chewing toast. Already she was feeling better.

Rory watched her like a hawk, his body braced for action.

As her stomach settled, the bites and sips became larger. The warmth of the liquid spread through her. She finished the toast and drained the cup with a relieved sigh. Shay balled up the paper and handed her trash and the cup to Rory.

"Feel better?" he asked, his concern evident in his furrowed brow.

"Yes." She snuggled down under the covers and closed her eyes.

"Well enough to ride with me to pick up your SUV? Riley texted and said the red Tahoe was best. It needs new tires and a tune-up, but otherwise is in excellent condition. It also had the best price and a bit of warranty left."

At that moment Shay couldn't care less about the details. She wasn't up to another two-hour ride, another hour of price haggling, and waiting while Rory had the car serviced before heading home. She had no doubts he'd handle everything today. That was his nature.

She opened one eye and met his gaze. "Can you take someone else with you to drive mine here? I do feel better, but I'm not up for another long ride. I'd rather stay home and chill."

He sat on the bed beside her and took her hand. "I can wait until you feel like riding with me. I'd rather not leave you home alone, knowing you don't feel well."

Shay opened the other eye and squeezed his hand. "My stomach is fine. A short nap and I'll be good as new. Go, don't wait. You return to work tomorrow," she reminded him. "I'm sure you'll have to work overtime to catch up since you've been out. That means it will be next weekend at the earliest before we can go get it."

"You won't be without transportation, Shay, if that's your concern."

She shook her head. "I know you'll leave me the truck. But the dealer will only hold the SUV for three days. You get it today, and we'll be done with the whole purchasing process."

He sighed. "Can I call someone to sit with you? If not one of the pack, then Shannon?"

Now she smiled. "No, I'm okay. I'll bother Kian if I feel the need for company."

Both his eyebrows shot up. "If you've got the ability to tease, then you're obviously feeling much better than you look."

Actually she'd been serious, but if it made him happier to think she was joking, who was she to disillusion him?

"Let me call Riley and see if he's free. If not, I'll give Caleb a call." He rose from the bed and left the room.

Shay eased out of bed and went to use the restroom. Catching a glimpse of herself in the mirror, she could better understand Rory's concern. She did look pale, and her eyes appeared sick. She washed her face and brushed her teeth, deciding there was no sense combing her matted hair when she was climbing right back into bed for it to flatten.

Rory returned to the bedroom as she was exiting the bathroom. "One of my crew is riding with me. I told Caleb to keep his phone handy. I'll program his number into your cell phone. You call him if you run into any trouble, and he'll come running." He gave her a look that enforced his command.

"Okay." Though Shay doubted she'd run into any problems.

Appearing relieved that she wasn't going to give him any argument, he went into the bathroom to shower. Twenty minutes later he was gone.

Shay dozed while Rory dressed, but the minute the door closed behind him, she was wide-awake. In the strange manner of pregnant women, she'd gone from wanting to barf at the mere thought of food to feeling like she'd die of hunger if she didn't get something inside her in the next instant.

Pausing only long enough to slip on a pair of shorts and an oversize T-shirt, Shay trotted down the stairs to the kitchen. A jumbo glass of orange juice, a banana, a muffin, and a container of yogurt later, she was still hungry.

She glanced down at her belly in disgust. "You're not even here yet, and already you're as demanding as your father."

Sighing in resignation, she pulled out a flat of eggs, a pack of sausage, and a bag of cheese in preparation for making an omelet. Shay could tell which one of them this little one took after.

She started the entire container of meat cooking and, as an afterthought, grabbed the bacon as well. If she was going to pig out, might as well do a thorough job of it. After turning the oven on to four hundred degrees, Shay lined a cookie sheet with wax paper and almost an entire pack of bacon strips—the thick, meaty kind. What else would a shifter buy?

As the aroma of cooking pork rose in the air, Shay eyed the basement door. In the short time she'd been here, she'd gotten used to sharing meals with another. She gave the mountain of food she prepared another glance, then looked back at the door. Inviting Kian to share a meal would be the nice, friendly, *family* thing to do, wouldn't it? It wouldn't constitute *bothering* him, would it?

Certain Rory would agree and approve, Shay had the door open and was walking down the stairs before her conscience could kick in and talk her out of it.

"Kian," she called as she cracked the second door open. "It's me, Shay—Rory's mate? I've come to invite you to breakfast. Thought maybe we could get to know each other since, you know, we live in the same house and all."

She nudged the opening wider and peeped around the wood.

"I know already we have one thing in common. We both dislike the pack. I know I shouldn't say this, but having met them, I don't blame you for not wanting anything to do with them. That's the reason I had Rory put a stop to them walking into this house anytime they got good and ready. From now on the doors are locked and they have to call first before coming over. I even had him change the locks." Shay paused. She couldn't hear any sound of movement. If Kian was there, he wasn't interested in making nice.

"Anyway," she said, her spirit drooping, "Rory left for Fort Knox this morning to go pick up a vehicle for me. I realized, after I started, I cooked way too much food for one person and thought I'd see if you wanted to join me. If not, I understand." She waited another moment for Kian to show himself, then, shoulders slumped, turned and went back up the stairs.

The sausage was ready to be flipped. After doing so, she got busy cracking eggs. Since Kian wouldn't be joining her, Shay cracked three eggs into a medium-sized bowl and tossed the shells into the trash. The timer on the oven went off. She checked the bacon to see how it was progressing, and set the timer for another three minutes. It was slightly golden, but Shay liked her bacon crispy. By then the sausage patties were ready to come out of the pan. She scooped them up and onto a paper-towel-lined plate. Running out of countertop space, Shay grabbed the eggs and turned to place them in the fridge and almost dropped the container.

Kian sat, not three feet away, quiet as midnight, watching her with those eerie blue eyes.

Chapter Fourteen

"Make some noise, will you? You scared the bejeebers out of me," Shay snapped, fear giving way to anger. She put the eggs on the counter before she crushed them and then closed her eyes for a moment, trying to catch her breath.

His ears flicked forward, and his head tilted to the side. Very deliberately he lifted his right front paw and then the left. His claws made a miniscule scraping sound when they landed on the wood floor.

"A jokester. Great," Shay said with heavy sarcasm.

His eyes laughed at her.

Shay studied him, her gaze narrowed. "Does this mean you've decided to join me for breakfast?"

He looked toward the stove, then back at her and nodded. The action looked so strange, for a moment Shay was taken aback. Reminding herself there was a man inside the wolf, she literally shook off her disconcertment, shaking her head so that wisps of hair flew into her face. She really needed to get a haircut, she mused.

"Fine. How many eggs do you want? I cracked three for me. You want me to add another three for you?"

One side of Kian's lip curled up. Great, he was sneering at her. "Four?" she guessed.

The beast yawned.

With another glance that took in his size, she asked, "Six?"

Kian only looked mildly interested.

"You do realize I'm cooking more than eggs, don't you? There's sausage and bacon too," she offered.

He actually rolled his eyes.

Stunned, Shay stared. How the hell had he done that? Finally she huffed and said, "Fine, but I'm not cooking more than nine for you. That's a total of twelve eggs. That's more than enough for any…" *Man*, she started to say, but trailed off, realizing Kian wasn't a man or a wolf, but a wolf-shifter with a healthy appetite. Since Rory usually cooked, she had no idea how many eggs he went through in one sitting. "Never mind. That's all I'm cooking. If you want more, cook 'em yourself."

Kian flopped down on his belly and laid his head on his front paws.

The timer went off, and Shay removed the bacon from the oven. "And I'm not putting food on the floor. You want to eat, you'll shift and sit at the table like civilized folk." She didn't glance back to see how he took her edict.

Shay resisted the urge to fidget as the weight of Kian's stare settled like an itch between her shoulder blades. Determinedly, she took out a larger bowl and a huge frying pan that she needed both hands to move, cracked the rest of the eggs, then picked up the whisk and strong-armed the mix until the yolks and whites blended seamlessly together. Cooking this many eggs at one time was a challenge, but she managed to do it without any getting scorched or worse, runny. She hated slimy eggs.

Since she'd made an issue out of "civilized behavior," Shay placed the bacon and sausage on a serving platter and the eggs in a serving bowl and set the table with plates, napkins, silverware, and cups. "You can wash your hands at the kitchen sink," she said matter-of-factly, praying he couldn't tell how uneasy she was.

Out the corner of her eye she caught a shimmer of light. There were a few muffled popping sounds in quick succession; then Kian stood before her in all his naked glory. And a glorious sight it was.

He stood a few inches taller than Rory but was just as heavily built. His hair was coal black and eyes a vibrant blue. Shay tried, really she did, not to let her gaze travel over the rest of him, but he was like, right there and she wasn't dead. She could appreciate an eyeful of masculine eye candy the same as any other woman. Kian's legs were long and lean like a runner, his ass high and tight. The way his muscles shifted as he crossed to the sink was pure poetry in motion.

Shay checked her hormone meter. Despite her appreciation of the view and her recognition of Kian's hunky appeal, she felt not the slightest bit of sexual attraction toward him. "Well, now, I guess this means I'm good and mated," she said aloud.

Kian turned and shot her a questioning look, and Shay saw that the front of him was just as delicious as the rear.

Shay waved a hand, indicating his body. "You're a mouthwatering, eye-catching male, Kian McFelan, and I'm ecstatic to announce I'm not the least bit attracted to you."

His face turned a fiery red, and Shay laughed in delight. "I'm sorry. I'm not trying to make you uncomfortable. I'm surprised the women around here aren't beating down the doors trying to get to you."

He frowned as he took a seat at the table. *I heard you tell Rory you know ASL*, he signed.

“Yes, but I’m a bit rusty,” she answered.

I’m mute.

“The rest of you appears to be in working order,” Shay said. She bowed her head and said a quick prayer, then loaded food onto her plate. As she finished with each item, she nudged the platters toward Kian for him to do the same.

It doesn’t bother you?

“Why should it? We all have some type of disability. Some are more obvious than others. I prefer the ones I can see to the mental kind.” Shay glanced at him, hoping he caught her meaning. She hated prejudice of any nature and considered it to be a disability of sorts.

Kian fixed a mountain of food on his plate, his expression showing he was thinking about what she’d said. He took a few bites of food, then signed, *This is good. How did you and Rory meet?*

Shay laughed and had to bring a napkin to her mouth to catch the food that almost fell out. “Sorry about that. It’s funny to me now, but when I first met your brother, I thought he was the most annoying asshole of a man I’d ever met.”

Kian’s eyes widened.

As they ate, she told him their story, from the first meeting in Kiesha’s store, through the blue moon, and her recent return to Refuge for her cousin’s wedding, leaving nothing out. Kian’s eyes never left her face.

You love him.

“Yeah,” she agreed in a soft voice.

He’s lucky.

Shay sighed. “I don’t know how lucky Rory is, but I do know he’s stuck. He wanted me, I’m here, and have no plans on leaving.”

You want any more of this?

“No, go ahead. I’m not as hungry as I thought I was.” Or maybe her subconscious had known she’d planned to entice Kian out of his hole with food. “Rory showed me your bedroom upstairs. I can understand a man wanting his privacy, but dude, you live like an animal. Why don’t you have any furniture down there? I’m sure Rory would have fixed the basement up any way you like.”

Kian shrugged. *I don’t like to be a bother. He has enough to worry about with the pack.*

Shay pinned him with a look. “Bull. He’s your brother. Your twin. You think he doesn’t love you, worry about you? You think you living downstairs like a lone wolf doesn’t hurt him?” she asked, startled to hear a hint of anger in her voice.

The pack doesn’t like me. It’s easier if I stay out of the way.

He appeared so uncomfortable Shay decided to take it easy on him. “That’s where you’re wrong. Rory needs you. From what I can tell, your brother has a lot of…if not enemies, well, they’re definitely not his friends. Let’s call his pack full of frenemies. He needs all the support he can get. He says you’re stronger than he is. If you won’t be alpha—and really, with those clowns, I don’t blame you a bit for not wanting the top position—at the very least you should have his back, be his beta.”

He has Caleb, and I don’t like fighting.

A gentle werewolf, Shay thought. Hmm…but then, most twins tended to be opposites in nature. Looks like

Rory got the aggressive gene. "Okay, I'll leave that alone. But Kian"—she reached out and placed her hand over his on the table—"I need you. Not only do we live in the same house, you're family. You're my child's uncle. No offense, but some of the Sparrowhawks are like a pack of hyenas. I think they'd turn on their own children if it would gain them something." Then, without giving herself much time to think about it, she told him about Conor's prophecy. Prediction? Hell, she didn't know what to call it other than a warning to watch her ass.

You want me to protect you and the babe? He seemed surprised.

"That's what families do," she said simply. "We protect and look out for each other."

He leaned back in his seat, studied her carefully. *No one's ever needed me before.*

Shay shook her head. "That's not true. You've been needed, by Rory and probably Shannon. They just didn't bother to tell you. I am."

The thought flashed across her mind that Kian might be one of the folks Conor had warned her of, but she immediately dismissed it. For one thing, she'd always had good instincts when it came to people, and her heart told her Kian could be trusted. For another, if Kian wanted to be alpha, he would be alpha. Rory might have fought his father for the pack, but she doubted he'd have fought his twin, not if Kian really wanted the position. From what Rory had told her, he'd stepped forward because there wasn't another suitable candidate.

I prefer being in wolf form.

Shay shrugged. "So be a wolf, but don't forget you're also a man."

There was silence as her words settled around them.

Going with her gut, she asked Kian, "You know these people, probably better than anyone else. People, even shifters, tend to lower their guards around those they don't consider a threat. Who do you think I should be watching out for?"

You wouldn't believe me if I told you, he signed, a hint of bitterness in his expression. *No one else does.*

A hint of excitement stirred inside. *He knows! Kian knows who my enemy is.* Shay leaned forward in her chair, her focus complete, her manner intent as she stared deeply into his eyes. "Yes I will. I'm not like the others. Rory thinks it's a man, but I don't think so. I believe it's a woman," she said carefully, watching closely for any change in Kian's expression.

His eyes flared before he could make his face blank. They stared at each other, taking each other's measure. Finally Kian's hands moved in a blur of motion.

"Whoa! Whoa! Slow down. You're going too fast. I'm rusty, remember?"

Kian's chest moved as he blew out a breath. He started again. Shay watched closely, her mouth dropping open the tiniest bit.

"Laurie Bell?" she asked faintly, hoping she'd read wrong.

You don't believe me. Kian's expression went flat again.

"No, I do. Shit! The tea!" Shay shot to her feet. She could see Kian's hands moving furiously, but she was in too much of a rush to stop and read. "Where the hell did I put it?"

The bag from the health food store was still on the countertop. She snatched it to her and peered inside. Not there. Turning, she almost bumped into Kian, who'd come to stand behind her. She tried to dart around him, but he grabbed her arm.

What is it? he demanded.

"She gave me this tea to drink. Said it was for the baby," she shouted as she snatched her arm free. Shay ran for the stairs, barely noting Kian keeping pace behind her. She tore into the bedroom, vaguely remembering stuffing the paper the man had given her into a pocket.

Jeans, jeans, jeans! Where are they? Bathroom! Dirty clothes hamper. She raced inside and flipped up the lid. They sat right on top. Shay dug into the pockets—front right, front left, back right, back left… *Jackpot!*

Shay turned to dash to the phone. Kian blocked her way. "Move," she ordered sharply.

He danced nimbly to the side as she charged him. Seconds later Shay's cell phone was in her hand and she was dialing the shop's number. "Please be open. Please be open," she prayed.

"For Your Health," a male's voice answered.

Shay breathed out a sigh of relief. "Hi, I was in the store yesterday evening, and Ken gave me his card. Is he available?"

"This is he."

"Ken, this is Shayla Morgan. I don't suppose you've had opportunity to analyze that tea I gave you?" she asked, crossing her fingers.

"Actually I have. I was going to give you a call when we closed up for the night. Hold on, let me grab my paper. I have it here, somewhere."

Shay clenched her fist in the bedspread while she waited. She could hear the sound of customers in the shop and, in the distance, the canned music they played in the mall. Ken answered a question or two, and then he was back. “Here it is. I need to ask, are you sure she gave you the right tea blend?”

Warily Shay asked, “She gave it to my fiancé to give to me. Why do you ask?”

“Because of some of the ingredients. She has peppermint and gingerroot—great for nausea, morning sickness, and flavor—in a base of ginseng for energy, chamomile, dandelion, and red clover. She also has red raspberry leaf and nettles, which while good for pregnancy, most herbalists, including me, recommend not be taken until your second and third trimesters,” he stated. “But there’s a few others here that confuse me.”

Shay stood and began to pace. “Like what?”

“She added black cohosh, angelica, motherwort, licorice, and a bit of rosemary to the brew.”

Shay’s wanderings brought her to the window. “And that’s bad?”

“Well…”

“Tell me, please.” It was evident he was reluctant to bad-mouth another professional.

“The herbs by themselves are good for menstrual and menopausal issues but, when taken during pregnancy, can cause miscarriage. Maybe she didn’t tell the vendor she purchased this from that you were pregnant?”

Shay dropped her hand to cover her womb. “How exactly do the herbs work?” she asked, knowing knowledge is power.

"Over time they can cause uterine contractions. Some, like angelica, force your menstrual cycle to come on. Like I said, she may not have known. I do recommend some of these herbs to pregnant women, but only those in their last few weeks. These are some of the herbs I mentioned that help speed and ease labor." He was talking fast, trying to be reassuring. "You haven't been drinking the tea long, have you? I think you said she'd just given it to you?"

"About a week," Shay murmured, her mind working overtime.

"Well, everything should be fine. Just switch to the pills I gave you and save the tea until you get closer to term," he said in a soothing voice.

"Can you fax or e-mail me a list of the herbs you found in the tea she gave me?"

"Sure. I have your e-mail address right here. I'll send it to you along with our weekly specials."

"Thank you for all your help," Shay said politely. Inside she wanted to scream.

"You're welcome. Glad to be of service."

Shay pressed the Off button and rested her forehead on the window. She'd been warned, and she'd still almost trusted the wrong person. She felt the heat of Kian's body as he came and stood close behind her.

"You heard?" She glanced over her shoulder.

He nodded.

"She tried to kill my baby, Kian. She's smart, I'll give her that. If something happened, if she were caught, she could say it was a simple error. But she knew exactly what she was doing. She's a naturalist. Owns a shop."

She hates us.

"Why?"

I don't know. She's always hated us. My parents too.

Rory's parents, Shay thought. Somehow it always seemed to come back to them. "She looked right into both of our faces and lied. Not even Rory caught it."

She's been living a lie for years. You need to tell Rory.

"Not yet."

He signed forcefully and with great emphasis. *He needs to know!*

Shay rubbed her forehead wearily. "I know, and I'll tell him, but not yet. He *trusts* her! Feels guilty about killing her mate. I need proof. This is going to crush him. But first I need to know that my child is safe."

She speed-dialed Kiesha's house number. They should be back from their honeymoon by now. Hopefully Alex would answer. Luck was with her. After three rings Alex picked up the phone. "Shay, I'll get Kiesha for you, but first, how are things?"

"Actually it's you I called to speak to, Alex." She plucked at the blind.

"Oh, what's wrong? You don't sound like your normal self." In the background she heard Kiesha call out, "Is that Shay?"

That put a faint smile on her face. "I have a bit of a situation. I need you to check and make sure everything's okay with my pregnancy. I'd come there, but Rory went to Fort Knox to pick up my vehicle, leaving me without transpo. I could call someone to bring me to you, but I'd rather no one know."

"Don't the Sparrowhawks have a midwife?" Alex asked.

"Yes." She left it to Alex to read between the lines.

"I see." He was silent. Miracle of miracles, even Kiesha was silent. "I'll be there as soon as I can."

"Thanks, Alex. Make sure you bring Kee."

He snorted. "As if she'd let me leave her behind." In a heavier tone, he added, "Shay, when I get there, I want to know what's going on. You're family."

"I'll tell you, both of you, when you arrive. Oh, and I went and had an initial workup done with Carol while you were gone. In case you need my chart or anything."

"Yes, that will help. What exactly am I looking for, Shay?"

"I'll tell you when you get here." She disconnected the call.

Kian tapped her shoulder to get her attention. *Alex Wolfe, alpha of the Raven pack?*

Shay didn't catch every word, but she got the general understanding of the question. "Yes, he's mated—married—to my cousin Kiesha."

His expression was dubious.

"Alex and Rory are friends. Have been ever since Shannon joined the Raven pack. More importantly he's a doctor. If he says the baby's fine, then she is."

She?

"Yes. I'm sure it's a girl."

Unlike Rory, Kian didn't immediately disagree. He simply stared at her bump.

"I need to call Shannon," she said and suited actions to words.

Kian shifted, his expression changing to one of unease.

"What?"

She's scared of me.

"She's your sister. I don't think you McFelans know the meaning of fear. She probably thinks you don't like her, and is wary as a result," Shay said before she switched her attention to Shannon, who'd just answered.

"Shay, what's going on?" she asked cheerfully.

"Trouble. I need a family powwow. Alex and Kee are coming. Can you come, and bring Nikolai?"

Shannon covered the phone, murmured something to her mate, and his deep voice answered before she came back on line. "We'll be there. Where's my brother? I don't hear him in the background."

"Which one? Kian's here. Rory's in Fort Knox," Shay said, looking Kian in the eyes.

"*You've met Kian*?"

"Yes," Shay stated with a hint of impatience. "We had breakfast together."

"He came out of his room and *ate* with you?" There was astonishment in Shannon's voice and maybe a tinge of jealousy.

"Yes," Shay said again, a little less annoyed. "We're all one big happy family now. See you when you get here." She clicked the phone off and tossed it on the bed. "You're not planning on making a liar out of me, are you? You will stick around for the meeting?"

He considered for a moment. Shay could tell he was weighing the pros and cons.

"I need someone on my side. Laurie Bell comes off as so nice and friendly I might have difficulty convincing them on my own," Shay said, although it wasn't exactly true. Kiesha would believe her. Alex might question, but he'd have no reason to go against her. It was Shannon and Rory she was concerned about.

Kian gave one short nod.

What about Caleb?

"What about him?" she asked, puzzled.

As Rory's second, he should be here helping with any plan of action you formulate.

Shay considered. "You trust him?"

He's a good man. Honorable.

"All right. I'll call and ask him to come over."

You still need to call Rory.

"Fine, but I'm not telling him about Laurie Bell. Not yet." First she called Caleb and told him she'd invited a few people over for a late lunch and asked him to join them. Once she had his agreement, she called her mate.

He answered the phone with, "Is everything okay?"

"All good on my end. I had breakfast with your brother."

"*Kian*?"

Shay's brow furrowed. "You have another one you didn't tell me about?"

"No, I just…never mind. Okay, so you two had breakfast. That's good. What's wrong? You sound strange."

Shay closed her eyes and forced herself to think cheerful, happy thoughts so her upset wouldn't show in her tone. "Nothing. Just called to warn you I invited Alex and Kee, and Shannon and Nik over to the house. They should be here when you return. Have any idea when that will be?"

Rory groaned. "Shay, you know your cousin wants my liver on a platter. How could you do this to me?"

He sounded so pitiable Shay couldn't help but laugh. "Just be your normal, charming self and Kee will get over her dislike," she said, tongue in cheek.

He sighed heavily. "I should be home in another two and a half hours. Haggling over the price didn't take as long as I thought. I'm just waiting on the last of the paperwork so I can leave. Riley will handle the rest of the maintenance work."

"Great," she said, relieved to know he was on his way home. "Now who around here can I call to deliver enough food to feed three hungry male shifters and two pregnant women?"

"Sam's Rib Shack. The number's online. Call him and tell him you need five slabs of ribs with all the trimmings for a meet up. He'll put it on the pack's tab. Or you can call Caleb and ask him to handle the arrangements. Sam's delivers. Look, I gotta go. The insurance binder just came through. See you soon."

"Okay. Be careful," she said, reluctant to let him go.

"I will."

Shay held the phone until the dial tone sounded in her ear. "It's all coming together," she told Kian.

He studied her, expression intent. *You have a plan?*

She frowned, hating the fact that she was so uncertain on something this important. "Maybe. I'm not sure it will work. That's where you guys come in."

What is it?

Shay bounced her ideas off Kian, trusting him to help her fine-tune her plan before presenting it to the rest of the group.

Might work.

"It better," she said determinedly. "Now while we wait for everyone to arrive, let's do something about your space."

* * * *

Caleb arrived first. Shay wasted no time roping him into helping her fix up the basement like a mini-apartment. While Kian and Caleb took Kian's king-size mattress and frame apart and reassembled it downstairs, Shay went through the house earmarking items to refurbish Kian's abode: a television, lamp, an easy chair—not Rory's—and love seat. She tried dragging a few of the heavier items to the basement entrance to make it easier on the men and got chewed out for her efforts.

"Fine, I'll stay out of the way," she said.

You show us what you want moved and we'll do it. No lifting, Kian signed.

"You are a bigger nag than Rory," she griped.

Kian smiled and winked at her. *That's what families do.*

With her own words being quoted to her, Shay could do nothing but get out of the way and let them handle things.

She made a note to purchase knickknacks, plants, area rugs, and accent mirrors to give the place a homey feel. While Kian was being so agreeable, she wished she had time to paint but knew none of the men would allow it. To feel useful, instead she found one of the rarely used bathrooms upstairs and stole the shower curtain, floor mats, and coordinating decor to fix up Kian's.

When the rest of the group arrived, literally within minutes of each other, Kian's basement retreat had been thoroughly cleaned and vacuumed and looked inviting. Best of all, Kian seemed pleased with the results.

"This doesn't mean you get to hide down here," Shayla warned Kian.

Kian smirked and nudged her up the stairs to greet her guests, going furry and four-legged before she could get the door open. Shay shook her head but didn't complain. She didn't have time. As soon as she opened the door, Shannon and Kiesha blasted her with questions.

"I'll explain everything as soon as Rory arrives," Shay told them. "Nikolai, Alex." She greeted the men with a nod as they entered.

"Explain what?" Caleb asked. "I thought this was a simple family get-together."

"So she didn't tell you either?" Alex mused. He held out a hand. "Alex Wolfe, alpha of the Raven pack." As Caleb gripped his hand, Alex continued with the introductions. "My mate, Kiesha Wolfe. You know Shannon, and this is her mate, Nikolai."

"Caleb Jones, Rory's second. We've seen each other but never officially met," Caleb said as he acknowledged each one. "Looking good, Shannon."

"Thanks, Caleb. Good to see you," Shannon said.

"That's Kian," Shay stated with a flick of her wrist to indicate the pony-sized wolf hovering in the background. "Now that the introductions are over—Alex, you brought your stuff?"

In answer he held up his medical bag in one hand and her file in the other.

"Good. Let's get this done." Shay crossed over to the stairs and headed up. Hearing too many footsteps trailing her, she stopped and turned. Behind Alex were Caleb, Kiesha, Shannon, and Kian. Only Nikolai seemed disinclined to follow. "Whoa! Back it up. Alex, you come. Kiesha, you too. Everyone else, scat."

Caleb shook his head. "While Rory's away, I'm responsible for you. Where you go, I go."

"I'm not getting a prenatal checkup with you in the room," she told him.

When he crossed his arms, a set look on his face, Shay groaned. "You werewolves are stubborn."

"Shifters," half the group corrected.

Rolling her eyes, Shay said, "Whatever. If Shannon comes with me, will that satisfy you?"

Caleb eyed Shannon thoughtfully before giving an abrupt nod.

"Okay, Shannon, you're with us. Now if we can get this over with?" She turned and started up the stairs, muttering, "Since when did doctors' visits become a group event? That's what I'd like to know."

"When you became mated to an alpha," Alex answered in a low, humor-tinged voice.

Kian came too, but somehow with him in wolf form, it was easy to overlook his presence. She headed for the master bedroom. Kian shot ahead, blocking access to the door while nudging her away from the room.

Before she could question him, Alex said, "If that's your bedroom, pick another. Rory won't be happy to have another male's scent in there."

Remembering how psycho possessive he went at the thought of Alex seeing her naked when they went to

Refuge for her first checkup, Shay swallowed hard and chose another room. No sense pushing Rory's buttons if she didn't need to. Not about something like this.

Shannon and Kiesha stood a distance away, giving Alex the room he needed to complete the exam and Shay some semblance of privacy. When finished, he jotted down a few notes in her chart, then told her, "Get dressed and come downstairs. I'll go over the results down there." Then he left the room.

The two women immediately ganged up on her. "Now tell us what all this is about," Kiesha said, and Shannon echoed with, "Yeah."

"Gee, guys, can I at least get my panties on first. Naked here," she reminded them with a glance at Kian, who immediately turned his muzzle in the opposite direction.

Fisted hands on their hips, Shannon and Kee stood side by side, an immovable mountain of female determination.

"Put your clothes on, Shay. But you're not leaving this room until we get some answers," Kiesha said.

Chapter Fifteen

Shayla narrowed her gaze at the two pains in her behind masquerading as female family members blocking the doorway. "I mean it, you two. I don't want to get into this, not without Rory here. He'll be pissed if I tell you before telling him, and he's going to be furious enough as it is," she said as she dressed.

"Tell us something," Kiesha appealed, switching from combative to pleading. "Shannon said you told her there was trouble." In a lightning-fast mood swing, Kiesha asked with a dangerous glint in her eye, "It's not Rory, is it? He's not starting with you again, is he?"

"Jeez, woman, let it go," Shannon said irritably. "You act like you and Alex never had a fight. She wouldn't be waiting for Rory to get here if he was the problem."

The two women glared at each other.

Shay sighed. "Kee, Rory loves me, and I love him. He'd be the last person to do me harm." She sat on the bed to tug on her socks and tennis shoes.

"Someone in the pack wants to hurt you?" Trust Shannon to latch on.

"Who?" Kiesha demanded.

She studied the both of them. They weren't going to quit unless she gave them something. And as crazy as they both could make her, she loved them. If the situation were reversed, she knew she'd be just as determined to get answers. "All right, all right. Sit down."

Shay waited while they relocated to the bed, both of them perching tensely on the mattress. Mentally she sifted through and decided what she could tell them. "At your wedding reception, Conor gave me a warning. You know how he is, Kee. He sees stuff. Usually he's dead on the mark," she added for Shannon and Kian's benefit.

Shay repeated Conor's warning without flourish.

Kiesha shot to her feet. "What! And you didn't tell me?"

"That's why you asked all those questions about the pack," Shannon stated.

"Yes. Though I would have wanted to know what I was walking into anyway, his warning gave me more incentive to learn," Shay said in response to Shannon. To Kee she said, "My pack. My problem."

"Spoken like a true alpha-fem," Shannon murmured, smiling in approval.

"Screw that! If you get yourself killed dealing with these yahoos, then it's mine. We're family. If they don't like it, tough. They'll just have to deal." Kiesha's face was flushed, and she breathed heavily.

"Kee, take a seat and calm down before Alex comes storming up here to see what the problem is," Shay clipped out. She refused to continue until Kiesha complied; then she said, "Kian and I now know one person behind the threat to my children. I've hopefully come up with a plan to flush the rest out."

"Who is it?" they both demanded.

"Unh-huh." Shay shook her head. "That's all you get until Rory arrives."

Both women argued and cajoled, but Shay refused to budge. Finally Shannon asked, “How soon do you expect him?”

“Not for another hour.”

Both Kiesha’s eyebrows shot up to her hairline, and her mouth dropped open. “An hour! You expect me to wait that long?”

“What are we supposed to do in the meantime?” Shannon asked.

“First, I’m going downstairs to get the results of Alex’s exam. When that’s done, you two can go shopping with me.” Shay strode for the door.

“Shopping!” they echoed.

Shay stopped at the door and turned with a grin, knowing she’d shocked them. “Yes. Kian’s allowed me to fix up his space, but he needs more stuff. I want to get it done before he changes his mind.”

All three women turned to look at the huge black wolf sitting quietly, watching them.

“Shopping,” Shannon mused.

Still staring at Kian, Kiesha said, “I’m down with that.”

Of course it wasn’t that simple.

The men were sprawled in various poses of relaxation, watching some type of sport on the big-screen. As soon as Shay appeared, Alex muted the sound. Kiesha crossed over to sit near her mate, and Shannon did the same with Nikolai. Shayla took her seat in Rory’s favorite armchair, and Caleb rose to take guard position near and slightly behind her right shoulder. Kian stretched out on the floor at her feet.

Inwardly rolling her eyes at her self-appointed bodyguards' behavior, she said to Alex, "Well?"

"It would help if I knew what you were looking for," Alex said in a tone of polite inquiry.

"Tell me what you found," Shay insisted.

Frowning, he said, "Your pregnancy is progressing more like a shifter than a human, which I'm sure Carol already told you. Other than that, everything looks normal."

"You're certain?" Shay pushed, needing to be sure.

Eyes narrowed in concern, he reiterated, "Yes. Now what's this about?"

"Hold up. What does that mean, progressing like a shifter?" Kiesha asked.

"It means shifter females have a shorter gestation period than human women. At the rate Shayla's progressing, even though you conceived before her, you'll be delivering around the same time," Alex explained.

"Have you told Auntie Yona?" Kee asked.

Shay's eyes widened. "Have you lost your mind?" she asked.

"Shay, you have to tell her," Kee fussed.

"I will." *Eventually.*

"What I want to know is why you didn't call Laurie Bell to check you out. She's the pack's midwife," Caleb stated.

When Shay glanced over her shoulder at him, she could tell he was displeased. Tough. "Alex is family."

"Pack is family," Caleb argued.

"I'd still like to know what this is about," Alex stated.

"And I'll be happy to tell you, after Rory arrives. Now, Shannon, Kiesha, and I are going shopping," Shay told the men as she stood.

"Shopping?" Caleb asked. "Does Rory know about this?"

"Rory's my mate, not my keeper. I don't have to report my every movement to him," Shay said, frowning.

"You're right. Which store are we going to?" Caleb asked.

"*We're* not going anywhere. I'm going with my two friends," Shayla said.

Caleb was shaking his head before she finished. "You don't have to report your every movement to him, but I do. Rory's not here, which means I'm your shadow until he returns."

She opened her mouth to argue, but the sight of Alex and Nikolai rising halted the words before they formed. "Where—"

"Where she goes, I go," Alex answered, pointing at Kiesha.

Shay turned to Nikolai. When he merely smiled, she gave up. She glanced down at Kian. "I suppose you're coming too?"

Kian shook his muzzle. Shay was getting used to having a wolf respond like a human.

"Fine! The one person that has a valid reason to ride doesn't want to. All right, if we're going, let's go," she ordered.

* * * *

The trip to the nearby dollar store took less than a half an hour. When they returned, the men couldn't simply let the women hang the pictures. No, they had to pull out measuring tapes and tap for studs. God forbid the females hurt themselves doing such dangerous activities. In retaliation the women hassled and teased the men. They were laughing and having fun when Shay heard Rory's truck pull into the yard.

It was a measure of her distraction that Shay didn't notice Kian disappear from the basement. He'd been doing so off and on the entire time everyone was present. Shay marked it down to Kian being a loner.

"Shayla!" Her name was roared loud enough to rattle the windows.

Realization hit. "Kian, you traitor! I told you not to say anything!"

Shay flew up the stairs and ran headlong into Rory at the door of the basement. He gripped her by the arms, snatched her off her feet, and gave her a shake. "*Why the hell didn't you call me*?"

"Take your hands off her, you bastard! She's pregnant. You can't be shaking her," Kiesha hollered, coming up the stairs behind her.

"Kee, this is mate business. Stay out of it." Alex's voice drifted up the stairwell.

"I'm fine," she said to Kiesha. "We're fine," she told Rory in a softer voice, cupping his face gently.

Rory pulled her close into a bear hug. He literally shook in her arms. "She could have killed the babe, and it would have been my fault."

"Shhh. She didn't, so stop talking stupid." Shay rubbed his back, nuzzled his cheek, and held him until he calmed. She understood his fear. She'd been frantic when she'd first found out, but now that Alex had verified everything was okay, she'd settled.

"We're blocking the doorway," she told him when the shaking stopped.

He backed farther into the kitchen, then slowly lowered her to the floor. His gaze staring calmly into hers, he said in a cold voice, "She's dead."

Knowing better than to argue with him when he was in alpha protective mode, Shay merely nodded. She'd talk to him about it later when he wasn't as furious.

"He's here now," Shannon said from behind her. "Tell us why you called us all together."

Shay motioned everyone into the living room. Caleb, in his role as the alphas' protector, lagged after. "The food?" she asked him.

"Should be here in another thirty minutes or so. I estimated for Rory's arrival," Caleb said. In his eyes she saw a curiosity as great as the others.

Rory all but carried Shay into the living room. He plopped down in his recliner and pulled her sideways across his lap. Kiesha, Alex, and Caleb claimed the couch, Shannon and Nikolai the love seat, and Kian slunk in, ears and tail low, and stretched out on the floor.

"You are so busted, Mister," she told the wolf.

He lowered his muzzle to the floor and placed one paw over his eyes. Shay bit back a smile at his antics.

"Leave my brother alone. At least one of you knew the right thing to do," Rory drawled. "Are you sure the babe's fine?" He placed a hand over her stomach and rubbed it in a circle.

Understanding his need for reassurance, Shay glanced at Alex and said, "Alex, you tell him."

"She's healthy. Her pregnancy is progressing at a nice, if accelerated rate," Alex assured him. Then he pinned Shayla with a steely-eyed gaze and said, "Now that your mate is here, will you be so kind as to tell me what this is all about?"

"You didn't tell him?" Rory asked.

Kiesha rolled her eyes. "She refused to tell anyone anything until you got here."

"Well now, thank you for waiting," Rory said, sounding mildly satisfied. "Go ahead and tell them."

With Rory's permission, Shay told the group about the tea she'd been drinking and what she'd discovered about the ingredients.

"Shay, I told you all that herbal stuff can be dangerous. It's not regulated the way medicine is and while I know you're extremely knowledgeable, some things you need to leave to the professionals," Kee said.

Her cousin Kiesha was a traditional sort of gal. She preferred pharmaceuticals over natural remedies. She also preferred junk food to the healthy stuff, but that was another issue altogether.

Alex was a bit quicker on the uptake. "Someone gave you the tea, hoping you'd miscarry," he guessed quietly. "That's why you insisted I come."

"Who would do such a thing?" her cousin asked, horrified.

Caleb stiffened and leaned forward out of his formerly relaxed but watchful pose. "Laurie Bell."

"Aye," Rory all but snarled.

"*Laurie Bell?*" Shannon's voice was high, filled with disbelief.

"Who's Laurie Bell?" Kiesha asked.

"The pack's midwife," Alex answered.

Shay laid her head on Rory's shoulder, and he stroked her back in a gentle caress. She wasn't sure which one of them the gesture was meant to calm—him or her.

"But that's—" Shannon sputtered.

Shay shared a glance with Kian. "Kian said she hates you—all of you—and always has."

Kian's gaze flicked past hers to Rory's, and Shay had the sense that they were communicating.

"Kian warned me and Da about her, but we never listened. Thought his dislike of the pack was skewing his perception. I'm sorry," Rory said to his brother. To the rest of them he said, "It didn't seem possible, and after my mother died, well, Laurie Bell was a great help. Almost a surrogate mother. She definitely smoothed my transition to alpha."

"And you felt guilty for killing her mate," Shay added.

"Why?" Caleb asked. "It was a fair challenge. He knew the potential outcome, even insisted on it. Why should you feel guilty for giving the man exactly what he asked for?"

"We outlawed death challenges a long time ago, but even so, there are times when you aren't given a choice," Alex said. "It's the nature of the beast."

"But I don't understand. Why would Laurie Bell do such a thing?" Shannon burst out. Nikolai pulled her closer to him and stroked her arm in a comforting manner.

"A woman scorned," Shay murmured.

They all looked at her.

"What did you say, Shay?" Rory asked.

"A woman scorned," she repeated a bit louder. "You know the saying, 'Hell hath no fury like a woman scorned.'"

"That doesn't make any sense," Shannon stated.

Shay shrugged. "It makes perfect sense to me. Rory told me Laurie Bell was raised with the expectation she and your father would mate. Can you imagine how she felt being tossed over, and for a lowly omega?"

Shannon scoffed. "Shay, everyone knows my father mated my mother because she was pregnant. Besides, he was a right bastard. Who would want him?"

Shay shook her head. "I don't believe that. I think what really happened is your father impregnated your mother because he wanted to mate with her."

There was a stunned silence in the room.

"I'm feeling a little lost here," Kiesha admitted. "Could you go back to the beginning for those of us who don't have a clue what you're talking about and explain?"

Very aware of Rory's silence behind her, Shayla explained her thought process. "When explaining the history of this house and its occupants, Rory mentioned that not only the alphas, but at one time the betas and members of the council used to live here. He said his father and Laurie Bell grew up together under this very roof, and it was always understood the two of them would mate."

Shay looked at Shannon, who appeared pale and shaky. "Shannon, you're the one who explained how shifter males valued strength in a female. The stronger the female, the stronger the pups," she reminded.

"Yes," Shannon agreed with a slow nod.

"So, that being the case, your father mating your mother because she accidentally got pregnant never made sense to me. She was a shifter. From what I've learned, shifter females can only get pregnant while they're in heat. Your father could have easily avoided her during this time if he'd really wanted to. Correct?"

Shay paused for a moment to let that sink in, still aware of Rory sitting entirely too still and quiet. "I think what happened is your parents fell in love. Maybe it started out as a casual fuck on his part, but something about her captured him. He knew his father, hell, the entire pack would never accept your mother as their future alpha's mate unless he had a pretty compelling reason so…"

"He got her pregnant, knowing how shifters feel about bastard children," Kiesha concluded.

"That's my take," Shay said in agreement.

"With twin boys," Shannon added. From her expression, Shannon was beginning to agree with Shay's analysis of the situation.

"Rory and Caleb will have to confirm if I'm right, but I'd imagine with the pack's mortality rate being what it is, your mother being a proven breeder would have given her instant status," Shay commented.

"It did for a while," Rory mused.

"But it wasn't enough," Shannon added. "Ma was always having to prove herself, prove she was worthy of being alpha-fem. The pack never fully accepted her as my father's equal, or his mate."

"How much you want to bet Laurie Bell kept things stirred up? Nothing that could be traced back to her. Just a few seeds of doubt planted here and there." When no one commented, she continued, "Again, this is all speculation on my part."

"It's a good theory and would explain much," Nikolai said.

"So what do we do now?" Kiesha asked. "I hope you plan to fry the bitch." She placed a protective hand over her rounded belly, and Alex's hand covered hers. Her expression showed her horror at the thought of anyone trying to harm her unborn child.

"I'll handle it," Rory said in a tone that said the issue was closed.

"Dead woman walking," Caleb said in an undertone.

"No," Shay disagreed, glaring at her mate. "We'll handle it together. My biggest concern is that she may not be the only threat."

That started another round of questions, this time from the men in the room. Ignoring the others, Shay kept her gaze on Rory's until he finally nodded. "We'll handle it."

She gave him a small smile. "Right answer."

Her phone vibrated in her pocket. The e-mail she'd been waiting for from the herbalist was in her in-box. "Kiesha, Shannon, tell Alex, Nikolai, and Caleb what Conor told me," she instructed as she opened the e-mail.

She vaguely heard Nikolai say in a grim voice, "Conor's involved in this?"

"What's that?" Rory murmured.

Turning the small screen where he could view it to, Shay said, "The herbs in the tea."

As Rory read, his hazel eyes sparkled with gold. A flush rose from his neck to fill his face. His gaze lifted from the screen. "You know I won't let her live for this insult. Don't even think of trying to talk me out of killing her. She threatened you, our child. Pack law allows me to exterminate her."

"You're alpha. You make the law," Shayla reminded him.

He bared his teeth. "Exactly."

Shay judged the others' conversation to be winding down, and handed her phone to Alex. "These are the herbs she placed in the tea." The herbalist had listed each ingredient and its effect on her pregnancy.

After reading the screen, Alex said, "She's canny. The mixture she gave you would have taken time to take effect, long enough that no one would have suspected her of being the cause. One of these herbs increases blood flow. There's a good possibility you would have bled out if help wasn't rendered in time."

"And in a crisis situation, we'd have called for the nearest medical personnel—Laurie Bell—leaving her on hand to ensure the results she desired," Shay said.

Shannon shook her head. "Say she did manage to kill you and the baby, Shay. What would be the purpose? What satisfaction could she possibly gain?"

It was Caleb who answered. "With you gone and Shay dead, Laurie Bell would once more be the most powerful female in the pack."

Could it really be that simple?

"All this to be top dog?" Kiesha asked in disbelief, then sheepishly added when Alex fired her a warning look, "No pun intended."

"It's possible," Shay answered, considering it. "Think about it. As...Magnus?" Shay shot a questioning glance at Rory to make sure she had the name right. When he nodded, she continued, "As Magnus's mate, she'd have been alpha-fem. When he mated your mother instead, she settled for second best, Magnus's beta. Being the pack's healer gives her a certain amount of clout. Rory said the healer is outside of the pack hierarchy, correct?"

"That's true with all packs," Alex agreed.

"I wouldn't be surprised if Laurie Bell was behind her mate's decision to fight for the position of alpha. Had he won, she would have stepped up to her rightful place, the one stolen by your mother," Shay said.

"That's a whole lot of evil attributed to one person," Kiesha said, her tone and the frown on her face showing her doubts.

"Women and men have done less for power," Nikolai reminded.

"All this is interesting conjecture, but what if you're wrong?" Caleb asked.

"I guess I'll just have to ask Laurie Bell why she did it," Shayla answered smartly.

Rory gripped Shay's chin and turned her face toward him. "You won't be getting close enough to Laurie Bell to ask her anything."

"Of course I will," Shay countered. "We have to continue on as normal, like we don't know."

"No." Very firm. Very final.

"Rory, be reasonable and think for a moment. I'm all for pack justice, but you can't just kill the woman, not without proof. She's damn good at what she's doing. She's the pack healer, for God's sake. She has almost as much, if not more, clout than you. Who's going to believe she intentionally tried to harm our child? By your own admission, Kian's known her true nature for years and no one believed him when he tried to warn you. You think the pack will believe you?" Shay asked, her eyes gazing appealingly into his.

Rory opened his mouth to answer, but she continued, pressing her point. "Some might, but there'll always be this question in their mind. This fear. Worse, you'll undo everything you spent these last years trying to build."

Eyes narrowed, a hint of gold around the pupils, he said, "Fuck the pack."

Shay shook her head and cupped his clenched cheek. "You say that now because you're angry and frustrated, but you also know I'm right."

He growled low and fierce, the sound rumbling through his chest. The gold edged out a little more of the hazel.

"We need to trap her. Force her into showing her true face, not only to us but to the pack," Shay finished.

"And how do you propose to do that?" Caleb asked. As the man most responsible for the alphas' safety, of course he'd want to know.

Shay's gaze was measuring, watching closely to see his reaction to her coming question. "Rory, do you trust Caleb?"

"Shay!" Kiesha protested.

"Aye, with both our lives." Rory's answer came swift, with no hesitation or qualifications.

Caleb's eyes crinkled with suppressed humor, and the corners of his mouth tilted up ever so slightly. "Shay, I have no desire to rule. I'm content where I am. Besides, if something happened to Rory, I'm not the one the pack would look to for leadership." He glanced pointedly at Kian, who showed no reaction to Caleb's claim.

Shay allowed a small smile to appear. "I thought so, but it doesn't hurt to be sure. Okay, first I think we should let Ms. Thing believe her plan is working. I'm sure half the pack knows you guys are here. Caleb, maybe you could let it leak that Alex examined me and is concerned about the progress of my pregnancy."

Rory's body turned to granite beneath her. "Not just no, but hell no. You will not set yourself up as bait."

Shay turned so they were face-to-face. "You know this is the only way. Conor said our enemies were treacherous. They won't come against us openly, so we'll have to outtrick them."

If possible, his face got even harder. His eyes were a brilliant gold now. "I said no. I forbid it!"

As his words sank in, her eyes popped wide open, then narrowed to dangerous slits. "What did you say?" she asked in an oh-too-soft voice.

"Oh shit, he's done it now," someone—probably Kiesha—exclaimed.

"I said I forbid it," Rory reiterated, a hint of belligerence in his tone. The pinprick of claws dug into her thighs.

Someone, a male, groaned. Shay ignored the byplay, totally focused on her mate. No one, absolutely no one dictated to her. She didn't tolerate it from her mother, and she wouldn't take it from this overgrown wolf trying to stare a hole into her.

Though her hands balled into fists in her lap, Shay forced her expression to show only the mildest hint of curiosity as she blandly asked, "Is that right?"

"Aye. That's what I said," he answered in a voice gone wolf.

“Ah, Rory? You might want to rethink that. Shay doesn’t respond well to orders,” Kiesha offered helpfully.

“She’ll bloody well follow mine.”

Out of the corner of her eye, Shay saw Caleb shake his head. His gaze flitted from Shay to Rory and back again. “Bro, if I were you, I’d sleep tonight with one eye open—in a different room.”

A tense silence fell as everyone watched the staring contest between her and Rory. No one moved. It didn’t even sound as if they breathed.

The doorbell rang, its loud, jubilant tones striking a discordant note.

“Food’s here,” Caleb announced, sounding relieved.

Chapter Sixteen

Rory took a calming breath and then eyed his furious mate. Her wolf had submitted to his dominance, but her human half needed to recognize his authority. As much as he loved her feisty nature, when it came to her safety and that of their children, he would not bend. Shay would obey him in this.

He allowed her to give him the cold shoulder and tolerated her snipes when forced to address a comment to him. Simply biding his time. She was safe. That's all that mattered.

His heart had stopped and the blood had iced in his veins when he'd pulled into the driveway and Kian had telepathed what Laurie Bell had done. All he could think of was seeing with his own two eyes that his mate and child were safe. After that terror, Shay thought he'd allow her to blithely put herself in the line of fire again?

What if Laurie Bell decided to use a more direct method? Shay was such a fierce little thing, with plenty of heart, but she was going up against wolves in human clothing. Compared to Laurie Bell, Shay was fragile.

Rory had no illusions. It was only his presence, his protection that kept others from coming after her. Shay was human. Humans were prey. Touching his mate meant an instant death sentence. He knew it. The pack knew it. But they also knew killing Shay would kill him. There were some in his pack bloodthirsty and power hungry enough to take the risk.

As they moved the gathering to the dining room and settled down to a meal of ribs, slow-roasted pulled pork, baked beans, corn on the cob, coleslaw, and garlic toast, Rory watched his fuming mate pick at her food. If there'd been any question in his mind, any doubt about the validity of his feelings for Shay, they were now gone. He even loved the crazy woman when she was in a snit.

They spent hours relaxing over their meal and though he'd enjoyed their company, it was time for his guests to leave. When the women rose to clear the table and put away the leftovers, Rory signaled the men his need of privacy with his mate.

Caleb left first, citing a previous engagement for which he was late. Rory smelled it for the lie it was. Fortunately Shay's senses weren't as keenly developed, or she was distracted by her conversation with Kiesha.

Nikolai must have telepathed Shannon, for she cut off midsentence in whatever she was saying, shooting a startled glance at her mate, then a wary one at him. "Nikolai's ready to leave. I'll call you tomorrow," she told Shayla.

"You sure you don't want any of this food? There's plenty." Shay indicated all the plastic containers being placed in the fridge.

"No, we're fine."

"All right. See you later. Don't be a stranger," Shayla said.

"We need to be going too," Alex said.

"Oh, but—" Kiesha began.

"It's getting late. We both have work tomorrow and a long drive ahead of us," Alex stated, giving her a meaningful look.

Kiesha pouted a bit, then said, "Let me finish helping Shay with this stuff. Then we can go."

Alex motioned Rory out the room and over to the living room door. "It should go without saying, but in case you didn't know, we're family now. More than that, we're friends. Your mate's blood kin to mine. You trusted your sister to my keeping, and now she's a valued member of my pack. Screw interpack politics. You need anything, *anything*," he stressed, "call and we'll come running. Friends watch each other's backs."

Rory mused on that a moment. Friends? He guessed they were. "I'll do that." Rory stuck out his hand. Alex clasped it hard and held. More than a handshake, it was an acknowledgment of the bond between them. A bond cemented by the women in their lives.

After Kiesha and Alex left, Kian took one look at Rory's face and disappeared. But Rory was sure he'd return. Rory didn't know what magic Shay had worked in his absence to pull his brother out of his shell, but he was glad to have his twin back.

Rory made sure the house was locked up good and tight, then followed his mate to their room. She had her laptop on her lap and seemed very intent on whatever was on the screen.

"Shayla."

No response.

"Shayla." This time Rory put a little force behind it.

"What?" Eyes that sparked fire glared at him over the top of the monitor.

"You are the air in my lungs, the very blood in my veins. There is nothing, absolutely nothing I wouldn't do to please you. But"—he captured her gaze with his and held it hostage—"when it comes to your safety and that of our children, I will be obeyed. Completely and totally," he finished in a firm tone that brooked no argument.

Shay's expression went from anger, to a blooming flush of pleasure, to something indescribable as he finished his statement. His gaze dominated hers until after a long, silent, tension-filled minute, Shay capitulated by looking away first.

He continued to stare at her, his will an invisible but weighty force.

"In matters of our safety," she reluctantly agreed.

He crawled onto the bed beside her. "Shay, don't you realize you hold both of our lives in your hands? Do you think after having known you, after loving you, I could live without you?"

"I..." Through the bond he felt her need for independence war with his need for her. Love decided the battle, and she surrendered. "I know. You're right. I love you too. I'd go crazy if something happened to you. I just want this over and done with. I want us to move forward with our lives without any threat to me or our child."

He pulled her close to him. Shay caught the laptop before it could fall off the bed, shut it down, and set it to the side on the floor. Once it was safely out of the way, she snuggled close and rested her head on his chest.

"I thought about what you said," Rory said as he stroked her hair.

"About?"

"About the damage it would do to the pack if I killed Laurie Bell," he said.

"Not to mention the difficulty of hiding the body. You can't just make people disappear like in the old days before computers," Shay added.

He chuckled at her naïveté. "Shay, people go missing every day. The law is the least of my worries. Besides, it's not like there'd be anything left of her to find."

She tilted her head back to look at him, eyes rounded in shock, mouth gaping.

Using the tip of his finger under her chin to close her jaw, he continued with what he was saying. "I wanted to modernize the pack, so we'll try doing this the human way first."

Still looking a bit shocky, she asked, "And if that doesn't work?"

"Then she dies."

Shay stared for another moment, then shook her head and sighed. "As much as I like the picture you plant in my mind of her being eaten"—he flashed a brief grin—"dying's too good for her. I want Laurie Bell to suffer and suffer hard for every second of panic she put me through. I want to find out what she desires most in life and take it from her. I want to watch her beg and plead until her tears turn to blood. Then I want to make her really pay," she finished in a growl, golden sparks lightening her eyes.

Bloodthirsty, vicious, full of vengeance, and all mine. His smile, when it appeared this time, was slow and full of promise. "I think I can manage that."

With one accord, they brainstormed the rest of the night.

* * * *

Ashley knelt on the bed, facedown, ass high, arms outstretched and bound. Michael mounted her from behind. The first surge of his cock was deep, hard, and punishing. The second took him in to the hilt. He alternated thrusts with stinging, openhanded blows to her hips that set her pussy ablaze.

The rougher he got, the more she loved it. She was addicted to his brand of dominance. Though she told herself she was still in control, deep inside she knew she'd crawl over broken glass if Michael beckoned.

She clenched her vaginal muscles, smiling into the pillow when he groaned, then praised, "Such a sweet little pussy. You like the way I fuck it, don't you, little girl?"

"Yes, alpha," she gasped.

"Beg me to fuck you," he commanded.

"Fuck me," she parroted.

He stopped, going motionless. She whimpered and pushed back with her hips.

"Say it like you mean it," he ordered.

"Damn you! Fuck me!" she screamed.

He laughed, a cold, cruel, mocking sound. Then he began to move. "Later I'll do something about that dirty, disobedient mouth of yours."

Punishment. A shiver of delight slithered down her spine, shaking her body, and caused her pussy to spasm.

"Oh yeah. You like that. You're a good little bitch." He spread her butt cheeks. "Look at the way your pretty pink pussy swallows my cock, leaving it all wet and shiny."

Ashley clenched her inner muscles again, trying to lock him to her. She'd never had a man like Michael. One that knew how to turn her body inside out and make her crave it. With him the lines between pain and pleasure burned in an ecstasy so sweet. She'd laid a trap for him, but she was the one ensnared.

He placed a hand between her shoulder blades and pushed down. She obediently lowered her cheek to the mattress, her nipples rubbing back and forth against the sheet. This new angle allowed him to plunge deeper. He thrust harder, faster, until he pounded into her. Sounds of flesh smacking together and wet suctioning with each withdrawal filled the air.

"Please please please," she begged. She was so close to the edge.

"Don't come," he ordered.

Ashley hung there at the pinnacle with every nerve ending screaming for release.

Michael reached a hand beneath her and viciously pinched her clit, ordering, "Now!"

She screamed as she erupted, coming so violently consciousness faded for a few brief seconds. Vaguely Ashley was aware of Michael drilling into her to the hilt, then grinding his pelvis against her ass as his cock pulsed and jerked in release.

Her breath shuddered. Aftershocks rocked her body. When he withdrew, she whimpered and her vaginal muscles tightened convulsively, trying to contain him.

Michael laughed and ran a soothing hand down her flank. "Such a greedy cunt."

He leaned forward and loosened the bindings. Ashley held her position, though every muscle quivered with the effort.

"Good girl. You can move," he said.

She immediately straightened her legs and eased onto her stomach, allowing tense muscles to stretch and relax before rolling to her side.

Michael had the lazy-eyed look of a man whose sexual appetite had been recently sated.

Ashley turned onto her back, spread her legs to draw attention to her sex, and raised her arms above her head, gracefully arching her spine in a languid stretch.

As planned, Michael's heavy-lidded gaze traveled from her breasts to her mound. He quirked an eyebrow. "More?"

She slid her hands down her torso, paused briefly to tweak her nipples, then rested one hand on her stomach while the other continued south. Ashley spread her legs wide, opening herself completely to his view, rubbing gently at her vulva before easing her middle finger inside her tender, swollen vagina. As he watched, a growing hunger on his face, she finger fucked herself.

When his cock hardened and he rose to his knees in preparation for mounting her, she withdrew her digit and slid gracefully off the bed. Eyes on him, she sucked the juice off her finger. "I have to go. Class in the morning."

His eyes narrowed. Inwardly she smiled. Power games. He might control her body, but she made sure she kept him wanting, kept him hungering. He gave a short nod. Ashley turned to walk out the room, feeling Michael trail behind her.

At the door he spun her around, lifted her by the thighs, and impaled her. Their fucking was fast and furious. Ashley clawed his shoulders and back. Michael's eyes changed around the edges, going wolf. The first sign she'd ever seen that he wasn't totally in control. Even as she thought how she could take that, use it, he gave a final jerk of the hips and pulled out, leaving her unsatisfied.

"Be careful who you tease, little girl," he warned. Seconds later she stood on the stoop staring at a closed door.

Damn it! What will it take to break that iron control of his?

Ashley shifted and loped the two and half miles to her small place. She lived in one of the efficiency cabins owned by the pack, cleaning the lodge and cabin rentals in lieu of paying rent. Though dark, there was still a spattering of humans, tourists mostly, out and about, so she crept up to her rear door, which faced the woods, shifted, then slipped inside.

The blow sent her sprawling. A growl sounded as her wolf came to the surface, ready to defend.

"Whore! You've been with MacDougal. I can smell him all over you." An irate Wesley stood over her, feet planted, fists clenched.

Reining in her wolf before it could spoil all her plans, Ashley made herself whimper instead. "I had no choice. I'm doing what you told me to do." Tears sparkled in her eyes and on her lashes as she cradled her throbbing cheek.

"What *I* told you? I never told you to whore yourself," he said in a furious whisper, his face flushing an angry red in the soft night-light she'd left on.

She held out a hand as though pleading for understanding. "Alpha, Rory's denied the pack access to the house. I haven't even been allowed in to clean. Only Caleb and MacDougal know why, and Caleb's not talking." Letting her voice go soft and shaky, she added,

"I can't get you his woman if I can't get in." Then she cast her gaze to the floor and waited.

There was a long silence. She could feel the intensity of his stare as he weighed her words, his jealousy warring with his thirst for power. Wesley didn't want her as his mate, but he still considered her his and was extremely possessive. She was the first woman, the first person to recognize his greatness. She was his tool, yes, but one he didn't want anyone else playing with. Ashley knew exactly how his mind worked.

Finally he sighed, reached down, and helped her gently to her feet. "I'm sorry. I should have known you'd never betray me. Forgive me for being such a jealous beast."

Ashley slipped closer and seductively rubbed her breasts against his chest. "Alpha, you know you're the only man for me. MacDougal took an interest in me after the howl. I couldn't say no, not without causing suspicion or worse, speculation."

"You're so beautiful," he breathed. "Your body lush and firm. It's no wonder he's drawn to you." Wesley ran his hands down her flanks, reversed directions, and brought them up to her breasts, which pebbled in his hold. "I missed you," he admitted, breath becoming heavy as his lust rose.

She palmed his erection, stroking it the way he'd taught her. "No one pleases me the way you do," she said in a throaty voice.

She walked backward, towing him by the cock until her progress was halted by the futon. Sinking onto the cushion, she spread her legs wide. "Take me. I need you. It's been too long."

Greedy eyes devoured her. Wesley dropped to his knees, gripped her hard by the thighs, and plunged inside.

She moaned and gasped, uttering praises meant to stroke his ego. He didn't last long, but it was enough to stir the dying embers of the fire Michael had started.

"I came inside of you," he mumbled, cheek resting on her chest as he sought to catch his breath.

"I wanted you to. It will cover MacDougal's scent." She languidly ran her fingers through his hair, her mind busy calculating her next move. "Did anyone see you come in?"

"No, I came in the back way through the woods."

That would work in her favor.

He raised his head and looked at her. "You hadn't been by to see me. Now I know why." He was still a bit disgruntled.

Stupid of her, she admitted to herself, but she'd never expected him to come looking for her. She'd always gone to him, or they met in the woods. Fortunately she'd had her excuses already thought out. "I've missed you. Missed having your cock in my mouth," she said, casting him a shy glance. Wesley liked it when she played the timid schoolgirl.

Another jealous glare. "MacDougal didn't—"

"It's not the same," she interrupted. Truer words were never spoken from her lips. Sucking Wesley's cock was simply a means to an end. Sucking Michael's was pure pleasure.

Ashley pushed steadily on Wesley's shoulders. "Lie down. Let me..." As he lay back, she flowed over him, her intentions clear.

As she sucked his cock, Ashley admitted once again to herself that she'd miscalculated. Caught up in her obsession with Michael, she'd forgotten her main agenda and Wesley's part in it. She remembered the anger that had sent her running to Michael. So what if Wesley wanted to fuck the little human before destroying her? The human would be gone, and that's all that mattered.

Besides, she had Michael in her bed now. The thought of him made the slumbering hunger in her awaken sharply. Lifting her gaze to Wesley's, she licked her lips. His eyes followed her every movement.

"I want you again. I've missed you," she said.

"You had him," he complained.

God, had he always been this whiny? "But he isn't you," she explained, somewhat patiently, which was difficult because his attitude was severely straining her patience. "He doesn't have your experience, your expertise."

She rolled sensuously onto her back on the throw rug, pelvis tilted invitingly. "Fill me," she encouraged.

Wesley hesitated the barest of moments before covering her, his hands and mouth greedy in their possession on her flesh.

This is power. This is what woman was created for. Men only thought they were in control, but let a woman flash some tits or spread her legs, and she ruled absolute. *Men are tools to be used to get what I want. Thank you, Momma, for teaching me that truth.*

Ashley let her body work its magic while her mind plotted her next step. Wesley had once more proven himself a liability. Worse, he was slipping the leash she had on him.

How dare he strike me! Not even Laurie Bell had dared raise a hand to her, and her mother thought Ashley was as worthless as the father who'd spawned her. But soon Laurie Bell would have to eat her words. Ashley would show her mother how important she was. The whole idea of sleeping your way to the top would work.

Wesley would get rid of the alpha's mate. Ashley would then be honor bound to turn him in, resulting in instant death for the man. In his grief Rory would turn to her, and if not, Michael would make a great alpha. Ashley was sure she could convince him to take her as his mate, making her alpha-fem. And once she was the alpha's mate, she'd rub her mother's nose in the fact that her worthless daughter had managed to achieve the one thing Laurie Bell had always wanted.

Wesley hit a spot that jerked her out of her contemplation. Fully engaged, she put all thought of plotting aside and focused on reaching orgasm. When fulfillment was obtained and their breathing had calmed, Ashley said in a low voice, "Michael said I'll be allowed back in the house on Tuesdays and Fridays to clean. Give me a week to let the alpha's mate get comfortable with me; then I'll get you into the house."

Actually it was Caleb who'd told her, but Wesley didn't need to know she hadn't learned anything important from her visits with Michael.

"A week? That will be perfect. Gives me time to set up things on my end," Wesley said. "Speaking of cleaning, when are you coming back to my place?"

"I'll come Monday, same time as normal."

"Good." He stood and gazed down at her. "I'll let myself out."

"Be careful. If you're seen..." She let the warning trail off.

"I know the consequences," he muttered. "I'll be careful.

He went to the door, cracked it open, and looked out, then with a quick wave, was gone.

* * * *

It had been a scorcher of a day. Even now, as long shadows faded to night, humidity hung in the air like a moist blanket. In deference to the heat, Ashley wore a thin, dark blue tank with spaghetti straps that bared her belly button, and a faded pair of denim short cutoffs.

It had been two weeks since the incident with Wesley. Two long, frustrating weeks and she was no closer to her goal of being top bitch. She inwardly cursed her lack of progress as she made her way to the pack's gathering place, deep in the woods in the state park.

The alpha, or rather his bitch, Ashley thought bitterly, had finally allowed her to come and clean, but *only* on Tuesdays and Friday at the time *she* designated. No more coming and going whenever it pleased her, and she was restricted to the first-floor common areas like she was some criminal who couldn't be trusted around the alpha's personal items.

Ashley could have made this new schedule work to her advantage, except every time she arrived at the house, the alpha had also been present, hovering over his mate. Seemed she suffered from a severe case of morning sickness, and it left her incapacitated. Weak! This was what happened when an inferior human was allowed to mate with one of their kind. Their puny bodies couldn't handle it. The woman couldn't even shift. She deserved killing.

A trio of voices called out, "Hello, Ashley,"

She waved in greeting, pasting a bright, fake smile on her face.

As she got closer to the meeting place, she ran into more pack members. It was the night of their quarterly howl, when the Sparrowhawks came together to run and socialize as a pack. The first thirty minutes or so was devoted to pack business. Then the floor opened for members to share news or bring issues to their leaders' attention.

As a rule, howl attendance wasn't mandatory, but no one missed if it could be helped, afraid they'd miss the latest news. From the many faces she'd seen, tonight would be no exception. Their pack was small compared to others, less than one hundred total. When Ashley arrived at the clearing, a quick scan showed a little over half of their numbers were present. More were arriving by the minute.

Another glance revealed the alpha, his bitch, Caleb, and Michael had yet to arrive. Wesley and the other elders were huddled in a group, talking among themselves as normal. There were other groupings as well. Some families stood together. The young, unmated males gathered in a small group, casting the occasional lascivious glance at the unmated females, who stood in another group. Ashley went and joined the unmated females.

The mood was jovial. Numerous conversations, the occasional burst of laughter, and called-out greetings filled the night. Wolves were social creatures by nature, and there was nothing like a run with fellow pack mates at night while the moon rode high in the sky. The ability to shed their human skins and run as the animals they really were. *That* was something Rory's human mate would never know.

Full dark had fallen. The muted glow of the moon shone on the clearing as the humidity gave way to a layer of fog hovering over the treetops and no breeze of which to speak. Deep in conversation with a female adolescent she was particularly fond of, Ashley was slow to note the change of atmosphere. Little by little there was a beat of stunned silence, then a wave of hushed whispers.

"What's he doing here?"

"Who's that?"

"Is that Wolfe?"

"…alpha…Raven pack…"

"…pregnant mate…"

"Kian, my God, haven't seen him since…"

"Thought he'd left…"

The alpha had arrived, and he wasn't alone. Rory strode into the center of the clearing. Behind him was the human. But it was the ones who followed that caused the uproar. Kian, his black hair unbound, dressed in jeans and a T-shirt that clung to delineated muscles that did nothing to hide his feral nature, trailed close—almost protectively—after the human female.

Ashley was so rattled by Kian's seldom-seen appearance, she barely noted Caleb and Michael bringing up the rear. Rory took his place on the mound, in the center with the human female to his immediate left and Kian on his right. Caleb and Michael took guard position in front of the alpha pair at the base of the small rise.

Then Ashley noticed the other four. A mixed-race, pregnant female stood next to Shay. Hovering possessively on her left...was that *Alex Wolfe*, the Raven pack's alpha? No wonder the pack was uneasy.

While Ashley was still recovering from the combined shocks, Shannon strode into the clearing with a tall man with dark hair, a goatee, and the face and body of a Playboy model less than a step behind, his hand at the small of her back proclaiming his ownership. Shannon walked to Kian and stood beside him, with the male to her right.

Rory made no move to quiet the group. He let the conversations continue until gradually, silence fell. Then his voice rang out. "As you know, from the time I became alpha, I've made changes in an effort to pull this pack into the twenty-first century. Many of our old ways were outdated. Some downright illegal. If we're to thrive and grow in this new world of instant messaging, camera phones, and global networking via the Internet, we have to change."

He paused, looked around at each group assembled before him. His gaze lingered briefly on the elders before returning to the rest of the pack. "Some welcomed the changes as long overdue. Others"—again his gaze went to the elders—"fought me tooth and claw, even as they benefited from the very changes initiated."

There were some murmurs from the pack, the tone of which seemed to acknowledge Rory's statement as being valid. The council appeared outraged but, after casting a leery glance at the still-muttering pack, remained silent.

"Tonight marks another new beginning for the Sparrowhawks. Even as the wolf who stands alone dies alone, so too does the pack without allies, destined to fade into obscurity." He pointed to the Raven pack's alpha. "A few months ago, Alex Wolfe found and mated his one,

Kiesha Morgan. His one is cousin to mine, Shayla Morgan." He gestured to Shannon. "You all know my sister, Shannon. She's now a member of the Raven pack, with my full approval and blessing. Based on the blood that binds us, the Ravens and Sparrowhawks have entered into an alliance."

While the pack was adjusting to the news, Rory nodded to Alex, who howled. A chorus of howls answered him, and more than just a few. Ashley spun with the rest of the pack, looking into the surrounding forest. A multitude of glowing eyes stared back. The outline of wolves formed as they drew closer—much larger, much stronger wolves. They surrounded the Sparrowhawks. Ravens, in wolf form.

There was more nervous chattering as the Sparrowhawks defensively drew closer together.

"This is an outrage," Graham snarled, a hint of fear in his eyes.

"You made a decision without discussing it with the council? Why weren't we notified of your intentions?" Bertram asked.

Wesley looked around at the wolves, then at his nephew. His face mottled with fury.

Rory's left eyebrow arched. "I'm alpha. I discussed the issue with those who mattered—my mate, my brother, my men—before approaching Alex with the offer of an official pack alliance."

It was a verbal slap in the face.

"And I, in turn, discussed it with my mate, my second, and my elders before agreeing," Alex added.

"Where is your second?" Graham asked.

"She wasn't needed for this," Alex answered.

"*She*!" the old fart choked. Ashley rolled her eyes. The ancient wolf needed to do everyone a favor and die. She didn't care that he was her uncle.

Alex didn't bother responding, but his mate leaned over and whispered something to the human. She, in turn, rolled her eyes, then whispered something back. With their faces that close together, Ashley could see the family resemblance.

"What, exactly, do we get out of this alliance?" Bertram asked.

"More resources, more business prospects, a bigger pool of mates to hunt in. The Raven pack has medical resources we don't. Their pack's larger, stronger, more modern. It's what we're trying to become," Rory said.

At the mention of mates, all the unmated males and several of the unmated females perked up. The females looked at the surrounding males with a gleam in their eyes, and some began primping. The Ravens' males returned their looks with interest.

While hunting outside of your pack wasn't forbidden, it wasn't always strategic to do so, as pack politics tended to come into play. This new alliance with the Ravens just opened up a world of opportunity. Not that she cared. She already had her sights set on a mate.

"What are they getting out of it?" Wesley asked. "Seems like everything's weighted in our favor."

The Ravens' alpha-fem spoke up. "We get the privilege of making sure you fuckers know if you touch my cousin or her child, there'll be hell to pay."

Alex closed his eyes, a pained expression on his face. Rory and his siblings grinned. Shannon's male didn't show any reaction. He kept watching the pack, his gaze going from person to person as though looking for something. And the human? Well, she laughed.

"That's not the way I would have phrased it," Alex amended, "but what she stated is the truth. Because of our mates, Rory, Kian, Shannon, and I are family now. Their enemies are mine," he finished in a hard voice with a cold stare. Gone was the affable persona, and in its place was the alpha that ruled a pack of over two hundred.

Ashley's gut twisted, and her blood ran cold. She took in the posture of the group standing before them, shoulder to shoulder, and felt her dreams go up in smoke. Only a fool would go after the human now, and though Ashley was many things, foolish wasn't one of them.

Chapter Seventeen

As the pack dealt with Wolfe's announcement, a confusing blend of scents swept through its midst, mirroring her own—fear, confusion, dismay, a hint of anger, and a whiff of trepidation.

"Which brings me to our next order of business. Laurie Bell, please step forward," Rory requested in a mild tone, breaking the silence.

The strangeness of the request had her forgetting her own problems. Laurie Bell, her slim body encased in jeans and a white T-shirt, long hair gathered in a ponytail at her nape, pushed her way through until she stood a few feet in front of Caleb and Michael, a quizzical expression on her serene, Madonna-like face. God, just for once Ashley wished others could see behind the mask her mother wore.

Alex and the male with Shannon moved to stand slightly behind and to either side of her. Ashley's, along with every other pack member's, interest sharpened. Why had they flanked her like that, she wondered as Rory stepped past his second and third until he stood directly in front of her mother. She moved to a better position that allowed her to see her mother's expression and still keep everyone in view.

If the two men standing behind her mother perturbed Laurie Bell, it didn't show. She kept the same placid, mildly confused but agreeable expression on her face. "Yes, alpha?"

"Laurie Bell, you've been accused of a heinous crime against the pack. How do you plead?" Rory asked, his expression neutral.

Her mother tilted her head to the side, a faintly amused smile on her face even as her brows furrowed in puzzlement. "All right. What's the crime?"

"Attempted murder of the alpha pair's unborn child," he announced.

There were gasps and cries of outraged denial from the pack. Ashley whistled under her breath. Man, that was ballsy, even for her mother. *Did she really believe she wouldn't get caught? What am I thinking? Of course Laurie Bell thought she'd get away with it.*

Laurie Bell's mouth dropped open, and she brought her hand up to capture her gasp. "You're serious? Someone actually accused me of doing something so…so dreadful?" Tears welled up in those innocent-looking eyes.

"How do you plead?" Rory repeated.

"My God, you actually believe…" Her voice trailed off, and she examined the alpha's expression. He didn't crack a smile. No mercy there, Ashley thought. Her mother's gaze slid past Rory to zero in on the human. "Shay, I'm a healer. I save lives, not destroy them. You can ask any person in this pack. I would never do something so…so…" She shook her head, apparently too overcome to speak. The sheen of tears sparkled in her eyes.

Bravo, Mother, bravo! Talk about an award-winning performance. If I didn't know you to be the viper you are, I'd believe you. I can't even smell your lies.

"You plead not guilty?" Rory asked.

"Of course I'm not guilty," her mother responded, her voice containing just the right amount of injured outrage.

"What's the meaning of this? Who would dare point the finger at Laurie Bell, after all she's done and continues to do for this pack?" Uncle Graham demanded.

Questions were shouted out as the pack demanded more information. Laurie Bell was a beloved member whose legacy as a pack healer went back several generations. Ashley wasn't surprised only she, and possibly the alpha, believed her mother capable of murder, and even Ashley wasn't sure. God knew her mother was cold enough to accomplish it.

Rory ignored Graham and the others and nodded. Alex and Shannon's male stepped closer to her mother, each one grabbing one of her mother's arms, holding her immobile. Then before the pack's shocked and horrified gazes, Shannon's male bit her mother on the neck, drinking her blood.

Vampire! Shannon's male was a vampire? Shannon had mated a vamp, for there was no denying the two were mated. Ashley stood frozen with shock, watching the tableau unfold before her.

Some of the men protested and moved forward as though they would put a stop to whatever was happening. Alex snapped his fingers, and quick as a blur, there was a wall of Raven pack wolves standing in the way. Knowing they were no match for the others, the

Sparrowhawk men settled down, resorting to angry mutterings and hostile glances.

The vampire raised his head, fangs showing clearly in the moonlight. He closed his eyes and licked the few drops of ruby-red blood spotted on his lips. There was a tense silence as everyone waited to see what would happen next. Ashley didn't know much about vampires and their powers. Most of what she'd heard was probably rumor. She did know that shifters had a natural immunity to some of their more powerful psychic powers.

Suddenly her mother shrieked, "Get out of my head!"

All movement ceased. Ashley's startled gaze bounced from her mother to the vamp. *He was in her head? How was that possible?* Unless it had something to do with the blood... Ashley glanced around at the older pack members. Their gazes were somber, knowing.

"Nikolai?" Rory asked.

"Guilty as charged," Nikolai stated calmly as his eyes opened.

"You can't prove anything, you bastard! Let me go!" her mother shouted furiously, the mask beginning to crack.

Ashley heard the mutters.

"He read her mind."

"That's impossible."

"He's a vampire."

"He took her blood. Never give blood to a vamp. It gives them a path in."

"On the contrary. We have proof. We took the herbs you gave Shay to an herbalist in Fort Knox. He's the one who told us what you did," Rory said in a voice gone as cold as his expression.

There were more gasps. More whispers, but opinions were divided. The mood of the pack shifted from angry disbelief to denial and uncertainty.

"He's a liar," her mother hotly denied. "I'd never do such a thing." Laurie Bell glanced at the council, the pack. "You know me. I delivered most of you, doctored the rest. There's been a mistake." She turned back to Rory.

"It's no mistake," he said in a flat voice. "You own a shop. You knew what that particular blend of herbs would do to Shay's body, to the babe."

Oh God, this was awesome. Damn, all she needed was popcorn. It was about damn time someone else knew what her mother was capable of. Ashley felt the gazes of others searching her reaction to the unfolding events. Seeing what she knew, if she knew anything at all. She held in a smile, struggling to look as horrified and stunned as the rest.

"I want to know why." The human's quiet voice cut like a knife through the uproar that had risen at Rory's words.

"Why what? I didn't *do* anything," Laurie Bell protested. "Shayla, I know you're new here, but believe me, this is all a terrible mistake. I'm a woman, a mother. A midwife, for God's sake. Bringing healthy children into the world is what I do."

The human stared at her out of a face set in stone. *No sympathy there, either, Mother.*

Laurie Bell glanced around wildly. "Why aren't you listening to me?"

"I'd also like to know why," Shannon stated. "Nikolai, can you…?"

All eyes turned toward Nikolai. He nodded. Then his eyes lost focus.

Her mother began struggling. "Stay out of my head!"

"She's fighting me," he said to Rory in a low voice that still managed to carry. "I need to get in front of her."

"Kian," Rory called.

Kian left Shayla's side, stalked toward Laurie Bell like the predator he was, and grabbed hold of her arm. From the way the muscles in his arms bunched, Ashley would bet money that his hold was painful. Nikolai joined Rory in front of her mother. As he stared into her eyes, her mother screamed her rage. Her eyes changed and jaw elongated. The scream morphed into a deep-throated growl.

"She's trying to shift," Alex warned.

Nikolai's eyes flashed red as he firmly ordered, "You will not shift!"

Ashley watched in horrified fascination as the wolf seamlessly faded away.

The scent of her mother's fear rose in the air. She stared at the vampire like he was the devil coming to steal her soul, eyes wide and glassy.

Nikolai's hand clenched on her jaw, and he leaned in close until they were eye to eye. His were a red flame of power. "Bitterness. Hate. So much hatred."

Laurie Bell shook her head and threw her body back, trying to escape his grasp.

"Betrayal," Nikolai continued, moving with her. "Love and hatred, intertwined."

"Noooooo!" she moaned.

"I see a man, one she loved heart and soul. He turned away, mated someone—"

She turned to Rory, hatred in her gaze. The mask was finally gone. "Stop! I'll tell you all. Just make him stop," Laurie Bell demanded.

Rory considered, then gave an abrupt nod. Nikolai released her and stepped back.

Laurie Bell angled her gaze up toward the alpha's mate. "You want to know why? I'll tell you why. Magnus was mine. Then she came along. She was nothing. Less than nothing, but he mated her. When I asked why, you know what he said? The bastard actually *fell in love* with her. An omega. A nobody."

At her words, Wesley protested. Magnus's mate had been his sister, after all. No one paid him any attention, too caught up in the drama.

She turned her venomous gaze on Rory, then Kian. "When she got pregnant with twins, Magnus was so happy. Even happier when it turned out to be boys. The pack began to accept her. I couldn't tolerate it. She had my man, my children, and what did I have? Nothing but pitying looks and questions about my suitability to be a mate." Laurie Bell's rage was palpable. Her voice and body trembled with it.

"He got his precious sons, but I made sure he didn't enjoy them, enjoy *her*." She smiled then at Rory and Kian, and it was purely evil. "If Magnus had been this much slower"—she held her thumb and forefinger less than an inch apart—"getting into the room, you both would have been…" She snapped her mouth closed as though realizing she'd said too much.

"Would be what?" Rory asked in a dangerous voice.

Laurie Bell tightened her lips, refusing to answer.

"You will speak the truth, all of it," Nikolai ordered. Ashley could feel the power in his words. They pressed on her mind and in her heart, and she had bite down on the urge to blurt out what she'd done. As insurance against confessing, she retreated farther into the safety of the pack, her hand covering her mouth.

"Dead. As it was, I damaged his precious firstborn so he couldn't lead. Told him it was because his bitch was so weak that his sons were flawed. He died believing it." She cackled, her laugh so manic Ashley felt the hairs on her nape rise. Her mother was well and truly crazy.

"No matter how much she tried, I never let her or anyone else forget she wasn't good enough," she continued. "I was happy as long as the three of you were miserable, but then you brought *her* here," she said to Rory, nodding her head in the human's direction. "Your pregnant mate. And you were *happy*—" She spat.

The interrogation began. The Raven pack's alpha and mate, Shannon, and the human all asked question after question, demanding answers when Laurie Bell hesitated or resisted. At one point she bit her lip bloody trying to keep silent, but in the end, the combined powers of the vampire and Rory were too strong.

The whole sordid tale came powering out of her mother in fits and starts as she fought the compulsion. It infuriated her, but she told them all, and she spoke the truth. How she'd tried to smother Kian to death at birth because she couldn't risk breaking his neck as she'd wanted. How she'd seduced and mated Magnus's beta so she could remain close to him. How she'd fed Magnus's mate, Susan, insecurities, causing trouble between the couple at every opportunity, and never let them know a day of peace.

When she got to the part of how she'd pushed her mate into challenging Rory for the position of alpha, Rory bellowed out, "*Enough*!"

The force of his power sent most of the pack to their knees.

Laurie Bell's mouth moved, but nothing came out. If looks could kill, the look she shot Nikolai should have incinerated him. She closed her mouth, a disdainful expression on her face.

Ashley was devastated. For the first time she realized that nothing she'd done and nothing she could ever do would make her mother love her, or approve of her. Laurie Bell hated her, not because she wasn't a healer, but because she didn't come from Magnus's seed.

Sick at heart, she turned and left the clearing. She didn't care what became of her mother, just as her mother had never cared about her.

"RORY," SHAY CALLED in a soft voice.

She knew her man, and he was all but vibrating with fury. His claws were out, and through the bond she felt the struggle he had to control his beast. Her mate wanted blood. No, he wanted to gorge on Laurie Bell's flesh and wallow in her blood.

"Rory," she called again, "I need you." Through the bond she pushed, hoping he'd hear her, *"Please, come to me. She's not worth it. Remember the plan."*

It was touch and go, but finally he returned to her side. Shay immediately burrowed close. Rory wrapped his arms around her and held her to him. Now that he was with her, Shay realized she was shaking.

So much hate. So many years of misery, attributed to one woman. It was sickening and so very sad. Shay still intended to make Laurie Bell pay for what she'd done. Justice demanded it, but she was woman enough to feel compassion. She couldn't imagine the pain of giving someone all of you, only to be rejected, tossed over for someone you considered less than your equal.

"You're shaking," he whispered in her ear.

"So are you," she told him.

He grunted, tightening his grip on her.

"I'll be all right in a bit. Just give me a moment," she told him in a soft voice, uncaring if others heard her.

The pack was enraged. Anger was a living, breathing entity in their midst. One wrong word and things would turn ugly. Mob justice would prevail, and Laurie Bell would be ripped to pieces. Even the Raven pack's wolves' fur stood on edge, their teeth bared and hackles clearly raised.

"Remember our plan," she murmured to Rory, her gaze on Laurie Bell's haughty expression. "Death is too easy for her. I want her to pay for what she did to you, Kian, Shannon, and your mother. And then I want to go home, me and you, skin to skin, and forget this night ever happened."

They'd determined Laurie Bell acted alone. She might not be the only threat, Shay mused, but after tonight anyone should think twice about coming after her and their children.

Rory slid his hand from her waist down to cup her butt. The sudden hardness pressed against her stomach told her that her words had their desired effect. She raised her face to his. "Kiss me."

The kiss was hard, brutal, tasting of the anger he tried to manage. But when it was over, both Rory and his wolf were more in control of themselves. He turned her so that her back pressed against his front, and wrapped his arms around her waist. Shay relaxed into his hold.

"Laurie Bell, I find you guilty as charged. Caleb?"

"Guilty."

"MacDougal?"

"Guilty." MacDougal's voice showed his disgust.

"Council?"

Wesley and Bertram's response was instant. "Guilty."

When Graham didn't answer, Rory asked, "Graham, how do you vote?"

In a voice so cold it made Shay shiver, Graham said, "Kill the bitch and be done with it."

Laurie Bell flinched and looked at her brother in shocked disbelief. "What?"

Graham kept his eyes on Rory. "She's dead to me."

He really is a bastard. And to think, she thanked me for saving your sorry, worthless life. "Finish this so we can go home," she told Rory, revolted by the whole matter.

"The penalty for the crimes committed against the alpha pair and their unborn child is death, but…" Rory paused.

The pack began muttering.

"What? What does he mean, 'but'?"

"Kill the bitch and be done with it!" Graham hollered again.

More cries of the same were called out.

"But," Rory continued in a louder voice, "as my mate stated, death is too kind for you."

All eyes swung toward Shay, taking her measure. When Rory remained silent, the quiet increased as anticipation grew. What could be worse than death? Shay knew what they were thinking by the expression on their faces.

"I hereby declare you outcast. All property is to be seized. You have three days to clear all your personal belongings."

Laurie Bell's mouth dropped open. "You can't kick me out! I'm the pack's healer. You need me."

"Three days!" Rory reiterated.

"My house! My shop! You can't take them from me," Laurie Bell protested.

"They belong to the pack, purchased with pack money. The house and its land, the shop and all the merchandise therein," Rory reminded her. Shay had the satisfaction of seeing Laurie Bell's face turn white as the impact of what she was losing hit her.

"But what am I supposed to do?" she wailed.

Did she really think they cared?

Behind her Rory seemed to expand. The heat of his flesh scorched hers where they touched. His power rose in the air, so heavy breathing became difficult. Her wolf stirred, rising to the surface in response to whatever Rory was doing.

"Don't fight it," he stated in her mind. Until then Shay hadn't realized she was. She relaxed, trusted herself to Rory's care. Her beast rose, joining with Rory until they were no longer two beings but one powerful entity.

Then Shay felt something else, someone else's wolf join with them. It felt like Rory, but there was a subtle difference. A glance at Kian showed his eyes were glowing pure gold and he'd partially shifted. He still looked human, but his mass was larger and he'd sprouted claws and fangs.

Shay felt a tug and realized Rory was pulling on the pack. Caleb, MacDougal, the council, then each member, one by one, eyes began to glow bright gold until the clearing was lit. Her hair whipped around her face, but there was no breeze. The sheer buildup of energy had Shay staggering, punch-drunk under the strength of it.

"*You. Are. OUTCAST!*"

At Rory's roar, something burst out of them and hit Laurie Bell straight in the belly. Shay could almost see the flow of power. The force of the blow bent Laurie Bell over, then bowed her spine. Head thrown back, she let out a high, agonizing scream that hurt Shay's sensitive eardrums. Laurie Bell collapsed to her knees. Would have fallen on her face if Alex and Kian weren't holding her upright.

Like a dimmer switch being turned, the brilliant glow of the pack's eyes slowly faded until everyone's irises were their natural color. Rory's heat, though still high, no longer felt as if it would scorch a layer of skin off Shay's back. The power rush faded, leaving her mentally tired but physically energized.

Shay turned to say something to Rory when there was a muffled scream, then a gurgling sound. Spinning around, she saw Laurie Bell on the ground, her bloody hand clutched to her throat. Kian casually flicked the blood off his clawed hand, his face impassive.

Her mouth gaped. That wasn't part of the plan. Shay glanced at Rory. "Did you know he was going to do that?"

He smiled grimly. "It appears Kian felt it necessary to inflict a bit of justice of his own."

"Did he kill her?" Shay asked, prepared to be pissed.

"No, she lives." He watched Laurie Bell continue to bleed out, then shrugged. "I don't believe she'll have much of a voice from now on." He glanced out over the pack. "Sanders, you and Davidson escort this outcast to pack up her belongings."

The crowd parted as the men came forward. When they reached her side, both recoiled slightly and gave Rory a look of terror-filled awe.

"What's wrong?" someone asked.

With a cautious glance at Rory, one of them answered, "She smells human." Then they picked her up and carted her off.

That started another round of shocked mutters. Shay mused that this day would go down in pack history, and prayed they'd never have to repeat it.

After Laurie Bell was gone, Rory turned to the rest of the pack and said, "Let's run."

The Sparrowhawks were slow to respond, but gradually they shook off the anger and lethargy, began to undress and shift. Once on four legs, they pranced restlessly in place, looking at Rory.

"Go ahead," Shay told him. "They need you."

"You wanted to go home," he reminded her.

"We will. After..." she said.

"You too, Alex," Kee called out as Rory shucked his clothes. "Go burn off some of that energy."

"I won't leave you unprotected," Alex said.

"I'll watch them," Caleb said.

Kian signed, *I'll stay as well.*

"Kian said he'd stay too. Go, run. Rory needs you," Shay said, eyes on the form of her mate. His ears were flattened, tail hanging low. "You're the only one who understands what he's feeling right now."

Alex followed her gaze, then without another word of protest, cast off his jeans. His body flowed seamlessly into that of a wolf, and he loped over to join the rest of the mingled packs. Rory arched his neck and howled. Alex did the same. Then the Sparrowhawks and Ravens charged off into the woods.

So, in a replay of her first meeting with the Sparrowhawks, Shay found herself once more sitting on the mound, waiting for her four-legged lover to return. This time instead of the women of the pack, she had Kiesha, Caleb, Kian, and Nikolai keeping her company.

"You can shift now. You didn't want to run with the packs?" Shay asked Kiesha.

Kiesha cast a wary look at the pine-strewn ground before reluctantly settling beside her cousin. "I'm still not that good at it, and Alex wants me to avoid shifting until after the babe is born."

"Why? Does it hurt the baby?" Shay asked, placing a protective hand over her stomach.

Kiesha shook her head. "Alex doesn't think so, but he's not willing to take any chances either. In fact, he hesitated on allowing me to come tonight—not that I wouldn't have come anyway—because he was concerned all the people shifting at once would force me to change as well."

"Did it?" she asked curiously, keeping to herself that she was able to shift at will. That was something only Rory and Kian knew. She'd shocked them with her capacity to shift easily from human to wolf and back, especially since her scent still proclaimed her to be fully human. One day that ability might save her life, and Rory wanted the element of surprise on their side. Not only could she do a full shift, but both Rory and Kian were teaching her how to do a partial one as well.

Digging her hands into the soil, Shay concentrated until she felt her nails shift to claws.

"I felt the tug on my wolf—God, it still feels so strange saying 'my wolf,'" Kiesha admitted with a laugh, "but Alex taught me how to control it."

Shayla hadn't felt a pull at all. Of course, she'd still been tightly linked to Rory when the pack shifted en masse, so that might have had something to do with it.

"Do you think she was the only one?" Kiesha asked Shay.

Shay glanced at the men, who stood in a group talking before answering. "I don't know. Conor said enemies, plural, so I doubt it. What I do believe is that after what Rory did to Laurie Bell, anyone else planning to betray him will think twice."

"And what, exactly, did Rory do? She screamed like someone was tearing her apart from the inside out," Kiesha said.

"He bound her wolf."

Kiesha's brows drew together as she tried to understand what Shay was talking about. "He did what?"

"He bound her beast," she repeated. "Locked it up so tight it can't come out. I told Rory as punishment I wanted everything taken away from Laurie Bell that mattered to her. Rory couldn't make her not be a shifter, so he did the next best thing. He made it so she couldn't access her wolf," Shay explained.

Kiesha's jaw dropped. "I didn't know that was possible."

Shay glanced at Nikolai, who watched them. "Neither did Rory until Nik told him," she said, gesturing toward the vampire, who winced at her abbreviation of his name. "I guess being older than dirt has its advantages."

He bared his fangs at her, and Shay burst out laughing. It felt good after the tension of the last few weeks.

She turned back to Kiesha to finish her explanation. "To the Sparrowhawks, the only thing lower than an omega is a shifter who can't shift."

"Not just the Sparrowhawks, but all shifters," Nikolai corrected.

"And this is something all alphas can do?" Kiesha asked.

"No," Caleb answered. "It takes a lot of power. More power than one alpha alone can command."

"So how…?" Kiesha asked.

The men all looked to Shayla. "Don't look at me. I know what he did and where he got the idea to do it because I read him while our bond was wide open. I still don't know how or why it worked."

Nikolai sighed and came and crouched down beside them. "Because of the wolf's bond with his pack, he's able to link with them on the spiritual plane and gain strength when needed. A pack's alpha also has a certain amount of control over his members' beasts."

"Like the ability to force a shift when necessary," Caleb added.

Shay remembered how Rory had forced her wolf to retreat when she hadn't known how to change back to her human form.

"Yes, exactly. The reverse is also true. Just as an alpha can force a change, he can also stop a change," Nikolai continued. "But the effect is usually temporary."

"Most alphas only use this ability to help omegas learn how to control their beast in situations where it would be dangerous for them to shift," Caleb said.

"So what Rory did to Laurie Bell, binding her beast like he did, is only temporary? It won't last?" Kiesha asked.

Nikolai shrugged. "It's difficult to say. It all depends on how strong the woman's beast is and how determined to break loose. Right now she's sense blind. Her wolf is there, but it can't connect with her. It's like being in a concrete box with no opening. The woman will still have better vision, hearing, and sight, and faster reflexes than the average human, but she won't be able to tap into the strength of her beast. And she won't be able to shift into her four-legged form."

"She looked down on Rory's mother all those years for being an omega, and now she's less, and outcast to boot," Shay stated with grim satisfaction. It wouldn't make up for all the damage the woman had caused, but it was a start.

"Thank you, all of you," she said, looking at Nikolai and Caleb in particular, "for all you did tonight. Nikolai, I know you and Rory have this whole vampire/shifter stuff going on, but I appreciate you not only allowing Shannon to come here—don't tell her I said 'allow'—but stepping in with much-needed advice and wisdom."

"Of course he did." Kiesha slung her arm over Shay's shoulder. "We're family. Family sticks together. You know how it is: we may argue and fight with each other, but let someone else threaten us and it's on."

"Hmm, I always wanted a vampire as a brother," Shay mused, eyeing the vampire thoughtfully.

Nikolai shook his head and smiled, a mere crook of the mouth. "The wolf has his hands full with you."

"Yep, but he's never bored," she said with a cheeky grin.

Caleb choked on a laugh. From the way Kian's eyes twinkled, she knew he was amused as well.

* * * *

Rory retreated, letting his wolf take control. Unlike the man, the beast saw things in simple black-and-white and wasn't conflicted by emotions. Betrayal was severely dealt with, then forgotten. Now it took joy in running with its brothers, its sibling at its side.

He brushed his side against hers in a show of easy affection as they ran through the dense woods, not minding that she had the scent of vampire on her. Even the vamp was pack.

The man inside the wolf knew that later he'd have to deal with fallout from tonight's actions, but for now he was content to simply revel in the multitude of smells—the rich soil, new and decaying leaves, pine needles and cones, the smell of small prey.

He chased after a rabbit, caught and killed it, and brought its bleeding carcass to Shannon before bounding off after another one.

As a pack, they roamed all over the state park, traveling miles and remarking territory that belonged to the Sparrowhawks. Occasionally Rory caught sight and scent of couples mating in wolf form, and missed Shay with a longing that was physically painful.

Both man and wolf made the decision to turn and head back to the clearing, to their mate.

MacDougal fell into step beside him. *"I contacted the Arizona pack's alpha."*

"And?"

"I'm going to go, check it out," MacDougal answered before trotting off.

Rory silently wished him luck. When he'd put aside his pride and gone to Alex for help, one of the issues they'd discussed was MacDougal and his discontent with the Sparrowhawks. Alex had put out feelers among his considerable contacts and discovered there was a small pack, numbering about thirty total, whose alpha was old and was looking for a strong wolf to take over. None of his males were strong enough. None of the men in Alex's pack were interested since it meant relocating. Rory had taken the information and passed it on to MacDougal.

MacDougal was a strong wolf and had the makings of an alpha. Unfortunately he'd focused his attention on the Sparrowhawks, where he had no hope of leading. Rory had no intentions of giving up control anytime soon, and when he did, there were others higher in the hierarchy—Kian, Caleb, and should enough time lapse, his unborn son.

If everything worked out, this would be a win-win situation for them all. The Arizona pack would get a strong male alpha to take over when their leader stepped down, and Rory would have peace in his pack.

He padded into the clearing in time to hear his mate say, "Kian, now that we know what caused your muteness, you need to let Alex or someone at his clinic examine you. They may be able to fix the damage."

It doesn't matter. I've been this way this long, he signed.

"It does too matter," Shay argued stubbornly. "Besides, you might meet a cute nurse or doctor who'll insist on loving you back to health."

One corner of Kian's mouth kicked up, indicating amusement, but he shook his head.

"You might as well give in," Rory telepathed him. *"She's not going to give up until you agree."*

"At least think about it." Shay proved Rory right when she said it in a manner that showed she had no intention of letting the matter drop.

"Let me know when you're ready, and we'll get it scheduled," Alex said.

"I'll call Carol and make an appointment," Shay said as though it were a done deal.

Shifting back to human, Rory laughed at the annoyed expression on his brother's face. "Told you."

He strode forward and lifted his mate into his arms. "Time to go."

"You're not waiting for the others?" she asked, eyes wide with surprise.

Rory stopped walking long enough to shove his tongue down her throat, letting her feel how much he wanted her through their bond.

"Oh!" she gasped when he ended the kiss and continued toward the truck, the perfume of her instant arousal scenting the air.

"But what about Kiesha?"

"I'm not into threesomes, and even if I were, I doubt Alex would agree," he answered.

"You got that right," Alex called out in response.

Shay slapped him on the back of his head. "You know that's not what I meant."

He pinned her with a look, allowing the heat of his lust to show. "Home or here? Your choice."

She swallowed audibly. "Home."

They made it to the house in record time. As soon as the front door shut behind them, Rory ordered, "Strip!"

The smile on her face should have warned him she was in a mood to tease. Shay undid the buttons of his shirt, one by one, taking her sweet time about it. By the time she reached the snap of her cargo shorts, he was panting and his claws were unsheathed.

She pulled down the zipper, then slid the tip of her forefinger beneath the slice of panties visible and gave her clit a stroke.

"Shay," he warned, control hanging by a thread.

"Hmm?" She gazed at him under heavy lids, her face flushed.

"Mate, now is not a good time to tease." He felt the shape of his eyes change and knew his wolf was close to the surface, as aroused as he. Her cream was driving them both crazy.

"Oh, I'm sorry," she said, striving to look innocent, but the devilish glint in her eyes gave her away. "I thought I'd indulge in a bit of foreplay."

By alternating sides, Shay used her free hand to push down her shorts and panties. Rory's gaze stayed glued to the triangle of pubic hair and her busy little finger circling her nub. When the clothing dropped to her ankles, she stepped out and kicked them to the side.

"Rory?"

He grunted, words beyond him.

"I'm naked." Spreading her legs, she tilted her hips forward and speared her pussy with her finger. Seconds later she dragged the glistening digit through her nether lips, circled it around her clit, then plunged it into her vagina again. It made a squishing sound. Shay threw her head back and moaned.

Rory's control snapped as with a roar, he scooped up his mate and bore her to the floor. He flipped her onto her belly, snatched her hips into the air, and like an arrow, pierced her glistening sheath to the hilt. Teeth locked onto her nape, he rode her like a bronco as she bucked, squealed, and screamed her pleasure beneath him.

After her orgasm ripped through her, he jerked free, lifted her into his arms, and carried her upstairs to their room.

"You didn't come," she panted.

"Not yet," he gritted out between clinched teeth.

"Why?" she asked, sounding sated but confused.

"Bed first," he explained, then had no more words.

He tossed her onto the mattress and followed her down. His mate's comfort seen to, he was free to satisfy his own desires. Rory loved her until they both collapsed onto the mattress in an exhausted heap, the emotional trauma of the night forgotten.

Snuggling close, Shay murmured into his neck, "Laurie Bell deserved everything she got tonight. There's no need for you to feel guilty."

He closed his eyes and tugged her closer, thanking the Creator for giving him a mate who understood him better than he often understood himself. "I know."

"More importantly, she's no longer a threat to us or the pack." She licked a bit of sweat off his neck.

"I know," he agreed, running his fingers lightly down her spine. "I just…"

"Feel like you lost your mother all over again," she completed.

"Yes," he admitted with a sigh.

Shayla shifted until she lay on top of him and cupped his face in her hands. "The woman you thought you knew doesn't exist. Eventually you'll realize this and not feel so bad. Right now it makes me happy to know that you can't do what was done tonight and not feel anything."

"I'm alpha, Shay. Tough decisions come with the territory. It's not the first time I've had to do something difficult."

"And it's not the first time your heart has suffered as a result. You know what this makes you, Rory?" she asked, their noses almost touching.

Eyes narrowed in suspicion, he asked a touch belligerently, "What?"

"Human." Then she kissed him, and Rory forgot about Laurie Bell, the pack, and his justifiable actions tonight and gave himself over to his mate's tender, healing mercies.

Epilogue

Rory stared at his brother, a half smile on his face.

"Your mate is a nag," Kian telepathed.

"She loves your mangy butt. God only knows why," Rory said.

Kian glared at him. *"This isn't funny. She keeps hounding me to let Alex's staff at the clinic look at my throat."*

Rory leaned back in his office chair. "And..."

He knew why Kian hadn't before, but none of those reasons were valid now. After Laurie Bell—four weeks later and Rory still couldn't think of her without his wolf bristling—had made her confession, they knew the cause of Kian's defect had nothing to do with genetics but was simply an injury caused in his infancy. One that could possibly be corrected. Since Refuge had a top-rate, fully equipped medical emergency center staffed with people who knew about shifters, most of whom were shifters themselves, there went Kian's only other reason for refusing.

"I'm doing it," his brother snarled in his head. *"It's the only way I'll get any peace."*

Smiling, Rory asked, "Want me to come with you and hold your hand?"

The heat in his brother's gaze should have scorched him. *"You want me to rip out your throat?"*

Arching his left eyebrow, Rory reminded Kian, *"You can try, but if you succeed, you'll be stuck running the pack by yourself."*

Kian's chest vibrated in a growl only Rory could hear. *"Should have drowned you as a pup."*

"Then you'd be alpha now instead of coalpha," Rory stated with unconcealed devilment, relishing having his brother in his rightful position, both in the business and the pack.

Snatching up his hardhat and clipboard off his desk, Kian gave Rory a look of disgust and stalked out the office door.

Rory stared unseeing at the empty doorway, the joviality of the moment fading away as concern took its place. He hoped for his brother's sake that things would work out well, fearing that disappointment would crush Kian and send him back into his lone-wolf shell.

At least one good thing had come out of the mess last month. Rory had his brother back as an active part of his life. No more did Kian hide in the shadows. Not only that, but after what they'd done to Laurie Bell, the pack no longer looked on his brother with disdain. Instead their actions had instilled a healthy level of fear and respect in all of them.

* * * *

Hours later Rory was knee-deep in the mountain of paperwork that had accumulated since Shayla's arrival. He glanced up, irritated, when the door opened and a spill of sunlight fell across his desk. Damn place was busier today than an inner-city bus station.

MacDougal entered the office, followed by Ashley. "You got a minute?"

With an inward sigh, Rory tossed his pen on a stack of papers. "Yeah, what's up?"

MacDougal strode forward confidently to stand before the desk. "Me and the Arizona pack clicked. I've been officially offered the position of alpha."

"Are you taking it?" Rory asked.

MacDougal nodded. "No offense, but I'm not like Caleb. I want to lead. Being third, and now with Kian being coalpha…"

"I understand," he said when the other man trailed off. "It's not easy, especially when the wolf is riding you." MacDougal was a strong beta, borderline alpha. Without him, Kian, and Caleb in the way, his wolf would grow into the alpha MacDougal was meant to be.

"You'll be missed," Rory told him sincerely. Now that Mac no longer had his butt on his shoulders, he'd proven to be a good man to have at your back. They might eventually end up friends once this dominance crap no longer stood in the way. "When do you leave?"

"I was able to get on with the electric company in nearby Phoenix. Gave my two-week notice today. I start work there in three weeks. The thing is, Ashley's coming with me," he announced.

Rory felt his eyebrows shoot up to his hairline. "Ashley?"

"I stood a better chance of getting and holding the position if I were mated. The pack there is small, and the alpha's daughter is too young to be mated. By the time she comes of age, I'll be so well established that it won't be a problem," MacDougal said, showing the ruthless cunning that could make him a force to be reckoned with in years to come.

In packs without a male heir, it was typical to mate with the alpha's female offspring as a means of securing the alpha position. It ensured continuation of the alpha line, while bringing in new, stronger bloodlines.

Still, MacDougal's reasoning, though it made perfect sense, concerned Rory. He glanced behind him to Ashley. "You're okay with this?" She was a part of his pack, and as alpha, Rory had a responsibility to see to her well-being.

Ashley's expression was serene. "He could have chosen someone else, but he wants me. That's all that really matters. And," she added, "I'm more than happy to be leaving this place and going somewhere no one knew my mother. It will be a fresh start for both of us."

Rory winced, seeing the truth of her words. Besides, the news of Ashley's leaving would make his mate a happy woman. "Well, I wish you both great success. Mac, you need anything, pick up the phone and call."

"We'll be all right, but thanks for the offer." He placed his hand on Ashley's back and turned to leave.

"Could you give me a minute? I'd like to speak to Rory…alone."

MacDougal glanced at Rory, then back at her. "I'll wait outside."

She smiled. "Thank you."

Ashley waited until the door closed with MacDougal on the other side of it before turning to Rory. Then she seemed to flounder.

Curious, Rory waited for her to gather her words.

"I didn't know what my mother was up to," she finally said.

"I never thought you did," he assured her.

"No, let me finish. I knew she was power hungry and that she had no respect for anyone she considered lesser than herself, like me." Ashley drew in a shaky breath. "I said…I did… Hell!" She cast her gaze down to the floor. After a few more breaths, she stiffened her shoulders and raised her head. "Mother wasn't the only person who was a threat to your mate. I'd rather not say how I know, but watch your Uncle Wesley. He wants to be alpha and doesn't particularly care how he accomplishes it."

Rory stared at her, his wolf in his eyes. She bravely held his gaze for a few seconds before lowering her stare to the floor, baring her throat in an act of submission. He considered her unfinished statement and remembered all the suspicions Shayla had about this woman-child.

Then he thought about what it must have been like being raised with Laurie Bell as a mother, knowing what he did about the woman now. Ashley's life must have been a living hell.

He sighed and felt the wolf retreat. "The past is the past. Thank you for the warning. You're a beautiful young lady. One day you'll be a formidable woman. Go show the Arizona pack and MacDougal what you're made of."

She gave him a brilliant smile. "Thank you, alpha."

"Go on. Your mate's waiting for you."

Ashley hesitated before giving him a quick hug and a peck on the cheek. Then she was out the door. MacDougal and Ashley. He was still reeling. But the two were gone now, and Rory pushed them out of his mind to return to his mountain of invoices and contracts.

That evening, as Rory thought over all that had happened today, he realized his only unfinished business was his mate and her procrastination in telling her parents of their mating. Rory allowed another month to go by before taking matters into his own hands.

While she slept, he eased out of bed, took her cell phone off the bedside table, and went downstairs to his office. An hour later, a smile on his face, he shook Shay by the shoulder. "Shay, your mom's on the phone."

She groggily held out a hand, asking, "What time is it?"

"Eight. I'll go get breakfast started." As he left the room he heard her say, "Morning, Mommy. What's up?"

He'd just cleared the bottom stair tread when his mate bellowed, "*Rory McFelan! Your ass is mine*!"

His laughter rang out while his mate continued to heap recriminations on his head, turning the air blue. Claiming Shayla was the best move he'd ever made.

THE END

Zena Wynn

I love to read. I love books that can take me out of my ordinary life into an extraordinary reality. I don't just read. I become. To me, a really well written book is like a mini-vacation, without all of the hassle. My greatest hope is that after reading one of my stories, you'll feel the same.

The mother of three (four, if you count Lady, our family dog) and grandmother of two, when not busy with family or church, I can most likely be found in front of the computer writing or escaping into a book.

You can read more about Zena Wynn at http://www.zenawynn.com, find out what she has to say at http://www.zenawynn.blogspot.com/, and hang out with her and her fans on Yahoo! at http://groups.yahoo.com/group/LoveThatLastsaLifetime

Loose Id® Titles by Zena Wynn

Available in digital format at http://www.loose-id.com
or your favorite online retailer

Reclaiming His Mate

The TRUE MATES Series

Carol's Mate
True Mates
Nikolai's Wolf
Claiming Shayla

Available in print from your favorite bookseller

The TRUE MATES Series

True Mates
Nikolai's Wolf
Claiming Shayla

CPSIA information can be obtained at www.ICGtesting.com
Printed in the USA
LVOW08s1748090315

429814LV00001B/41/P

9 781611 189803